Shooting Marmalade

Roger Kirk

authorHOUSE®

AuthorHouse™ UK Ltd.
500 Avebury Boulevard
Central Milton Keynes, MK9 2BE
www.authorhouse.co.uk
Phone: 08001974150

© 2010 Roger Kirk. All rights reserved.

No part of this book may be reproduced, stored in a retrieval system, or transmitted by any means without the written permission of the author.

First published by AuthorHouse 9/13/2010

ISBN: 978-1-4520-3488-1 (sc)

Published in memory of Roger

1. Blue Peter

Drawing himself to attention, he stared out to sea. After a moment he grimaced and shook his head. He was standing like a four-year old playing at soldiers, holding his breath, with his shoulders up round his ears and his body rigid. It was embarrassing despite the fact that there was no one to see him. All he needed was a cocked hat fashioned out of newspaper, an inverted broom for a crutch and a toy sword stuck in his belt and he'd look like one of the outlaws in *Just William*.

His left nostril was still blocked. Gulping breath as best he could he dropped his shoulders, waggled his head gingerly from side to side and tried to relax. It was years since he'd stood properly to attention. He glanced down quickly to check that his toes were together and precisely in line with the edge of the cliff and that his thumbs were parallel to the seams of his jeans. Chiefy Watkins, scourge of the Naval Section in his old school Cadet Corps had been hot on toes and thumbs. Satisfied, he continued trying to breathe as deeply as his damaged ribs would allow. No matter how he stood his chest was sore.

Despite the heavy clouds overhead it was clear offshore. Even with only one eye he could make out the gas platforms on the horizon. Had anyone been on the deserted beach nearly three hundred feet below it was doubtful whether that at such a distance they would be able to discern that his head was swathed in bandages. Fresh dressings covered his left ear and eye and his broken nose was taped. For the most part the bandages successfully concealed evidence of a frighteningly close encounter with a discharging firearm. By some miracle the lead pellets had missed him. But something, wadding, they had assumed at the hospital, had raked the left side of his head. So close had been the discharge that he'd suffered tissue damage from combustion gases and lost a small piece from the very top of his ear. It had also left him deaf. He was well aware that he was lucky to be alive.

Life was all pluses and minuses, he thought. His survival would definitely be at the top of his 'plus' column. Another millimetre or two and it would have been all over. He didn't continue with the thought. There was little to be gained by dwelling on what would be writ large at the top of his list of minuses.

The injuries were something of a minus but they could have been worse. They were temporary. His nose was extremely uncomfortable and it irritated him that he couldn't really figure out how it had happened. Still, the painkillers helped. His eye looked an awful lot worse than it was. He hadn't been blinded. That was another plus.

It was Saturday, 15th September 1980; a full year to the day that he'd buried his mother. The day of the funeral had been unseasonably cold. Ellen had been fifty-nine. Her death had come out of the blue, a real shock to everyone. It was no age. That was a minus. Equally upsetting, he hadn't seen her for over a year before she died. She had been chafing for him to visit for ages. Sadly, there was nothing to be done about it now. It was his fault entirely and a serious minus.

Back on the plus side though, he'd met Margaret at his mother's funeral. Despite recent events, that had to be more of a plus than a minus.

A lot had happened in the last twelve months. His wife Abigail had left him. He'd lost his job. But he'd started a new career and he was enjoying it. Gabby had come into his life. He grimaced. Thinking about Gabby wasn't entirely comfortable. He still had to face her.

There was another plus. He'd discovered that his father was still alive. And this after more than a quarter of a century during which nothing had been seen or heard of him. Another possible plus or minus, yet to be determined, was the discovery that he had a half-brother and a half-sister. They had come as something of a surprise.

He glanced down briefly. There was something else. Oh yes. There it was again, the big minus. It kept intruding, forcing its way into his consciousness, but he didn't want to think about it.

He stood stock-still on the edge of the cliff for some time. Eventually the image faded. That was just about the extent of it, really. Oh, except for King and the rest of his half-witted relations, two doors down. That was another problem and something else he preferred not to think about.

Slowly he raised his arms until they pointed to the sky. The ribs didn't protest too much. Absurdly, it crossed his mind that he must look rather like a diver at the business end of a springboard, with a high-tariff dive coming up.

It was peaceful on the cliff top. A gentle breeze played at his back and somewhere a long way behind him a tractor droned back and forth across a field. Even further away gulls squabbled half-heartedly at the rubbish tip. He could just make out the gentle swash of waves on shingle far below him.

He took several deep breaths, quickly, painfully, one after another. Then he dropped his arms, screwed his eye tight, opened his mouth wide and roared.

'Aaaaaaaaaaaaaaaaaaaaah!'

He paused, gasped and gulped in more air.

'Aaaaaaah....' His head throbbed. He swallowed. 'Aaaaahaaahahah!' He soon ran out of puff. 'Aah-ah-ha, heh,

heh, heh.' As the by-now-feeble roar became no more than a coughing fit he was forced to bend forward, struggling for breath and clutching at his damaged ribs. He opened his eye and almost overbalanced. With his heart racing he stumbled away from the cliff edge.

The coughing eventually abated. Still bent over he cupped the front of his neck with his hand and groaned. The vocal abuse had hurt his throat. He gulped in more air and fumbled for a handkerchief. Finally locating one in his jacket pocket he dabbed his nose and mouth and wiped his right eye. His handkerchief was spotted with blood again. The split in his upper lip must have reopened.

It was still peaceful. The waves sighed on the beach below; the gulls had settled their differences temporarily and the tractor droned on. Peter Fincham looked around, but he needn't have worried. There was still no one about. Even if anyone had seen or heard him it would have been unclear whether they had just witnessed a cry of ecstasy, anger, agony, frustration or despair.

2. Old Nick

It was just after nine o'clock on the evening of 30th January 1953 when Monica Nichols☺ saw her husband, breadwinner and father of Louise and Raymond for the very last time. It was not a cheery leave-taking.

'That's right,' she shouted, 'bugger off. I don't know why you don't set up a bloody camp bed in the corner of that pub and then you wouldn't have to bother coming home at all. You're down there every night....' The door slammed, cutting off Monica's screeching and Raymond's howling.

Nick Nichols paused on the back step and fumbled at the buttons of his raincoat with shaking fingers. His breathing was fast and shallow. Blood hammered in his chest and pulsed at his temple. Something twitched persistently above his right eye. He paused, closed his eyes, took a deep breath and then rested his head on the door-jamb. The chill night air was welcome. Eventually he calmed. He straightened up and fished out his tobacco tin and lighter. In the dim light from next door's living room window he rolled himself a cigarette. The worn Zippo sparked into life but shook in his hands as he took the first deep and welcome drag.

It really wasn't fair. He'd never been much of a drinker, even in the army. It was only recently that he'd taken to going to the pub in an effort to seek out a little peace and quiet, temporary relief from Monica's nagging and the constant bickering at home. He could do nothing right. If the weather had been better he could have gone to the allotment, but that wouldn't have been right either. In the recent bitter cold and wet he'd spent many an evening alone in the corner of the pub, hunched over a half and a crumpled paper or a Max Brand. He'd had enough of the Westerns now though and was well into 'The Grapes of Wrath.' Louise had found the paperback on a train returning from a school trip to London. Nick was captivated and could hardly leave it alone. He patted his pocket to make sure that he had it with him.

Behind the flaking green door and in the absence of Nick, Monica had turned her attention on the children. Louise had given Nick a look as he passed the table where she was doing a composition for English.

'The Oddest Person I have ever met.' She could have taken her pick from those assembled in the cramped living room of their terraced house in Leeds. Monica sat with her knees in the fireplace, her fat legs horribly mottled from sitting so close to the fire. Furiously smoking a cigarette, painting her nails and thumbing through the *Radio Times*, her pale face was suffused with anger and disappointment. She looked far from her best in a white top, vivid pink skirt, red cardigan and worn fluffy mules. Her red hair was netted and in curlers, and her roots were in need of attention.

Perched in the sagging armchair on the other side of the fireplace and looking like some deranged chicken, was her mother. Every few minutes she'd cackle and call out. 'Come on, come on.' It was the latest of numerous unwelcome developments in her inexorable decline with dementia.

Nick's son Raymond had been lying on his back on the floor playing with a couple of plastic toys from a cereal box. It entailed much gurning, muttering and gibbering interspersed with yipping and whooping. He'd begun to cry as Nick put on his raincoat and headed for the door. This was all played out against the radio quacking in the corner and beside it on the sideboard the budgerigars twittering and squawking and ringing their wretched little bell. No wonder Louise had difficulty concentrating.

'Raymond! Will you stop that noise and go and get ready for bed.' Monica shouted. 'I won't tell you again. And you need to finish what you're doing, miss, if you want me to….'

Nick shook his head, closed his eyes and held his breath for a moment.

'Ah Mum, can't I….'

'No, you can't.' The wheedling wasn't going to work tonight. 'I'm sick of having to tell you. If your father hadn't…. Just do as you're told for once.'

'Ah. Ha-ha-ha-ha-ha. Come on, come on.'

Expelling blue smoke Nick pulled up his collar. He crossed the yard, stepped out of the back gate and turned towards *The Murderers*.

It was well after closing time when he left the pub. After some deliberation and the careful counting of the change in his pocket he made a minor diversion to the chippy. He ate his bag of steaming chips and scraps as he hurried home along the frosty pavements.

The house was dark and silent. He couldn't face Monica. She probably wouldn't speak anyway but if she did communicate it would be more barbed comments, more hurtful cracks. It was much more likely to be the turned back and silence, but he couldn't face that either. The usual course of events now would be several days of non-communication, making his own sandwiches, getting his own tea. She'd be off out every night. As he grew accustomed to his wife's hostility her enmity would give way to hurt looks, muttered complaints and then plates slammed down on the table, the preface to yet another blow-up and the next inevitable vocal broadside.

Nick stirred the fire into life and banked it up with an off-cut of wood and what dross was left in the coal scuttle. He shivered, then went to the sideboard and took out the half-bottle of whisky that they kept against emergencies. Just a nip would do. The bottle was empty. He rummaged around and pulled out a sweet sherry and a Ruby Port that each contained no more than a dreg. Monica had been tippling again. Returning the bottles he then cleared the piles of old papers, magazines, toys and the cat's ball off the sofa and made himself comfortable beneath his raincoat.

Nick had never had trouble sleeping and he slept well until he was forced up just after 5 o'clock by a sore hip. He'd been lying on Raymond's mouth organ. After emptying his bladder he poked the fire into life with more off-cuts and padded through to the kitchen to make tea. Returning to the sagging sofa he made and lit a cigarette. As he sipped his tea his eye fell on the untidy mound of old magazines, calendars and Christmas cards piled precariously on the sideboard. Raymond was to sort through them and take some to school for collages.

Shooting Marmalade

Nick got up and flicked through the pile until he found what he was looking for. He had been surprised when the card arrived out of the blue. It was from Wormy Dale, one of his fellow NCOs years ago in the Royal Engineers. They hadn't been in contact for some time. Wormy had never married and was now foreman of a contractor's gang building sea defences on the north Norfolk coast. He'd written in the card that he was presently quartered in the very same Nissen huts at the old Royal Engineers depot on the cliff tops that they had inhabited in 1940 when they were laying mines on the cliffs. Wormy had enclosed a photo of him and his workmates in front of the huts. It looked as though little had changed. They were starting a new contract shortly and since Nick had once expressed an interest if something should come up, Wormy wondered whether he was still interested. The money was good and the work wasn't onerous, so long as the weather behaved and he didn't mind being away from home.

Nick had tried discussing it with Monica, but she wouldn't countenance the idea of him working away. Back on the sofa with his tea he realized suddenly as he stared into the flickering fire that he'd give anything to go. His life was awful. He was miserable at home and he loathed his job at the drapery warehouse. The pay was barely adequate, the work was tedious and the foreman was giving him far more time out in the yard in the cold and wet than anyone else. He was well aware that the man was looking for any excuse to get rid of him so that he could bring in yet another of his cronies.

By the time he had finished his cigarette and his tea Nick had made up his mind. Suddenly he was excited. Ever since leaving Norfolk years ago he'd wanted to go back. He'd suggested they go there on holiday but Monica had always poured scorn on the idea.

'What on earth do you want to go down there for?' She supposed that Great Yarmouth might be all right but she preferred the familiarity of Scarborough or Blackpool.

Nick had never seen a wide, open and more beautiful sandy beach than that below the tall north Norfolk cliffs which they'd planted with mines in 1940. He'd dreamt many times of returning. He couldn't get out of his mind a particular afternoon he'd spent on that very beach with Ellen. He'd coaxed her down the heavily mined cliffs onto the sands. Unsurprisingly it was deserted and unspoiled, well before it was fouled with fuel oil and the other detritus of war. The tide was out further than Ellen could ever remember and she'd lived there all her life. There was a gentle breeze off the land and the sea was like glass. It had been warm enough to paddle and they'd walked arm in arm for miles. He'd never been happier. Afterwards they'd lain together in a tiny derelict potting shed on the cliff tops.

He'd go. Wormy had said drop in any time. He might even see Ellen, if she were still in the village. He'd often wondered what had become of her-and what might have become of them both if he'd gone back after the war, instead of returning to Leeds and Monica.

Nick looked at the clock on the mantelpiece. If he went by way of the allotment and fed the pigeons; he could leave his bike in the shed and hitch down to Norfolk. With an early start he could be down and back in the same day. He was supposed to go in to work until lunchtime but he no longer cared. No one would miss him beyond cursing him since one of the perennial idlers would have to venture out into the yard from the stuffy warmth of the foreman's hut. A new job away from home, plenty of money; he'd learn to drive and buy a nice little car. He jumped up and set about washing and shaving. After another quick cup of tea and a slice of bread and syrup he took a banknote and a handful of change from the biscuit tin on the sideboard and left the house before it was light and well before anyone else had stirred. He thought briefly about leaving a message but given his sudden urgent need to leave; he decided against it. He'd be home that evening, and besides, it wouldn't hurt to let them all stew.

*

It wasn't until the afternoon of 31st January 1953 that the very last sighting of Nick Nichols occurred. Two eight-year-olds, Peter Fincham and Philip Holt came upon him in the lee of the Lord Nelson pub, sheltering from a heavy shower and what was developing into a vicious northerly gale. The boys had met him earlier, albeit briefly, at Cowper's Cottage. They'd left him there beside the fire, deep in conversation with Peter's mother, Ellen.

They were soaked, frozen stiff and breathless from running, after a brief but ill-advised visit to the cliff edge to look at the stormy sea. After lunch they had assured Ellen that they would go directly to the Holt's to finish the Meccano dragline they'd been working on for weeks. Now anticipating a telling-off from Philip's mother Kathy, they were happy enough to delay the inevitable by chatting to Nick for a while. They wiped the rain from their streaming faces and rubbed their hair with their gloves and handkerchiefs.

Nick had rightly assumed that there wouldn't be a bus for ages and he kept dodging out from behind the pub wall on the lookout for a car. He was hoping for a lift to the old army depot below Beacon Hill but as usual early on a Saturday afternoon in winter, there was little moving on the coast road. Sated with roast meat of their choice, cabbage, carrots and potatoes, the majority of villagers would be dozing over the

Eastern Daily Press or the *North Norfolk News* in front of their fires. The village was as dead as a doornail and this particular afternoon the foul weather and forbidding forecast offered little incentive for anyone to stir far from their fireside.

The boys and Ellen had just finished boiled eggs and toast at the Fincham's cottage at the top of Back Lane when they'd heard heavy running footsteps in the front yard. Rain was just beginning to slash noisily across the tiny living room window. Peter had hurried to the door.

Ellen had been flustered at Nick's unexpected arrival but she was obviously pleased to see him. She thought he looked older than his thirty-nine years and indeed, he did. Too many roll-ups, a poor diet and lack of exercise had left him with bags under his eyes and a pastiness that would benefit from a week or two in the sun. The troubled marriage and home life too, had taken their toll.

His greying hair was combed straight back and thinning at the temples and crown. He still favoured the severe army-style short back and sides from his service days, but it did him no favours.

Ellen helped him off with his raincoat. She put it carefully on a wooden hanger and hung it up on the picture rail. Beneath the coat Nick was wearing a suit of sorts but the cheap grey jacket and the dark blue trousers were not of the same provenance.

Peter and Philip left the adults together in front of the fire, nodding and smiling at each other over their teacups and Nick smoking a cigarette and complaining about a tooth he'd broken that morning.

'That's my dad,' Peter whispered excitedly as the boys ran out of the gate and turned down Back Lane.

'Oh, yeah.'

Philip had heard it before. Both boys were without paternal relatives and the identity of Peter's father was a

Shooting Marmalade

subject that exercised them both from time to time. The sighting of any male stranger about the village had Peter wondering whether it was his father that had finally come to see him. In his continued absence the missing parent had taken many forms over the years. He had been an explorer, a spy, a deep-sea diver, a fighter pilot, a footballer and a sleuth. The errant father had changed career in step with Peter's particular enthusiasm at any given time. There had been supposed sightings before but in over eight years Peter's father had never yet put in an appearance.

Philip knew exactly who his dad was but he too, had never actually met him. He was unlikely ever to do so since the unfortunate Dave Holt had been fatally wounded in the African desert after driving over a mine just after the end of the war. Terribly injured and not missed for days, Dave had been discovered eventually and taken to an aid station. Kathy had received a handwritten note from a nurse by the name of Hoda saying that her husband was not expected to live more than a day or two and that she would care for him until the end. She never heard from Hoda or anyone else again, until an official letter turned up informing Kathy that Sgt David C. Holt was believed by the authorities to have perished.

'It is. I recognize him from that old photo mum's got upstairs in her writing case.'

'You said Harry Littleboy was your dad, but he wasn't.'

'Yes, but that was different. I'd never seen the photo before Harry arrived. Mum never showed it to me. I definitely recognize this one. Nick was… is his name anyway.'

Running into Nick later that afternoon would stick in the boys' minds forever. He gave them money, a florin for Peter and a like amount in change for Philip. They'd both been told countless times not to take money from strangers but since they'd already seen him that afternoon in Ellen's company and Peter was convinced that the man was his father anyway;

they considered that the warning didn't apply. Nick asked them whether Annie still ran the village shop and if she still sold liquorice whorls and bootlaces. They confirmed that she did and that they would be able to buy a barrow load each. Generosity on such a scale was quite unexpected and they were both taken aback at Nick's largess.

As the rain eased they decided to take advantage of the lull and hurry on to the Holt's cottage at the foot of Back Lane.

'Goodbye, Mr Nick,' called Philip as they crossed the road. 'Thanks for the....'

'Bye,' called Peter. 'Thank you.'

'You're welcome.' Nick waved a hand. 'Bye, lads. Mind how you go.' He called something else but it was whipped away in the wind.

The boys glanced round moments later to see Nick setting out determinedly across the pub car park towards the lane that led to the cliff tops. He'd wondered whether he might not be quicker walking along the beach to the depot, if he could get down the cliff. They had agreed that he could do it in less than half the time it would take by road. What exercised Nick though was that the cliffs were still dangerous. Ellen had told him that they were not yet cleared of mines. He hadn't expected that.

Philip nudged Peter as they flapped along in their Wellington boots. 'Why didn't you ask him?'

'What?'

They began to run as heavy spots of rain heralded another squall.

'If he's your father, of course.'

Peter glanced at his friend for a moment before replying. 'I know he is. I told you.'

Philip shook his head and brushed rain from his eyes. 'You're mad, you are.'

Shooting Marmalade

He looked back and caught Nick glancing round. They exchanged waves. Peter turned but Nick had disappeared from sight, shielded from view by the pub garages. It was the last time anyone saw Nick Nichols.

*

They were all wholly unaware as they went their separate ways that they were about to be overtaken by one of the most devastating natural disasters ever recorded in the United Kingdom. It had already begun, originating in the early hours of 30th January when an unexceptional depression measuring 996 millibars began to develop to the south of Iceland. The system caused no comment until it began deepening rapidly as it headed eastwards. By that evening the depression was close to the Faeroes and had deepened to 980 millibars.

At 7.45 the next morning, despite the bad weather the *Princess Victoria*, a British Railways roll-on, roll-off ferry left Stranraer for Larne. By 9.46 the ferry was in difficulties and requesting the assistance of tugs. The stormy seas had damaged the stern doors and the vessel was listing to starboard. It had a shifting cargo and was taking on water and at 10.32 a.m. the ship sent out an SOS.

At 11.30 the Meteorological Office at Dunstable warned of exceptionally strong winds. By midday the depression, now measuring 968 millibars was centred over the North Sea. With each decrease in pressure of a single millibar the sea level had risen by one centimetre. It was a huge volume of water and it was being driven on by storm force winds.

At approximately two o'clock in the afternoon the order was given to abandon the *Princess Victoria*. But it was already too late for 133 souls.

Within hours the east coast of England would experience the full force of an event reckoned to occur only once in every two hundred and fifty years. Almost 1,000 miles of coastline would be damaged, sea walls would be breached and over 3,000 sq miles would be inundated. More than 30,000 people would be evacuated, 24,000 properties would be damaged and 307 people would lose their lives in Lincolnshire, Norfolk, Suffolk and Essex.

In the late afternoon, as he descended the cliffs in north Norfolk, Nick Nichols was just one of many thousands of people without the benefit of this intelligence.

3. Nick Redux

After a disturbed night with the wind booming in the chimney, tiles careering off the roof and corrugated iron sheets rattling and banging on the outhouses, Henry Ball wasn't at his best when he took the dogs out early next morning. The old outside lavatory had finally collapsed and the wind had torn the roof off one of the sheds. A couple of windows had gone and the tarpaulin on his boat was ripped from stem to stern, dumping six inches of filthy water and rotting leaves into the hull. Apart from the tiles though, his ramshackle smallholding on the cliff tops just below Beacon Hill looked largely untouched by the storm.

His wife and sons had been glued to the wireless since early. Given the level of devastation up and down the coast they'd got off lightly. As he picked up some fruit trays that had blown out into the yard he realized that the dogs had disappeared.

'Damn it. Sam! Bonnie! Here gal, come on.'

He could just make out Sam barking above the wind. It sounded as though they were out in the field or on the cliffs.

He made his way across the muddy yard and staggered in the gale as he stepped out from the lee of the outhouses to cross a track and a narrow strip of rough grass to the cliff edge. There was no sign of the dogs but Sam's dysphonic barking was closer and to his left. Henry paused for a moment to peer at the sea. He had never seen anything like it. The light had an ominous yellow tinge and the sea and sky were melded into one impenetrable smear in which he couldn't actually make out the water at all.

The dogs were in the minefield, upwind. He turned into the gale. Blowing straight along the cliff edge it buffeted him and took his breath away. Leaning hard into the wind, with his head averted and cupping his eyes he made slow progress.

He found the dogs together below a finger of clay, about forty feet down, he calculated. Sam was agitated, barking, dodging and feinting beside what looked like a sack of logs. As Henry skirted the cliff edge in an attempt to get a better look it quickly became clear that it was a body that was exciting the dogs.

'Bloody hell,' Henry muttered. 'Get off, you two!' he shouted.

Bonnie spotted him and stopped nosing at the corpse. Affecting disinterest, she moved a short distance away, squatted and relieved herself. Sam began tugging at the corpse's trouser leg.

'Get off, Sam! Leave it.' Henry shouted again, but the wind whipped his voice away.

'Hello! Hello?' The figure never stirred. Foreshortened as it was, it looked like a man.

'Shit!'

Henry peered right and left along the cliff tops and sighed. There was no one in sight. He hated the minefield. It frightened him. Over the years he'd heard too many explosions. They always took you by surprise, bigger and more violent than you remembered. He'd felt the pressure-wave numerous times. The shock from any mine detonated close by invariably broke windows. He'd seen shrapnel fly up from the beach higher than the cliff tops, well over two hundred feet high at this point. And he'd seen the police bring up the pitiful remains of one of two boys blown up ten years earlier. Of the other child there had been no trace other than a bloodied brown leather sandal.

Living as close to the cliffs as they did there was no stopping the dogs from going into the minefield. They did it all the time. Although he doubted the veracity of his belief Henry had convinced himself that the dogs were too light to set off a mine. Despite his many warnings his sons went on the cliffs too, after rabbits, but Henry had never ventured more than a foot or two beyond the sagging barbed wire fence that ran along the cliff tops.

He groaned again. There was nothing for it. Fortunately the body wasn't too far from the top. After casting right and left Henry found a place he thought he could descend. The surface wasn't too greasy and the slope was gentle enough until it met the foot of the clay finger where it steepened suddenly. With numerous arthritic joints causing him discomfort and much difficulty he clambered over the cliff edge and began the descent. Despite his caution he ended up slithering the last few feet on his backside.

'Damn it, Sam. Get off! What's the matter with you?' The dog backed away as Henry levered himself up and approached the body. He wafted a hand at the dog and looked around for visible signs of mines. There were none, but it was of little comfort to Henry. That was the point of burying them in the first place.

'Hello! Hello?'

It was a man. He looked lifeless. His hair was matted to his skull and beneath the mud caked on his face he looked deathly pale. He had lost a shoe and a heel poked through a hole in his sodden grey woollen sock. His raincoat and trousers were torn and smothered in clay. Henry didn't like the idea of touching him but taking a deep breath and wrinkling up his nose he felt the man's right wrist. He wasn't really sure what he was looking for but he'd seen them do it in films. There was nothing to feel but he detected a flicker of some sort in the man's face. He straightened up and poked the body gently with the toe of his boot. Yes, there it was again, definitely a reaction.

With little enthusiasm Henry tried to lift the man but he was deadweight. He'd need help.

'I'll be back in a minute, mate. Hang on.' He patted the man's shoulder and then straightened up. 'Come on,' he called the dogs and set off up the cliffs. 'Sam! Come here! Come on. Good boy.'

He tried to walk in the scrapes and footprints he'd left on the way down but since speed was of the essence he didn't try too hard.

*

Between them they carried, pushed, dragged and bundled the man up the cliff. He was definitely alive. He'd gasped and cried out a couple of times in the manhandling that had been necessary to get him up the steep cliff and over the edge. They carried him quickly but with rather more care over the field, through the muddy yard and into the house. With both boys galvanized Henry had been able to leave most of the heavy work to them. It was just as well since his hip was by now very sore.

While his wife saw to the stranger Henry limped down the lane to the telephone kiosk on the coast road to phone for the doctor. The phone was dead. He supposed that the lines had been brought down somewhere. Sighing, he retraced his steps, got out the lorry and drove to the surgery in Mundesley. After an age the doctor's wife answered the door. She was in her dressing gown and had wet hair and looked exhausted. Her husband was up the coast somewhere. She hadn't seen or heard from him since before nine o'clock the previous evening. When Henry explained she suggested that he take the man direct to the hospital at Cromer. There was no point in trying to get an ambulance; the phone was off and they would all be busy anyway.

By the time Henry arrived home the man was still damp from a bath. Propped up in an armchair beside the fire, wrapped in an eiderdown he seemed feverish and drifting in and out of consciousness. Henry's wife had got him into an old pair of pyjamas and slippers but she was very agitated.

'I'm glad you're back. His name's Vic, I think. You ought to take a look at his shoulder. It's all funny.'

'Vic? What's wrong with it?'

'There's a lump. I don't think it'll work. Is Dr Milner coming?'

'No. He's out. Been out all night.'

Henry had a quick look at the shoulder. 'It's broke, I think. That'll be the least of his worries though. Mrs Milner said we'd better get him straight to the hospital.'

'Yes.' Betty Ball nodded and wrung her hands. 'He's got exposure, I reckon. I think that would be best. I don't like the look of him at all. We don't want him dying on us now… not after we've….'

'No, gal. You're right. Get the boys.'

'You don't think we did it, do you?'

'What?'

'Broke it, his shoulder.'

Henry looked at his wife. 'Don't be so bloody soft, woman.'

With his elder son's help Henry got the man into the lorry cab and the three of them set out for Cromer.

They made good time but ran into trouble in Suffield Park, over half a mile from the hospital. Making wretchedly slow progress they discovered that the road outside and the entrance to the hospital were jammed with vehicles. With Henry shouting out of the window and his son slapping the outside of the cab door with the flat of his hand they gradually made headway, partly on the pavement. A policeman and a harassed porter were doing their best to keep traffic moving. The policeman hurried over in response to Henry's call. He shook his head.

'You can't stop here, sir. We've got to keep a way open for the ambulance.'

Henry explained. After glancing at their passenger the policeman quickly cleared the way to the entrance where after a brief wait they were seen by a nurse and a couple of auxiliaries.

After ushering another unfortunate into the hospital a young doctor clambered up to the cab and cast an eye over their passenger. He shook his head immediately and jumped down.

'We need him in. Quickly, now!'

*

Some days later the patient was staring at the ceiling from a bed in the Men's Ward at Swaffham Cottage Hospital. A nurse chattered amiably as she busied herself with squash, pills and potions nearby. He was lucky to be alive, she said.

He'd been in a sorry state, what with exposure, a broken collarbone and a dislocated finger, a sprained ankle and numerous scrapes and bruises. Now, apart from a horrible cough he was on the mend. She called him Vic and asked him what had happened. He couldn't remember a thing, least of all that his name was Vic.

It wasn't until two days later at about four in the morning that his eyes snapped open suddenly and he remembered the cliffs, the beach, the fall and above all, the bitter cold. After leaving the boys and descending the mined cliffs without mishap he'd set out along the beach with the wind and stinging sand at his back. It all went well at first, but the sand was disappearing at an alarming rate as the tide surged in. He'd never seen the sea like it. Trying to dodge round a headland between combers he'd tripped in soft sand and been swamped. The waves knocked him over and soaked him with icy seawater and covered him with filthy scum. He had never felt cold like it. It left him breathless and almost unable to move. Then he was scrabbling up the cliff for dear life, battered by the wind and rain and with the waves at his heels. He had slipped on a streaming outcrop of clay and for what seemed like an age he had frozen, afraid to move backwards or forwards, buffeted by the wind and paralysed with fear. Eventually his tensed muscles cramped and he had been forced to stir. He had fallen. It must have been all of thirty feet or so, and in the dark. It knocked the wind out of him. That was when the shoulder and finger went. He had been frightened. But he did manage to drag himself back up again... until he was overcome by the cold and exhaustion and could go no further.

Where had the black and white dog come from? He had laughed when he first saw it, thinking that it was just typical that it was not a St Bernard bearing a welcome brandy barrel round its neck. He had been pleased to see it... and the people. He wondered who they were and then drifted off again.

In the morning he asked about his clothes and a grey-haired woman in a suit came to see him. She said she would need a name and address. He said someone had said he was Vic. She didn't pursue it.

'You had no clothes or belongings of any sort when you arrived, Victor. Do you not have any idea where you came from, what you were doing?'

He really didn't and it was easier to allow himself to drift off again than try to explain.

They moved him to a convalescent home near Dereham where he eventually filled in most of the gaps and pieced together what had happened. Late one morning as he awoke from dozing he was filled with misery when he had no difficulty recalling who he was and where he had come from. He also remembered where he had been going. It was in the gloom of the late afternoon that it occurred to him that almost no one else knew these things. And those that did know something actually knew very little. The more thought he gave it the more inclined he was to think that this had the look of a golden opportunity that was not to be dismissed out of hand.

As indefensible as it was; he had little inclination to go home to the nagging and unfaithful Monica, the thoughtless and thankless Louise and Raymond and the dead-end job. His parents were both gone. Things had never been the same between him and Monica after he came home from the war to find her carrying on with Little Jack, an old flame from her schooldays. The only one that might have missed him was the dog, but he had died. There were his father's pigeons, but he'd only kept them out of some sort of loyalty. He had no real interest in them.

If he didn't go home to Leeds, didn't communicate with Wormy, Kathy, Ellen or their sons, or the people that rescued him, and he didn't know who they were or exactly where they were; he was free. He could start a new life. True, he had no clothes, money or papers. But if he didn't worry about those things, they were of little concern.

Vic. He smiled and wondered where it had come from. He'd known one or two Victors in his time. None of them had been mad or deserving of scorn. No, Vic would be okay. He could live with it. There were worse names. What about Peter, his real name? No. He'd never used it. He preferred Vic. Vic Nichols? No. If he was going to make a new start Nichols would have to go. He slept.

During his waking hours he spent a lot of time chewing over alternative surnames. For a while he toyed with Gosling but finally concluded that it was too open to ridicule. Somehow the same logic failed him when he hit upon Codling. Vic Codling. What more propitious initials could there be?

Eventually though he decided against Vic. He wasn't convinced that he'd answer to the name out of the blue.

'You all right, Vic?' He wasn't sure he'd respond. He'd have to return to being Nick. Stick with Nick. He smiled, savouring the possibilities of a new life-not that it would be without difficulties.

There was Monica and the children, for a start. He felt guilty about leaving Monica. Fourteen years of marriage down the Suwannee. But in truth there had been precious little between them for ages. Certainly there was no love. There hadn't been anything of value since her affair with Little Jack, the jobbing builder she'd known since school. He was the caller down at the Bingo in the evenings. Not for the first time Nick wondered whether it was back on again. That might account for all the misery lately.

Shooting Marmalade

What about his little Lou and Ray? What would they make of his disappearance? It saddened him but they'd long since stopped being his or little. He concluded despondently that they'd hardly notice that he'd gone… until they had to clean their own shoes for school.

The house wasn't a problem. It belonged to Monica's mother and Monica would inherit it eventually.

For a moment he toyed with returning to Ellen's and trying to make a go of it with her. But he really didn't know anything about her these days. He hadn't been in touch since sending her a postcard at the end of the war and then he'd baulked at putting his address on it. She'd been fine when he saw her recently but you could never tell.

There seemed to be no man on the scene but Peter's father might be around. No. Nick was convinced that a new start would have to mean a new place. Somewhere no one knew him and where there was little likelihood of anyone from his old life stumbling across him. It was exhilarating, but daunting at the same time.

*

The woman spooning a poached egg onto his toast at breakfast became quite excited when he announced that his name wasn't Vic but Nick, Nick Codling in fact and that he'd lost everything in the floods. That much was certainly true. In addition to his clothes he'd lost his wallet and his watch. He wondered whether his rescuer had kept them. There had been ten shillings in the wallet and the watch was only a cheap one, but they had been his. He decided that there was nothing in the wallet by which he could be identified. What irked him most of all though was the loss of his cigarette lighter, his beloved Zippo, his *Windproof Beauty*. It had been talismanic since the beginning of the war when he won it off a GI. He hadn't smoked for days and he felt no inclination to do so, but he felt the loss of the lighter keenly.

When the home administrator eventually came to see him he gave a bogus address in Cromer. In return she arranged for him to have a haircut, his own razor and shaving things, some clothes and thirty shillings. The clothes, although new to Nick, had all been worn before. However they were clean and serviceable. They gave him a shirt he recognized as ex-RAF, a dark blue V-neck pullover, a maroon tie bearing a single discreet motif in pale blue, charcoal grey trousers and a pair of excellent quality black closed Oxfords, the best shoes he'd ever had in his life. There was no jacket that would fit him but they said they would find him one. In the meantime he had a heavy dark blue overcoat, a tartan scarf and a pair of grey woollen gloves. He politely refused the offer of a knitted woollen hat in duck egg blue.

Later in the day he had his tooth mended. He'd broken a molar eating a bacon sandwich in a café in Sleaford on the way down to Norfolk and had been aware of nagging toothache for days.

For a further two days Nick rested and ruminated over whether to go and where to go. He couldn't come easily to any conclusion. Without money and the means of earning some and with nowhere to live he would be faced with severe difficulties immediately, this bitterly cold February. But he was feeling much better and apart from a cough, some residual soreness in his shoulder and a slight limp he felt almost back to normal. It was while he was ambling round the gardens one afternoon, his first outing without the sling, that he decided that he would just have to take a chance. He could ill afford transport so he'd simply go wherever a lift would take him.

*

The following morning after breakfast Nick exchanged pleasantries with the porter and said that he was off out for a walk. He left the convalescent home wearing all of his clothes and with just over twenty-eight shillings and a banana in his pocket. At that moment it was everything that he owned in the world.

It was a walk of just over a mile to the A47. Things almost went awry immediately when he arrived at the main road and one of the nurses pulled up beside him on her bicycle.

'Good morning, young man. And where do you think you're off to?'

'Hello, Iris. It's a nice morning.' He stretched gingerly, yawned and massaged his shoulder. 'I'm trying to ease the battered body back into action, something like normal.'

'Well, don't you go overdoing it. We don't want you hanging around the home any longer than absolutely necessary.' She grinned at him and gestured behind her. 'If you take the second on the left it'll bring you round in a circle and back to the Post Office. I think you'll find that will be quite far enough without the sling.'

'Very good. That sounds about right. I don't want anything too challenging. See you later.'

'You're looking better.' Iris pushed off and wobbled across the road.

'See you,' she called.

'Yes, bye. Get the coffee on.' Nick stared after her. He hated the deceit. They had all made him very welcome and they'd helped him enormously. He felt shabby. If his father wasn't exactly turning in his grave he'd certainly be raising an overgrown eyebrow. Iris had been kind and friendly during his stay but he couldn't really tell her he was off. He watched her until she was out of sight and then turned out onto the

A47. Since he had no particular plan in mind he decided that he might as well stay on the side of the road that he was on.

He got off to a modest start with a ride for about twelve miles in an Austin Healey with a retired Army Colonel. The man had served in Africa during the war and was interested to hear of Nick's experiences in the Royal Engineers. After being dropped and a wait of nearly half an hour at the roadside Nick was heartened when a muddy Land Rover with a covered trailer pulled up just ahead of him. He hurried towards the waiting vehicle. The driver leaned over and opened the passenger door.

'Where are you going?' he shouted.

'Hello,' Nick poked his head in the door and hesitated for a moment. He shrugged his shoulders. 'Anywhere. Anywhere down south.'

The driver cackled. 'South? You're going the wrong way, old mate. This is northbound.'

'What?'

'I'm going just north of Skegness.'

'Oh.' Nick sighed and looked back along the road. Nothing was going that way.

'Do you want a ride or…?'

'That would be fine, thanks.' Nick made up his mind quickly and waited while the man moved all manner of stuff off the passenger seat by the simple expedient of sweeping everything into the foot-well with his meaty arm.

The inside of the Land Rover was a tip but it was warm. The man waited until Nick was seated and then with a broad grin stuck out a large and calloused hand.

'Stanley Riggall, Yellowbelly, philosopher and farmer. People call me Stan.'

Awkwardly, Nick turned and took his hand. He couldn't avoid wincing as the farmer shook it.

'Nick… Nick Codling.'

'I'm pleased to meet you, Nick. Are you all right?'

'Oh.' Nick tried to organize his left arm gingerly as the farmer put the Land Rover in gear and pulled out into the road with a jerk. 'I've just come out of hospital. I got caught up in the floods. Broke my collarbone, among other things.'

'Oh, sorry. I'll take it a bit steady. What happened?'

'I got cut off by the sea. Had to climb the cliffs. Then I fell, knocked myself out, broke my shoulder and did a few other bits of damage. I lay on the cliffs all night. Got taken into hospital with exposure.'

'Grief! You were lucky someone found you, weren't you? What on earth were you doing on the beach in that muck?'

Nick stuck to the truth where he could and as best he could. He was determined to keep fabrication to the bare minimum.

'Sea defences. Contract's done now though. I ended up in the convalescent home in Dereham. Lost my clothes, wallet, everything. Didn't seem to be any point in going back.'

'So where are you off to now? Home?'

'No. Got nowhere I have to be. I thought I'd have a few days off and then see what comes up.'

'Ha!' The farmer beamed and slapped the steering wheel. 'Wish I was that footloose and fancy-free.'

'It's been bad up your way too, hasn't it?'

'Terrible.' The farmer frowned and shook his head. 'It's been awful. Mablethorpe, Sutton, Skeg, all flooded. Lot of people killed, and beasts. Everybody knows someone…. It's been a bad do.'

'Were you affected?'

'We were lucky. We're a few miles inland at the foot of the Wolds. The drains backed up and flooded here and there but it didn't reach us, fortunately.'

'You're a farmer, you said?'

'We've got a small farm just outside Alford. Do you know that way at all?'

'No. I went to Skeg on holiday once but that's it.'

Stan chuckled. 'Everyone went to Skeg on holiday once.'

He was an easy man to talk to and the time passed quickly.

'I must say I'm a little bit peckish,' Stan announced as they approached Boston. 'Could you eat something? I've been up since before five.'

'I could probably eat a bun or something… and a cup of tea would go down well.'

The farmer looked at Nick and raised an eyebrow.

'They do a good breakfast here. Daisy's.' He nodded at the sign as they pulled off the road in front of a café.

'Hello again, Stanley. If I didn't know any better I'd think you were having trouble staying away from me.' Stan was greeted cheerily by a small blonde woman as they pushed open the door into the clean, warm and welcoming café. 'Seems like no time at all since the last time I saw you.'

Stan chuckled and pushed up the peak of his cap.

'Hello, my lovely.' He turned to Nick. 'I stopped for a cup of tea and a piece of toast on the way down. I've been looking forward to my breakfast ever since.'

He led the way to a table by the window and called out to Daisy. 'I was telling Nick here I've been looking forward to my breakfast.'

Daisy smiled. 'Hello, Nick. I don't think we've seen you in here before.'

'No, I don't think I've ever been this way.'

'Well, you're very welcome.'

After a moment Daisy called. 'Is that the full kit and caboodle for two, Stan?'

'Yes, thanks.' He looked at Nick. 'You'll eat something, won't you?'

Nick was taken aback. He hesitated.

'My treat,' said Stan.

'I can't let you….'

'Sit down and enjoy it. You won't find a better breakfast anywhere.'

'Well, thank you very much, Stan.' Nick struggled with his coat. 'I'm sorry. I wonder if you could…. I seem to have seized up sitting in the car.'

The farmer helped Nick with his coat and chair then sat down himself. He took off his cap and leaned back. He was a short, stocky, ruddy-faced man with wispy fair hair. He looked at Nick for a moment before speaking.

'So, Mr Codling. You're not actually on your way anywhere in particular at the moment, just wherever the fancy takes you, so to speak.'

'I suppose so.' Nick didn't really know what else to say.

'And you haven't got a job at present.'

'No. I'm a free agent.'

'And, let me get this right, you've got nowhere you ought to be?'

'That's right.'

The farmer paused for quite a while, then leaned forward and lowered his voice. 'There isn't an empty… cell somewhere, with your name on the door?'

Nick looked up, startled. 'No. Why?'

There was a definite twinkle in Stan's eye.

'Or you're not, what shall we say, just one step ahead of our friends with the pointy blue hats?'

'No! Whatever…?'

The farmer leaned back, studied Nick for a moment and then grinned.

'Well, Nick. You've got to admit it's a bit.... Man standing by the roadside midmorning on a workday. No luggage. Going he doesn't know where, north or south, no home or family to go to.' He paused again and looked Nick up and down. 'I hope you won't mind my saying but the clothes are a bit.... Not that it's any of my business, of course.' Stan looked out of the window before fixing Nick with a look and resuming.

'I like you, Nick. And I like to think I'm a fair judge of folk.' He took a handkerchief from his pocket and blew his nose before resuming. 'If all you've told me is true, I was wondering whether you'd be interested in a little proposition. I wondered if you'd done any farm work at all, or a bit of general handyman stuff, this, that and the other. You look handy enough, apart from your arm, at the moment of course. And you seem as though you could turn your hand to most things. It sounds as though you might be looking for a bit of work.'

Nick was surprised.

'Well, I am pretty good with my hands, and I'm a quick learner.'

'Can you drive?'

Nick decided that this was not the time to stretch the truth.

'No. I can't. Not properly, anyway. I did start in the army during the war, but then I was posted. Then with one thing and another I never got back to it. I wish now I'd....'

'You could though? Thank you, my dear.' Daisy's girl arrived with tea and two plates of toast.

'I should think so. Like I said I'm a good learner.'

The farmer started in on the toast and then looked round as Daisy appeared behind him bearing two plates of breakfast.

Shooting Marmalade

'Ah, splendid,' he said, rubbing his hands as she put the plates down.

'Mind your fingers, they're very hot.'

Nick goggled at the plate Daisy placed before him. It was a magnificent sight. Crispy bacon, black pudding, two sausages, fried bread, tomato, beans, two huge field mushrooms, all topped off with two fried eggs. Opposite him Stan beamed first at his plate, then at Nick and finally at Daisy who was standing behind the farmer with her hand on his shoulder. He looked up at her and took her hand.

'Thank you, my dear. That looks....' He turned to Nick and reached for the HP Sauce. 'Dig in,' he said. 'I think you'll agree that looks just dandy. And I'll tell you something. You'll not get better anywhere. Even Mrs Riggall would have to go a bit to match this.' He winked. 'But don't ever let on I said so.'

He reached up again and gave Daisy's hand a quick squeeze before addressing his meal.

'Enjoy your breakfast, boys.' Daisy returned to the counter.

Given the opportunity he'd been offered Nick decided to be completely honest with the farmer. Here was a man who seemed on the point of offering him a job, in addition to having given him a lift and what was proving to be every bit as good a breakfast as had been promised. As they ate he told Stan that he had a wife and family but that in view of his wife's infidelity he had no home or job that he wished to return to. He also explained that he had been on his way to see about a new job but he had never got there after his difficulties on the cliffs. He related, to the best of his knowledge what had happened since. Stan listened carefully. He wiped his mouth with a paper napkin.

'Well, thank you for being honest, Nick. I'm rarely wrong about people, fortunately for me.'

Worryingly for Nick they finished their meal in near silence.

After they'd both finished their refills of tea Nick fished in his pocket. 'I know you said it was your treat, Stan, but....'

'No.' The farmer shook his head. 'Put it away.'

'Oh, come on, Stan. You've been good enough to give me a ride. It's the least....'

'No, Nick. It's my treat.' The farmer took out an untidy wad of notes from his cord trouser pocket, selected two and placed them on the table.

They took their leave of Daisy, Stan's leave-taking so protracted that Nick wondered whether there was or had been something between them. She was certainly a comely woman.

Stan poked his teeth once they were back on the road. He took his time returning to the topic of a job. It turned out that he had been thinking.

'I suppose what I'm looking for is a fairly adaptable sort who could run our new caravan site and help out on the farm when the site's not busy. We hope the site's going to develop and do well, get busier. That's why I need someone. I haven't the time at the moment. It's close to the farm and we only started it in the middle of last summer. It's not big at present, but we've got plenty of room to expand.'

'It sounds interesting.'

'Have you ever stayed in a caravan?'

'No. I never have. I must say I'd like to.'

'Well, if you want the job we've got our old van in the yard. It's parked up beside the barn and it's got water and electric and so forth. It would do to get you started, wouldn't it?'

They talked wages, rent and covered numerous other topics. Later that afternoon the farmer parked the Land Rover in the yard at Grange Farm on the edge of the Lincolnshire Wolds. Nick's shoulder was painful and he felt exhausted as the farmer helped him out of the cab. He took some comfort though from the fact that he now had a friend, he had a job, he had a home and no one from his old life knew where he was. At the age of thirty-eight, wearing all that he owned and with nothing but a bruised banana in his pocket, Nick Codling was ready to begin life anew.

4. A Letter to America

Peter gazed out at the North Sea from the cliff tops behind the Lord Nelson. He yawned, took his hands out of the back pockets of his blue jeans and ran his fingers through his fair hair. Thirty-five years old, he was tall, lean, slightly stooped and at the moment in need of a shave and a haircut.

He had let himself go over the last three months and it had not gone unnoticed. Kathy had made the odd pointed remark. A qualified and one-time fulltime stylist she'd even offered to cut his hair. He'd nodded and smiled and agreed to let her tidy it up in time for Christmas, acknowledging at the same time that he would have to snap out of the ennui that seemed to have overtaken him since his mother's death.

Since the funeral he'd got into the habit of making his way down the overgrown lane beside the pub after his lunchtime pint and sandwich. There was no need for justification but he'd told Kathy that he enjoyed the fresh air and exercise and he liked to look out at the sea. She'd looked doubtful and wondered aloud how much in the way of exercise there was in the couple of hundred yards between the Lord Nelson and the cliffs. Otherwise she held her counsel. Peter was quite sure that she was well aware of why he was drawn so often to that particular spot on the cliff tops.

When Ellen died Peter had hoped that his father would turn up for the funeral. He had only met him once in his life and then very briefly. He suspected that Nick didn't know at the time that he was his son. But Nick had failed to put in an appearance and Peter had learned that no one, including Nick's wife Monica or his two other children, had seen or heard anything of him for over twenty-six years.

Peter scuffed at the damp grass beneath his feet. The balding toes of his olive green desert boots were dark with moisture and he could feel the cold dampness seeping into his socks.

It would be Christmas shortly and then 1980, a whole new year. On balance it would be a good thing to draw a line under 1979. A return to work would probably help. He'd been away too long. Over the last few years he had accumulated a huge amount of holiday. At the time of Ellen's funeral it had seemed a good idea to take extended leave, to use up the backlog. But his normally well-ordered life had become something of a shambles over the last three months. The long holiday hadn't been a complete success.

Kathy hadn't mentioned it yet but he hoped that she would invite him for Christmas Day. He wasn't given to melancholy but he didn't want to spend Christmas alone, with memories of earlier festivities with his mother and his ex-wife. Until very recently he'd assumed that he'd be spending every minute of the holiday with Margaret, but that wasn't going to happen now.

In theory everything should have been tickety-boo. Since Ellen left him Cowper's Cottage he now owned a very desirable property in a charming part of the country, in the north Norfolk village in which he had grown up. She had also left him a not insignificant amount of money and a Morris Minor, elderly but still serviceable. He had a decent job and some friends. But as soon as the New Year's celebrations were over he would be off, back to the supposed glamour of the movie business. It was all right; he got to meet some interesting people and it wasn't badly paid. He could do it standing on his head, but the endless travelling and hotel life had become tedious almost to the point of being unbearable.

In addition to his father's connection with the spot on the cliff tops where Peter now stood, it was also the place where he and Margaret had clambered up and down the cliffs during their brief but exhilarating affair. He had heard nothing from Margaret since the night he'd ambushed her as she left work.

When she admitted that she was pregnant Peter had been overjoyed, feeling at that moment that things could hardly get any better. He had long wanted to father a child with his wife Abigail, but she had been wholly against it. She was much more interested in opening another boutique in Brighton.

But Peter's joy was short-lived. Apparently convinced that the baby was her husband Tom's, Margaret wouldn't see Peter again. When he wondered aloud, although tentatively, whether he could have fathered the child; she was adamant that it was Tom's baby.

So he had lost Margaret, with whom he thought there was some possibility of a future. He felt as though he had lost a child too, albeit one so ephemeral that had he blinked he might well have missed it. He was bored, and unsettled.

Perhaps he should hurl himself off the cliffs. The thought skittered across his mind briefly but it wasn't serious. He guffawed quietly to himself. If he jumped from where he presently stood the worst he would achieve was no more than getting mud on his clothes.

Below him the cliff face sloped at a gentle angle to a ridge about ninety feet down. The state of the cliffs below the ridge was anybody's guess since the contorted mass of sands, gravel and clay was constantly eroded by groundwater and wave action.

There would be little in the way of wave erosion today though, with only a gentle breeze blowing off the land and no more than a moderate swell on the grey water in front of him. The sea was calm for December and the day was mild. It was just after high tide and judging by the sands that were visible away to his right it looked as though the water hadn't come far up the beach. Out of his vision immediately below, the waves wouldn't have got within twenty feet of the foot of the cliffs before swashing shingle back down the gentle slope into what had been a low only a few hours before.

Peter shivered suddenly. He turned away from the cliff edge, stamped his feet and zipped up his denim jacket. It was time for a cup of coffee and few minutes with the crossword.

*

Back at Cowper's Cottage he yawned, stretched, tapped his teeth with his pen and then tossed it down on the kitchen table. He rose and wandered over to the kettle with his coffee mug.

While he waited for the water to boil he picked up his mother's letter from the table and reread it. For some reason Ellen hadn't begun a response until September, some six months after receiving a letter out of the blue from Louise Stark. Recovering in the convalescent home at the time, confused and exhausted only days after suffering a stroke; Ellen had asked Philip to respond on her behalf. He had taken the letter home with him but Ellen died before he could do anything with it. When Peter returned from abroad for the funeral Kathy gave him both letters along with the rest of Ellen's personal effects from the home.

Dear Mrs Stark,
Thank you for your letter which came as something of a surprise.

I'll bet. Peter smiled and shook his head.

I'm sorry that it has taken me so long to reply but I have not been in the best of health. My name is Ellen Fincham. I am 59 now and I did know your father, Peter or Nick as we knew him during the war. We became friendly when he was stationed nearby.

Friendly? His mother had always been a great one for understatement.

He was one of the soldiers laying mines on the cliffs.

I never lived at the Lord Nelson but we often met there in the evenings. I still live in the village a short distance from the pub.

You say that you last saw your father on 31st January 1953. I know that 25 years have passed and my memory is not as good as it once was but I think that it was on that same day that he came to see me. I have talked to a friend who also knew him during the war and we are sure that was the date.

Kathy had confirmed this at the wake and they'd talked about it several times since but Peter had reason enough to remember it himself.

It was a surprise. I was not expecting him. I hadn't seen him since 1944 or heard anything of him since the end of the war.

When he sent the miserable postcard that was still upstairs in Ellen's writing case, saying he had survived the war. His hope that Ellen had survived too seemed to Peter almost an afterthought. There was no return address. The postmark was Bradford.

He arrived in the afternoon on 31st and only stayed for a short while. He didn't stop long because the weather was bad.

He had a cup of tea and a piece of cake and we chatted for a little while. Then he left to go to see someone about a job on the sea defences or something like that. He said he might look in the next day if he had the time, but I never saw or heard from him again.

And after they had cleared up the storm damage and rounded up the chickens Ellen had had taken considerable care with her appearance and waited in for him on 1st February, her thirty-third birthday. And she was more disappointed than she let on when he didn't turn up. And so was Peter. The previous day was the only time he ever saw his father in the flesh.

Peter rocked back on his heels and stared out of the window. He wondered, not for the first time, what could have happened to Nick. Drowned and lost in the floods, buried in a cliff fall, blown up by a mine on the cliffs? They'd never know now. Anyway, all of this was what he had to find words for, to tell Louise Stark, Nick's daughter.

I assumed that he had returned home.

The letter stopped at this point. Those words were the very last that his mother ever wrote. Looking at the familiar careful handwriting made Peter's eyes prickle.

He helped himself to a teaspoon of *Nescafé* from the jar on the worktop and stared out at the garden at Cowper's Cottage. It was a bright and sunny now, but chilly. The apple trees cast sharp shadows on the grass which was already showing signs of shagginess here and there. Soon it would be time to get Ellen's old Suffolk Colt out. He wondered whether there was any petrol in the shed. There probably was. His mother had always been well organized so far as the garden was concerned.

He must stop thinking about Ellen's old this and Ellen's old that. Almost all of her stuff was gone. He'd spent weeks clearing out. What remained was now his.

He watched a wren busying itself among some plant pots near the steps that led from the patio down into the garden. A couple of doves were canoodling on the shed roof and a green woodpecker was rooting about beneath the apple trees at the bottom of the garden. Peter loved seeing the woodpecker. There was something particularly earnest and engaging about it as it bounded about the grass feeding. He watched it for a moment until a sudden movement to the right beneath the lilac caught his eye.

The cat was crouched beneath some straggling ivy, his tail twitching. He was some distance still from the woodpecker but he was watching it intently. Peter had always been fond of animals but it was difficult to like the big ginger tom that belonged to George, his mother's younger brother and his slatternly wife Janice who lived two doors down from Peter. He had never cared for his aunt and uncle or his cousins Kingsley and Jeannie. Peter and Kingsley in particular had a long history.

He felt an intense antipathy towards them all at the moment since none of them had seen fit to attend his mother's funeral. In the months since there had been nothing from them, not a word, a card or a note. There had been no expression of sympathy and no interest whatever. It confirmed Peter's belief that Ellen had always been far better to them than they deserved.

Their cat was monstrous and ugly as sin. He was also extremely aggressive and cunning. When Toby, Ellen's old Labrador was still alive the cat tended to shun Cowper's Cottage and its environs. But Toby had died just before Ellen went into hospital. Heartbroken, she had buried him at the bottom of the garden beneath a flowering cherry tree where she could see his grave from the cottage. Now the cat was in the garden every day, apparently fervently committed to stamping out the entire avian population. Ellen had once seen the creature actually pull down a thrush in mid-flight.

The cat wasn't even well thought of in feline circles. Most of the local cats bore the scars of altercations with the tom. Peter had seen him send Mr Rump's two greyhounds packing. Other excesses included the prolonged torture and bloody despatch of Topsy, a pet rabbit from further down Back Lane and the untimely death of numerous of Mr Weller's pigeons.

The thing that really irritated Peter though was the cat's habit of defecating on the lawn and then walking away and leaving it. The tom made no concession to the generally held belief that the species was clean, that cats dug holes and buried their waste and tidied up after themselves. He obviously hadn't read the book.

Despite Peter's watchfulness after the first time he trod in the cat's copious leavings he'd traipsed muck into the cottage on two occasions in the last ten days. One night he'd gone up the stairs and into his bedroom before he noticed the stink and spotted the marks on the carpet. He'd spent the next half-hour on his hands and knees with a bucket of hot water and disinfectant.

Peter rapped sharply on the kitchen window. The cat's head whipped round. He gave a long, and it seemed to Peter, contemptuous stare. His tail twitched back and forth in agitation and then, as he turned his attention back to the woodpecker, resumed its earlier more studied motion. Peter rapped again, harder. The woodpecker and the doves flew away. The cat ignored Peter and continued to stare after the departing birds. Finally he turned again to glare at the window, then sat up and licked his privates.

'You horrible creature.'

As he turned away it occurred to Peter that simply tapping on the window was never going to discourage the cat. Not wishing to hurt the animal he'd hurled a handful of gravel in its general direction a few days earlier just to see it off. It had been curiously satisfying to see the tom bolting as the stones clattered into his next-door neighbour's wooden fence. George's head had bobbed up from his garden further over.

'What the hell was that?'

Peter had looked up, shaken his head, then called 'phone' and gone indoors. His mother was quite right about George's head. She had often referred to her brother as Mr Potato Head. From the bathroom window Peter had watched the cat scramble over his uncle's fence. He could hear George talking to the creature.

'Hello, my man. Who's the best boy in the world, then? Did he frighten you? Poor old boy.'

George stooped to fondle the creature and glanced up at Peter's window and almost certainly spotted him before Peter had ducked away.

Throwing stones wasn't the answer. There was an old Milbro catapult in a box out in the shed or the garage. It had belonged to Kingsley. It would be a nice irony to shoot the cat with his cousin's catapult. Perhaps he would seek it out sometime although he doubted that the elastic would still be any use. One well-aimed pebble… ah, there was the difficulty. Even as a child Peter had never been able to hit anything with a catapult. As the kettle clicked off and the cat stalked away Peter poured water into his mug and went back to the letter on the table. He sighed.

It was a difficult letter to write. So far he'd managed his address and the date, 15th December 1979. After a sip of his coffee he sat down and picked up the airmail envelope and read the return address again.

10981 W. Kiowa, Ventura, California, 93004 USA. He'd passed Ventura several times driving between LA and Santa

Barbara or San Luis Obispo. There had never been any reason to stop. He read the flimsy letter again.

Dear E. Fincham,

I am writing to you largely out of desperation. My name is Louise Stark. I was born Louise Nichols in Leeds in 1939. My parents were Monica (née Oldfield) and Peter, or Nick (as he was known) Nichols. I don't know whether you ever knew mother but I believe that you may have met my father during the war in Norfolk. This is something of a last ditch attempt to discover his whereabouts since nothing has been seen or heard of him since the morning of Saturday, 31ˢᵗ January 1953. You may remember it because it was the time of those dreadful North Sea floods.

Peter certainly remembered. He'd never forget that sea and he had recognized Nick as soon as he saw him standing in the doorway, hunched against the wind and rain.

He left home early that morning as usual on his bicycle. He was going to see to his pigeons at the allotment and then go on to work. Normally he would have finished at lunchtime and come home for something to eat before going to the rugby or the football in the afternoon. However, the night before he and mum had had a row.

A dog walker saw him briefly at the allotment but they didn't speak beyond saying 'Good morning'. The man didn't really know father but he had seen him about. He said that father seemed normal and cheerful enough. Whatever happened afterwards, father left his bicycle in the allotment shed and never arrived at work that day. No one saw him at all after the sighting at the allotment.

The police were involved. They searched for days, even digging up part of the allotment, but to no avail. Father still remains a missing person to this day. Mother spent years expecting that he would return. Eventually the stress made her ill.

After she passed away last year we found an old wartime pocketbook of father's among papers in the loft. Your name, alongside the Lord Nelson's address, was among a number of others written in the back.

There was no indication whether you are male or female or that you lived or worked there. You may have been a guest. We have traced or accounted for all of the names in the book except yours. Sadly most are dead. Yours was a name with which no one was familiar and I am writing in the hope that you or someone at the Lord Nelson can throw some light on father's movements or present whereabouts. I know that he was stationed in your area for a while during the war but people who knew him from that time are few and were unable to help. He would have been 38 at the time. He will be 64 now.

I realize that after all this time the chances of even finding you are slim but I thought I would have one last go at trying to obtain news of my father. If you are able to help with any information at all I will be delighted to hear from you. Please feel free to call collect (reverse charges). I look forward to hearing from you.

Yours sincerely,
Louise Stark.

Peter had known nothing of the letters or their contents until Kathy and Philip mentioned them in the bar of the Lord Nelson after Ellen's funeral. He'd been exhausted and distracted at the time. The shock of Ellen's death, the fatigue of flying home from Hawaii, the flattering attention of Margaret Graver; all of these proved a rather heady mixture.

On reading Louise's letter for himself Peter had been astonished to discover that he had a half-sister. He'd definitely have to look her up next time he was in California. They each had a different mother but Nick was father to them both.

*

'Bye boys. See you this evening.'

After ushering the last few old lags out Kathy Holt closed and bolted the door to the public bar of the Lord Nelson.

'Good grief, I thought they'd never leave.' She turned to Peter, the sole remaining Sunday lunchtime patron. 'How was the steak and kidney?'

Seated on a stool at the bar Peter put down his cutlery, pushed his plate away and shook his head as he finished the last morsel. He wiped his mouth, crumpled up his paper napkin and tossed it onto the plate.

'It was very, very tasty, thank you.' He patted his stomach appreciatively. 'And now I'm very, very full.'

'You don't want any crumble and custard?'

Peter snorted. 'I'd love some but not at the moment, I'm afraid. As you know I do like crumble. But I am F-U-L, full. It was excellent, thanks.'

'Double ell. Good. Well, you know us. You know our motto.'

They grinned at each other and chanted Dalek-like, in unison.

'Excellence comes as standard.'

Peter laughed and drained the last of his bitter. He was wearing a shapeless roll-neck navy blue sweater and light grey jeans. His hair was uncombed and curled over his collar. He hadn't shaved for days. Otherwise he looked fit and well, if a little tired.

Kathy rounded the bar, took his empty plate and glass and switched off the main lights. Every movement was well-rehearsed, quick and purposeful, belying her sixty years. She had worked at the pub in some guise since she left school at fourteen.

Before her time in the early 1900s the Lord Nelson had been one of the finest and busiest hotels in the area. The fields behind the hotel, between it and the cliffs, were often crowded with tents during the holiday season. Many were drawn to the village by the magnificent beach with its wide, golden sands, safe bathing and lows for paddling.

The hotel was still popular in the mid 1930s when Kathy began cycling to Cromer to work all day at Norah's Noted Hair Salon before returning to labour at least three evenings a week in the Lord Nelson kitchens and bar. Since that time she had worked at the pub without a break, other than for a few days after giving birth to Philip. She had experience of every aspect of hotel and bar work.

The place remained busy throughout the war but it fell into serious decline afterwards. With the cliffs still mined and the beach inaccessible the holiday trade went elsewhere. The closure of the railway in the 1950s was the final nail in the coffin. The bedrooms and the restaurant fell into disuse and the bars were treated to a succession of the worst excesses of brewery initiatives and the latest in pub chic. When Kathy took over as licensee in 1975 she ripped down all the old nets and fishing tat that festooned the public bar. To general acclaim she replaced the red plastic seating and chrome and smoked glass furniture with the old solid wooden chairs and tables which fortuitously had been stored out in the garages. Each item was repaired and refinished by the local carpenter and returned to the bar.

The beach eventually reopened in 1966 but the cliffs remained off limits. With no way down to the sands from within the village the holidaymakers continued to stay away. However, Kathy was once again offering a few rooms and meals at the Lord Nelson. She was not slow to notice that an increasing number of people had cars and stopped to enquire whether the pub did food. If and when trade picked up she hoped eventually to be able to reopen the dining room.

To the male drinking populace Kathy was the archetypal barmaid. She was friendly, talkative, a good listener, smart and sexy. She looked good and could flirt or commiserate with the best of them. Despite her age, seen from behind she could easily pass for a woman in her 40s. Petite in stature and naturally mousy-haired, she had learned long ago that image was of great import in keeping the patrons happy.

It paid to give them what they thought they wanted and Kathy never failed them. Her hair was currently ash-blonde and today worn up in her own interpretation of a French twist. Together with the four inch heels that she customarily wore in the bar it gave her all the height and authority she needed. A selection of discreetly padded bras, low-cut necklines and close fitting skirts formed Kathy's everyday uniform. Coupled with bulky costume jewellery and makeup tending towards the exuberant it gave her the appearance of the boozer's delight and everybody's friend. Men were very happy to spend much time and money in her company and women able to see past the façade, recognizing the warm and generous soul within.

Kathy was no dizzy blonde or anyone's fool or floozy. A lifetime of hard work, the early loss of her husband and bringing up Philip alone had toughened her. It had kept her sharp, her body trim and supple and her posture enviable.

Peter had known Kathy all his life. She and Ellen had been best friends since their schooldays and Peter had always loved her.

'You'll come to us for your Christmas dinner? We'll be eating in the evening. I'm not going to open Christmas night. It's always a waste of time and energy.'

'Oh. That would be great. Thanks, Kathy.'

'There's just the two of us, me and Phil. Bryan's going to stay with his sister in Cornwall. Will you be bringing anyone? Margaret?' She looked at Peter speculatively.

'No, just me. I haven't seen her recently. Not since….'

'Ah.'

Kathy had a last quick look round and turned off the bar lights.

'Are you coming through? There's a nice fire in the back and I'm going to have a cup of tea and put my feet up for a bit. Bryan's gone to see Marian. We can have a natter. And then if our eyes should happen to close and we nod off for a few minutes, well, who's to see or care.'

'Sounds good. Is there anything I can bring, or do?'

'No. Go on through and sit down. I'll bring the tea in a minute.'

*

'Can you believe it's going to be 1980?'

'I know. It doesn't bear thinking about. I'll be thirty-six next year.'

'Oh, Peter.' Kathy pretended exasperation. 'You've only just had your thirty-fifth, last month.'

Peter grinned. 'That's true.'

'Wait 'til you're sixty. You'll discover then that time really does fly.' Kathy took a sip of tea. She stared into the fire. 'Has Phil told you about this madcap scheme of his-trying to find out what happened to his father? He's found some organization, down in London, I think, that specializes in finding folk that went missing, especially during the war- people that were never properly accounted for.'

'Yes. He told me… he said he was going to look into it, at least.'

'I don't know why he wants to, what he hopes to accomplish.'

Peter frowned. 'Can't you? I can. Perhaps it will lay the ghost. It's not so very different from me and my dad. Perhaps they'll be able to turn up exactly what did happen to Dave and where he is.... Where he's buried.... You never really....'

'You could get him to find out what happened to Nick while he's at it.'

'I suppose so. I'm pretty sure he's dead. He must be.'

'Not knowing can grind you down. It did me, over Dave, for years. But you can't go on living at that sort of pitch.' Kathy shook her head. 'I don't want all that over again. It would be too upsetting and anyway, I'm settled with Bryan. I'm not sure it isn't better to let sleeping dogs... sleep.'

Bryan was a retired brewery representative. The Lord Nelson had been on his patch for years and he had known Kathy a long time. He was still married to Marian, but she had been in a near vegetative state in a mental hospital for most of their marriage. There were no children.

Bryan was older than Kathy. A quiet, retiring, self-effacing man, ruddy of face and with salt and pepper hair; he was destined always to look a good deal younger than his age. He continued to live in the bungalow in Overstrand that he once shared with Marian but otherwise he spent much of his time at the Lord Nelson with Kathy. He had recently developed an interest in cooking and often helped out in the kitchens. It was a curious arrangement but it seemed to suit everyone well enough.

Kathy finished her tea and placed her mug on the floor beside her.

They were ensconced comfortably either side of the fire in the living room in the back premises of the Lord Nelson. Kathy had kicked off her shoes and was propped up among numerous cushions and with her legs stretched out on an ancient and threadbare *chaise longue*. A magazine lay in her lap and others littered the floor. Peter was slumped in an armchair with his feet up on a tatty leather pouffe. He levered himself up in the chair and hooked the pouffe closer.

'I finally sent a letter to Louise Stark yesterday.'
'Oh, yes? The woman in America….'
'Yes.'
'What did you say?'
'Well, it took me an age.' Peter shook his head. 'In the end I just sent what mum had written and added a little bit of my own. I told her that mum had died, that we had all seen Nick that day in January 1953 and that no one's seen or heard from him or anything about him since. I also mentioned that it seems as though we're related since we have the same father.' Peter tutted and shook his head again. 'That should come as a bit of a surprise but the poor woman probably gave up any hope of a reply ages ago. She should get the letter before Christmas.'

'Yes. Ellen received the letter in March, didn't she?' Kathy frowned. 'I don't know why it took her so long to get around to answering. She was very odd about it altogether.'

Peter nodded. 'I said I'd try to look her up, Louise, next time I'm in LA. It's not far. I'm bound to be over there before too long.'

'Ha!' Kathy chortled. 'So you're finally going back to work then, after New Year?'

'Yes. I phoned the London office. I'm off to Iceland for a bit, first week in January. I'm looking forward to it. I've never been there. It's just a short term thing. Presumably after that they come up with something a bit meatier.'

Kathy laughed. 'Iceland. That'll be a bit on the chilly side at this time of year, won't it? You'll find it hard after all this time, getting up in the morning and shaving and so on. When did you stop? September?'

'Mid September, when I came home for the funeral.'
'Oh, yes. Still, you've had a good holiday.'
'Mm. I'm not sure holiday is quite the right word.'
'No, perhaps not. Break, then.'

'Yes.'

They sat in silence for a while, staring into the flames.

'I do miss Ellen.' Kathy pulled a dramatically sad face and sniffed, then promptly roused herself. 'How are you getting on with the clearing out? Do you need any more help?'

'No, thanks. I'm just about done. That reminds me though.'

'What's that?'

'Mum's paintings.'

'What about them?'

'Didn't she usually enter paintings in some exhibition at Christmas? I thought it might be nice to put some in, if we can.'

'Oh, yes. That's a good idea. She had some watercolours she wanted to show this year. Did a couple in the summer up at Wells and Cley. She had three, I think. She was really pleased with how they'd turned out... had them framed. They were jolly good, I thought.'

'Who organizes it, do you know? Who would I need to get in touch with?'

'Well, anyone from the art class. They meet every Thursday morning at ten down in the old school. The exhibition will be in there, in the big room. Your best bet would be to take the paintings along this Thursday. Or you could always phone what's her name? She still runs it. Manfredi, Gabrielle... Gabby Manfredi. She lives at The Old Rectory.'

'Gabrielle Manfredi, Gracious. What's that? French? Italian? Sounds a bit exotic for these parts, at any rate. I think I saw her name and number on the notice board in the kitchen. I'd better get on with it or we'll miss the boat.'

'I think Manfredi's Italian. It's her husband's name but they both sound English. She's English, certainly. Born in Norwich, I think. She's a nice girl. You've probably seen them in here. They're in occasionally. Most Sunday lunchtimes, but not today.'

In the warmth and flickering light of the fire and the companionable silence that followed both Kathy and Peter fell asleep. When Peter awoke some time later he found Kathy studying him.

'What?' Peter found her gaze disconcerting.

Kathy shook her head. 'Nothing.' She continued to stare. After a moment her expression softened. 'I was just thinking how well you've done.'

'Oh? How do you mean?'

'Well, you've just lost your mum, comparatively young, totally unexpected, while you were away. And you've had the funeral and all the clearing out and so on.'

'I do wish I'd seen her before she died, but I suppose everyone says that. I really do regret not seeing more of her though. I could have… should have made more effort.' A pained look crossed Peter's face. 'It never occurs to you that you won't see someone again. You say, "bye, take care, see you next time," and it never even enters your head.'

'Well, of course. But you can't live like that... as though you're never going to see someone ever again. You have to get on with your life and take some things on trust or you'd never actually go anywhere or do anything.'

'True enough.'

'Then there's you and Abigail splitting up. After all this time it can't have been easy even if your marriage wasn't all that great. Do you think you'll get back together?'

'No.' Peter was emphatic. 'No way. Not a chance. She's got someone else, anyway. We haven't been close for years. I can't remember the last time we slept together.' Peter screwed up his eyes and peered up at the ceiling. 'Hang on a minute. I tell a lie. I do know. It was when she flew out for the weekend when I was in Holland. The Rijnhotel, if I remember rightly.

That would have been nineteen-seventy-five, no six. Yes, six.'

'It's a shame.'

'Ah! I'm glad it's over.'

'Will you get a divorce?'

'I suppose so. But I'm in no hurry. I'll wait until I hear something from her.'

'And then there was Margaret. That really was a…. You seemed so happy together.'

'Yes, but it rather failed to take into account the fact that she was married, is still married, and is now pregnant.'

After a long pause Kathy gave Peter a sideways look.

'Do you… do you believe her?'

'What? That it's her husband's child?' Peter looked sceptical. 'There's no way of knowing, is there? He was at home a few days before mum's funeral, apparently. But he'd gone by the time I met her and… well, things did move quite quickly, I suppose.'

'Hmm, within hours, I heard.' Kathy rolled her eyes and shook her head. 'I don't know, such goings on in Back Lane.'

'But she said the baby is his. She was adamant. I thought it had to be mine but that wasn't based on anything other than… and of course I can't prove it, if she says it isn't.'

'Well. It all seems to have been a bit of a rich mixture in such a short period of time.' Kathy smiled at Peter. 'You seem to be holding up pretty well though, I must say. I was just saying the same thing to Phil.'

'Oh, well. I can't say I haven't been a bit down from time to time. But you just have to get on with it, don't you?'

'Ellen would have been so proud. She was terribly proud of you.'

*

Back at Cowper's Cottage that evening Peter placed his mother's paintings along the foot of her bedroom wall. Fortunately she had been meticulous in signing and dating them and it was a straightforward matter to identify the likely candidates for the art exhibition. He got the number for the Manfredi's house from the kitchen notice board and after speaking to a young girl was passed to Gabby, who was obviously on her way out.

'Yes,' she said. 'Can you bring them down to the school on Thursday? Twelve, or just after would be good.' Peter heard the repeated click of a cigarette lighter and a moment later the hiss of exhaled smoke. 'The old dears will have gone by then.'

Fired by the sight of his mother's paintings he dragged his old art portfolio out from beneath the wardrobe in the spare bedroom. The large rectangular folder, clad in grey, white and black swirling Fablon, looked as though it had lain there untouched since he left school. He had been tempted to toss it out of the carriage window as the train crossed the bridge over the river near Knapton on his last journey home from school. It was the custom for leavers to empty their school bags and dispose of at least some items of uniform in such fashion on the last day.

Peter had balled up his tie, his cap and his threadbare blazer and hurled them from the carriage window. Something similar was going on, accompanied by much whooping and yipping at each window along the train. He had been gratified to see his bundle land in the water. Some claimed that timing was everything, but in Peter's case it had been pure luck. He smiled as he recalled that for years later a pair of navy blue knickers had hung among the branches of a dying elder on the bank beside the bridge, thrown from the train by someone over-exuberant at leaving the girls' high school.

After wiping the dust from the folder he placed it on the bed and opened it up. His nostrils were filled immediately with the smell of printing ink from his old lino and wood engraving prints. There within the portfolio, he found his old O and A level efforts, the wood engravings that had taken months of painstaking work, the bolder lino prints and numerous careful compositions of twigs and flowers in Indian ink and wash. Beneath them were the results of earlier forays with powder paint, gouache and pen and pencil and his efforts at abstract painting. He'd got an A grade in Art and there was a time when old Charlie Barley, the Art teacher, tried to interest him in going to Art College and perhaps a career in graphic design. Barley apparently had an old college friend who was principal at some fashionable College in London and he was keen to call in a favour. Peter had been excited about the prospect for a while but it turned out to be no more than one of his many short-lived enthusiasms.

Spread out on the bed now he thought that his A level work still stood up quite well, rather better than the swirly Fablon, which looked distinctly dated. He was glad that he hadn't thrown the folder out of the train.

Later that evening he dug out Ellen's brushes, watercolours and oil paints and after shunting the furniture about set up her easel in the conservatory. He spent much of his time in the following days sketching and painting what he could see. The cat came and went, stalking through the garden several times but since it neither defecated nor harassed any birds Peter did no more than watch the creature and mutter to himself.

It was just after noon on the Thursday when he parked Ellen's Morris Minor immediately behind a bright red but slightly battered MGB convertible, outside the old school. Deep in conversation, a number of elderly women and a handful of men were still leaving the hall, almost all encumbered by drawing boards, easels and capacious bags and boxes. They nodded and smiled as Peter took Ellen's paintings out of the boot. He realized that the car would be all too familiar to them.

As he entered the old schoolroom the only person he could see was a tallish, slender woman with blonde hair scraped up into a knot and held in place by a large tortoiseshell comb. She half turned from the flyblown mirror over the fireplace.

'Hello, can I help…?' She turned back to the mirror.

She wore a pair of gold-framed spectacles and was elegantly dressed in a dark brown sweater, a long oatmeal skirt and high boots in tan leather.

'Oh,' she called, her voice echoing in the empty room. She finished applying lipstick and turned back to him. 'You must be Ellen's son. Peter?'

'Yes. I've brought the….'

'Come on through. Bring them into the other room. Do you need a hand? We can put them in our cupboard for now.' Snapping a compact shut she gathered up a huge handbag and led the way through to the adjoining room, the heels of her boots rapping the pale dusty floorboards. Having unlocked the cupboard door she turned to take the paintings.

'Ah good, you've brought the mill… and the church. And I like this one very much.' The third painting was a watercolour of poppies in the field beyond the bottom of the garden at Cowper's Cottage. Gabby held the painting at arm's length for a moment. 'Are you sure you don't want to keep any of them?' She placed the paintings carefully beside some others on the floor of the cupboard.

'There are quite a few on the walls at home. I like the poppies too, but there are several similar paintings that I like better. I think mum enjoyed painting them.'

'Phew. There's a terrible smell of damp here somewhere. Still they won't be here long.' She closed the cupboard door, locked it and then thrust out a pale bony hand. Each fingernail was elegantly shaped and varnished the same dusky pink as her lips. 'I'm Gabby Manfredi.'

'Peter Fincham.' He shook her hand and grinned. 'How do you do? It's good of you to take mother's pictures.'

'Oh, we're glad to. She was one of our stalwarts. We were so sad at your loss, our loss. Ellen was lovely. She was much loved and greatly admired. We will miss her. She always entered something in the Christmas show. Usually sold one or two. You might be lucky this year. Did you price them?'

'No. I didn't really....'

'I'll take care of it.'

Gabby tiptoed to the door in rather a dramatic fashion and peered into the larger room. She turned back and smiled. 'I think they've gone. Someone usually forgets something.'

She went to her handbag and took out a packet of Benson & Hedges and a slim gold lighter. 'One or two of them invariably make a fuss if I smoke. Do you?' She offered the packet to Peter.

'Oh. Thanks.'

He hadn't smoked since he and Margaret finished the packet of Lucky Strikes he'd brought with him from Hawaii. As Gabby lit the cigarette he noticed that it smelled faintly of expensive perfume.

'So,' Gabby exhaled extravagantly, 'do you paint at all? Ellen was quite talented and she certainly got a kick out of it. Have you inherited the gene, or the interest?'

'Not sure about any talent but I've just spent the last few days splashing and mudding about with her watercolours and oils. Enjoyed myself enormously.'

'Oh? What have you been painting? Of course, you're in the film business, aren't you? It's creative.'

'Just ideas from the garden. I'm not sure that what I do takes much in the way of creativity. But when I was getting mum's paintings I dug out my old artwork from school. I was so fired up I got her easel and stuff out into the conservatory and got going. I must say it was fun.' Peter looked at Gabby and grinned. 'What do you paint?'

'I don't,' Gabby shook her head. 'I used to. Now I'm reduced to this.' She gestured at the empty room. 'What is it they say? If you can, do, if you can't, teach. Most of the old dears haven't got a clue, bless them, but they enjoy themselves. It's more a social occasion than an art class. No matter how many times I point out to them that tree trunks are usually green or grey, if they're painting a tree, they invariable reach for the tube of poo brown.'

Peter laughed as Gabby grinned and continued.

'I worked in a couple of galleries for a while too. I may not paint but I can teach a bit and I do know good painting when I see it.' Gabby screwed up her nose and shook her head. 'Sadly, I just can't do good painting, myself.' She marched across to a window, opened it and tossed her cigarette end out. 'I haven't the patience. It's like me and gardening. I can't stand gardening. It's so slow. Everything takes so long. I like quick results.'

'Ah,' Peter found himself nodding sagely. 'But anything creative usually takes time.'

'Why don't you join the class if you're going to be around? We could do with some new blood.'

'Ah. Sadly, I'm not stopping. I go back to work in the New Year.'

'Oh, that's a shame. It'd be good to have someone nearer my own age. Most of them are geriatric.'

They sat on the battered wooden trestles and stacked table tops in the empty schoolroom for as long as it took Gabby to smoke a second cigarette. Peter found her easy to talk to and she seemed much at ease with him.

He was surprised as they left the school together when she called to him as he was getting into the Morris.

'Are you going home now?'

'Yes. Why?'

'I'll follow you. I've got to go to the shop anyway. You can show me your paintings.' She gave him a quizzical look.

'Oh.' Peter was nonplussed, but pleased. 'Okay. You know where...? I'll see you there.'

*

He managed to tidy away the worst excesses of his bachelor lifestyle before the MGB skidded to a halt on the gravel in front of Cowper's Cottage. He'd left the front door ajar and called out when he heard boot heels on the quarry tiles in the porch.

'Hello? Come on in.'

'Hiya. Where are you?'

'Come on through. I'm in the kitchen.'

Gabby took off her gloves and unbuttoned her long coat as she entered. She looked around. 'This is nice.'

'Have you not been in before?'

'No. I've been as far as the door collecting for something or other, but I've never been in.'

Peter took her coat.

'Would you like coffee? I've put the kettle on.'

'Oh. Yes. That would be lovely.'

Shooting Marmalade

'*Nescafe?* Is that all right?'

'Yes. I prefer instant.' Gabby rooted in her handbag for her cigarettes and lighter.

'Me too. Do you take milk or sugar?'

'No, black thanks. Do you want one?' She offered the packet of Benson & Hedges.

'Thanks.'

Gabby lit their cigarettes and then turned away.

'So where are these paintings?'

'They're in the conservatory.' Peter gestured through the sitting room. 'Go on through. I'll bring the coffees.'

He found Gabby standing well back from the painting on the easel with her head tilted to one side. She stared at the picture for some time. Eventually she spoke.

'Did you say you had some others?'

'Yes. A couple. I'm afraid that none of them is finished though.' Peter replaced the painting on the easel with another and propped a third against the easel legs. Gabby moved little further away and then frowned as she backed into the wall. 'You need more room. This place is far too small.'

'It is a bit.'

Again Gabby spent several minutes smoking silently and concentrating on the paintings.

'And these are original?'

'Yes. They're probably not up to much but I enjoyed painting them.'

Gabby gave Peter a stare.

'Do you really think that, or are you just being a pain?'

'What?' Peter wasn't sure what to say. 'Why? Why do you ask?'

Gabby didn't answer immediately. She wandered over to look out of the windows at the garden. Eventually she turned and looked at Peter.

'Did you say you had your old portfolio?'

Peter nodded.

'Is it handy? Can I have a look?'

Peter fetched the shabby Fablon folder and took it into the dining room where he opened it up on the table. 'What you have to remember is that I was but a callow youth when I did this lot.'

'I know.' Gabby leafed carefully through the contents of the portfolio, pausing occasionally to dwell on one or two pieces. Beside her Peter groaned at the sight of some of his old offerings.

'Oh, don't.'

Having been through the entire folder once; Gabby leafed through it again.

'You've certainly matured,' Gabby said.

'Oh?'

'Your painting.'

'Ah.'

'Have you ever thought about painting professionally?'

'No. Well, not since I left school.'

Gabby turned and looked up at Peter. 'You should. I know a number of galleries that would be interested in the paintings in the conservatory, without a doubt. O and O would, for one. Lavinia would love them.'

'Who is… are O and O?'

'Opie O'Grady. Gallery in the City. I used to work for them.' Gabby poked Peter in the chest. 'Try some even more imaginative stuff.' She looked at her watch. 'I must go. Thanks for showing me your paintings. You should paint on canvas though and give abstract a go.'

Peter saw Gabby out to her car. She was on the point of leaving when she opened the driver's window.

She frowned for a moment. 'What are you doing on Christmas Day? Got anything lined up?'

'Well, I…' the lie came easily, 'not really.'

'Why don't you come to us?' Gabby paused for a moment, fumbled in her handbag and then thrust a business card through the window.

'Come about noon. We usually eat mid-afternoon. Give us time for a drink and a chat. Spencer will be pleased to meet you.'

5. Father, where art thou?

Peter was interested to see that even after her death Ellen received more Christmas cards than he did. There were obviously still people unaware that she had died. But he was in reasonably good spirits on Christmas morning, given that it was his first at Cowper's Cottage without his mother or his wife.

There had been a card from Abigail. It was just one of the many company cards that she sent to customers each year. She had written that she would be in Milan for Christmas, returning to London on New Years Eve. This intelligence left Peter unmoved.

The final post before Christmas brought an unexpected bonus in the shape of a card from Margaret Graver.

'With much love and best wishes for a very Happy Christmas, Margaret. XX'

Her neat and stylish Italics and the double kiss left Peter far from unmoved.

They'd first met at Ellen's funeral when Kathy introduced them beside the lych gate. He'd invited Margaret back to the Lord Nelson to join the rest of the mourners for a drink and a bite to eat. Kathy said later that the attraction between them was almost embarrassingly obvious. It had been immediate and mutual and after everyone else had left the Lord Nelson they spent the rest of the afternoon together drinking and chatting. Eventually Margaret drove Peter to Cowper's Cottage. There they continued until in view of the lateness of the hour and the fact that they had both drunk quite a lot of alcohol Peter invited Margaret to stay the night.

It was while they were preparing the guest bed that they kissed and rather quickly thereafter ended up together in Peter's bed. It was the beginning of a particularly intense affair. During the following weeks they were almost inseparable. Then suddenly in late October, without any explanation, Margaret disappeared off the radar.

Eventually an unhappy Peter went one evening to the convalescent home where Margaret worked as Administration Manager. He caught her as she was leaving. They sat in the dark in Margaret's Mini outside Cavell House and she told him that she was pregnant and that she couldn't possibly see him again. Peter immediately assumed that the baby was his but Margaret was adamant that her husband Tom was the father.

Tom Graver was a marine biologist and his prolonged absence in the Antarctic had facilitated Peter and Margaret's romantic activities. However he had apparently been at home the week before Ellen's funeral. Margaret apologized for not letting Peter know but she said that it had to be over between them. It wasn't fair on her husband and besides, she wasn't sure that she could trust herself in Peter's company.

Peter was devastated. He had been under the impression that little remained of Margaret and Tom's marriage, not unlike his own with Abigail. He had been hopeful of some sort of future with Margaret although nothing had been promised.

He was therefore a little taken aback to receive a Christmas card since there had been no contact at all between them since that wretched evening in November. He wondered what it meant, if anything.

*

He was sauntering round the garden killing time until he could reasonably set off for The Old Rectory when he came across the pile of fresh excreta on Toby's grave.

'Ugh! You filthy creature.' He cast about the garden but there was no sign of the cat. It was as he was on his way to fetch a garden spade from the shed that he changed his mind and decided to go to see his Uncle George and Aunt Janice. He'd had little to do with them since arriving but it was Christmas morning after all, and they were family. Hopefully he would find them in good humour. Perhaps they could resolve the cat poo problem over a festive glass of something or other. Despite the fact that George and his family had never given his mother so much as a greeting card he felt that he should extend the hand of friendship. He'd already poked a card through their letterbox and he'd bought a white poinsettia in order to have something by him should he need an unexpected present. It would be the work of a moment to write a gift tag.

Armed with the poinsettia Peter knocked at No 3, Back Lane.

'George! Someone at the door,' Janice shrieked from inside. 'I can't go, I'm….' Aunt Janice sounded fraught. Eventually the door opened and George appeared. A short, balding, thickset man with huge shoulders and stomach, and a neck rather wider than his head; Peter's uncle cut a less than impressive figure. He appeared unwashed, unshaven, and had obviously been plucking poultry of some sort earlier. There was a well-thumbed *TV Times* and the cardboard tube from the centre of a toilet roll tucked under his arm.

He had feathers and down in the remains of his hair, on his clothes and on the hairy backs of his arms. Returning from the lavatory he was still tucking the tail of a collarless shirt into a pair of brand new shiny green trousers. Having completed that operation he struggled with his braces. He was also sporting new carpet slippers in a regal shade of purple, undoubtedly this years' Christmas present from Janice, May or Jeannie.

'Morning, George, Happy Christmas to you.' Peter exuded a jocularity and *bonhomie* that he really didn't feel.

'Why-up,' George said. He looked at Peter suspiciously then turned away. 'I suppose you'd better come in.'

'Who is it?' Janice squawked.

'Peter.'

'Don't go letting him in here.' Janice shrieked. 'I haven't got no clothes on and I haven't got time to be sitting around chatting.'

Actually Janice was still in her nightdress. A short, burly woman with short curly hair, Janice always gave Peter the impression of being angry and in a hurry. As he stepped down into the tiny kitchen he could see his aunt's broad back at the sink. Even from behind she looked hostile. She was up to her elbows in a plucked cockerel and busy dropping bloody innards onto a newspaper spread out beside her on the floor. Perched precariously on a tray on the draining board a second freshly-plucked cockerel awaited the same fate. The smell was appalling.

'Happy Christmas, Janice.' Peter almost gagged at the stench from the cockerel's entrails. 'I've brought you a little something.'

As Janice turned to peer over her left shoulder something disturbed the balance of the precarious construction on the draining board. The sequence of events thereafter was hard to follow, but the floor immediately around Janice was suddenly covered in water, potatoes, peelings, sprouts, stuffing and the corpses of two cockerels.

'Ow!' Janice howled. 'Look! Look at what he's made me go and do now.'

'Blast, gal,' George shouted, hopping about from one foot to the other. 'What the bloody hell….'

'Ow, I'm all wet. And look at the stuffing. Ow, I've just trod in it.'

'I'll just put this down in the living room.' Peter muttered apologetically from behind his poinsettia. 'Sorry if I've come at an inconvenient….'

'I told you not to….'

'Stay there! And mind them new slippers. If you want any Christmas dinner today, George Fincham, you'll stop right there.' Janice sounded dangerous.

'I was just….'

'Yes. I know what you were just. You're just the same idle bastard that you always were. Useless. All you bloody Finchams are the same.'

'I'm sorry,' Peter said. 'Is there anything I can do to help?'

'Yes,' said Janice, as she dropped to her knees and began picking up potatoes. She glared at Peter. 'You can bugger off. It's your fault anyhow. If you hadn't come round here we wouldn't be in this bloody pickle would we? And I've got Kingsley and May coming and our Jeannie and Greg and the kids and….' And Janice was red in the face and sweating profusely and looking like she might very well blow a gasket at any moment.

Peter stared at his aunt and uncle and then turned abruptly and let himself out. Now would be a poor time to raise the issue of cat poo, he felt. He could still hear his aunt and uncle as he closed the front door to Cowper's Cottage.

'Numbskulls,' he muttered.

*

Having gathered the cat turds onto a garden spade he was about to toss them over the fence into the field at the bottom of the garden when he had a thought. Penny Hunt; his next door neighbour was away on voluntary service in Africa. Peter had seen neither hide nor hair of her during the time he'd been at Cowper's Cottage. No one seemed to know with any certainty where she was or when she would be back. She was certainly not at home this Christmas morning though.

After a moment of deliberation Peter retraced his steps. A quick look round confirmed that there was no one about so after another brief pause he tossed the cat faeces carefully across Penny's garden into George and Janice's backyard. The fence prevented him seeing precisely where they landed but he was fairly sure that at least some of the mess would be on their path.

'Happy Christmas. So shall ye sow, so shall ye reap,' he muttered. 'And with any luck one of you will tread in it.'

After he had cleaned the spade and put it away in the shed he set about looking for Kingsley's old catapult. He found it without much difficulty, but as he had feared the elastic had perished. It was useless and he tossed it into the rubbish bin. His mood improved immeasurably though when he spotted a small red and blue striped cardboard box spilling its contents among numerous rusty tools and DIY detritus in the bottom of an old enamel breadbin. He lifted the box out.

'BEATALL,' he read aloud, '*WAISTED Air gun pellets, .177 or No 1 bore.*' And there, nestling among the spilled pellets at the bottom of the breadbin he spotted the chromium-plated barrel of his old Diana air pistol. Ellen had confiscated it years ago. He took it out, blew and wiped the dust off it and spent a moment or two gloating over it just as he had more than twenty years earlier. After several unsuccessful attempts to spin the gun on his index finger in the manner of a practised gunslinger he gave up, carefully compressed the barrel, took aim at the light bulb hanging from the shed ceiling and pulled the trigger.

'*Bok!*' It still worked.

The air pistol looked as menacing as it had the day he first saw it in the window of the sports shop in Cromer. He was thirteen at the time. He'd coveted it for months but Ellen had forbidden its purchase even if he saved up his pocket money and paid for it himself. But he'd been determined to have it. His mother would just have to remain ignorant of the fact. Week after week he went out of his way to pass the shop window to make sure it was still there. Eventually he managed to scrape together the money. As he handed over the seven shillings and sixpence he assured the shop assistant behind the counter that yes, he was indeed sixteen. The man had had some difficulty not laughing but the transaction had been concluded with the dignity of both parties remaining intact. Peter had taken the pistol out of its bag on the bus on the way home for a surreptitious look and had been forced to bundle it away hurriedly when the conductor came past.

Once home he hid the pistol in an old shoe box in his bedroom. The box was labelled '*Fossils, Shells & Stones*' and had once contained examples of each, gathered from the beach. He knew that his mother would never look in it since she claimed that the few original contents remaining smelled of rotting fish.

Having cleaned and oiled the pistol Peter loaded it and compressed the barrel. He looked around the garden for a suitable target and eventually took an empty oilcan from the shed and placed it on the garden fence. It took him five attempts, moving closer to the target each time, before he hit it. On the successful occasion the can clanked very satisfactorily but it fell irritatingly just out of reach in the field.

He took a few more pot-shots at targets further away and was disappointed to see that he could follow the flight of the pellet quite easily as it looped in a leisurely fashion in an arc high and to the left, before dropping low and right. Rather illogically he had hoped that in the intervening years the pistol would somehow have become more powerful and more accurate than he remembered.

He wasn't going to be able to hit anything with the little Diana, but that suited him well enough. It wasn't killing that he was interested in but it should be possible to get a pellet close enough to the cat to frighten him off.

It was well after eleven-thirty when he looked at his watch. He took the Diana and the box of pellets inside and left them in the conservatory. His shoes were sodden from the wet grass so he changed them and after some deliberation decided he'd be a good deal quicker going to Gabby's on Ellen's old bicycle. He'd tidied up the old black Raleigh and used it occasionally for nipping down to Annie's shop.

After accepting Gabby's invitation for Christmas Day he'd had to make his peace with Kathy. She and Philip had hooted when he explained.

'Ah well,' said Kathy. 'You're right to go. It's not every day you get called to the top table. I shall look forward to hearing how it goes.' She laughed. 'You'll get a good dinner at any rate, what with Spencer being in the trade.'

'Oh, is he a chef?'

Philip laughed. 'He's got a fish and chip shop.'

Kathy shook her head.

'No. He's got several now, restaurants too, and I think he's about to open another.'

Peter apologized and said he would look in later on Christmas night if that was all right.

He had just placed a couple of bottles of wine in the cane basket on the handlebars and mounted up at the gate when a car crested the rise at the top of Back Lane. It was travelling very fast. He decided to wait in the gateway until it had passed but the brown Rover 2000 skidded to a halt just past the gate and with much revving of the motor the car backed up. The driver leaned over and wound down the passenger door window a few inches.

'Get off and milk it,' he shouted. 'You want to get yourself a proper bike.'

Neither understanding what was said nor recognizing the car; Peter dismounted and bent down. The driver had a big, pasty moon face and the same unsettling washed-out blue eyes as his mother.

'Oh. Hello, King.'

Peter's cousin Kingsley leered at him through clouds of blue smoke.

'What are you up to, Pedro?' he shouted. 'Are you coming round to ours for your dinner?'

'No, I'm….'

'Why not? Don't you want a good feed?'

'I wasn't invited.' And frankly, Peter thought, I'm extremely glad that it isn't me that has to put up with a day of the worst excesses of you and your family in the close confines of No 3 Back Lane.

Something stirred on the seat beside Kingsley and another big silly face, brown and white and hairy, suddenly reared up and hurled itself at the window. Taken by surprise Peter lurched backwards. It was Archie, Kingsley's Basset hound. The creature barked hysterically, and then all aquiver, stared sidelong at Peter through the slobber on the glass, willing him to put his hand through the narrow opening.

Kingsley said nothing but grinned around the stem of what was obviously a brand new pipe. The odour of burning tobacco wafting through the window was sickly sweet and reminded Peter of something, custard creams, perhaps. He realized there was someone in the back of the car.

'Oh, hello May.' He gestured at her. 'Merry Christmas.'

'Hiya, Merry Christmas.' Kingsley's bovine wife was already stuck into a box of chocolates in her lap and didn't look up.

'What do you think of the new motor?' Kingsley shouted. 'Good innit?'

'Oh, yes. It's very nice.'

'Got it yesterday. You want to get yourself one. Be better than pissing about in that crappy old Moggie of your mother's.'

'Yes,' Peter laughed. 'I expect you're right.'

'Is that your mother's old bike?'

'Yes. Why?'

Kingsley snorted. 'Thought so.'

'Well, I must be off.' Peter mounted up again. 'Have a good Christmas.'

As he made to leave Kingsley revved the motor and edged the Rover across his path forcing him into the wall. He almost fell off the bicycle, saving himself only by propping himself up on Penny Hunt's front wall.

'What?' Peter staggered, hauled the bike upright and then bobbed down to peer through the window. 'What are you doing?'

Kingsley grinned, puffed on his pipe and backed off slightly. Both he and Archie watched expectantly and when Peter remounted Kingsley repeated the manoeuvre.

'Oh, very funny.'

Shooting Marmalade

Kingsley was laughing like a drain. Archie was smearing nose all over the passenger window. Behind Kingsley's shaking shoulders May cackled. Kingsley kept on until Peter lost his balance and fell, the bicycle handlebars scraping the car's nearside wing and passenger door, gouging scratches almost a foot long. Kingsley backed up, leapt out of the car as though scalded and hurried round to examine the damage. Peter picked himself up and remounted.

'Shit! Look what you've done!' Kingsley was furious. 'Best bloody car in the street and you go and do that. I've only had it five minutes.'

Peter shook his head, rolled up his right trouser leg and examined the scrape and developing lump on his shin. He was shaken and angry.

'It's your own fault.' He rubbed his leg. 'You've only got yourself to blame. If you had just let me go about my business it wouldn't have happened. You would keep on though, wouldn't you? As usual. You could never leave anyone alone. Always got to be goading. You could have killed me.'

'It was only a sodding joke. I was just having a laugh.'

'Yeah, that'd be right. Well, you can laugh at that.' Peter nodded at the damaged car. 'You're a bully, Kingsley and an idiot. You always were and you always will be.'

'What's happened, King? What's he done?' The nearside rear passenger door opened and May levered her considerable bulk out. Tottering in white sling-backs she was otherwise resplendent in a pale blue satin suit that was obviously too small to accommodate her adequately.

'Ow, look at that,' she wailed. 'Did he do that?' She turned on Peter, spilling chocolates from her Black Magic. 'What'd you want to go and do that for? Ow, look. Look what he's made me do now.'

Peter shook his head disbelievingly and turned away as his Aunt Janice, hearing raised voices, appeared hotfoot from her gate. She was now dressed in an outfit not dissimilar from May's, only peach in colour and by all appearances, with the same provenance.

'What's going on?'

'And here comes another idiot,' Peter muttered under his breath. 'Bye, Happy Christmas,' he called as he made good his escape.

Even half way down Back Lane he could make out Janice screeching. Before he turned out onto the coast road he concluded that the total IQ of those gathered in and around the Rover 2000 at the top of Back Lane equalled exactly the number of wheels on the car, and that included the Basset. He checked the wine in the bicycle basket. Fortunately, despite Kingsley's intervention, it had remained intact.

*

The Old Rectory was a huge house standing in extensive grounds on the corner of Station Road and the main coast road. A wide gravel drive ran from the wrought-iron gates in the five-foot boundary walls up to the front door. Beyond, the drive passed between neat lawns and formal flower beds to what had originally been the kitchen garden and the stables where fish and chip entrepreneur Spencer Manfredi now kept his collection of classic cars.

Peter's old English master had lived in the Rectory once. He'd kept pigs in a sty at the bottom of the garden until the neighbours complained. Once the pigs had been sent packing the sty had made an excellent den and the boys of the village congregated there to smoke cigarettes, read racy magazines and boast and speculate about girls. They sometimes lit a fire and had on one memorable occasion cooked a stew. It all came to an abrupt end after Kingsley set fire to the sty.

The resulting conflagration spread rapidly and consumed numerous trees and bushes in the vicinity. Everyone got away successfully before the fire brigade and the police sergeant turned up but Kingsley's instantly recognisable bulk and triangular head had been spotted. When the police sergeant called round at Uncle George's cottage later he found Kingsley standing naked in six inches of water in a galvanized bath in the middle of the kitchen floor while his mother bathed him. Given stern looks by his inquisitor and badgered by his mother it had taken Kingsley no time at all to grass on everyone who had been present. Somehow though, the fact was overlooked that he had been responsible for starting the fire in the first place.

*

Peter propped his bike beneath a fig tree beside the front door of The Old Rectory and rang the bell. Eventually two dark-haired girls dressed in coats, hats, scarves and gloves came to the door.

'Oh,' said one, 'hello.' The other gave Peter a tight-lipped smile.

The girls left, heading off down the drive, leaving the door ajar and Peter standing on the doorstep. After a minute or two no one else had appeared so he ventured inside and closed the front door behind him.

'Hello?' he called.

The hall was in near darkness. Only the feeble light penetrating a sagging stained-glass window halfway up a wide staircase at the far end provided illumination. Even so, it was evident in the gloom that the hall was spacious enough to accommodate a cricket pitch. Huge doors were let into the walls either side and there were double doors at the far end some way past the foot of the stairs. Peter knocked tentatively and opened the first door on the right. It was a cloakroom. The second door on the same side opened into a huge dining room containing a groaning sideboard, two Hostess trolleys and a highly polished table set for five. The walls were festooned with holly, ivy, other greenery and many a festive paper chain and gewgaw.

He was heading for the next door on the right when a large ungainly man backed into the hall from behind a green baize door on the left. Peter heard Gabby's raised voice. '… bloody great turkey… and I can't be expected to….' The rest was lost as the door closed. The man was dressed in an opennecked white shirt, dark business trousers and black shoes. He was smoking a small cigar and was bent beneath the weight of a huge tray loaded with bottles and glasses.

'Blah, blah, blah, blah, blah.' He muttered round the stub of his cigar. '…for God's sake woman… give it a rest, do.' He suddenly noticed Peter looming up beside him. 'Whoa! Good grief… didn't see you there… gave me a bit of a turn.'

'Sorry. I didn't mean to….'

'Nearly lost the good stuff.'

The man put the tray down on a monstrous dark wood settle in the hall.

'We'd all get on so much better with a little light.'

He marched over and flicked numerous switches beside the green baize door, then turned, took the cigar out of his mouth and after surveying Peter for a moment stuck out his hand.

'You must be Peter… Fincham, isn't it? I'm Spencer. Manfredi. Happy Christmas, and welcome to our humble abode.'

'Happy Christmas to you, Spencer. Thank you. I've brought a couple of….'

'Oh. Good man.' Spencer took the bottles and without so much as a glance at the labels placed them on the tray.

Gabby's husband was a very big man. He was balding, with what remained of his black hair over-long, oiled and curling over his collar. He had a small and finicky moustache and was very red in the face, presumably Peter thought, from the exertion of carrying the heavily loaded tray.

'Gabrielle's in the kitchen buggering about with sauces. We've got brandy sauce, cranberry sauce, bread sauce and I know not what other kinds of sauce. There are pots and pans and dishes and trays and crap everywhere. She is not a tidy or methodical cook. I don't know how anyone can work like that. I can't stand it. It's not safe to go in there. Come on into the sitting room. There's a nice fire. I'll get you a drink. Gin?'

'Yes. Thank you.'

The door on the right, opposite the green baize door opened into a large sitting room that boasted two huge sofas and several armchairs arranged around a large TV and an open fire. An enormous Christmas tree adorned the corner of the room diagonally opposite the television and what looked like hundreds of Christmas cards hung from strings on the walls. More paper chains and lanterns hung from the ceiling. Spencer handed Peter a gin and tonic and ushered him into one of the chairs. He put an *Abba* LP on the stereo, threw Peter an enormous packet of salted peanuts and then disappeared. Somewhat bemused, Peter sipped his gin. It was eye-wateringly strong.

Gabby appeared from the kitchen with a tall glass brimming with something alcoholic. She dabbed delicately at the thin film of perspiration on her forehead and upper lip. Her hair was gathered up into a complicated knot on the back of her head but it appeared to be in danger of escaping. Otherwise looking very attractive in a dark blue dress and heels she appeared to Peter a little on the smart and precarious side for serious cooking. She fanned her face and blew at an errant strand of hair as she approached.

'Peter,' she called. 'I'm hot.' Peter scrambled up from his chair and returned the rather clumsy embrace. Gabby kissed him on the cheek. 'Happy Thingy,' she cried.

'Yes. Happy Christmas.'

'Has Santa been good to you?' She detached herself and took a cigarette from an open packet of Benson & Hedges on the mantelpiece. 'Spencer has gone to fetch some logs.' She had just sat down and lit her cigarette when something began pinging in the kitchen.

'Oh, piss pots,' she said.

It turned out to be a strange Christmas and a long day. Both Gabby and Spencer had obviously been at the gin long before Peter arrived. There had also been some kind of altercation between Gabby and Spencer's daughters resulting in the two girls stumping off to spend Christmas Day with Spencer's sister in her cottage in Church Street. With the two girls gone there were only three for dinner in the huge dining room. There was far too much food, not to mention the sauces. Gabby had obviously lost interest in the meal long before it appeared on the table.

After a brief moment of forced hilarity when they pulled crackers, read out the mind-numbing jokes and put on silly hats Spencer and Gabby largely ignored each other and the meal descended into the sound of eating and drinking interspersed with questions and answers. Both Gabby and Spencer drank steadily, Gabby at one point drinking both red wine and gin. The meal and the conversation became increasingly chaotic until Gabby suddenly lurched up and rushed out. After she failed to return Spencer eventually left the table to look for her. He returned with the news that she'd been as sick as a dog in the cloakroom and had now taken to her bed.

'I should use the upstairs loo, if I were you,' said Spencer. Peter thanked his host for the meal and said that perhaps under the circumstances it might be best if he left. Spencer wouldn't hear of it. He bustled through to the kitchen and returned with Christmas pudding and brandy sauce so fierce and alcoholic that it was almost inedible. This was followed in short order by port and Stilton during which time Spencer treated Peter to a detailed *résumé* of his career in fish and chips. Peter found it not wholly uninteresting.

Spencer had been working behind the counter at *Capaldi's Fish and Chips* in Great Yarmouth when he got what he called his 'little stroke of good fortune.' He'd been there for some time and although the work was tedious and not particularly well paid the owner Mr Capaldi was a decent enough bloke and a fair employer. The shop was in a prime location but it was too small and never did as well as it could. Spencer often dreamed about what he would do if it were his.

One day during a busy lunchtime Mr Capaldi went through to the back premises to fetch more chipped potatoes and failed to return. Almost run off his feet alone in the shop Spencer was eventually forced to seek more chips himself. Mr Capaldi was lying face down on the floor among thousands of raw chipped potatoes. He'd obviously knocked over the bin as he fell.

'I felt his pulse but he was dead.' Spencer said. He gave a short laugh. 'I went looking for my chips and he'd cashed his in.' Peter wondered how long it had taken his host to polish that one up and how many times he'd told it.

'We were that busy I just shovelled the chips up off the floor and used them. I didn't have time to do any more. Mind you, it was his heart that had gone. There wasn't any blood or anything. Just as well really.' He had to replenish the chips twice more and it was only when the rush was over that he called the ambulance and the police.

Mr Capaldi's wife had money of her own, no interest in the shop and no head for business. As soon as the old man was buried she was off to stay with relatives in Scotland. She sold Spencer the business for next to nothing. He'd long had a business plan and he persuaded the bank to help him purchase a couple of boarded up shops beside *Capaldi's*. Within weeks Spencer had developed the site and opened a sizeable fish and chip emporium. There was a restaurant and a take-away downstairs and a bar and rather classy restaurant upstairs. Out of respect for and gratitude to his previous employer he continued to call the place *Capaldi's*.

Since then Spencer had opened three more *Capaldi's* fish restaurants along the coast and was on the point of opening yet another. Apart from the original *Capaldi's* which he would never change; he was considering re-branding the rest. Over brandy and cigars he and Peter tried to devise suitable names. Spencer favoured *Chips Ahoy, Chip Mates* and *Chip Shapes*. Peter countered with *Fission Ships* and *Cod 'n' taters*. Spencer liked *Piscine and Potato* once Peter explained.

Late in the afternoon they rose from the table and Spencer took Peter to inspect his collection of shotguns, fishing rods and golf clubs. After that Peter was treated to a guided tour of the house and the car collection out in the old stables. By the time they'd been round everything Peter could hardly keep his eyes open.

They returned to the sitting room where Spencer stoked up the fire and produced Christmas cake and yet more alcohol, this time a bottle of *D'Oliveiras, Reserva*.

'1968.' He quacked as he put his feet up on the coffee table. 'I hope you like Madeira.'

Peter had never seen such enormous feet as Spencer's. His shoes looked about eighteen inches long and slightly other-worldly. Peter laughed and made the mistake of saying that he liked anything alcoholic. He was having a jolly good time.

*

It was after three o'clock in the afternoon on Boxing Day when he was woken by the telephone. Totally disoriented, he was surprised to find that he had been sleeping fully dressed on the sitting room sofa. When he glanced at his watch he thought at first that it was very early in the morning. But it was daylight still, all the lights were on and he had an appalling headache. By the time he had struggled upright the telephone was silent.

It was only after a bowl of cereal and a couple of mugs of black coffee as he lay in the bath that Peter recalled some vague memory of Spencer driving him home in a big red car. How on earth had the man been able to drive? It must have been after the Madeira that they began tasting and discussing the relative merits of Scotch and Irish whiskeys. Beyond that memory failed him. He spent the evening quietly.

The news had started when the phone rang again. He'd just eaten some scrambled eggs on toast and was feeling rather more human.

'Hello?'
Silence.
'Hello? This is….'
'Hello, Peter.'
'Oh. Margaret. Hello. How are you?' Peter could imagine her sitting on the second step at the foot of the stairs in her hall, tall, angular, slightly awkward looking but sexy, with her dark hair falling over her pale face and bold makeup. She

would be raking her hair back, a ring on every finger on her right hand and several on the ring finger of her left.

'I tried you yesterday. Just to wish you a Happy Christmas. And then I rang earlier. I expect you were out.'

'Yes. How are you feeling? Is everything going okay… with the baby? And you… yourself, are you all right?'

'I'm okay-ish. Tired. No not tired, exhausted. I'm anaemic apparently, and thoroughly sick of being sick. It's so wearing. Anyway, what about you?'

'Oh, I'm fine. I'm off back to work once New Year is over. I've got a short term contract in Iceland. What else? Ah. I've more or less finished clearing out. I'm going to be living here when I'm in the UK. I've been doing a bit of painting-pictures, not walls and ceilings. I had far too much to drink yesterday and I'm going to bed early any time now.'

'Did you go to Kathy's?'

'No. I should have. I wish I had. I was invited to the Manfredi's. Do you know…?'

'Oh. Yes. No wonder you had too much to drink. I've met Gabby once or twice and… what's her husband's name? Spencer? I don't know him well but I've heard…. What did you think of him?' She laughed.

'Well, I have to say it was a bit odd. Unlike any other Christmas I've experienced.'

'What happened? Did they…?'

'Oh, yes. Let's just say I've never seen anyone put away so much booze in so short a time. Gabby didn't even manage to make it through lunch. She was as sick as a dog and had to take to her bed.'

'That sounds about right.'

'And I think that Spencer could best be described as a drinker of… heroic proportions.'

'So I've heard.'

'So, did you want something… anything in particular?'

'No. It just occurred to me that it would be your first Christmas there without your mum. I was just calling to say hello and make sure you were all right.'

'Oh. Well, that's very kind. I suppose you wouldn't countenance coming over and keeping me company? Or is Tom at home?'

'No,' Margaret paused, 'to both questions.'

*

Philip Holt's face took on a pained look. Peter looked across at him and laughed. He reached for his glass.

'So you're going to get in touch with these people?'

'Yes. I don't see why not. They've had quite a bit of success and they seem optimistic. Their fees are not unreasonable. If they think they can help find Dave, or exactly what happened, why not?'

'Hmm. What about Kathy? She didn't seem too keen. She was telling me the other day.'

'Oh, she'll be all right.'

'You'll get your ankles nipped.'

'Well, it won't be the first time, and I don't suppose it'll be the last.' Philip frowned. 'I don't know why she's so opposed to it. I'd just like to find out, once and for all, if possible. And frankly, I suspect she would too. Then we can forget about it. Or I can forget about it.' Philip's plump face glowed red in the flickering firelight. 'Not knowing just keeps… festering… gnawing away at me. Not badly, but… you know.'

'Oh, yes. I know… all too well.' Peter nodded. He looked at his friend and wondered, not for the first time, how Philip always managed to look so blessed neat and tidy. He positively gleamed. They'd been slumped in armchairs on either side of the fire in the lounge bar of the Lord Nelson since closing time and Philip still contrived to look fresh and dapper. He was on the short side and stocky, with closely cropped fair hair and a neatly trimmed moustache. They were both dressed in much the same way, leather jackets, denim shirts and blue jeans. There the similarity ended. Peter looked down at himself. Whereas Philip looked crisp and clean, he was just the opposite. The flickering firelight danced off Philip's burgundy leather bomber jacket. Peter's jacket was worn, scuffed and dull and the dark brown leather seemed to suck the life out of the light. Philip's jeans were good quality and comparatively new. They fitted him well and were freshly washed and ironed. Peter's were worn and crumpled, with evidence of the odd mud spatter and beginning to fray around the bottoms. Philip wore highly polished burgundy slip-ons. The nap had worn from the toes of Peter's desert boots leaving a baldness which no amount of cleaning or brushing would ever remedy. Peter sighed and consoled himself yet again with the thought that it must be a homosexual thing. He'd never known many but most of those of his acquaintance seemed like that, taking great care with their appearance and clothing, buying quality items which fitted. They tended to be very coordinated.

It was almost two in the morning a couple of days after Boxing Day, during the dead time between Christmas and New Year.

'Another drop?' Philip picked up the bottle of Bells from the low table beside him.

Peter hesitated. He sighed. 'On Boxing Day I swore I was never going to drink again. I thought I was going to die. I've seen some pretty serious drinkers over the years but I have never seen anyone put it away like Spencer Manfredi.'

'Oh, yes. He's a serious toper all right and Gabby's no slouch. I think he drinks all the time, just keeps himself topped up, like a battery.' Philip gestured with the bottle again. At Peter's nod he leaned over and poured a small measure into his friend's proffered glass.

Peter looked appreciatively at the golden liquid in the light of the fire. 'Actually this is slipping down rather well.' He looked across at Philip. 'The clients have obviously been good to you again this year.'

'We tend not to get much in the way of Christmas presents. Coming to see the dentist is not most people's idea of a good time. It's only the Benoits. They always do us proud at Christmas. Last year they gave us each a bottle of Famous Grouse. This is very good. They always come up with something eminently drinkable.'

Peter chuckled and shook his head. 'And if I remember correctly we sat here in these seats until morning and emptied that very bottle, putting the world to rights. I'm not sure I'm up to doing it again.'

'Well, why not? You haven't got to be anywhere in the morning.'

'No. That's true. Maybe we can get Kathy to do us a fry-up again. Do you remember last year's?'

'Ah, yes. She makes a good breakfast. Mind you, you would, wouldn't you, if you'd run a pub for years.'

They sipped their drinks in silence for a moment.

'I'm off back to work next week, back to the factory.'

'Well, you've had a pretty good break…'

'Yep.' Peter shifted his weight and reached out a toe to hook a chair closer. He put his feet up. They stared in silence at the fire for a while, the only sound the occasional settling of the coals and the metronomic ticking of the grandfather clock in the corner.

'It's weird, isn't it?'

'What's that?' Philip looked up.

'How we are all minus our fathers, you, me and Margaret.'

'Yes. Mind you, she did discover what happened to hers.'

'Yes. Can't have been easy, finding out that the father you never knew drowned himself in the churchyard well.'

'No. True enough. And that he'd been all that time in a POW camp, when everyone thought he was dead.' Philip paused. 'How is she? Have you seen her?'

Peter pulled a face. 'No. Not since she told me she was pregnant. But she phoned the other night.'

'Oh, really?'

'Yes. She sounded all right apart from being sick and anaemic apparently.'

Philip paused, trying to frame his next question.

'Was she absolutely…?' He paused again. 'There's no way it could have….'

'Been mine? Apparently not. We haven't discussed it again. Not since… She was adamant about that. It's her husband's. Tom's.'

'Hmm. Oh, well, I suppose she'd know.'

Peter looked askance. 'And just how do you suppose…?' He lost interest in finishing and shook his head. 'Never mind. It was fun while it lasted.'

He stared into his glass and frowned. 'It was more than that though. I thought it might actually go somewhere and I'm certain she felt the same. I know she's married but he's never there… and I don't there's anything much remaining of the marriage. And she definitely gave me the impression that he wasn't….'

'Couldn't get it up, hey?'

'No, it wasn't that. I suspect he was pretty much firing blanks, or something else… just something she said… or *didn't* say.'

Peter yawned.

'We are all the same.' Philip dragged them back to the subject again. 'She never knew her father, you never knew yours and I never knew mine.'

'Not exactly the same. Margaret was simply too young to remember Harry. He left before she was old enough to remember anything about him. But he knew that he had a daughter.'

'Yes.'

'You never knew your father. And as far as we know he never knew anything about you. And I never knew Nick except for that one time we met when he called round. But I suspect that he didn't know that I was his. I'm pretty sure mum never told him. She was going to tell him when he came back the next day, but he never showed up. And he's never been seen since.'

Philip snorted and shook his head.

'We were so distraught the day we went to collect your mum's things from the convalescent home we were joking on the way back in the car about her burying Nick under the patio.'

Peter cast a glance at Philip, then grinned. 'You might be right.'

'Don't you ever wonder whether he is still alive somewhere? Wouldn't you like to see him, if he is?'

'I don't think he is still alive,' Peter said flatly. 'I can't believe that he wouldn't have come to mum's funeral if he were still upright and breathing.'

'Perhaps he didn't know.'

'Gordon Bennett, Phil!' Peter expostulated. 'We had this same conversation last year… and the year before, word for word. It's like wiping your arse on a wagon wheel. You just get done with one bit and here comes some more.'

'Ah, you're right.' Philip grinned across at Peter. 'Watch out for those splinters. Still, I am going to see if I can find out, once and for all, what happened to Dave.'

'Well, good luck with it. I hope you find what you're looking for.'

*

Nick Codling lay on the floor of the caravan and stared at the ceiling. His back was sore again. He'd spent much of the day on the forklift and had sought out the floor as soon as he arrived home. He was pondering what to do with himself in the summer. In three months time, on 17th March 1980 to be precise, he would celebrate his 65th birthday. He would be retiring from full time employment.

His leaving date didn't quite coincide with his 10th anniversary with the company but they'd agreed to give him his pin and award anyway. Almost ten years he'd been at the gas terminal tucked behind the sand dunes on the Lincolnshire coast. Stan had been forced to lay him off so he'd started work as a security guard. When the opportunity of transferring to a job in the warehouse came up he took it. The work was much more interesting, he didn't do shifts and the pay was better. He'd been there ever since.

It was what he was going to do with himself in his retirement that was exercising him. A contractor at the terminal had offered him a job but he really didn't want anything full time. Stan had said he could work part time on the caravan site if he was so minded. It had grown enormously over the last few years and now employed several people full time. He could do as much or as little as he wanted. Money wasn't a problem for Nick. He'd saved, he would have a modest pension and Barbara had left him a tidy sum in her will. She hadn't been able to leave him the cottage they'd shared and he'd had to move out because of the family, but she'd done him proud otherwise. He was living in one of the rental caravans at present and waiting for his new home, a brand new static, to be delivered.

Nick had decided that the first thing he would do after retiring was have a holiday. But there was another knotty little problem. Where would he go? And who would he go with? There was no one. A couple of years ago he and Barbara had driven up to Inverness and stayed in a B & B on Ness Bank. It had rained incessantly but they'd had a really good time. They'd gone nowhere last year because Barbara hadn't been up to travelling. Nick sighed. He missed Barbara. They'd been together a long time.

His back was feeling easier. He'd get up in a moment. He almost drifted off to sleep and then suddenly his eyes snapped open. The thought had floated back into his head.

For some time he'd been chewing over the idea of a visit to Leeds to take a surreptitious peek at Monica, Louise and Raymond, if they were still there. He admitted to himself that he would have had a hard time explaining his interest in his erstwhile family after all this time.

Nick had been completely successful in his attempt to disappear from his old life. He'd scarcely given any of them a passing thought since February 1953 when he first arrived in Lincolnshire. Now he felt the urge to go and look them up. He didn't know why he wanted to see them after all this time and he wasn't really sure that he wanted to actually speak to any of them. It was more a case of seeing them one last time, he supposed.

As he lay on the floor of his caravan in the gathering darkness he knew that he would go to Leeds. In the meantime he had Christmas to get through, without Barbara.

6. *You're him, aren't you?*

It was after two o'clock in the morning on 1st January 1980 when Peter arrived back at Cowper's Cottage with his brain reeling. His condition was not only a response to the usual over-excitement, over indulgence and euphoria of New Year's Eve. Certainly there had been much of that but he'd also experienced the most electrifying snog that he could recall, certainly since he was a schoolboy. Snog was exactly the right word, he decided. Kissing and cuddling just didn't meet the case. He had gone weak at the knees. As he shambled up Back Lane he had muttered to himself that it had been rampant snogging of the very highest order. Unbridled lust sadly would not fit the bill since anything more than snogging and a bit of urgent fondling had been suddenly and irritatingly bridled. But it had been made extremely obvious that more of the same would be welcome and much, much more was possible, should he be so inclined. Peter sniffed his shirt and grinned. He could still smell expensive perfume, *Aliage* she said, *Estée Lauder*.

Even without such a bonus it had been a good night, reminiscent some said of the times they enjoyed during the 1950s and 60s when the Saturday night dances at the Lord Nelson were *de rigueur* for anyone seeking a good night out, a bit of romance or some good old fashioned fun. The pub served excellent beer and a wide range of drinks. Kathy invariably provided a good spread on such occasions. The tickets for the New Year's Eve bash were always eagerly awaited and snapped up in no time. People turned up in droves and those without tickets cursed their luck and determined to do better the following year.

Kathy had opened up the old dining room for dancing. An earlier landlord had been sufficiently far-sighted to have a proper sprung dance floor installed during the late 1950s. On New Years Eve the carpets were removed and the tables were arranged around the walls. Kathy gave five local Grammar School boys their very first public gig. *Athletic Support* had been practicing for months every Sunday afternoon and Wednesday evening in the old garages beside the pub. Philip was appalled at what he viewed a foolish gamble. However it hadn't been pure chance that led Kathy to venture out to the garages most Sundays in mid-afternoon, bearing three halves of bitter, a lager and lime, a Coke and five bags of crisps. It came as no surprise to her when the band was an outstanding success.

Peter's night was marred only briefly early on when he bumped into his uncle in the toilets. George gave him an odd look and asked him if he'd been throwing stuff into their back yard. Peter affected not to know what he was talking about but his uncle had gone on his way with the warning.

'You know bloody well what I mean. You want to be careful. Coming round here with your big city ways; I shall be keeping an eye on you.'

Peter frowned and shook his head.

'Big city?' He decided not to return to the bar but to give the music a go.

The Manfredis arrived just after eleven with another couple and a single woman. They'd obviously come on from, or were going on to, a fancy dress party and were in high good humour. Gabby was dressed to kill in a cowgirl hat, tasselled suede mini-skirt, a white shirt gathered into a knot at her belly and high suede boots. Spencer was dressed as a butcher in a straw boater and striped apron. He was carrying a cleaver which Kathy insisted he put behind the bar for safe keeping. The other couple had come as Tweedledum and Tweedledee and the single woman appeared to be a witch. Gabby gave

Peter a wave as they made their way to the temporary bar set up at the end of the room.

Spencer paused briefly as he returned, bearing drinks.

'Hello, mate,' he muttered round a stub of cigar. He shook his head. 'Have you seen my wife? Silly cow. What in God's name does she think she looks like?'

Peter grinned and lifted his glass in salutation.

'Hello, Spencer. Happy New Year. Not like that daft beggar that's come dressed as a butcher....' But Spencer had moved on and was having the same conversation with some one else.

When the band returned from their break they began the second half by slamming into *Twist and Shout*. Gabby appeared in front of Peter, took him by the hand and dragged him out onto the dance floor. She was a good dancer, energetic, stylish and enthusiastic and it was no hardship for Peter to stay for *I'm Alive* and *You Really Got Me*. She was the best looking woman in the room by a mile and he was delighted to be her partner.

Gabby insisted they remain on the floor for the slower *House of the Rising Sun* during which she put both arms round Peter's neck and snuggled into his chest. Peter realized suddenly that he was happier than he'd been for some time. Gabby smelled and felt wonderful in his embrace. Surreptitiously he pushed his face into her hair and neck and breathed in deeply. She looked up at him and shook her head.

'Naughty,' she said but her eyes were sparkling.

Then it was time for the famed Lord Nelson Twist competition. A knockout, it was held every New Years Eve, the final purposeful activity of the year. Heavily dependent upon the amount of alcohol consumed and the commitment and effectiveness of the judges it usually went on for ages and the winners often owed more to their talent for pacing themselves and their stamina than to any artistic flair or gymnastic ability. Some looked forward to the competition but for most of the males it was the signal for a smart exodus to the public bar or the gents' lavatory or even outside for a breath of fresh air. Gabby raised an elegant eyebrow at Peter and he felt he had no option but to remain on the floor.

Despite the cowards and the absentees there was a good turnout and as things progressed and tension rose so those that had left returned to stand in the dark at the edge of the dance floor. Initially Peter did little more than go through the motions but when Gabby began really to put her back into it he felt himself responding. Her enthusiasm was infectious. Gradually the less able or less attractive combinations were tapped on the shoulders to sag off to the sidelines in embarrassment or resignation.

Suddenly the dance floor was much less congested and there were only four couples left. The spotlights blazed on those remaining and more spectators crowded into the dark extremities around the floor, clapping and cheering on friends or their favourites. Then there were three couples. Eventually another pair was removed and only two couples remained. Now the spotlights held each writhing couple in their glare and the dance floor was greatly reduced in area. By now Peter was sweating and blowing hard and looking forward to someone bringing the tortuous business to an end. After what seemed an eternity the judge stepped forward smartly and the other couple were shown off the floor. Peter and Gabby had won.

Far from stopping proceedings though the judges egged them on and the crowd roared for more. They wanted an exhibition which Peter and Gabby gave with a will, each drawing on new reserves. Finally the band decided that they at least had had enough. They got progressively faster until they were galloping and then they stopped in disarray. The drummer looked in wonder at a crop of brand new blisters, the lead guitarist manipulated his left hand, vainly trying to ward off cramp and the rhythm and bass guitarists shoved their aching fingers up under their armpits seeking relief. The singer downed the best part of a pint of bitter and mopped his brow.

Exhausted, rolling their eyes at each other and with their tongues hanging out, Gabby and Peter sagged to a halt. They embraced clumsily for a moment to stop each other falling over. Dripping after their exertions, they gracefully accepted from Kathy the worn and dented cup that was habitually presented to the winners. Originally a tennis trophy it had the names of numerous successful mixed doubles inscribed upon it. There had at one time been a small plate bearing the winners of the Twist Competition but it had come adrift and been lost. At the end of the evening the trophy would be placed back on the shelf in the public bar until the following New Year celebrations. They also received a bottle of sherry and a box of chocolates. Waving and bowing in all directions to great applause and the odd cry of 'fix' they picked up their drinks and took them outside to cool off. After a few minutes of heavy breathing and silence they sat on a low wall together and exclaimed over their success. Eventually Gabby took Peter's hand.

'It's a lovely clear night. Let's go and see if there are any ships.'

They made their way round to the terrace at the rear of the Lord Nelson and looked out across the dark fields to the sea. The lights from two ships were visible. One was close in to the shore. Peter thought that it was probably the dredger that had been about for some time. The other lights were away out on the horizon.

'It must be an odd life. What will they be doing now? It'll be midnight shortly.'

'I suppose there'll be someone on watch. The rest will probably be having a drink or two, like us.'

Gabby shivered and leaned into Peter's chest. He put an arm round her.

'Mm,' she said. 'You smell nice.'

Peter nuzzled Gabby's hair.

'Mm, so do you.' Gabby gave off the delicious odour of warm female, a heady mix of quality soap and cosmetics and expensive perfume overlain with the merest hint of sweat and a faint smell of cigarette smoke.

It was at this point that Gabby turned to Peter suddenly, put her arms round his neck and kissed him full on the mouth. They remained locked together in this fashion until a group of rowdies staggered round the corner. While their girlfriends watched and squealed the boys cavorted round the terrace shouting and laughing and trying to stamp on balloons they'd pulled down from the dining room ceiling.

'Oh great,' Gabby exclaimed.

'Good-oh,' muttered Peter, 'buffoons with balloons.'

Gabby laughed. 'Oh well, put the kibosh on that. We might as well go back to the party.' She took Peter by the hand again and led the way past the sniggering and whispering group of rowdies, round to the front of the pub. She stopped in the shadows by the garages and gave Peter another kiss.

'I've wanted to do this since the first time I saw you. I shall have to make sure I'm not wearing any knickers next New Year's Eve,' she whispered, grinding her groin against his hip. 'And you can shag me up against the wall.'

'Mmm,' Peter responded.

Holding hands they wandered back across the car park. They moved apart quickly as someone came out of the public bar. It was George, Janice, Kingsley and May making their way to the dining room for Big Ben. Janice said something and they all laughed.

The crowd on the dance floor was counting down as Peter and Gabby arrived at the French windows which were now flung wide open.

'Five... four... three... two... ONE.'

Across the land the same tableau was replicated. The momentary hush, flushed expectant faces... until... BONG... the room was filled with the first chime of Big Ben, emanating in the case of the Lord Nelson from the radio brought into the dining room specifically for the purpose. BONG... BONG.... Cries of 'Happy New Year,' were general, interspersed with the shouts, cries, squawks, sighs and whispers of folk wishing each other well. Husbands turned to wives, mates turned to each other, hands were proffered and shaken, lovers embraced.

'Maybe this year.... Health, wealth.... Let's hope this one's a little better.... All the best.... Happy New Year, son.... It's got to be better than the last.... Cheers!'

Gabby and Peter kissed briefly and chastely and then Gabby grabbed at the witch who was passing, clutching a glass of cider and a bent roll-up cigarette.

'Happy New Year, Dani,' she cried.

'Ah, piss off,' the witch responded. She looked as though she hadn't recognized Gabby at all.

'Thank you so much,' said Gabby, 'and the same to you, sister dear.' She turned to Peter and shouted in his ear. 'My lovely sister, Danielle,' she said by way of explanation. 'She enjoys ill-health and misery generally. Her glass isn't half empty; she doesn't even know where the bloody thing is. She couldn't even be arsed to come in fancy dress tonight.'

The singer waited a few seconds after the last chime before shouting 'HAPPY NEW YEAR, everybody.' The band launched into a madcap version of *Knees up Mother Brown* that got faster and faster until like the twist competition it too concluded in mad confusion. Peter looked around for

Gabby but she was in the midst of a throng getting organized for the inevitable *Auld Lang Syne*.

He ran into her again on his way to the Gents. She was returning from the Ladies' cloakroom with a coat.

'Oh, I'm glad…. Someone said you're leaving, going abroad?'

Peter explained.

'Well, give me a ring when you get back. We need to do something about your paintings.' She gave him a look. 'If you're interested, that is.'

'Oh, yes. I'm certainly interested.' Peter grinned. Gabby grinned back. She kissed her fingers and patted Peter's mouth.

'I'll look forward to it.'

He didn't see her to speak to again that evening. After a while he went to seek out Kathy, gave her a hug and a kiss and then spent the next hour or so helping her and the kitchen staff clear up.

He was far too pumped up to sleep when he arrived back at Cowper's Cottage. He poured himself a whisky and water, watched TV for a while and then after some indecision picked up the phone. It was some time before it was answered.

'Hello?'

'Hello, Margaret. It's Peter. Just called to wish you a Happy New Year. I didn't wake you, I hope?'

At the other end of the line Margaret sighed.

'Do you know what time it is?'

'Oh, pretty late, I suppose.' Peter laughed. 'I'm sorry.'

'Oh, well. It was a kind thought. Happy New Year to you too, Peter.'

'Yes. I just wanted to let you know that I'm off on Friday. Flying to Iceland.'

'Yes, so you said the other day.'

'Oh. Anyway, I wanted to wish you well with the baby. Hope all goes well. I'll write and perhaps you can let me know how things go.'

'Yes, of course.'

There was a short silence.

'I miss you, Margaret,' said Peter.

'Yes. I miss you too.'

Peter was suddenly chastened as he recognized the familiar maudlin stage that he had now entered. But he couldn't help himself.

'I could be there in twenty minutes.'

'Oh,' Margaret laughed. 'And how would you propose to do that?'

'It's only twenty minutes in the car, give or take.'

'Yes, but I have my doubts whether you could get it out of the garage, let alone drive over here.' She paused. 'And anyway, you know very well what we agreed. It couldn't go on. I'm pregnant.'

'Yes,' Peter nodded and then added under his breath 'with our baby.' After a brief silence there was an exasperated exclamation at the other end and Margaret put the phone down.

*

Peter was strap-hanging in a crowded carriage on the Piccadilly Line when the train stopped in a tunnel just outside Green Park station. He was on his way to Knightsbridge to pick up some documents before heading for Heathrow for his flight to Reykjavik. The journey seemed to be taking forever. The train had already stopped several times. He was uncomfortably hot in his big coat but there was insufficient room for him to remove it so he carried on trying to read his paper.

Eventually the train jerked into motion. It travelled a few feet and stopped again. The carriage was crowded but silent, save for the regular ticking of a motor beneath the floor. There was a metallic tang in the heavy air, a combination of electrical charge, stale cigarette smoke, workday socks and armpits and burned dust. Suddenly without warning Peter was dizzy, his heart was pounding, he was breathless, his legs were buckling and he was soaked in sweat. It was a heart attack for sure. He had to get out of there.

The train jerked into motion again and trundled slowly out of the tunnel into Green Park station. Fortunately for him the doors opened directly opposite a seat against the tiled station wall. Peter staggered off the train and collapsed on the wooden seat. He was faint and nauseous, his nose had filled with mucous and his clothes felt as though they were sodden. If he had had the energy he would have taken off his coat but it was all he could do to unbutton it.

He was slumped on the seat for some time with his head bowed. He thought that he might be sick at any moment but he was relieved that the feeling that he might lose control of his bowels had passed. It had been truly frightening. Trains came into the station; their arrival heralded by a welcome, if all too brief breeze. They disgorged passengers, took on more and left, leaving in their wake rearranged dead air.

'Are you all right, dear?'

Peter looked up. A small middle-aged woman in a dark blue coat and unfeasibly red hair was bent over him. He smiled weakly and shook his head. She took off her gloves, felt his brow with the back of a white bony hand and then took his pulse.

'What happened, dear? You haven't been drinking?'

She sat down beside him.

Slowly and haltingly Peter described the experience.
'I think it's a heart attack.'

The woman smiled in a kindly manner. 'I don't think we need to worry about your heart. Just sit still and take some nice, slow, big deep breaths. You'll feel better in a minute.' She sat down beside him, took his hand, patted it reassuringly and then cupped it between her own.

'Slowly in, then out. In again, deep, slow, and out.' He did as he was told and was grateful that she didn't appear to want to talk beyond the odd encouraging comment.

After a while he felt stronger and stood up to remove his coat and take a handkerchief from his pocket. He wiped his face and neck, blew his nose and then sat down again.

'Phew. I do feel a bit better, thanks. Still a bit wobbly, but definitely better.'

'I should sit quietly for a few more minutes, if I were you. Do some more breathing.'

It transpired that the kindly woman was Joan. Peter couldn't make out her surname. It was double-barrelled. She had once been a midwife but was now on her way to do a morning at Help the Aged.

'Well, what on earth was that about?' Peter asked. 'I've never had anything like that happen before.'

'Well, I'm not qualified, dear, but since you ask, I'd say you've just had a little panic attack. Anxiety. Stress.'

'What? Why on earth would I panic while I was reading the paper on a tube train?'

'Oh, it's very common. You'd be surprised. I should go and see your doctor.'

*

The second attack occurred a few days later aboard a small plane as Peter was returning to Reykjavik from Heimaey. It was every bit as distressing as the first episode but this time he didn't worry quite so much about it being a heart attack. He closed his eyes, leaned his head against the window of the aeroplane and concentrated on deep, even breathing. Even so it was a bad experience. Eventually the attack passed but it left him soaked again and feeling very shaken and exhausted- and not a little fearful of the next attack.

He had hoped to take a trip to Greenland in his spare time but in view of recent events he decided against it. He really couldn't bring himself to endure the close confines of yet another small aircraft. Instead he went out and bought a set of watercolour paints and a pad of paper and contented himself with driving out into the countryside to take photographs and do a bit of sketching and painting.

He was fine for several days. The next incident occurred in an office block in the early morning. He had been increasingly wary of crowds and enclosed spaces since the first panic attack. Lifts had become difficult and he almost took the stairs on this occasion. But the doors to the lift opened invitingly as he was passing. The lift was empty and there were few people about. He thought that it might leave almost immediately and decided to chance it.

The lift was small, dark, old and tired and it became obvious that it was going nowhere in a hurry. More and more people piled in until Peter was wedged in a corner, far from the door. The cramped space was completely full by the time the door slid haltingly to a close and the lift began its creaking ascent. When it reached the second floor it shuddered to a stop and the doors limped apart again. Yet another person insisted on getting in. Peter was dressed for the bitter weather outside and was now uncomfortably hot, stuck in the corner of the lift and unable to move. On this occasion he felt himself beginning to panic. Suddenly he was overwhelmed with the now familiar horrible sweats, the shakes and the feeling that he had lost control of his bowels.

As the lift came to a stately halt yet again and the doors took an age to open Peter struggled to move and tried to shout. Barely a croak issued from his mouth.

Fortunately the girl beside him spotted his problem and shouted for the door to be held and people to get out of the way. She and a middle-aged man helped Peter out of the lift, fetched him a chair and a cup of water.

It was the last straw and Peter took himself off to the hospital where he was seen quickly, examined, prescribed tranquilizers and told to see his own doctor on his return to the UK.

*

As the date of his retirement grew nearer Nick dwelt increasingly on his proposed trip to Leeds to look up Monica, Louise and Raymond. Suddenly he was eager to go, to find out how they were and what they were doing. He acknowledged to himself though that had anyone asked why, after all this time; he would not have known quite how to respond. He was under no illusions about what kind of reception he could expect after walking out on his family all those years ago.

Late one Friday afternoon he was chewing it over again. He had nothing planned for the weekend. The forecast was poor. He decided that he might as well go. Why delay? He'd get up early on Saturday morning and drive over. It wouldn't take much more than a couple of hours.

*

Peter lay on the bed in his hotel room in Reykjavik and wondered what his next course of action should be. He had received a phone call from London that morning and a flurry of telexes in the late afternoon from Los Angeles and London with news that the studio had been taken over. The last telex to arrive, from LA, was a good deal more illuminating than anything he'd had from London. The entire company was to be restructured. The process had already begun and apparently there was no place for Peter in the new organization.

Perhaps given recent events it was a blessing in disguise. It had been on the cards for a while. He was surprised that he had survived as long as he had.

The studio had come up with a generous severance package. He knew plenty of people in the industry and was sure he could get another job without much difficulty. But he wasn't convinced that he really wanted to carry on. He kept thinking about what Gabby had said. In fact he spent a good deal of time thinking about Gabby, full-stop. He certainly enjoyed painting and he wondered whether she might be right and that he should start an entirely new career. He'd put in several afternoons visiting a few galleries and had come away convinced that he could do as well or better than many of the exhibits.

He rolled off the bed and fetched his sketch pad. After topping up his glass from a bottle of *J & B* he lay back again and looked carefully at his paintings and sketches. One or two were certainly worth developing and a number of the sketches might eventually form the basis of some exciting abstracts.

There had been no more panic attacks. He'd been taking the tranquilizers and avoiding crowds, lifts and enclosed spaces. In fact he had become quite solitary. He had also not been near an aeroplane. The thought of flying home was preying on his mind. He was by no means certain that he could get onto a plane again. It occurred to him that perhaps he could return home by sea.

*

Late Saturday afternoon found Nick eating cod, chips, mushy peas and bread and butter. As he ate he watched the citizens of Leeds going about their business. He was keeping half an eye out to see whether he recognized anyone. So far he'd seen no one he knew.

He'd set out from Lincolnshire in his green Cortina estate later than he intended and he'd only had a doughnut since breakfast. On the dark blue wall of a railway bridge across the road dozens of defaced posters caught his eye. He could just make out bills advertising The Clash, Joy Division and a forthcoming rugby match between England and Wales at Hull.

The chip shop was only a short distance from where he'd lived. He was astonished at how much things had changed. His old street had been demolished to make way for shops and a car park. The Murderers had disappeared and a new pub had sprung up some distance down the road. The old allotments had survived but unsurprisingly his shed had not.

He'd gone into a fruiterer's to enquire about the Nichols family. It had been an anxious moment when the man looked at him as though he might have recognized him. But the fruiterer suggested that he try the baker's down the road. There were a couple of elderly women who worked there that might be able to help.

Nick found the baker's without difficulty. He hung around for a bit looking in the window. There was an elderly woman serving but he didn't recognize her at all. One of the customers addressed her as Daphne.

He went in. After some indecision he asked for a doughnut.

'That the jam or the cream, dear?'

'Jam please.'

The woman put the doughnut into a crisp white paper bag and rang up the sale.

'I don't suppose you know where I could find the Nichols family, used to live just round the corner here. Number Twelve?' Nick inclined his head towards the door.

'Nichols? No, I don't think so. When would that be?'

'Well, they were certainly here twenty five years ago.'

Daphne laughed. She looked a jolly soul.

'Oh, you're going back a bit. That's before my time.' Daphne looked at Nick and sucked her teeth. 'I'll ask… Josie. She's been around here for ever and….' Daphne put her head through the door behind her and called out.

'Jose. Josie!'

'Yes, dear?'

'Can you come through a minute, please?' Daphne smiled at Nick conspiratorially. 'She'll be here in a minute.'

A squat elderly woman in a pink overall and a hairnet appeared at the door. Nick recognized her immediately. She had been a dinner lady at Louise and Raymond's school and sometimes helped out behind the bar in The Murderers.

'Yes, dear? What can I do for you?'

'This gentleman's looking for the Nicholson family. Used to be here, round the corner.'

'Nichols, not Nicholson.'

'Nichols, that's right.' Daphne's head bobbed up and down in agreement.

Josie frowned and closed her eyes. She wiped her hands on the front of her overall.

'Nichols. Nichols,' she intoned. 'Oh, now wait a minute. Do you mean, what was her name? They used to call her Bunny? Lived in....'

'No. I'm trying to find Nick and Monica, used to be at Number Twelve. They had two children, Louise and Raymond, I think.'

'Was she married? Well, I suppose she must have been.' The old lady frowned again. 'Oh,' she said. 'You don't mean what's his name, him that... he disappeared. The police dug up the allotments looking for him. Never found him. That's right. That was Monica. Oldfield, she was before she married him, what's-his-name Nichols.' Josie nodded and looked Nick up and down.

'I remember Raymond from school. He used to bring the paper. He married... someone from... hmm, I can't remember. Down south, somewhere. Buckinghamshire, I think. Yes, that's right. They moved down there, close to where she was from. He had a... not a garage exactly... he did up old cars. It was near High Wycombe, I think.'

'Do you remember a Louise at all?'

'Well, there was a girl but I couldn't tell you anything about her.'

'What about Monica? Does she still live locally?'

The old woman looked at Nick for a moment and then at Daphne.

'I'm almost certain she died, dear. Quite recently. She was on her own in one of the flats. They'd know down at Poole's, the funeral director. He's just down the road here.'

'Oh.' Nick was stunned. It had never crossed his mind that Monica wouldn't still be living.

'Are you a relative?' The old lady looked at Nick again. Suddenly her eyes hardened. Her hostility was palpable.

'Yes.' Nick picked up his doughnut and his change from the counter. 'I will go down to the funeral place…. Thank you very much for your help.'

He was almost out of the door before the old lady called out.

'You're him, aren't you? Him that disappeared and left them to it.'

7. Rook Pie and 'taters

It was after 6 p.m. on Monday 4th February when a mud-spattered Eastern Counties double-decker bus from Cromer halted in the murk and deposited an exhausted Peter at the bus stop outside the Lord Nelson. With some difficulty he hauled his cases out of the luggage compartment beneath the stairs and stepped down straight into a huge puddle. The bus was now empty except for the wizened conductor who affected to be absorbed by something on his ticket machine. Offering assistance would have necessitated him leaving the hot air blower in the bulkhead between the driver and the lower deck, at which he was warming his backside. As soon as Peter was clear the conductor took a coin from his leather satchel and rapped sharply on the bulkhead and the bus drove off leaving Peter shrouded in diesel fumes and pitch darkness since Kathy hadn't yet turned on the outside lights or the hotel sign.

It was bitterly cold and drizzling and Peter was not a little weary, having travelled that day down from Newcastle, missing his connection at Peterborough and changing again at Norwich. On the far side of the car park the lights were on in the pub and the curtains were not yet drawn. Despite being empty that early in the evening the bar looked warm and inviting. He thought about popping in but promptly decided against it. Kathy would want explanations. It wouldn't be a quick drink. He felt in need of a bath or a shower and some clean clothes. Once that was accomplished he would wander down. It would be nice to see Kathy and have a pint and hopefully something decent to eat.

After lugging his cases the length of Back Lane Peter found Cowper's Cottage warm and welcoming, if a little airless at first. He'd left the heating on for a short period twice a day to keep things ticking over. Philip had obviously been in since the post was stacked neatly on the sideboard and the plants in the conservatory had been watered. Peter put the kettle on and then hurried upstairs.

He was astonished to find a Red Admiral butterfly on the wall on the landing. He wondered whether he should let it out but concluded that it was probably best left alone. It would freeze to death outside.

It was while he was towelling himself down after a shower that something made him glance out of his bedroom window. He had the impression that someone was out there, just below the steps from the patio down into the garden. It was real enough to send a shiver up his back. He opened the window and leaned out.

'Hello?'

There was no response. Nothing moved and there was nothing to see. All he could hear was the heavy drip of water from the sodden trees.

'Anyone there?'

All was quiet. It was still drizzling. He supposed that it must have been his imagination, or tiredness. However, he felt better after closing the curtains.

*

When Peter returned to the Lord Nelson the car park was no busier than it had been when he got off the bus. As he opened the door to the public bar the welcome warmth and the familiar, comforting smell of food, ale, wood and tobacco smoke made him smile. There was something else… just the merest suspicion of Kathy's perfume.

'Good evening, I'll be with you in a moment.'

Peter grinned as he caught a glimpse of Kathy hurrying through to the back premises with an ice bucket. He took off his coat and hung it on the rack beside the door and then made his way to the log fire crackling in the grate. The bar was empty but somebody had obviously been in since cigarette smoke still hung in the air at the far end by the dartboard and a couple of empty pint glasses stood on the bar. He could hear Kathy rattling about getting ice from the freezer. He smiled again, warmed his hands at the fire and then sauntered over to the bar.

'What-ho there, doxy' he called.

'Hello? Who's that?'

''Tis nought but a weary traveller; a poor and weary cove with a powerful thirst, seeking a stoup of ale, a slice of rook pie and some neeps and 'taters. If you can see your way to sparing them, that is, missus.'

The scrabbling and rattling stopped.

'Who is that?'

Peter heard the freezer close and the tap of Kathy heels.

'A poor Christian soul down on his luck, seeking vittals.'

'It is you! I might have known. I thought….' Kathy's face lit up. 'I thought I recognized your voice, but I wasn't expecting you. And just who are you calling a doxy? You think I don't know what a doxy is, but I'm not as green as I'm cabbage-looking.' Kathy put down the ice bucket and rounded the bar. 'Come here and give your Auntie Kath a big hug and a kiss. Rook pie, indeed. Where did you get that from? Do they eat it in Iceland?'

'I don't know. I doubt it. But they do like a puffin pie.'

'Really? Those lovely little birds, with the chubby cheeks?'

'Yep. That's your man. Very popular in a pie, apparently.'

It always surprised Peter just how little there was to Kathy these days. He wondered briefly whether she had lost weight but then put it from his mind.

'It's lovely to see you. How are you?'

Kathy leaned away from him and looked him in the face.

'I'm fine. What about you. I wasn't expecting you back quite so soon.'

'Ah, well. There's a bit of a tale there, but first I'd like….'

'I know, a stoup of my excellent ale.' Kathy rounded the bar, picked up a glass and went to the pumps. 'Have you eaten?'

'No, I haven't. I was rather hoping you'd be able to oblige. There's nothing in at home except a few cans. Get yourself something.'

'Well, puffin pie might be a bit of a challenge but I can knock you up some chicken and chips, or I've got a nice piece of ham. There's cold beef. An omelette, sausages and pork pie…. What do you fancy? Something on toast? We don't usually do a great deal on a Monday night but I can make you something.'

Kathy handed Peter his drink. 'I won't have a drink just now, thanks.'

'Mm, thank you. I've been looking forward to this since about Doncaster. Cheers. What's easiest?'

Shooting Marmalade

'Whatever you fancy.'

'You couldn't knock up sausage, egg and chips or something like that? I just fancy something tasty.'

'Coming up. Bryan's in the back and he's a dab hand these days in the kitchen.'

'How is he?'

'He's fine.'

'And Marian?'

'The same.'

Kathy went through to the back and Peter heard her talking to Bryan. She popped her head round the door.

'Could you eat some mushrooms? We've got some field mushrooms, real beauties, but they won't last much longer.'

'Oh, yes. That would be lovely.'

It was no surprise to Peter that Bryan never showed his face. In all the time they'd known each other they'd barely exchanged two words. He was a shy and retiring soul and he and Kathy shared a strange life together.

Kathy returned with the local paper.

'Here's the EDP. You can catch up on all the local news and gossip.'

'Thanks, good health. It's great to see you again.' Peter sipped his beer. 'How's Phil? He's obviously been to the cottage recently. Has he made any progress with those London people, about Dave?'

'Phil's fine, so far as I know. I'm not sure how that's going. He hasn't been here much recently. He's got a new friend. Spends most of his time up in Norwich. Anyway, tell me about your trip to Iceland. Did you manage to keep warm?'

'Oh, keeping warm was the least of my problems.' Peter took a long pull at his beer and then proceeded to explain how he was no longer an employed person. He told Kathy about the studio take-over, his panic attacks and how he'd returned to the UK by a scenic, if extremely circuitous and leisurely route.

From Reykjavik, Peter had travelled by fishing boat to Heimaey in the Vestmann Islands. After a couple of days of pounding round the comparatively recently reconfigured Eldfell volcano and the harbour he caught another fishing boat to Seydisfjordhur on the west coast. He spent a bitterly cold day there, enchanted by the people and the scenery but nauseated by the smell of fish oil. Then he picked up a ferry to Torshavn. Following a brief stay under lowering clouds in the Faeroes he set sail for Bergen in Norway. There he took another ferry to Newcastle, where he caught a train to Peterborough and later another for Norwich.

'Kathy.' A quiet voice called from the back premises.

'Here we are. Do you want to sit at a table or at the bar? I'll bring you some cutlery.'

'I'll stay here, thanks. I'm quite comfortable.'

Kathy returned with a small plate bearing bread and butter and a huge white platter laden with sausages, fried eggs, two monstrous mushrooms and a mound of freshly cooked chips.

'Gracious, look at that. That does look rather splendid.'

Kathy laughed. 'I think the bold Bryan's found his niche. He's a decent cook, and what's more he enjoys it, although he'd be the first to admit it's come as a bit of a surprise.'

'Well, you'd go far before you'd find anything that looked much more appetizing than that.'

Kathy stole a chip. 'Oh,' she flapped a hand in front of her mouth, 'hot.'

Peter too took a chip, bit into it and gasped. 'Mm. Good though. Just needs a little salt….'

'Do you want any sauces?'

'Ah. Maybe some tomato ketchup, please.'

'So what are you going to do with yourself? Are you going in with someone else? You'll be able to get another....'

'No.' Peter set about his meal. 'I've had plenty of time to think about it since they told me-and on the way back. I'm done with the movies. It's a complete change for me.' Peter grinned at Kathy and paused for effect. He drained his pint of bitter and nodded when Kathy gestured at the pump. 'Yes, please. And get something for yourself and Bryan.'

Kathy looked round and then whispered conspiratorially.

'I'll have a small brandy, then, thank you. His nibs won't want anything just now....' She topped off Peter's glass expertly. 'Well, go on then.' Kathy urged Peter to continue. 'Don't leave us hanging.'

'What?'

'Peter! You can be a right royal pain when you want to be. You know very well. What are you going to be doing with yourself?' Kathy almost handed Peter his bitter but then stopped, just out of reach. 'Tell me, or you'll get this over you. I mean it.'

'All right, all right.' Peter laughed and held up his hands. He knew that it wasn't that likely but Kathy wasn't above dumping beer in his lap, especially since there was no one else present. He'd seen her do it before. He grinned and nodded and took the glass from her. 'I'm going to paint.'

Kathy stared.

'Paint? Paint what? Houses and stuff?'

'No, for goodness sake. An artist, I'm going to become an artist, full time. I'm going to make my living painting pictures, or at least try to.'

'Oh.' Kathy was plainly surprised. 'For a moment there I was struggling with the vision of you in a dusty flat cap and an apron. Will you be able to make enough to live on? It'll be a bit dodgy, I'd have thought.'

'I think so. It may take a little while to make the necessary contacts but I've got a pretty good severance package from the studio and I'll be okay for a while. And Mrs Manfredi, Gabby, said she thought her old gallery would certainly be interested. She had a look at one or two before I left.'

'Oh, yes. That's right. She used to work for that gallery in the city, didn't she? Opie's. Opie and... someone. When did you see Gabby? Just now?'

'No. Before, when we were getting mum's paintings for the Christmas exhibition. Speaking of which, do you know whether any were sold?'

'Two, certainly. They had red dots on them when I was there.'

'Ah, excellent.'

'So what sort of things are you thinking of painting? Are you going to do portraits or landscapes or some of this modern stuff-or cards? They sell well, don't they?'

'Yes. I suppose so. I'll need to look around and talk to people. I'm not sure I want to spend all my time turning out windmills and wherries. I'd quite like to try my hand at something a little more imaginative, but you're right, I'm going to have to pay the bills.'

'Well, that's a bit of a surprise, I have to say. Mind you, you were always good at art, weren't you?'

'Well, we shall see whether I'm good enough.'

Kathy raised her glass and grinned at Peter. 'Good luck then, young feller me lad. I hope you can make a go of it. If it's what you want to do…. You only get one shot at life. You might as well do something that interests you and that you enjoy-if you can. Cheers.'

'Thanks, Kathy. Cheers.'

*

Peter rose late and breakfasted on a couple of bread rolls and some ham that Kathy had pressed on him as he left the pub the night before. He unpacked, did some washing and took his time over coffee while he read the mail. The morning was cold but dry so he hung a few things out on the whirligig and then wandered round the garden. He found evidence of feline bowel movements, but irritating as it was, it came as no surprise. There were two on the lawn and another squarely on top of something he couldn't name in what had been his mother's herb garden. After clearing them up he walked down to Annie's to buy a few staples for the fridge and his cupboard.

As he was crossing the road from the shop towards the church the sun broke through. Instead of going straight home it occurred to him suddenly to visit his mother's grave. He hadn't been back to the church or the graveyard since the funeral and he had never seen Ellen's headstone.

When Ellen was buried a year earlier hers had been the first grave dug in the new graveyard. Peter was surprised and in a way, comforted to see that four others had now joined her. She was no longer alone. Absurd as it had been his sadness on the day of the burial had been compounded by the irrational thought that Ellen would be lonely.

In Loving Memory of
Ellen Eliza Fincham
1920-1979
Beloved mother and friend
'The best portion of a good woman's life
is her little, nameless, unremembered
acts of kindness and love.'

Kathy and Philip had gone together to see to the headstone. The quotation had been Kathy's idea.

'It's not accurate, strictly speaking. It should be "the best portion of a good *man's* life...." But I thought it was nice.... I don't know where it comes from originally. Very fitting though.'

She had gone once to see the headstone after it was installed, but had never returned to Ellen's grave since.

'No,' she said. 'I prefer to remember her alive. What possible difference could it make to her now, whether I go or not.... It can't help her and I'm damn sure it won't do me any good.'

Peter tended to agree. Philip was obviously a regular visitor though, since the grave was neat and tidy and adorned with an earthenware pot of evergreens.

Peter was sauntering along the footpath beside the coast road when a red sports car accelerated fast past him, only to screech to a halt and lurch to the side of the road ahead.

'I thought it was you.' Gabby Manfredi clambered out of the car and stood on the verge grinning at him. She had her hair up and was wearing a long waxed-cotton coat, a charcoal skirt and yet another pair of boots. 'Why didn't you let me know you were back?'

'Hello, Gab.' Peter put down his bag of shopping. 'I only arrived last night. I was going to phone you later.'

'Are you going home? I'll give you a lift. Get in.'

Once Gabby moved her handbag and numerous items of clothing Peter managed to lever his long frame into the low-slung passenger seat of the MG. The interior of the car smelled strongly of perfume and cigarettes.

After much revving of the engine Gabby took off with neither a look to the side or to the rear.

'Mirror, signal....' Peter jerked backwards, gripped the door handle and shook his head. He couldn't help himself.

Gabby gave the rear-view mirror a belated glance.

'And there was I thinking the mirror was for doing my make-up.' She laughed and turned right into Back Lane on the wrong side of the road. The tyres screeched and the MGB fishtailed alarmingly, almost clipping the bank. Peter's feet were performing all sorts of ghostly movements in the footwell as he braked, declutched and braked again while Gabby performed similarly, but late and in the wrong order.

Once she'd straightened up Peter cautiously relaxed a little. In the distance ahead he could just make out George and Janice's cat stalking across the top of Back Lane near Cowper's Cottage.

'You can redeem yourself.' He nodded at the cat. 'A bottle of gin if you can nail him.'

'What, dat poor litter puddy tat?'

'There's nothing poor or little about him. He's big and ugly and he keeps crapping in my garden. And he belongs to George and Janice.'

'What? Jan the Obese?' Gabby laughed. 'Sorry. That's what Spencer calls her. She used to do some cleaning for us but she was hopeless. Always late, did a lousy job-and I'm not sure she didn't help herself from time to time. We had to get rid of her.'

Gabby began to slow. 'So you'll be related to that what's-his-name, Kingston? Kingsley?' She laughed. 'And the dread Jeannie.'

'Kingsley and Jeannie. Sadly, yes. They're my cousins.'

'What a stupid twat that Kingsley is. He came to give us a quote for some plumbing and we never saw him again.'

'Sounds about right.'

'And that Jeannie. My God, she's even bigger and uglier than her mother is. And nastier, if that's possible.'

As they neared the end of the cottages Gabby slewed the car hard right and skidded to a halt on the gravel in front of Cowper's Cottage.

'Thank you very much. I haven't so nearly filled my knickers since the door fell off a helicopter I was travelling in, over the Pacific.' Peter gathered up his bag. He looked at Gabby. 'I'm about to make some coffee. Have you got a few minutes or have you got to run...?' Peter waggled his eyebrows at Gabby. 'I have news.'

Gabby glanced at the elegant gold watch on her wrist. 'Well, I've got a hair appointment.'

'I've got something to tell you.' Peter gave her what he considered a conspiratorial look.

Gabby stared at him through her huge driving glasses. 'Really?' She grinned. 'Go on then. Just a quick one. Since it's you. I've got a bit of time.'

*

'Kathy said that a couple of Ellen's paintings sold. Did the other one...?'

'No. It's in the cupboard at the school. I don't know why it didn't go. I've got a couple of cheques for you at home. We did quite well overall.'

After congratulating themselves on both taking their coffee black and without the benefit of sugar they were sitting at the kitchen table each with a cigarette. Gabby looked at Peter and grinned.

'I can't tell you... what a lovely surprise.' She smiled and shook her head again. She had indeed been taken aback at Peter's news. 'When will you make a start? Where will you work? What...?'

'Whoa, Trigger. Slow down.' Peter laughed. 'I need to catch my breath a bit.'

'You could work in one of the old outhouses in our garden. We've got loads of space. Plenty of room for a studio.'

'I was hoping I might be able to work here somehow.'

'It's a bit poky.' Gabby looked around the room. 'You'll need much more room than you think.' She got up from her chair and wandered through to the conservatory. 'No, this is no good….' She paused and looked across the garden to the left. 'Is that all shed this side of the garage? Do you use it for anything?'

'Not really.'

'Would it do? Is it big enough? Let's go and have a look.'

Peter led the way out to the shed. It was a long, low, single story brick and cobble building with one large window, one small window and a pantiled roof. The shed door had dropped on its hinges and Peter had some difficulty opening it.

He flicked the light switch. A single sooty bulb suspended on an ancient piece of cable in the centre of the ceiling responded with a dim glimmer.

'Oh, look at this.' Gabby looked round at the gloomy shed interior, the walls and ceiling hanging with cobwebs and the corpses of a million insects. 'This would be perfect.' She was ecstatic. 'Coat of paint. I can give you a hand. There's lots of space-and a long wall. It's tall enough for some serious canvasses.'

'Need to do something about this.' Peter stared down at the compacted earth that formed the floor.

'Mm. Yes. Get the builders in to lay a floor.' Gabby walked about the shed excitedly. 'We can do something about the windows. This will do very nicely.'

'Hang on a minute, missus.'

'What?'

'We're in danger of trying to run before we can walk, aren't we?'

'Well, no point in hanging about. What's the problem? I can talk to what's-his-name Bullimore. Ed, Ed Bullimore. He owes us. Spencer's put no end of work his way. Should be able to get mate's rates.' Gabby looked again at her watch and gulped the remains of her coffee. 'I must go.'

They went back into the cottage so that Gabby could get her bag. She picked up the ashtray and emptied it into the swing bin.

'There's that cat again.'

'What?' Peter was at the window immediately. 'Where?'

'He's just gone down the steps.'

'Right.' Peter rushed through to the conservatory and returned brandishing the Diana and the box of pellets.

'What on earth have you got there?'

'My old air pistol.'

'Ha. I haven't seen one of those for years.'

'It's useless actually, hopelessly inaccurate. But it ought to be possible to give him a bit of a scare. He keeps crapping all over the garden.'

The pistol was already loaded so Peter carefully opened the kitchen window a crack, just sufficient to take the barrel. He waited for the cat to reappear. Gabby stood beside him with her arm resting on his shoulder. He was very aware of the closeness of her.

'There he is,' she whispered in Peter's ear. 'Go on, then. God, you're right. He is big. That's not a cat, it's a small heifer.'

'Wait just... a minute.' Peter squinted along the short barrel in what he hoped was a convincing manner.

'He'll be gone in a minute if you don't get on with it.'

'*Bok!*'

The cat paused briefly, looked round and then continued on his way.

'Well, what happened there?' Gabby was grinning. 'Did anything come out?'

'Think so.' Peter looked at the pistol. The barrel was fully extended. He undid the screw and peered down the barrel. It was clear. 'Yes, the pellet's gone.'

'You must have missed by so much he didn't even hear it.' Gabby laughed. 'You're never going to do any good with that silly little thing. You want to borrow one of Spencer's rifles, or better yet a shotgun. That would really put paid to buggerlugs out there. I'll bring one round. But in the meantime I'm late. I'm late, for a very important date.'

Gabby gave Peter a quick kiss on the lips.

'I'll see you later, Dead-Eye Dick.'

8. Surprise turned to disbelief...

Directory Enquiries were very helpful. There were several R. Nichols' in the High Wycombe area but only one R. T. C. Nichols. He lived in Princes Risborough.

Raymond Trevor Charles. Before the christening Nick had boggled at Monica's insistence on three names. It turned out that one of the women in a group to which she aspired had just christened her son with three names and Monica felt the need to do likewise. It would raise their son above the common herd, she said. Several cricketers had three initials and they went to university and were nicely spoken. Nick struggled with both the logic and the relevance. He never liked Raymond or Trevor as names but Monica had been adamant. Raymond was for her father and there had been some logic behind the choice of Trevor which now escaped Nick. Charles had been his contribution, grabbed out of the air. Monica hadn't liked it much but she couldn't deny it having chosen the other two names.

'They'll call him Charlie,' she said.

'I doubt it,' had been Nick's rejoinder. 'They'll call him Ray.'

'Well I shall call him Raymond, his proper name.' And true to her word Monica invariably did.

Retreating from the accusing stares in the baker's shop in Leeds Nick had scurried along the street to the undertaker's office. There an aged woman with almost translucent skin and loose dentures dug out records confirming that Monica Nichols, née Oldfield, had been cremated in January 1978. Nick declined her invitation to find someone to accompany him to the crematorium gardens to see where his wife's ashes were buried. As he left Nick felt strangely disoriented. He couldn't get out of his head the last image that he had of his wife, sitting in lumpish fashion and in ill-fitting clothes with her legs almost in the fireplace. During all the years he'd been away, on the odd occasions that he gave any thought to Monica; it was exactly how he remembered her.

They had shared some good times. It had been the war and coming back to find her having an affair with Little Jack that had killed the relationship. It must have been the same for countless couples.

He set out early the following Saturday morning for Buckinghamshire in the Cortina Estate. As he neared Princes Risborough he became increasingly jittery. He stopped in a lay-by near Wendover and poured a cup of coffee from his flask.

Raymond's house wasn't at all difficult to find. After leaving the car in a pub car park he wandered slowly the length of the road and identified his son's house. A semi-detached property, it was neat and tidy with the front door opening directly onto the pavement. It looked as though no one was at home. He was sauntering back to his car when a woman rode up on a bicycle. She dismounted at the kerb and began to let herself in the side gate next to Raymond's house.

'Excuse me.' Nick waved an arm and broke into a trot towards the woman.

'Yes?' The woman paused as she was about to close the gate behind her.

'I'm sorry to bother you. I don't know whether you can help.'

The woman looked anxious.

'I'm trying to find Raymond Nichols' garage… or repair shop. I was told to try down here.'

'Oh,' the woman looked relieved. 'The workshop's not here. He lives here.' She nodded towards next door. 'But he'll be at work. I know his wife is out. I've just seen her in the butcher's in the town with one of the boys. If you want the workshop it's just off Aylesbury Road on the other side of the town. It's right behind the Shell station, *RTC Autos*, you can't miss it.'

Nick didn't miss it and twenty minutes later he was sitting in the Cortina at the side of the petrol station forecourt wondering what to do next. There was a roughly-daubed home-made sign on the fence beside him advertising RTC. An arrow pointed towards a narrow gravel lane at the back of the petrol station. Nick decided to take a look.

He was edging slowly along the lane when a battered recovery vehicle loomed large in his rear-view mirror. There was nowhere that he could stop to let it pass so he simply preceded it into the potholed yard in front of *RTC Autos* and pulled over among a jumble of parked cars and vans. The truck passed him and stopped in front of the workshop. Nick was about to turn round in the yard when a chunky red-faced man in torn and greasy overalls jumped down from the truck, slammed the cab door and called out something as he wiped his hands on a piece of rag.

Nick had no difficulty in recognising Raymond. He almost panicked. It wasn't what he had planned.

Raymond strode over and was soon beside the Cortina. There was nothing for it but to wind down the window.

'Yes sir, and what can we do you for today?' Raymond bobbed down to peer in the window.

Nick stared. He couldn't find the right words.

'Hello. I….' He didn't know what to say. 'I….' Any words at all would have been useful. In the end he couldn't help himself.

'Hello, Raymond.' Nick gazed in wonder at his son's face a couple of feet or so from his own. Raymond had obviously broken his nose at some point and there was a poorly knit scar beneath his left eyebrow. He looked like a boxer. 'It's been a long time.'

Raymond was having difficulty. He frowned and stared at Nick. 'Do I… do we…?'

Nick felt sorry for his son. He was swamped for a moment with compassion and guilt.

'I know this….' Nick licked his lips and turned away to peer through his windscreen. 'I know this might come as a bit….' He frowned and rubbed at a speck on the dashboard. Eventually he stopped fiddling and turned back to Raymond. 'It's me, Raymond, Nick, your dad.'

Still Raymond frowned. He stared at Nick. Suddenly he blinked, as though someone had slapped his face. Blankness became surprise. He continued to stare at Nick. Surprise turned to disbelief and then quickly became derision. Raymond's face turned nasty. He stood up and backed away. It was a long moment before he spoke.

'Get out of here,' he said dismissively, 'you miserable bastard.' He turned away shaking his head and stumped across the yard and into the workshop.

Nick sat for a moment or two stupefied. He sighed and muttered to himself. 'Well, that went well.' But he couldn't leave things like that. He began to get out of the car.

'Ray?' he called. 'Raymond?' Agitated, he began to make his way across the yard.

Raymond reappeared in the workshop doorway, his face contorted.

'Haven't you gone yet?' he shouted. 'I told you to bugger off. You ought to be able to do that. You've had plenty of practice.'

Another man appeared at Raymond's elbow. Stooped and pale and badly in need of a haircut, he too was dressed in filthy red overalls. He asked Raymond something.

Raymond pointed a finger at Nick.

'Get rid of that bastard,' he shouted. 'I want him out of here now. Otherwise I'll swing for him.'

The second man placed a hand on Raymond's arm. 'All right, all right, calm down, mate.'

Raymond shook himself free. He pointed at Nick again. 'Get him out of here! Now!' He turned back into the workshop. He looked livid.

Raymond's colleague hurried across the yard in some agitation.

'I don't know…. I think you'd better go, mate. You don't want to be around here if he really kicks off. I'd get out of here quick smart, if I were you. Ray's a good mate but you don't want him for an enemy.'

As Nick drove slowly out of the yard he saw his son in the Cortina's rear-view mirror. Raymond was glowering. He was standing, legs apart in the workshop door, drinking from a large white mug. He looked less than at ease with the world.

As he negotiated a deep water-filled rut in the yard Nick heard the mug crash to the ground beside his car. He didn't hear what Raymond shouted but he could have made an informed guess at the sentiments expressed.

*

Thoroughly shaken, Nick drove into the town and parked the Cortina just off the main street. He walked around the centre looking in the shop windows but little of what he saw made any impression. However, it had the desired effect. Eventually, somewhat calmed, he went into a café for coffee and a sandwich. It was while he was eating that he decided to try Raymond's house again before setting off home.

He parked in the pub car park in the same place as before and perambulated the length of the street in both directions. There was no car or truck parked near Raymond's house but there was obviously someone in. An upstairs window was now open and he heard the TV as he passed the front door. He walked half the length of the road again before turning, retracing his steps and finally stopping at the house. After a moment's hesitation he pressed the bell push.

'I'll get it.' He heard the shout from within. The door opened and a boy appeared, a smaller version of Raymond, clutching a bag of crisps. He stared at Nick and fed another greasy crisp between his crumb-encrusted lips.

'Oh, hello. Is your mother in?'

'Mum!' Nick was treated rather fulsomely to the sight of a mouthful of partly masticated fried potato. The boy stared at him for a moment and then returned abruptly to the TV, which was clearly visible since the front door opened directly into the sitting room.

A large jolly-looking woman appeared, wiping her hands on a hand-towel.

'Hello? Yes?' She dabbed her face. 'Phew. I've been baking. It gets warm in there. What can I do for you?'

'I'm looking for Raymond Nichols.'

The woman looked Nick up and down. It was a moment or two before she spoke.

'You're his dad, aren't you?' She subjected Nick to another lengthy and rigorous appraisal before moving to one side.

'You'd better come in. Ray said you might turn up.' She laughed. 'From what he said at dinner it sounds as though he lost the plot for a bit.'

'Oh, well.' Nick wasn't sure how to respond.

'He's like that. Goes off like a cracker. But he's calmed down now.'

'Are you quite sure it's…?' Nick tried to peer past the woman.

'Oh. He's not in,' she laughed. 'It's quite safe.'

She ushered Nick inside and then held out her hand. 'I'm Sheila,' she said, 'your daughter-in-law.'

*

Sheila turned off the TV, sent her son on an errand down to her mother's house and offered Nick a mug of tea. She said that Ray was at the scout hut with their other son and wouldn't be back until five o'clock. After she'd taken scones out of the oven she brought their tea through to the sitting room and motioned Nick to take a seat on the sofa.

'So, you're Ray's dad.'

She flapped her hand in front of her face and perched on the arm of an armchair beside the fire. She looked to Nick like one of those women doomed always to look slightly overheated. Otherwise she was an attractive woman, somewhat overweight but apparently happy in her skin.

'Yes.' Nick sipped his tea. It was very hot and he put it down on a low table beside him. 'I expect you're wondering why I'm here after all this time, and where I've been and what I've been up to. And why I never....'

Sheila stared at him for a moment.

'Well, it's natural enough, I think. But it ought to be Ray you're talking to.' She stared again at Nick over the rim of her mug and then shook her head. 'But he really doesn't want to know.'

'Ah.'

'Still,' Sheila sat up straight, 'what can I do for you?'

'Well, I've located Raymond-not that it's done any good. I really don't know quite what I expected to achieve. Anyway, I was wondering whether you had any information about Louise, Ray's sister. I know no more about her than I do Ray.'

'Well,' Sheila put down her tea and smoothed her apron. 'There I can help you. Louise is in California. She's been there several years now. She lives in a town called Ventura. It's right on the coast north of Los Angeles. I've got her address. She keeps in touch at Christmas and birthdays. With any luck we should be going over next year for a holiday. We last saw her when she was over for Monica's funeral. You do know about that?' Sheila looked at Nick enquiringly.

'Oh. Yes.' He nodded. 'California? What on earth is she doing there?'

'She married an American. Nice fellow. Jerry Stark. She met him in London, I think. He's in the oil business. Drilling

Superintendent these days, I think she said. Or something like that.'

Sheila went to the sideboard.

'I thought I'd try to be ready, if you did come, after what Ray said. I found you these.'

She sat down beside Nick and proffered some photographs.

'You can keep them, if you want. And here's Louise's address.'

*

It was dark and drizzling when Nick finally left. He had just got into his car in the pub car park when a Ford van turned off the Wycombe Road. It was red and blue and had RTC Autos emblazoned in white on the side panels. In the light thrown by the street lamps Nick caught a fleeting glimpse of his son and grandson as they passed. For a moment he wondered whether he should go back and try again to talk to Raymond. But Sheila had been emphatic. Ray didn't want to see him. She hadn't been able to persuade him at lunchtime. And she said that to be fair, she understood how he felt. He would never be able to forgive Nick. There was nothing between them. She said this in a very matter-of-fact way, without being at all judgemental.

Nick had enjoyed talking to his daughter-in-law. She was a straight-forward soul and they had got on well together. He'd learned that he had two grandsons, Andrew and Stephen. Andrew was the elder and wanted to be a vet. The younger boy, Stephen, was a bit slow and had difficulty learning. But he was interested in cooking and they wondered whether he might eventually train to be a chef. Raymond seemed just to be Raymond. He had once been interested in motorcycles but had lost interest after a friend had been badly injured in an accident. Now he helped out at scouts and cubs.

Louise was married to a man considerably older than she was and had no children. However she seemed to lead a very busy and comfortable life out in California. Sheila even talked about Monica. He got the distinct impression that she hadn't cared much for his wife although she was careful not to say so. Monica, it seemed, had divided her time between Little Jack and bingo. Little Jack was still going strong apparently.

The afternoon had slipped by. Nick's visit was brought to a conclusion when the phone rang. It was Sheila's mother to ask whether it was all right for Stephen to return.

Nick was well on the way home before he realized that at no point in their conversation did Sheila ask where he had come from or where he lived. He smiled and shook his head. She was a smart girl, that one. Raymond was lucky with her.

Even before he arrived back in Lincolnshire he had decided that he would go to California as soon as he was retired. Having had an encounter with his son, no matter how brief, he was looking forward suddenly to seeing his daughter once again. He thought that his passport was still in date.

*

It was a bitterly cold and frosty night in late February when just before closing time; Peter decided to pop down to the Lord Nelson for a quick drink. It wasn't so much that he needed anything, more that he'd spent the entire day on his own starting to clear out the shed and hadn't seen or spoken to a living soul. The bar was warm and welcoming but he found little in the way of good cheer or distraction since the few souls hardy or desperate enough to brave the cold night left even before Kathy rang the bell.

To her irritation someone had put a couple of logs on the fire just before they went. There was no way of removing them. Bryan had gone so Peter helped clear up and then made them mugs of hot chocolate and stayed with Kathy beside the fire to chat. Eventually she saw him out and he heard her lock the door behind him. She normally left the outside lights on for a moment but this night since the moon was shining brightly she was very prompt in switching them off.

As Peter pulled up his collar and hunched his shoulders against the bitter night he was suddenly aware of someone standing in the shadows beside the garages.

'Goodnight,' he called as he hurried across the car park. It was so cold that the frozen gravel no longer crunched or gave beneath his weight. There was no response from the shadowy figure by the garages.

In relating the tale to Kathy later Peter said that he felt he had to investigate.

'It didn't feel right,' he said. 'Why would anyone be there, at that time of night? They might have been up to no good.'

'But it might have been anybody,' Kathy said. 'Just think. You might have been murdered or hit over the head.'

But it wasn't just anybody. When Peter approached, the figure in the shadows moved neither towards him nor away and he elicited no response to his enquiries. He fished in his pocket for his lighter. As he flicked it into life, through the plumes of his own breath Peter was astonished to recognize the pale and pinched features peering back at him from beneath a woolly hat.

'What on earth…?'

In addition to the hat the woman was bundled up in a long dark coat, scarf and gloves but she looked absolutely frozen.

'Margaret. What are you doing here?'

Margaret Graver's big eyes stared back at Peter in the flickering light.

'Where's your car?' Peter cast around but could see no Mini or any other vehicle. The car park was empty.

'Are you all right? Can you walk?' Clearly something was amiss. Peter took Margaret by the arm and led her gently out onto the coast road.

'Come on. Come back with me. We'll go home and get you warmed up… and sorted out. You must be frozen.'

They walked slowly up Back Lane, in silence apart from Margaret's boot heels clicking loudly on the icy road. She clung tightly to Peter's arm and would answer no questions. She seemed unable to go any faster.

When they got in Peter was aghast at Margaret's appearance. Ordinarily she wouldn't dream of being seen without makeup, jewellery and a carefully coordinated outfit. When Peter helped her off with her woollen hat and coat, her dark hair was greasy and matted; her face was pale and pinched. It occurred to him that she looked very like her father Harry Littleboy, when he first arrived back in 1950 after years in a Japanese POW camp. Margaret looked terrible.

Cowper's Cottage was warm but she was still shivering. Peter switched on the heating and poked the fire into life. He put on the kettle, fetched a travelling rug, placed it round her shoulders and sat her in an armchair beside the fire. After making cocoa he filled a hot water bottle which Margaret took gratefully and clasped to her stomach.

'You look as though a small brandy might be welcome.' He looked at Margaret but again got no response. 'I wouldn't mind one myself.'

He poured two small measures and placed one beside her.

'Get that down you. It'll help warm you up.'

Margaret stared into the flickering fire and nodded. She sniffed and dabbed at her nose with a handkerchief. After giving the fire another prod Peter rubbed his hands encouragingly and sat down opposite her.

'So.' He gave her a smile. 'I haven't seen anything of you for a while. How's young Graver coming on?' He grinned and nodded in the direction of Margaret's belly. 'Still cooking? Not ready yet, of course.' There was no response. 'Still got a bit of a way to go….' Peter knew he was beginning to gabble.

He tried to keep things light and sipped his brandy. Margaret sniffed again. She held her mug with both hands and stared into the fire.

Eventually she looked at Peter and whispered. 'I've lost the baby.' She closed her eyes and was racked by shuddering sobs.

*

Peter sat on the arm of Margaret's chair with his arm round her. He held her hand and tried to comfort her as she sobbed her way through what had happened. She had felt unwell for a couple of days and eventually miscarried in the early hours of 4th February, after taking to her bed the afternoon before with nausea, crippling cramps and back pain.

'Oh, it came as no surprise.' She dabbed at her eyes. 'I just knew something was going to go wrong.' She shook her head and wept anew. 'I'm not meant to have a baby. I might as well forget all about it. It's not going to happen.'

'What about Tom? Does he know? Were you able to contact him? Has he been home?'

Margaret shook her head wearily. 'Tomorrow. He'll be home tomorrow. Not that there's anything....'

She stopped speaking abruptly and stared into the fire. After a while she looked at Peter and gave him a tight little smile. 'This is nice.' She closed her eyes. 'I've always liked Cowper's Cottage.'

'So, have you been on your own since...? Have you got anyone who can help at all?'

'Next door's been good. I'm all right.' Margaret shook her head.

'You're not at work at the moment, are you?'

'No. The doctor gave me a certificate.'

'So… what were doing outside the Nelson? Had you been there long? Where's your car?'

'At home.'

'So how did you get here?'

'I walked.'

'You walked, in the dark, on a night like this?' Peter was incredulous. 'All the way from Cromer?'

Margaret shrugged. 'I just wanted to go somewhere. I couldn't stay at home.'

'Have you eaten?'

'I'm not hungry.'

'Can't I make you something? Soup? Something on toast?'

'No. I'm fine.'

'Let me fix up a bed for you. Stay here tonight.'

'This is fine. I'll just stay… by the fire. If that's OK.'

'Of course.'

Margaret put down her mug, turned on her side, pulled her knees up to her stomach and closed her eyes. She opened them briefly.

'I'm beat.' She gave Peter another tight smile.

'Get some sleep. I'll take you home in the morning, but there's no rush to get up.'

'Thanks, Peter.' Within seconds she was asleep.

Peter found another blanket and placed it over her. He banked up the fire, put the guard in front of it, turned off all but one table lamp and then went to bed. Margaret never stirred. She was obviously far away.

Peter had difficulty dropping off and then woke up sweating and looked at his bedside clock. It was just after three o'clock. After listening for a moment he got up and went downstairs. Margaret was much as he had left her. She looked peaceful enough but far from the elegant, confident and sexy woman with whom a few months earlier he'd hoped he might share the rest of his life. He looked at her sorrowfully for a moment then put a few more pieces of coal carefully onto the fire and returned to bed.

It was after nine when he woke again with a start. The living room was empty. Margaret had left a note on the kitchen work-top.

'Much better now. Thanks. Sorry for last night. Love, M.'

Peter thought about going into Cromer to check that Margaret was indeed all right, but if Tom were there…. He decided against it. There was a lot to do if he was going to turn the shed into a studio.

*

Dear Louise,

You'll never guess. Your father Nick turned up here this afternoon. He arrived out of the blue at Ray's workshop, but Liz next door said he'd been here asking before that. Well, you know Ray. He did exactly what he always said he would if your dad ever turned up. He didn't want to know and told him to b----- off. He can't find it in him to forgive his dad after all this time and what it did to your mum. He doesn't want to know where he's been or what he's been doing.

Anyway, Nick turned up here later after Ray went to scouts with Andy. He seems a nice enough chap and he looked well. I gave him your address, I hope that was all right, but you always said you'd like to see him again. He's almost retired and when he does retire he's going to try to come and see you. He's a Senior Warehouseman at a natural gas terminal in Lincolnshire. Stupidly I didn't get his address but if you wanted to contact him I imagine he lives close to the terminal.

From what he said I think he's been in Lincolnshire all the time from when he left home. He was living with a woman called Barbara but she died. He went to Leeds before he came down here and he knew that your mum had died. (He found out there.) He was interested to hear about you and where you were.

If I were you I'd be on the look out for your dad getting in touch soon.

Anyway, regards to Jerry. We're all well. Looking forward to coming over. I'll write with more news later. I just wanted to get this off to you quickly. I expect you'll be excited!

Love,

Sheila, Ray, Andy & Steve.

PS His name is Nick Codling these days, not Nichols. I didn't ask why.

*

Peter was sitting at the kitchen table in his dressing gown and moth-eaten moccasins when a car crunched to a halt on the gravel out front. A single car door slammed and after a moment he heard heels on the quarry tiles in the porch. A quick look through the window on his way to the door confirmed the identity of the caller.

He whipped open the door as she was about to ring the bell.

'Good morning.'

'Hiya.' Gabby eyed him up and down. 'Aren't you up yet? I thought you might like to offer me a cup of coffee.'

She swept in, trailing expensive perfume.

'Nice dressing gown.'

Gabby was looking very *Doctor Zhivago* in a fluffy fur hat, a long waxed raincoat, a scarf stylishly around her neck, leather gloves and boots.

'God, it's cold this morning. The main road's OK but the side roads are like glass. I don't know,' she said, dumping a capacious handbag on the table and unfurling her scarf, 'it's all right for some. I've been into Cromer, done the shopping, looked in on Spencer's mum and dad, had a quick coffee with them, bloody horrible-as usual, and you're still sitting here on your backside like lord of the manor-doing nothing and going nowhere. What am I going to do with you?'

Gabby smiled, divested herself of her coat and hat and sat down at the kitchen table.

'Hello, Gabby. Why don't you come on in, insult me and make yourself right at home?'

Peter grinned and shuffled over to the worktop to put the kettle on.

'I was just about to have a shower and get on.'

'Not before time. What are you doing today?' She rooted in her handbag then jumped up, went to the dresser and returned with an ashtray.

'I'm halfway through clearing the shed. Thought I might get on with that. It's bitter out there but with any luck I might get it finished today.'

'I could give you a hand.' Gabby took a cigarette and lit it. She pushed the packet towards Peter.

'Thanks. What? Dressed like that?'

'You are joking. Do you know how much it costs to look this good?' Gabby goggled. 'I'll go home and change into my grubby things. It'll only take a few minutes.'

'Oh. Well, any help would be very welcome.' Peter finished pouring their coffee and set a mug down in front of Gabby.

'Thanks. Have you talked to Ed yet, Bullimore, about the shed floor?'

Peter sat down and lit a cigarette.

'Yes. He's got a couple of blokes coming this weekend. Straightforward, he said. There's a good layer of hardcore down already, apparently, under about an inch of soil. They should be done in a day. That's why I need to finish clearing everything out. You haven't got a trailer by any chance, have you?'

'What for?'

'To take stuff to the tip.'

'We could use Spencer's pickup. He hardly ever uses it these days. I think it's still taxed.'

'That would be ideal. He wouldn't mind? Can't get much in mother's old car.'

'You'll need to get something else, won't you? You won't be able to carry much in the way of paintings with just the Morris.'

'I will. It's just about done. I had to get some welding done, and wheel bearings, cost a fortune. It won't pass another MOT.' Peter sipped his coffee. 'Actually the reason I'm all behind this morning is because I was a bit late to bed.' He told Gabby about Margaret's visit.

'Oh? I don't know her very well. I've seen her about. Doesn't she work at Cavell, the convalescent home?' Gabby gave Peter a sidelong look. 'She's very attractive. Weren't you two a little bit… cosy, not so long ago?'

Peter glanced up quickly.

'Yes.' He nodded reflectively and gave a little laugh. 'I… I had hoped….' He grimaced and shook his head.

Gabby tapped the ash from her cigarette carefully and paused for a moment before continuing. 'You never wondered whether the baby might not be yours.'

'Oh, yes. I thought it was. I was under the distinct impression that there was little in the way of… what shall we say, normal relations, between Margaret and her husband. And he's hardly ever there anyway.'

Gabby continued to twirl her cigarette in the ashtray.

'Hmm.'

'What?'

'Well, they do say-and I'm not saying that this is necessarily the truth-but they do say that Tom is… a little bit… the other way inclined.'

'Oh, really?'

'Gabby shrugged. 'It's not just me. I think it's a common enough view, I believe.'

'Oh. Well, anyway, she is married, and now she's lost her baby. I really felt for her last night. She looked terrible and she didn't seem entirely on the ball.'

'Yes. Well, that's understandable. It must be awful.' Gabby took out a compact and looked at herself in the mirror. 'Did you not wonder why she came to see you?' She put the compact away, stubbed out her cigarette and then shook her head. 'None of my business.'

'I think it's hit her hard. She was probably not thinking all that clearly.'

'Ah.' Gabby finished her coffee and stood up.

'Right. This is no good. You go and get showered, shitted and shaved and above all, dressed. I'll nip home and change and we'll finish that shed. I'll bring the pick-up and we can get rid of all your junk.'

9. *Up your pipe*

The MGB crunched into the yard as Peter was opening up the shed. By now the sun was shining brightly and the temperature had struggled above zero. In the shade the gravel, the path and the shrubbery were still mantled with rime. Gabby slithered to a halt, scattering gravel. She clambered out of the car resplendent in a white boiler suit that had obviously served as a painter's cover-all at some point. The thighs, right buttock, left breast and sleeve boasted impressive multicoloured impastos. In fact there was evidence over much of the garment of a good deal of carelessness with oil paint generally.

Peter had never had much time for the daubers who carefully encrusted themselves in such a fashion. It was so exhibitionistic and in the end no better than a badge or a uniform. *I'm a painter,* it screamed, *look at me!* It was a criminal waste of paint too. However this was Gabby, attractive, sexy Gabby who seemed happy to spend some time with him so Peter kept his lip firmly buttoned.

Sitting sideways on the driver's seat Gabby changed yet another pair of boots, brown lace-ups this time, for a pair of elderly suede slip-ons. She then tucked her hair up into a green baseball cap with a yellow peak and pulled on a pair of bright yellow rubber gloves. Whatever his reservations Peter admitted to himself that Gabby looked pretty eye-catching in her get-up.

'Right,' she called as she levered herself out of the MG. She stumped robot-like across the thawing gravel with her hands held vertically in front of her, in the manner of a surgeon, freshly scrubbed and about to conduct an operation.

'Lead me to my next victim.'

'I thought you were bringing the pick-up?'

'Sadly not.' Gabby reverted to human form. 'According to Spencer it isn't taxed and it's got a flat tyre… and a flat battery… and it's probably got a flat gearbox for all I know… and very likely fourteen other things that are very flat indeed. My husband can be a right royal pain sometimes.'

'Oh, well. Never mind. Thanks for trying. We'll just have to cram the stuff into the Morris. There's probably not that much anyway.'

With two of them working it didn't take long to finish clearing the shed. There were a few items that would have to go to the tip but they decided that a good deal of the rubbish could be burned. They stopped for lunch and Peter produced scrambled eggs on toast. After a quick cup of coffee and a few minutes with the Telegraph crossword they wheeled all of the combustible rubbish down the garden and built a fire on Ellen's vegetable patch. Peter worried briefly about the smoke but it rose almost vertically into the clear blue sky before drifting off across the field.

They went at the shed walls and ceiling with brushes and brooms, knocking down years of accumulated spiders' webs and skeletal insect remains. Since Ellen had kept her coal in the shed until she bought a concrete bunker everything was coated with coal dust. These activities were interspersed with periodic breathers outside when the dust became intolerable.

Among the items they had saved were several cans of emulsion and a number of paint brushes. The studio would need ultimately to be painted white but there were enough ends of various shades of cream and magnolia for them to make a start on a base coat. Gabby sent Peter in for a radio so they could listen to music while they worked. She quickly found a station on Ellen's old Roberts portable that was playing 1960s pop and they sang along, or droned in Peter's case, as they worked. They'd finished the two end walls and one long wall and were on the point of stopping for a cup of tea when there was a hammering at the shed door. It opened before Peter could move and a red-faced and angry Janice stood in the doorway. She glared at Peter.

'So here you are. What on earth do you think you're playing at?' Janice's pale blue eyes skittered rapidly over Gabby and round the shed interior before they narrowed and finally fixed on Peter.

He was taken aback. 'Hello, Janice. What's wrong?'

'I'll tell you what's wrong. That stinking bonfire of yours, that's what's wrong. There's smuts all over my washing.'

Peter went to the radio and turned it off.

'Really? I'm sorry. We checked to see which way the wind was blowing, not that there is much. I thought it was just going straight up or away over the field.'

'Well, it's not. There's bits all over my washing.'

'Oh. Well,' Peter shrugged, 'as I said, I'm sorry, Janice. We'll put it out.'

'It's a bit late now, isn't it?'

Peter clambered down from his stepladder.

'I'll come and do it now. As I said I'm very sorry.'

'Well, it's not good enough.'

Peter stopped and looked at her.

'I'm not sure what I can do apart from put the fire out. What would you…?'

'Well, I want to know what….'

'Oh, for goodness sake, woman.' Gabby had been no more than a disbelieving onlooker up to this point. 'He's said he's sorry. We are sorry. What more do you want? Blood?'

Janice rounded on Gabby.

'And just exactly what has it got to do with you, madam? I should like to know.'

'Well, since you ask, it was my idea to have the fire in the first place.'

'Was it now?' A look of triumph crossed Janice's face. 'And what exactly do you think you're doing here anyway?'

'I fail to see that it's any of your business, Mrs Fincham, but as you can see, as indeed anyone with half a brain can see… we were cleaning out Peter's shed and now we're painting it.'

'That don't alter the fact….'

'Oh, piss off, you stupid cow. We've apologized. Go and waste someone else's life.' Gabby obviously didn't suffer fools gladly. She turned away dismissively and went back to her painting.

Janice gave Gabby's back a long and venomous look. Her mouth hung open and she wiped furiously at spittle on her chin. It appeared to Peter that her face took on a worrying mix of cunning, malice and spite. He'd seen it before. Janice could be a nasty piece of work, if crossed.

'Right! You've been and gone and done it now. You'll be sorry. I'm telling George… and our Kingsley. He'll soon come and sort you out, madam.'

Gabby turned and choked back laughter.

'Your Kingsley? Don't make me laugh. He hasn't the brains of a gnat. We're still waiting for him to send us an estimate from last year.'

Janice gave them both an ugly look and then left, shaking her head and muttering.

'You'll see.' She called and she gave a short laugh. 'Don't say you weren't warned.'

Bewildered, standing paintbrush in hand, Peter frowned.

'What do you suppose we should do?'

'Oh. Ignore her. I know she's your aunt but she's plainly batty. The whole family is.'

'Well, we probably have messed up her washing. Maybe we should go and douse the fire.'

They hurried together down the garden but the fire was almost burned out.

'Well, that's not going to cause much of a problem to anyone.'

Peter looked across Penny Hunt's garden to Janice's washing line. It was bare.

'She's taken her washing in anyway.'

'Yes, and I suspect that the smuts were no more than a pretext. She just wanted to have a nose, see what was going on in the shed.'

'Oh. Ah.' Peter stared at Gabby for a moment. 'Maybe you're right.'

By now the sun had disappeared behind a bank of clouds in the west. The temperature was dropping rapidly and it was beginning to get dark. In addition Janice's intervention had broken the mood.

'We might as well call it a day, I think.' Peter looked at Gabby and laughed.

'What?'

'You are absolutely filthy, and you've got a moustache.'

'You can talk. Look at the state of you.'

'You'd better have a shower before you go, and put your boiler suit in a bag or something.'

As they washed out their brushes Gabby pointed out the wisdom of disrobing before they went into the cottage.

Shooting Marmalade

'Yes. We'd better go round the back. We can take these off and go in through the conservatory. God bless mum for having a shower put in downstairs.'

'That's handy.'

'You go first. I'll get some towels. Have you something to wear?'

'Yes. I've got jeans and a sweater under this.'

*

Peter wasn't totally surprised when in spite of the chill; Gabby had no compunction about disrobing in front of him. Outside the conservatory door she slipped out of her boiler suit and kicked off her shoes. She began removing her sweater and jeans as soon as she was inside.

'You go ahead,' he called. 'The shower's just through the kitchen… in the cloakroom. There should be plenty of hot water.'

As Gabby switched on the light Janice's husband George appeared in the field at the bottom of the garden. He couldn't fail to see Gabby prancing about in her bra and knickers, but he hadn't come from the direction of his cottage so it was unlikely that Janice had yet reported the most recent local difficulty. Stopping and taking out a handkerchief and wiping his nose, George stood for some time in the gathering dusk, apparently peering over the fence at Peter and Gabby.

'Pull the blinds, Gab.' But Gabby hadn't heard.

'Can I help you?' he called to George.

'No.' George replied. But he remained where he was.

Peter removed his boots. George still hadn't budged.

'What do you want?' Peter called again.

'Me?' George snorted briefly and then gave a little laugh. 'I don't want nothing.' He was typically unhelpful. Peter however was beginning to feel aggrieved. He put his boots back on and shuffled down to the bottom of the garden. Just as he arrived at the fence George glanced down to his right.

'You can stop that bloody nonsense, as soon as you like,' he called, irritably.

'Stop what?' Peter frowned. 'I don't see that it's got anything to do with you what….'

'I told you to stop it.' George was shouting now.

'What?'

'Come on, you little bugger. I won't tell you again.' George yanked savagely at something and then turned away, heading for the gate in the fence at the bottom of his garden.

As Peter leaned over the fence George cast back.

'I was talking to Archie.'

'Oh.'

'Yes. Oh. I should think so.'

George was returning from walking their son's Basset. Kingsley left the creature occasionally when he and May were both out at work. It caused George and Janice endless inconvenience, since understandably, there was little love lost between Archie and the cat.

'Oh, good-oh.' Peter rolled his eyes, shook his head and turned away. He stumped back to the conservatory and took his boots off again. Now he had irritated both Janice and George.

'Have you got shampoo?' Gabby reappeared. 'I think I'm going to have to wash my hair. Look at this.' She turned towards Peter and raked a hand through her hair.

'You do indeed look like the wild man of Borneo. Yes. There's shampoo in the rack. And there are towels in the cupboard opposite the shower. Help yourself.' Peter tried to sound blasé. He looked round. George had gone. 'I'm off upstairs. There's another shower in the bathroom.'

By the time Peter returned, dressed in jeans and a sweater, Gabby was dressed and her hair was swathed in a towel.

'I've put the kettle on. Have you got a hairdryer?'

'I've brought one down.'

'Oh, good man.' Gabby went to her handbag. Producing a hairbrush and a makeup bag she took the hairdryer and returned to the cloakroom. While it hummed Peter made tea and delved around in the cupboards until he found some biscuits. The hairdryer stopped.

'Peter,' Gabby hissed. 'That cat's back. Where's your gun?'

'Where is he? It's almost dark out there.'

'He'll be on the patio by now. Can I have a go?' Gabby's eyes shone with excitement. Peter fetched the pistol from the sideboard.

'Come on, come on.' Gabby was impatient. 'He'll be gone in a minute and it'll be too dark to see.'

He handed her the pistol. 'It is loaded.'

'Where's the best place?'

'Kitchen window, I should think.'

They hurried back into the kitchen and peered out into the darkening garden.

'I can't see him. Yes! There he is.' Peter carefully opened the window and moved aside. Gabby leaned over the sink and adopted what looked to Peter, a very professional double-handed grip.

'Now you little sod, let's see how you like this.'

Bok!

There was a screech from the garden and a crash as the tomcat leapt sideways into the boards between Cowper's Cottage and Penny Hunt's. He careered up the fence and disappeared at speed.

'Bloody hell! I must have hit him.' Gabby turned to stare at Peter. 'I could hardly see him. How on earth…?'

'Ah, just lucky chance, I expect.'

'I think not.' Gabby smirked and blew on the gun barrel in the manner of a professional gunslinger. 'I think you'll find that it was sheer skill. Having to allow for the wind, the tendency for the gun to aim high and what? Right?'

'Mmm. And the fact that there's an R in the month and you're wearing your lucky knickers, and de-dah, de-dah de-do.'

'Never mind my knickers.' Gabby chewed her lower lip briefly. 'Hope I didn't hurt him.'

'I doubt it. That pellet was travelling so slowly it couldn't do any real harm. He was probably surprised as much as anything. Well done anyway. I've never seen him move so fast. Tea?'

*

Peter phoned Margaret's number several times throughout the evening. There was no response. He considered driving over to see her but decided that if a conversation with her husband were at all likely he'd rather conduct it by telephone. There would be less chance of a misunderstanding, he felt. And if there were a misunderstanding, well; distance might, if not lend enchantment-at least give him a head start. He was on the point of going to bed when he decided to give it one last try.

'Hello?' A male voice.

'Oh. Hello. I'm sorry to trouble you so late. I did try earlier. I was just calling to see how Margaret is getting on. I know she hasn't been well recently.'

There was silence at the other end of the line.

'And you are?'

'Peter. Peter Fincham. Is that Tom? Tom Graver?'

'It is.'

'Hi. You won't know me but Margaret mentioned you. She got to know my mother, Ellen, Ellen Fincham in Cavell House, the convalescent home. Last August, September. I met Margaret at mother's funeral.'

'Oh yes.'

'Anyway,' Peter ploughed on. 'How is Margaret?'

'She's fine, feeling much better now.'

'Oh. That is good news.'

There was another short silence. Peter was wondering how, or even whether to proceed when Tom Graver spoke.

'Naturally enough she's feeling very silly, but otherwise she's okay.'

'Silly? Why's that?'

'Well, the pseudocyesis. You have to admit… bit rum that, enough to make anyone feel foolish.'

'The what? I didn't catch…'

'Pseudocyesis. P-S-E-U-D-O-C-Y-E-S-I-S.' Tom rattled the letters out far too quickly for Peter to catch most of them.

There was another silence. Peter got the impression that Margaret's husband was enjoying himself.

'Yes,' he said. 'I hear what you say but it doesn't mean anything to me.' He tried to keep the testiness that he was beginning to feel, out of his voice.

'Phantom thingy… you know.'

Peter could hear the sound of gulping. Margaret's husband was obviously drinking.

'Sorry to be a pain but… I'm….'

'Pregnancy,' Tom Graver barked. 'Phantom pregnancy.' He laughed. 'Thought she was up the duff, but she wasn't. It was bound to be though. I can't imagine why she thought she was.'

'What?'

'Pregnant. Margaret's pregnancy.'

'Oh?'

'Yes. Couldn't have been the real McCoy for the very simple reason that I was away and we hadn't done the needful... the business... you know.'

*

So had Margaret been pregnant or not? As he lay in bed Peter chewed it over again and again. He couldn't get it out of his head. Did she really believe that she was pregnant or had it been no more than make-believe? One of Ellen's old home medical books mentioned the condition but dismissed it in a few lines. Hippocrates had recorded a dozen cases of the disorder as early as 300 B.C. Peter also learned that Mary Tudor had apparently believed on numerous occasions that she was pregnant when she was not.

He wanted to talk to Margaret but didn't relish questioning a woman about her pregnancy, real or imagined, while her cuckold of a husband stood by. He chaffed and fretted and early next morning phoned Gabby. She looked it up and talked to a friend who was a midwife and was able to give Peter an informed view later as they sat at the kitchen table over coffee.

'Oh, it's a serious thing, a recognized disorder. A woman can believe she's pregnant and show all the signs, morning sickness, sore boobs, putting on weight, the works. Even feeling the baby moving. It can happen at almost any age, from about twelve to eighty or so, as likely as that would be. But it isn't real. I'm not sure what they do about it. Sadly I think a trick-cyclist is probably the only answer.'

'What causes it?'

'Oh, desperation. Fear. Desperately wanting a baby or scared stiff of having one, apparently.' Gabby dragged on the remains of her cigarette and then stubbed it out. She wrinkled her nose and blew out smoke.

'It sounds complicated.' She had clearly lost interest.

Gabby was by now a regular caller at Cowper's Cottage every weekday morning. After looking in on Spencer's aged parents *en route* to Cromer to ensure they were upright and breathing and see if they needed anything, she delivered their odd bits of shopping on her way back. After a foul cup of coffee with them she called in at Peter's for something to take the taste away. Peter quickly got into the habit of having the water boiled and a couple of mugs ready for instant blacks.

After he was thoroughly briefed on Spencer's parents' latest excesses they sat at the kitchen table smoking Gabby's Benson and Hedges, drinking coffee and fiddling with the Telegraph crossword.

'Faggots. The old bat wanted faggots. I had to go all the way up to Wilson's to get them… and marrowfat peas, for goodness sake.'

'Ah.'

'And last week, you know the pilchards that she couldn't live without. They're still on the shelf in the pantry.'

'Hmm.'

At weekends Gabby rarely visited and if she did, she would always phone first. The Manfredis often went to the Lord Nelson for a pre-prandial at noon on Sundays so Peter often ran across them there. He usually ate his Sunday lunch at the bar. Gabby made noises about inviting Peter for Sunday lunch but it never came to pass, which was something of a relief. The memory of Christmas Day was still strong in Peter's mind. He didn't press for an invitation.

On these morning visits Gabby was always fully made-up and elegantly dressed. When Peter commented on her appearance she admitted that she never went out in the morning without first washing her hair and applying her makeup.

'I couldn't face the world. If I was stuck on a desert island I'd have to have mascara. I couldn't bear it otherwise. I've got terribly piggy little eyes without it.'

Ed Bullimore put a new floor in the shed. Peter had overlooked the need for all of the numerous other jobs that needed attention but everything was accomplished quickly and easily and more to the point, at reasonable cost. The builder was keen to stay in Gabby's good books and she drove him hard on some of the prices.

She also sent round her 'little man' from the council houses. A real jack of all trades, he could turn his hand to almost anything. He ran a water supply out to an old butler's sink that Gabby donated, having found it at the bottom of her garden.

'You might as well have it. Spencer said he'd make a water garden or a thing for heathers and stuff like that but he never has. And he never will. And I can't be arsed with gardening anyway.'

The shed was rewired and the telephone and shelves installed. The door was replaced and finally a heavy-duty carpet was laid over half of the floor area. The other half was sealed with floor paint to keep the dust down. This was where Peter would paint.

Gabby set about calling up ex-colleagues in the art world and quickly turned up a second-hand studio easel, a radial easel, several frames, an enormous scrubbed pine table and a couple of chairs. She donated an elderly sofa and was able to persuade Spencer's potato merchant to collect everything in his lorry and deliver them to Cowper's Cottage.

They eventually gave the walls and ceiling a final coat of white emulsion and the new studio was complete. Even as they stood, tired and triumphant in the centre of the room their breath was visible. It was obvious that some form of heating would be necessary so Gabby's man installed a wall-mounted electric heater.

Finally, one Friday afternoon following a trip to Norwich for paint and brushes and numerous other items of equipment Gabby judged the studio ready for use. While Peter had gone in search of painting supplies in the city Gabby had spent her time, and a not insignificant amount of money on a manicure, a makeover and a bit of shopping.

Peter placed a charcoal drawing on the studio easel. He was excited. It was something that had been inspired by the drawings and photos he'd taken in Iceland. He'd been poking away at it occasionally in the conservatory and now he knew exactly how to proceed. It was his intention to get to work on an oil painting on Monday, his first full day as a professional artist.

It was late in the afternoon and getting dark when Gabby excused herself. She returned after a while with a bottle of champagne, glasses and salted cashew nuts. It was warm and comfortable in the studio and the fan heater was giving off that faint smell of scorched dust, characteristic of new appliances. Gabby had obviously touched up her makeup and the air was heavy with newly sprayed perfume. She pulled down the blinds and switched off all the lights except for the Anglepoise on the table. The lamp, which now gave off a warm glow, had been her gift to Peter, to wish him well in his artistic endeavours.

'That blind needs some attention. It won't come down any further than that. Will you open it?' Gabby handed Peter the bottle.

'Hmm. Thank you. Wow! *Dom Perignon*, very nice indeed.'

'Well, it's been kicking about at home waiting for some suitable occasion. This rather fits the bill, I think.'

Peter smiled.

'It's a kind thought. Thank you.'

The champagne cork gave Peter little trouble. It came out with a very satisfying pop and with a deft touch he managed to pour a couple of glasses without losing any of the precious liquid.

'Very impressive.' Gabby nodded appreciatively and took the glass that Peter offered. 'Not the first time you've done that.'

'No.' Peter laughed. 'I've been to a few serious bashes where eventually they stop pouring and you have to do it yourself.'

'Cheers,' Gabby raised her glass, '*salut* and bottoms up. Here's to your new venture.'

'Cheers, Gab. And thank you for all your help.' Peter suddenly cracked out laughing.

'What?'

'Oh, it's ridiculous. It just popped into my head. When I was at university there was a guy there who always responded to, or proposed a toast with a rather dubious….'

'What?'

'Up your pipe.'

'I beg your pardon?'

'That's what he said.' Peter raised his glass again. 'Up your pipe.'

'Oh, really.' Gabby looked puzzled for a moment but then raised her glass.

'Well, to each his own. Cheers, then, up your pipe.'

'Yes indeed, up your pipe.'

They grinned at each other across the table and toasted the easel, the brushes and the fan heater. Their glasses were soon empty and Peter refilled them.

'Sorry they're bog standard wine glasses. We could have done with some flutes. I know mum had some.'

'No matter. These were all I could find. Do you want a ciggy? Pass them over.'

They smoked and drank in silence for a moment.

'Oh,' said Gabby, 'my shoes.' She and Spencer had been invited to some black tie do and she'd bought the dress but hadn't found the right shoes. However she had discovered what she was imagining in Norwich. She went out to her car and returned with a shoe box.

'Good grief, it's cold out there now.' Gabby sat down again, opened the box and took out the shoes. She put them on and walked carefully to where Peter could admire them.

'Well, what do you think?'

'Well, apart from astonishment at how on earth anyone can walk in shoes like that, they certainly look very nice.'

'Very nice? Why don't you damn them with faint praise? They're gorgeous. Do you have any idea how much they cost?'

'I don't.' Peter shook his head. 'I don't think I want to know and I doubt whether Spencer will either. It'd probably make him very ill.'

'Spencer may have his faults but he's very understanding about some things. I told him before I married him, that if he expected me to look my best it was going to cost. You can't expect to look good if you're not prepared to pay.'

'No, I suppose not.' Privately Peter had doubts but he inclined his head and inspected Gabby as she walked carefully up the studio.

'They're more than very nice, Gab. Elegant is the word. You do look very, very sexy.'

Gabby twirled at the end of the room.

'That's more like it. Well done, you.' Gabby returned to her chair and was about to remove the shoes when Peter went over to the radio and switched it on.

'Hold 'e hard a minute. If I can find something suitable we'll see if you can dance in them.'

Peter quickly found Radio 1 and took Gabby's hand as Frankie Valli and co warbled and thumped their way through *'Walk like a Man.'* They grinned at each other and reached for their glasses and gulped more champagne before Abba launched into *'Dancing Queen.'* Gabby nodded when Peter suggested that they might jive. She was a good dancer, even in new and insane shoes.

They were both puffing slightly as they sipped their drinks again. Then they were off once more with Ian Dury advocating the benefits of being beaten with a rhythm stick.

'Hit me, hit me,' they intoned together.

Peter was topping up their glasses when Stevie Wonder broke into *'You are the sunshine of my life.'* He took a quick gulp of champagne and hurried round the table to take Gabby's hand once more.

'Oh, what?' She protested.

Peter wasn't about to let pass the opportunity of holding Gabby close. She took his hand again but then stopped and removed her shoes. When she stood up Peter put his arm round her.

'Madam has shrunk.'

Gabby looked up at Peter.

'Don't get smart with me matey.'

'I never realized you were really such a short arse.'

Gabby bared her teeth in a snarl and then grinned.

'I'll set your aunt Janice on you. And Kingsley and the dread what's-her-name.'

'Jeannie. Flora Morag to be precise.'

'What?'

'That's her full name.'

'You jest. They're not Scottish, are they? Are you?'

'No. As my granny used to say, "There's not a Scottish bone near any of them."'

Wide-eyed and shaking her head in wonder Gabby was speechless for a moment. Eventually she spoke.

'I know they're your relatives but they're certifiable, aren't they?'

'Oh, yes. Mum used to say they were barking mad, the lot of them. Absolutely woofing.'

Gabby snuggled into Peter's chest. Her perfume was strong in his nostrils and he was very conscious of the warmth of her body. Suddenly she was looking up at him. She smiled and caressed his ear lightly with her fingernails for a moment and then undid a couple of his buttons and slipped her hand inside his shirt.

She was staring hard at Peter's mouth. He kissed her on the tip of her nose. She stood on tiptoe to kiss the tip of his nose and then wrapped her arms around his neck, pulled his face down and kissed him hard on the mouth.

After a moment she broke away, removed her glasses and placed them on the window sill. She took off her top and moving directly in front of Peter she reached up, put her arms round his neck, kissed him again and pressed her body into him.

Peter rubbed the back of his hand against her bra and within seconds her nipples were hard and erect. Gabby moaned gently, closed her eyes and sagged against him. She ran her fingers lightly over Peter's crotch, then undid his belt and zip and fondled his scrotum.

Breaking free of him she took off her bra, skirt and slip and tossed them onto a chair. She returned to him in pants, suspender belt and stockings, lifted his shirt, pulled down his jeans and pants and then took his swelling penis in one hand and cradled his balls in the other.

'Mmm.'

Peter gasped. His toes curled and his sphincter tightened with pleasure as Gabby circled the root of his penis and gently manipulated his foreskin back and forth. He kneaded her nipples and then ran his hand over her buttocks and briefly between her legs. It was her turn to gasp.

'He looks eager.'

Gabby kissed Peter again and then suddenly snorted.

'What?' Peter was a little alarmed.

'I've just got it,' she said.

'What's that?'

'My brother,' said Gabby, still giggling. 'The toad. He used to call his the *Mighty Wurlitzer*. It's only just occurred to me.'

'The organ? The world famous organ?'

'Why's it taken me all these years?' Gabby laughed and shook her head. 'It's not as if I'm a prude.'

'I don't know. Never mind that. What are we going to do about this?' Peter nodded down at his swollen penis.

'Oh, I think he's more than up to it, don't you?' Gabby took Peter's hand and led him to the sofa. He waddled behind her with his jeans and pants round his ankles and his penis wagging like a signal arm in a high wind.

Gabby turned, leaned against the sofa back and parted her thighs.

'Oh. Hang on a minute.' She reached down for her new shoes and put them on. 'There, now we're the right height.' And indeed so it proved. She gently fed Peter between her legs and into her knickers. She sighed and closed her eyes.

'Hmmm. Ooh. That's nice.' She opened her eyes briefly and looked enquiringly at Peter. 'I bet it's a while since you last had a knee-trembler.'

Peter closed his eyes and groaned an acknowledgement.

It didn't take them long since they were both in a state of heightened excitement. Gabby's rhythm went all to pieces first and moments later Peter lost control in the most delicious way.

'Aaaagh.' Gabby gasped. 'Ah, ah, ah. Oh, my God!' She reared up and detached herself from Peter.

'What?' Peter's eyes snapped open.

'Someone at the window. I just saw a face, under the blind. There.' She pointed.

By the time Peter gathered his senses, pulled up his jeans and opened the door there was nothing to be seen. The moon shone over the frosty front yard. It was as silent as the grave.

10. Marmalade on toast

Predictably, Ellen's old Morris Minor failed its MOT. When Peter asked the Service Manager in the garage in Cromer what it would cost to put right there was a sharp intake of breath and a despairing shake of the head. Peter almost chortled. The man's reaction was of pantomime proportions. There was no escaping the fact though that Ellen's pride and joy was beyond economic repair. The best the man could offer was to take it off Peter's hands for £10-and then he was being a fool to himself. He advised Peter to buy something more modern.

As luck would have it he had just come by a tidy Hillman Avenger that he could let Peter have very reasonably. Peter listened attentively and walked round the Hillman. He even went so far as to give a couple of the tyres a polite prod with his toe. However he declined the offer and eventually talked the man into parting with £20 for the Morris Minor. Even so he knew that he'd been had.

Philip had a client on an American airbase that was repatriating and had a Ford Granada Estate for sale. It had done a lot of miles but it had been cared for and regularly maintained. They went together to look at it and Peter bought it on the spot. It would suit all normal requirements and be ideal for transporting paintings.

He puzzled over who had been at the shed window and concluded that the culprit probably lived no further than a couple of doors down. Gabby hadn't been able to say whether it was a man or a woman since she'd only caught a fleeting glimpse. Peter wouldn't have put it past any one of them. It was worrying and dispiriting though, that someone had been watching their intimate moments. He felt sure that even if it wasn't made public immediately it would eventually become common knowledge. There would be the inevitable staring, whispering and conversations drying up abruptly at one's approach. And then, of course there was Spencer. He hadn't struck Peter as being the most balanced individual. And further, the man possessed some fearsome weaponry.

Following Gabby's bulls-eye on the cat Peter changed his anti-feline tactics. Eschewing the air pistol he took to hurling stones or a handful of gravel and occasionally, if he was sure no one was watching, charging after the cat, shouting and flapping his arms. The creature invariably took off at speed but none of these measures deterred or discommoded him in any serious way. He was often in evidence again within hours.

Peter's career as a painter began less than auspiciously. Even before he made a single brushstroke the studio easel broke and he spent over two hours fixing it and then couldn't use it because he had to wait for the glue to set. Following his abortive first morning at work he fell asleep after lunch and eventually woke just as it was beginning to get dark. He managed a bit of painting on Tuesday but again fell asleep in the early afternoon. Things improved as the week progressed but he admitted to Kathy that he would have to discipline himself properly in future.

'You certainly need to do something, from the sound of it.'

'I'd like to work from nine until one, have a sandwich and do whatever needs seeing to and then again from two or so until five. Or something of that sort-pretty much like a normal employed person. If I do that as a minimum, I should make progress and be quite productive.'

'Yes, but don't you need to wait for inspiration, you artists?'

Peter snorted.

'Don't you need to be inspired?'

Peter shook his head and laughed. 'Ah, that old chestnut. So I've heard.'

'Well, how…? How can you…?'

Peter laughed again.

'Oh, that's simple. I'll just make certain that I'm good and inspired by nine o'clock every morning.'

'Oh.' Kathy looked at him and then laughed. She took Peter's hand across the bar.

'You're a funny feller, Peter, sometimes. But I do love you.'

Gabby continued to call round each morning but the dynamic had changed. Now she demanded a hug and kisses both before and after coffee. Sometimes things became a little steamy.

There was no fallout following their altercation with Janice until a Saturday lunchtime when Peter decided to stop for a quick pint at the Lord Nelson on his way home from Cromer. He'd been to buy hardboard and timber. Philip had mentioned that he would probably be around over the weekend and Peter was interested to see whether he'd had any information about Dave Holt.

There was a coach in the pub car park and the bar was noisy with a party of some sort. The visitors turned out to be birdwatchers. A Sabine's gull had been spotted on the beach at Mundesley. Peter had been down to take a look himself and had left somewhat disappointed. He wasn't sure what he expected to see but if it was the one that had been pointed out to him by a helpful twitcher it looked pretty much like any other seagull.

Neither Kathy nor Philip was about. Heather, a widow who lived in Church Street was behind the bar. She was happy to stand in as and when required and she confirmed that Philip hadn't yet arrived.

Peter borrowed the *Eastern Daily Press* from behind the bar and took his pint to a table in the corner. A second coach arrived and the bar became even busier and noisier. He was contemplating the wisdom or otherwise of a second pint when he looked up and saw his Uncle George accompanied by Kingsley, May and Jeannie's husband Greg. There was no sign of Jeannie herself but they were heading his way.

'Ah,' George croaked, 'just the man. I've been meaning to have a word with you.'

While Greg went to attend to their order the trio of Finchams loomed over Peter.

'Good morning, George, May, King. What can I do for you?'

Kingsley opened his mouth to speak but George held up his hand and shook his head. He turned to Peter.

'I've been meaning to ask, have you been having a go at our Marmalade?'

Peter was dumbfounded. He had expected some kind of accusation about the altercation with Janice over her washing.

'What?'

'Marmalade.'

'What marmalade?' Peter frowned.

'Our Marmalade. Have you been having a go at our Marmalade?'

Peter shook his head. 'What would I want with your marmalade?'

'That's what I'm asking.' George stared at him. Peter stared back.

'George. I haven't the faintest idea what you're talking about.'

'You haven't been kicking or hitting…?'

'Your marmalade?' Peter frowned again.

He noticed that Kingsley seemed on the point of bursting.

'Yes. He's been limping and I know you're none too keen on the poor old beggar.'

'I told you, he's been shooting at him,' Kingsley could contain himself no longer. 'Mum heard the gun. She said it sounded like an airgun.'

The penny dropped as George thrust his face close to Peter.

'Well, if that's true, you haven't any call to go shooting at him.' George shook his head. 'If there's any more of it, I'll get the law on you.'

Peter could see the crusty residue of dried coffee at each corner of his uncle's mouth and there was a smear of something on his tie. The trio glared at him. There was obviously no point in lying or beating about the bush. Peter leaned back in his seat.

'I've never shot your cat. I've got a silly little air pistol I've had since I was thirteen or so. You know the one, King. I've used it once or twice to frighten him off. That pistol won't hit anything and it wouldn't harm a fly even if it did. It's hopelessly underpowered and wholly inaccurate.' He smiled. 'The wretched creature keeps crapping in my garden. The number of times I've had to clear up after him, and I've trodden in it and tramped it indoors....'

Kingsley placed his knuckles on the tabletop and thrust his big face forward.

'You go shooting at Marmalade again Pedro and you'll be in deep shit.'

'Well there is a simple solution of course. Just keep him out of my garden.'

The trio looked at him as though he were mad.

'Don't talk so bloody daft, boy. How can you be expected to keep a bloody cat in any particular place, unless you lock the bugger up? You mark my words. Any more shit from you, I'll be round with my mates to fix your little game.'

Peter drained his glass. He'd decided against a second pint. He shook his head again in disbelief and got up from the table.

'Where do you think you're going? Do you hear what I say? You better take heed or you'll be sorry.' Kingsley prodded Peter in the chest with a stubby finger. He had never known when to stop. Peter noticed that he was wearing a fingerstall. He paused as he put on his jacket.

'Well, you keep your idiot cat away from my property and there won't be a problem.' Peter was suddenly angry. He thrust his face at Kingsley. 'If I catch the little sod crapping in the garden again he'll be the one that's sorry.' With that Peter pushed his way past his relatives and the coach party and stumped out of the bar, banging the door behind him.

It opened again immediately.

Shooting Marmalade

'Fucking arty-farty clever dick.' Kingsley had followed him.

'Language! There are ladies present.'

'I say....'

Kingsley turned to glower at someone in the bar.

'Oh, eff off, you stupid old bat.'

Quietly seething, Peter set off down the lane beside the pub. The thorn bushes on either side were overgrown and he had to force his way through in places. Finally he gained the cliff tops. As usual there had been more falls through the winter, although there appeared to be nothing major and the beach looked magnificent as usual, and serene.

He sauntered along the cliff edge for a bit, through the rough grass and brittle remains of thistles and cow parsley. Here and there were still the rusted remains of the barbed wire fence that once ran unbroken along the cliff tops from one end of the village to the other and beyond. Eventually he came upon the remains of an old brick potting shed. It had been a fixture on the cliff tops since before he was born and now it was marooned, stuck out on a slender finger of marl that couldn't possibly last another winter. Although in truth it was the spring thaw and high tides that wrought the real destruction on the cliff face.

Kathy had once intimated that over the years the old potting shed had probably hosted more than its fair share of 'goings-on.' It was especially true throughout the war when sappers of the Royal Engineers and later any number of RAF radar operators used the potting shed for entertaining. Peter had been under the impression that as she told the tale she gave him a rather meaningful look, sufficient for him to wonder whether there was something behind it. He had thought about asking her, but then it had slipped his mind. Perhaps one day he would.

The potting shed roof had fallen in and the door had rotted away almost completely. Absurdly, here and there, several layers of paint still clung to the sodden timber of the door and window frames. Peter concluded that some of that paint must have been applied long before he was born.

He wandered back the way he had come. Having calmed down a little his thoughts returned to fingerstalls. He hadn't seen one for years. Ellen made him one when he was a boy. He'd sliced the end off his left index finger with a carving knife while he was trying to cut a square of chocolate from a giant bar of fruit and nut. She'd cut a finger from one of her own buckskin gloves and attached a piece of shoelace. Later in the day Peter had spotted the remnant of his finger beneath the kitchen table. Delighted, he retrieved it and discovered that it still had a triangle of nail attached. He carried it about for days in an old matchbox and showed it to anyone who was interested and quite a few who were not.

Back at the Lord Nelson car park the twitchers were leaving. Peter was interested to see laughing faces at the windows as their coaches slowly crunched across the gravel towards the main road. He followed their gaze to the large rubbish bin upended on the roof of his Granada estate. It was one of several ordinarily kept beside the wall outside the pub kitchen. The foul liquid that dribbled down the sides of the Granada indicated that the bin was full. If he tried to lift it off the contents would cascade all over the car. Peter sighed. Cousin Kingsley had been busy in his absence.

He struggled to slide the bin off the back of the car to minimize the mess. It wasn't a simple matter. Chips, peas, fish skins, chicken bones and all manner of other foulness cascaded down the back of the car and the front of his jeans. As he grappled with the unwieldy bin the big silly faces of Kingsley and Greg appeared at the pub window. He could see them laughing and gesticulating and mouthing 'wanker' at him.

He picked up the worst of the stinking mess, repacked it and carried the bin back to where it belonged. There were still a few peas, fish bones and batter and what looked like tomato ketchup on the gravel but it was the best he could do. He decided against going into the pub to clean himself up for fear of getting into a further fracas. With as much dignity as he could muster he walked across the car park and crossed the road with the intention of washing his hands at the old village pump.

He was astonished to find that the pump had gone. All that remained was a circular steel plate set into a square of concrete that was diminishing in size as grass and weeds engulfed it. Presumably the pump was no longer required after the water main was laid in the mid 1950s. Peter wondered how he didn't know that the pump had been removed. He concluded that it must have happened while he was away. After wiping his hands in the grass he returned to his car and drove out of the car park giving his smirking relatives a hard look as he left.

'Right, you cretins,' he muttered. 'If that's the way you want it, I'll be happy to oblige. And as for you Marmalade, you're toast.'

*

For several days Peter worked hard. He saw no one but Gabby and he saw very little of her. Spencer's mother was in hospital for some procedure or other and Gabby was busy looking after old Mr Manfredi. She arrived later in the morning and was unable to stop for longer than a single mug of coffee and a cigarette.

'Do you know?' she said one morning, 'that old beggar is as fit as a flea. He gets up at sparrow's fart and she waits on him hand and foot until he goes to bed at night. He can't do anything for himself. He's absolutely useless. He can't cook. Making tea or coffee is a mystery to him. Wants his lunch at 11.30 on the dot every day, and that's a cooked lunch, a roast preferably. Tea at four. Then bloody dinner at 7 o'clock. He's a right selfish and miserable old bugger.'

'Hmm,' said Peter. 'It sounds to me as though he's not so much useless as bone idle. Anyone can make a cup of coffee. The clue is in the word 'Instant.' And I've got no time for these people who can't cook. Frankly if you're not physically incapacitated and can read; you can cook. It ain't brain surgery.'

He finally got down to painting. Fired by the photos and sketches he'd done in Iceland he produced a series of organic abstracts in acrylic. He'd never used it before and found it greatly to his liking once he'd got used to its tendency to dry rather quicker than one might like. As soon as he'd finished a couple he wished he'd painted them larger. He went out and returned with three eight foot boards tied to the roof-rack of the Granada. After priming them he set about the subjects again.

He had a strange experience one morning while he was painting. He'd been at work for a while; the studio was warm and comfortable. Music was playing on the radio and things were going well. He concluded later that there was absolutely no reason for the thing that popped into his head.

When he was at primary school he and a few other children from Back Lane were collected and dropped off by the school coach each day in the Lord Nelson car park. This particular afternoon Peter had changed his books in the school library and he was reading as he got off the coach. Ellen had drummed into him countless times the need to take great care every time he crossed the road, and never, ever to walk out into the road from behind the coach. This afternoon he had been last off and so engrossed in his book that he had walked out, without looking, into the road from behind the still stationary coach. There had been another coach coming the other way.

It wasn't until a couple of the older girls shrieked that he looked up from his book. To his left the driver of the by-now-stationary coach was shaking his head in disbelief, as were the two elderly ladies in the front seat beside him. One of the older girls rushed at him, grabbed him by the arm and dragged him to the roadside. There he was told in no uncertain manner how stupid he had been. As both coaches got under way the girls shouted 'thank you' and waved at the driver of the coach that had narrowly missed killing Peter.

As all this flooded back Peter felt his legs weaken. If it hadn't been for the vigilance of that driver…. Next moment he was slumped on the studio floor with his back against the wall, bathed in sweat and in the throes of another panic attack.

Other than for that slight setback Peter had a most productive time and soon had the makings of a reasonable portfolio.

*

After threatening all morning the rain arrived suddenly, just before noon, in the form of a squally shower. The Granada was parked some distance away so like many others Peter sought out the warmth and shelter of the *Singing Kettle*.

It had been a popular tea-room in Cromer for longer than most people could remember. Ellen and Kathy had been loyal patrons all their lives. They'd first gone as girls in the

1930s. During the war they dallied there with Nick Nichols and Dave Holt and they continued taking refreshment there long after the men in their lives moved on. Peter and Philip had been introduced to the delights of the tea-room at an early age. They'd eaten a significant amount of doughnuts there, both cream and jam. Margaret's parents Harry and Eve had spent many a Saturday afternoon there before Harry went off to war. For most of the folk shopping or in Cromer on business from the surrounding villages, a visit to the *Singing Kettle* was an integral part of the day. To return home without the benefit of a restorative cup of tea or coffee and a treat in the form of a buttered scone or an almond slice would have been unthinkable.

From the glossy black-painted door on the High Street one stepped down into a large half-timbered room where tables and chairs were tastefully arranged and gleaming copper kettles, warming pans and horse brasses adorned the walls. As intended, the room looked irresistibly cosy and welcoming through the Dickensian window frames and elegant curtaining. In earlier times a veritable posse of black and white uniformed ladies took orders on small pads and hastened back and forth with trays groaning with teapot, milk, sugar (in cube form and accompanied by tongs), crockery and a selection of fancy cakes. A pot of boiling water with which to replenish the teapot was *de rigueur*. These days a succession of overweight, gum-chewing and bored teenage girls fresh out of school provided a less focused service.

So popular was the *Singing Kettle* that the owners extended out into the back premises. There they created a long narrow coffee-bar behind the tea-room. Tall stools provided the only seating and it was in the gloom at the very back of the coffee bar that Peter found an empty stool.

The rain hammered with some vigour on the stained and crusted skylight above his head. It was heavy enough to be audible above the hissing coffee machine, the clank of crockery and the persistent cacophony of raised voices.

An exhausted-looking woman in a pink overall and a hairnet had just brought his cup of coffee and a scone when he spotted Margaret at the entrance. She peered along the bar looking for an empty stool. Like Peter she had hoped to get a table in the front room but it was a wet Saturday morning and the place was heaving. Peter waved.

Margaret's face lit up. He gestured at the stool beside him that had just been vacated and placed his scarf on it to reserve it. Margaret smiled, nodded and headed towards him, numerous shopping bags held high against a milling group of elderly women making their way slowly from the toilets towards the exit.

'Peter. Thank you. It's like a rugby scrum. How are you?' Margaret put down her bags, wafted a few crumbs off the stool and sat down.

'I'm fine, thanks.' He turned and smiled as Margaret unbuttoned her coat. 'More to the point though; how are you?'

'I'm well, thanks.' She gave him a quick smile and looked away. It was true that she did look more like her old self. She was pale by nature but there was a touch of colour in her cheeks and she was immaculately dressed and made up. Her hair was newly tinted and cut and she seemed in altogether better spirits than when Peter saw her last.

'What can I get you?'

While they waited for Margaret's coffee she explained that she was now back at work. Peter brought her up to date with the changes in his life. She was interested but seemed distracted. It was only when she was well into her macaroon that Peter felt able, albeit tentatively, to raise the subject.

'I talked to Tom on the phone the other day. He picked up when I called. Didn't say where you were but he mentioned the… what's it… pseudo… thingy.'

Margaret nodded.

'Yes. He said you'd called.'

'Is he still…?'

'No.' Margaret shook her head. 'He's gone.

'Oh?' Peter cast a quick glance at Margaret. 'Has he gone back to South America or the Southern Ocean?'

'Montevideo, yes. He's gone back to work.'

'Wasn't he able to get time off? You'd think after travelling all that way he'd be able to stay awhile.'

Margaret shook her head.

'I didn't want him here. We had an almighty row. I told him to,' Margaret lowered her voice to a whisper, 'bugger off. He's gone for good.'

'Oh.' Peter glanced again at Margaret. Her pale face was flushed and she was staring hard at the coffee cup before her.

'And good riddance too, the lying bastard.'

'Oh?' Peter looked askance.

Margaret screwed her eyes tight, bit her upper lip and sighed. After a moment she turned towards Peter. She licked at a tiny piece of rice paper on her lower lip in a vain attempt to remove it.

'You might as well know. Tom and I are finished.' The fragment of paper wouldn't budge. Peter offered to help. 'Here. Let me.' He carefully removed the scrap with a finger nail.

'Thanks.' Margaret dabbed her lips with a paper napkin. 'The marriage is over.' She held Peter's eye for several seconds. 'I told him it was a phantom pregnancy. It was a lie.' She paused again and looked away, poking macaroon crumbs around her plate. 'I really was pregnant. I lost the baby. I couldn't tell him the truth because we hadn't had sex… made love… for ages.' She gave Peter a crooked smile. 'He never knew about the real pregnancy.'

Catching Peter's frown she shook her head slowly from side to side and smiled again, fleetingly. 'Don't ask. I know it doesn't make any sense. I have no better idea now than I ever did about what I was going to tell him. But I wanted that baby. I was determined to keep it no matter what. I thought he might accept it. He's always been really good with children. I thought we might still have a future together… but we most certainly do not now. It turns out he's far more interested in… someone else.'

Margaret stared glumly at the coffee machine behind the counter.

'So,' Peter frowned, 'does that mean that the baby…?'

Margaret nodded her head up and down slowly. After a long pause she continued. 'I'm so sorry. Yes. You were quite right. The baby was yours.'

Peter stared hard at his coffee cup. It was a long moment before he spoke.

'You said it wasn't, and you wouldn't see me again.' Peter grimaced and took her hand. 'Why didn't you…?'

'Because, for some insane reason, I suppose I wanted to try to save my marriage.' Margaret became animated. 'I know it might sound stupid, given that it wasn't his baby, but it did make sense, to me at least… sort of… at the time. I wanted to have the baby and keep Tom.'

'Well, what's changed-with Tom.'

'Oh, well, I suppose there's no reason why you should know. Although you must be the only person who…. I thought I was the last. Tom's… you know.' She lowered her voice again. 'He likes young girls, and boys. Apparently some of our so-called friends have known, or at least suspected for years. Not one of them saw fit to tell me. He was never going to father a child with me, or stay with me. He's been shacked up for ages with someone.'

She turned to Peter and took both of his hands in hers.

'I'm so sorry. I know how excited you were. It was unforgivable. I can't tell you....' There were tears in her eyes. 'I wanted both the baby and, God help me, Tom. I've lost them both and it was my own fault. I've got no one to blame but myself.'

'You can't possibly believe that. You lost the baby through no fault of your own. It would be just one of those things surely. And as for Tom, well, I never met him but I have to say I didn't take to him on the phone. Sounds as though you're well rid of him.'

'I know. I know.' Margaret was now wringing her hands and sniffing audibly. The woman beside her cast Peter a hostile look and turned her back on them. Peter took a handkerchief from his pocket and offered it to Margaret. He put his hand on her shoulder while she dabbed at her nose.

'Come on, cheer up. You don't need to apologize either for losing the baby or Tom.' He patted her shoulder vigorously. 'But you did need to apologize to me for lying about our baby. And now you have, so let's mosey on.'

Margaret flashed Peter a brave but still teary smile.

'I'd better go to the loo and tidy myself up.' She looked up at the skylight. 'It looks as though it's brightening. I've still got to get some fish.'

*

One morning as Peter was heading for the studio; Gabby appeared at the door. She had a gun-case slung over her shoulder.

'Hiya. I can't stop. I've got to pick up the old bat from the hospital.'

'Hello, shweet-heart.' Peter tried a Humphrey Bogart greeting and gave her a kiss on the cheek. 'What on earth have you got there?'

'I've brought you one of Spencer's guns.'

'Oh?'

'You said you wanted to get rid of that cat.'

'Yes, but….'

'It's a Greener. 12 bore. Shoots well, apparently. I brought you some cartridges too.' She handed over a broken cardboard box, tightly wrapped in polythene and what looked like a mile of brown sticky tape.

'You'd better come on in. Good grief. You didn't want these to escape did you? Won't he miss it? Some of those guns of his are worth a fortune.'

'Oh, the daft beggar's spent thousands on them. I don't know what this one's worth. He's been pleased with it though. It'll certainly do for that stupid cat.'

Peter puffed out his cheeks doubtfully but he took the gun-case from her, placed it on the table, opened it up and half lifted the gun out.

'Heavens.' Even to Peter's untutored eye it looked an impressive weapon.

'You know how to use one don't you?'

Peter grunted noncommittally. He had never actually even held a shotgun before. But how complicated could it be? Not that it mattered since he had no intention of ever using it.

Gabby strode over and put the kettle on.

'I will have a quick coffee. The old bat will just have to wait. How's your painting going? Can I have a peep while the kettle's boiling?'

Gabby was extremely complimentary about Peter's latest efforts.

'Yes, the larger ones are excellent. Opie will definitely be interested in those. You could still go bigger though. And paint with oils, on canvas. We could do something with the smaller ones too. Leave it with me.'

As Gabby was driving out of the yard Peter took the shotgun and the heavily wrapped cartridges upstairs and placed them under the bed in the guest bedroom. He had a nagging suspicion that Gabby had taken the gun without Spencer's knowledge.

She phoned later in the day to say that she had made appointments in three weeks time with Opie and a couple of other galleries.

'Better get your head down, Peter. Oh, and make sure you take really good photos of every painting. You'll need to make slides for galleries to look at-and if you want to put something into a show.'

*

The fact that it was his last day at work didn't influence the time of Nick's arrival at the gates of the gas terminal. He drove into the car park at 8.10 a.m. as usual and reached for his packed lunch from the back seat of the car before he remembered that he was having lunch out today. As was the custom with anyone leaving the warehouse he was treating his workmates at the Red Lion. After exchanging some banter with the Security Guard and a couple of Maintenance men loitering in the guardroom he walked across the terminal to the warehouse and opened the door at 8.20. He'd done the same thing for almost ten years. The rest of the warehouse staff usually trailed in by 8.30 or so but this morning they had been cajoled and bullied into a special effort and had arrived before him so that they could clap, cheer and jeer as he walked through the door. There were cries of 'lucky beggar, wish it was me' and 'demob-happy.'

At 11.30 he was called to the Conference Room in the main office building for a brief farewell ceremony. The Warehouse Supervisor said a few words and presented him with a Safety Certificate and a pen and pencil set. The Administrative Superintendent said how greatly he would be missed and wished him well for the future. Then the Terminal Manager presented him with a ten year pin and a company penknife in a leather sheath despite the fact that Nick was actually a few weeks shy of the requisite ten years service. The Americans were good like that. Nick had found them to be friendly and generous people and had enjoyed working with them. He said a few words himself in response, about how he had enjoyed his time at the Terminal and that he would miss them all. He expressed the hope that perhaps he would still see a few of them in the pub at lunchtimes where he at least would be able to enjoy an alcoholic beverage.

Nick shook hands with almost everyone in the room as they left and that was it. He took the warehouse staff out for lunch as planned and then spent the afternoon clearing out his locker, handing back various items of clothing and equipment and saying a proper goodbye to one or two people with whom he had developed something of a bond over the years. At five o'clock he gave one last wave to the guys in Security and drove away down the access road past the firewater storage pond for the very last time.

He had planned originally to go to California the following week but Stan Riggall had a lot on at the caravan site and had asked him if he could help for a bit. He was always willing to help Stan whenever he could so he had decided to postpone the trip to Ventura for a while. The money would come in useful. It was not going to be a cheap holiday but it had now become, in Nick's mind, essential.

He hadn't been retired a week when he went down with the flu. It was the real thing, the fever, the weakness, the feeling like death. He had to take to his bed while Mrs Riggall and her daughter brought him onion gruel and paracetamol. The caravan stank of onion-larded sweat. Eventually he recovered but the virus had left him feeling weak and watery and with a horrible racking cough.

11. *A little something for Archie*

Lavinia O'Grady met them in the foyer of the Opie O'Grady gallery at 9.15 a.m. A small, dark-haired woman in a white blouse and a grey pinstripe trouser-suit, Lavinia greeted Gabby as an old friend. She twinkled at Peter and was all charm but he quickly formed the opinion that Miss O'Grady was a serious businesswoman and a tough nut to boot. She was about his age, quick, precise, knew her own mind and, he suspected, did not suffer fools at all. He'd come across women like her in the movie business, Americans mostly. When she said 'jump,' he guessed everyone within earshot leapt with a will, no one pausing for querulous inquiries about height.

The gallery had just undergone an extensive refurbishment. The smell of paint, glue, newly sawn timber, varnish and brand new carpet commingled into a heavy and nauseating atmosphere. The gallery seemed to Peter oppressive, overheated and airless. He had a momentary wobble when Lavinia invited them all into the lift to ascend the two storeys to her huge corner office. Despite the renovations the lift had not yet been replaced. It was small, old and desperately slow. Fortunately the three of them were the only occupants. Peter concentrated on deep breathing and staring fixedly at the threadbare carpet between his desert boots.

Lavinia's PA greeted them with coffee, freshly brewed and served in heavy hand-crafted earthenware mugs of a type that Peter loathed. They were terribly fashionable but it was impossible to tell whether they were clean.

Peter and Gabby were invited to take a seat on the sleek leather and chrome furniture that formed what was intended to be an intimate meeting area centred on a low table to one side of Lavinia's vast glass and chrome desk. She gathered up from his office a slender, raffish and alarmingly assured young man by the name of Clem, who Gabby hadn't met before but who turned out to be the assistant manager. He brought with him a slide projector and a portable screen. Once the blinds were adjusted and the room was in near total darkness they ran slowly through Peter's slides. Then they spread the contents of his portfolio the full length of a long wooden table and together with a couple of backroom staff spent a good deal of time examining Peter's work. Occasionally Lavinia or Clem would mutter something, make some comment or direct a question at Peter. Sometimes he wasn't sure how he should answer but they seemed satisfied and once or twice Gabby nodded approvingly.

Eventually Lavinia decided she would take seven of the Icelandic-inspired abstracts. For some reason Clem wouldn't budge on the eighth. He was however sufficiently excited about three of the paintings to phone a client right away. Peter was at first horrified at the rate of commission Opie's would be taking but Gabby whispered that it was not unreasonable.

Lavinia suggested that Peter give some thought to making limited edition prints of some of his work and she talked about the possibility of him participating in her autumn show later in the year. As they left the gallery Gabby took Peter's arm. She tapped him on the forearm.

'Well done you. She likes you. That's important. If Lavinia makes you an offer, be sure you accept.'

'Well, it might not come to anything.'

Gabby shook her head vigorously.

'She's interested. She knows as well as I do that those paintings will sell. And she damn near offered to take you on. The autumn exhibition is very prestigious. Loads of influential people attend. Lavinia's got a lot of clout nationally... and internationally.'

'I thought this was just a local gallery.'

'No. There's an O & O in central London and she used to be involved in another gallery in Richmond. I don't know whether she still is. And she's got stuff going on in the States and Europe. People try for years to get on Opie's books. You've made it in record time.'

'Well, thanks in no small measure to you, Gab.'

'Maybe, but Lavinia wouldn't have wasted any time on you if she hadn't seen evidence of talent. She's just spent the best part of an hour looking at your work and chatting to you. She doesn't do that lightly. It's a good start, but you need to be ready to build on it.'

From Norwich they headed to the coast, to Aldeburgh and Southwold. Small, discreet galleries in both locations were sufficiently enthusiastic to take some of the smaller paintings. They also asked about prints. By the time Peter and Gabby had finished with business it was lunchtime. They considered getting a bite to eat at Snape but eventually, in view of the unseasonably sunny and warm weather decided to seek out a pub in the countryside.

They came across one without much difficulty, an old hostelry with stables and a walled garden. One or two people were already sitting outside. Gabby found a table in the garden, fully in the sun and sheltered from what little breeze there was. Peter went into the comparative gloom of the bar and returned with a pint of Adnams for himself and a dry white wine for Gabby. They grinned at each other.

'Well, this is nice. Cheers.'

'Up your pipe.' Gabby took a sip of her wine, lit a cigarette and studied the bar menu. She took off her scarf and jacket. Over her shoulder Peter noticed a weary-looking middle aged woman sitting across a table from what Peter took to be her mother. An elderly dog lay at the older woman's feet. They were clearly on holiday and it was equally obvious that mother had had enough.

'I'll be right glad to get home again, back to my own bed, and so will Lucky. Won't you boy?' She bent to fondle the dog's ears. Lucky twitched his tail obligingly.

'That bed's given me backache and my arthritis is giving me gyp. All my joints ache. Even the tea doesn't taste right. It's the water. I haven't had a decent cup of tea since we left home.'

The ancient droned on. The daughter looked pale and stressed. Peter saw her jaw set and her lips tighten into a thin line. Suddenly she caught his eye. He gave her a sympathetic smile and an imperceptible shake of the head. The daughter rolled her eyes, smiled back and let her shoulders sag briefly. She straightened up almost immediately, opened her eyes wide and stared hard at her mother, paying dramatically close attention. Her mother droned on, never missing a beat. Just then their lunches arrived.

'Is that mine?' The crone squinted suspiciously up at the waitress. 'I didn't ask for that. I ordered a steak wing. And I can't eat all those chips.'

'Well, eat what you can. We decided against the skate wing, didn't we? Scampi was what we both ordered, a small portion for you. And that's exactly what they've brought.'

The daughter was getting dangerously close to snapping. 'Just leave what you can't manage.'

She smiled briefly at the waitress. 'Thank you very much.'

'Where's my knife and fork? And I'll want some vinegar. Don't go bringing me none of that Tartar muck. I can't eat fish without vinegar.'

Something pulsed in the daughter's cheek.

As he sipped his beer Peter thought that at least he had been spared that with his mother. Gabby tapped him on the arm and nodded towards a sports car that was pulling into the car park.

'Look at that. Now, that's what I want,' she said, 'only green, British Racing Green. A friend of ours just bought one something like that. Do you know the McKillops?'

Peter turned to look. The gleaming car crunched slowly into the car park and halted beside his Granada. He'd heard Gabby mention the McKillops once or twice and was on the point of saying that he had never had the pleasure when she continued.

'Good grief,' she exclaimed. 'It is McKillop. But that's not Laura. Who's that he's got with him? The randy old bugger.'

Peter knew that the McKillops owned a huge agricultural machinery business and were reputed to be as rich as Croesus. That was all he knew of them.

'Ah,' he said, looking round over his shoulder again.

Gabby waved at the newcomers.

'Ah, he's seen us.' She straightened her handbag and patted her hair.

'Hiya,' she called as McKillop sauntered down the path between the tables with his young female companion beside him. He was a tall slim grey-haired man, probably in his mid fifties, in a leather bomber jacket, blue denim shirt and jeans.

The man exuded wealth and confidence. His companion must have been less than half his age, blonde, willowy and attractive. To Peter, she looked the perfect passenger for a drive in an open-topped sports car on a sunny day.

'Gabrielle, lovely to see you,' said McKillop, bending to give Gabby a peck on her cheek. 'Hello,' he nodded at Peter. 'Beautiful day, isn't it?' He turned his attention back to Gabby. 'What brings you to this neck of the woods? Shopping trip, good works, or just a crafty day out with the fancy man?'

'Hello, Julian,' Gabby said. 'It's alright for some, out swanning about. I don't know.' She nodded towards Peter. 'This is Peter Fincham. He's an artist; he's a friend of ours. I've just been introducing him at a couple of galleries.' She nodded at Peter again as though to confirm her statement.

'How do you do, Peter?' McKillop smiled.

'Hi. How are you?' Peter half rose and leaned across the table to take the proffered hand.

'This gorgeous creature by the way,' McKillop continued, gesturing towards his companion, 'is my new assistant, Morag. It won't come as a complete surprise to you to learn that she is a Scot, a Kelso lassie. She's only been with us a fortnight. I've been taking her round to meet a few people.'

Peter and Gabby nodded and smiled at Morag. Gabby's eyes narrowed as she took in the girl from head to toe. With a practised eye she assessed Morag's looks and sourced and priced her clothes, shoes and accessories, all in minute detail. Morag smiled back at them, said 'Hi,' and offered a surprisingly limp hand to be shaken.

In response to Peter's invitation McKillop and Morag joined them. The four of them sat in the sun and ate an enjoyable lunch. Julian McKillop said that they had left before 6 a.m. They had made a number of calls before finally fetching up at the Lotus factory down the road.

He was thinking of buying his daughter a sports car for her birthday. Someone told him that there was a waiting list at Lotus so he thought he would look in at the factory to see whether it was possible to come to some arrangement with them.

'Kaaark!'

They were distracted by the elderly dog, Lucky.

'Kaark. Ahaaark.'

The old lady had been feeding him titbits from her scampi and chips and he obviously got a piece of something stuck at the back of his throat. He staggered out from beneath the table and lurched towards Morag.

'Kaark, Kaaark!' Concerned and irritated diners looked round from neighbouring tables.

'Kaak. Ahaaagh.' To everyone's relief an errant piece of chip was expelled. Half-chewed and shiny with saliva, it bounced off the toe of one of Morag's expensive taupe suede shoes. Lucky staggered over and vacuumed up the sodden mess. Obligingly he licked the greasy mark on the toe of Morag's shoe and had a half-hearted go at its companion for good measure.

'Oh,' said the old lady. 'I am sorry, dear. You!' She gave Lucky a stern look. 'Come here.'

McKillop wafted a hand ineffectually in the dog's direction.

'Don't do that,' said Morag. 'Say hello to the wee dug! It's alright. He's a nice wee soul, aren't you boy?'

Morag was quick to assure everyone that it really didn't matter. They were only old shoes anyway. As she dabbed at her toes with a paper napkin in a resigned manner the look on her face said otherwise.

However, the chip incident seemed somehow to relax Morag and she thawed sufficiently to accept a cigarette from Gabby. She struck Peter as brittle and a little over conscientious in playing the ice-maiden, although he was prepared to concede that it may well have been no more than reserve or shyness. He was surprised to see that eventually she struck up a rapport with Lucky, although that may have owed much to the dog's interest in the leftovers of her lemon sole.

Eventually Lucky and his party left. The old lady was still complaining as she stumped along arthritically in her daughter's wake. Staring rigidly ahead, the daughter was white of face and tight-lipped. She looked ready to scream, or kill.

Peter, Gabby, McKillop and Morag remained talking in the garden over their coffees until after three o'clock when the sun dipped behind a bank of clouds and both Peter and McKillop started glancing at their watches.

During the leave-taking in the car park Julian McKillop noticed the paintings stacked up in the Granada.

'Are those some of your work?'

'Yes,' Peter nodded in the affirmative. 'Not a great deal left now....'

'Oh, let's have a wee peekie.' Morag had lost her inhibitions of earlier. 'Can we? I'd love to see them.'

'Yes, that would be nice. Would you mind?' McKillop glanced at his watch. 'We've got a few minutes. You're not in any particular rush are you?'

Peter removed some paintings from their bubble wrap and leaned each one against the sides of the car. It served well enough as a gallery since their cars were by now the only vehicles left in the car park.

After they all promenaded slowly back and forth the length of the Granada several times McKillop decided that there were two that he particularly liked. While Peter began packing away the remainder McKillop stood with Morag and Gabby, trying to come to a decision about which one to buy. Gabby urged him to buy both if he couldn't make up his mind.

'You'll be very glad you did,' she whispered. 'You won't see them at these prices again.'

McKillop looked at her quizzically. 'Really? That promising?'

'Oh, yes.' Gabby continued in a whisper. 'Between the two of us, we've just come from Opie's. Lavinia's very struck. She took seven. Offered the autumn show and she only met Peter and saw his work for the first time this morning.'

'Hmm.'

In the end McKillop took Gabby's advice. He thought that they would do very well for the wedding anniversary coming up.

Since McKillop was buying two and Peter was feeling expansive he knocked £50 off the price. Morag produced a chequebook from a capacious black leather bag and wrote out a cheque. McKillop signed it with a flourish and handed it to Peter.

Gabby then insisted on a comprehensive tour of McKillop's TVR. She was completely smitten and demanded to be taken for a ride. McKillop shot quickly up to the end of the road and back and despite Gabby's entreaties to let her take the wheel he, very sensibly in Peter's view, wouldn't even consider it. Gabby almost stamped her foot but Peter guessed that no matter what she said or did McKillop wouldn't budge. Somewhere, sometime, he had almost certainly witnessed Gabby's cavalier approach to driving.

After repackaging the two paintings and installing them carefully in the sports car hands were shaken and cheeks kissed. Peter and Gabby led the TVR a short distance until after a cheery wave, a brief flicker of lights and toot of his horn; McKillop overtook them. The sports car shot ahead and was soon out of sight. Peter drove more sedately. It had been a good day and he was in no hurry to bring it to an end.

'Bet you're glad I came along.' Gabby was rightly convinced that she had been instrumental in persuading McKillop to buy both paintings.

'Yes, indeed. Well done. Thank you. Perhaps you should be my agent.' Peter looked across and squeezed her knee.

'Maybe I should. You can thank me properly later,' she said with a grin. 'Do you mind if I smoke? I'll open the window and blow the smoke out.'

'I'd rather you didn't,' said Peter, 'but if you have to, I suppose I'll just have to put up with it.'

'I'll make it worth your while.' She fumbled with her cigarettes and a plastic lighter that she had bought in Norwich.

It was the fact that Morag had produced a company chequebook from her bag that persuaded Gabby that she really was McKillop's PA and not just his bit on the side.

'I bet he is shagging her though.' It was almost Gabby's final word on the subject. Peter wondered whether she was jealous and whether at some time in the past Julian McKillop had been rather more than simply a friend.

*

Peter had just packed up for the day and was letting himself into the cottage when Philip crunched across the gravel in front of Cowper's Cottage. As ever he was smartly dressed and looked freshly scrubbed and laundered.

'How now, Rembrandt?' He grinned and rubbed his hands.

'Well, if it isn't the old dental retard. What are you doing here? Are you lost?'

'Ouch.' Philip staggered and clutched his chest. 'That's a fine way to greet your old friend. However,' he held up his hands. 'Guilty as charged. No. I haven't seen you for a bit. Thought I'd pop in since I had a moment.'

It was some time since Philip had been about. Even Kathy had commented. But she rarely said much about her son these days so Peter wasn't necessarily up to date with what was going on.

He grimaced, shook his head and laughed. 'Tea, coffee?'

'A mug of tea would be most acceptable, thank you. Small one. I can't stop long.' He paused, searching his pockets for something. 'I hear from mama that the painting is going well. I've just come from there. On my way back up to Norwich.'

'Yes, not too shabby.'

Philip spent all of his free time in Norwich these days. He had been living up there and commuting to work in Cromer for some weeks. Whatever his living arrangements he hadn't shared them with Peter and if Kathy knew she certainly hadn't imparted any intelligence. Peter assumed that Philip had a new boyfriend in the city and was staying with him.

Philip pulled out a small folded piece of paper. He had obviously found whatever he was looking for.

'You've sold some, I believe.'

'Yes.' Peter switched on the kettle.

'You'll be so rich and famous soon, you won't want to talk to us mere mortals any more.'

'Mm. I don't think so. I won't be holding my breath. Do you know what some of these galleries take in commission?'

'Oh, I'm sure. Still, it's a bit like tax, isn't it? You only pay commission on what you make.'

'I suppose. I shall be upping my prices however.'

'Any other news?'

'Yes. Opie's want a series. Harbours, boats, beaches, broads-windmills and wherries, that kind of thing. Big, splashy watercolours that can be printed.'

'Well, that'll be a nice little earner round here, won't it?'

'Hmm. Hopefully. I always said I wasn't going to paint windmills and wherries. But if they're big and bold and splashy….'

'Anyway,' Philip took his tea and led Peter through to the conservatory. 'I thought you might be interested in developments with the Holt research.'

'Yes. What did you discover?'

Philip waved his piece of paper. He paused dramatically.

'He may still be alive.'

'Really?'

'Might have survived. Those people in London have come up with three possibilities. Two can definitely be discounted. One's black and the other is a David Vaughan Holt. Pity, because he's rich. But we're looking for a D. C. Holt.'

Philip was becoming increasingly animated.

'Anyway, they've turned up a D. C. Holt in Rye in Sussex, or at least that's the last address they have for him, and he sounds encouraging. He's the right age; he was in the RAF and he was stationed in Iraq and Egypt during the war. Trouble is; he's married to someone else.'

'So what are you…?'

'Well, they're going to keep on it, but I'm going to drive down there and see if there's anyone about. Whether he's there or if anyone knows anything about him, or where he might be. There's no phone at the address apparently. I thought of writing but it won't take long to drive down.'

'Oh, well, you'll be encouraged then….'

'Yes. You should think about doing the same for Nick.'

Philip didn't stay long enough to finish his tea and he volunteered no information about his life in Norwich. Peter felt unable to ask.

*

The following morning Peter was mooching about the kitchen and waiting for the kettle to boil when something outside on the grass caught his eye. He hurried out. There on the lawn, directly in front of the patio steps was a pile of large, sticky turds. The wretched cat hadn't made even a token attempt to bury them.

Peter bent to inspect them more closely. They were very fresh and smelled appalling.

'Oh yes, thank you so much.'

It was definitely Marmalade.

Although angered Peter didn't do anything about them immediately. It wasn't until he'd been at work for a while that he stopped suddenly and sought out a plastic bag and a trowel. He scooped the turds into the bag and after tying it securely he placed it in the garage. At that moment he had no clear idea of what he intended but he felt that sooner or later something would present itself.

After a good morning's work he decided to run into Cromer to the bank and then reward himself with lunch at the Lord Nelson. There was no one in the bar when he arrived. Kathy and Bryan had gone to some brewery do in Suffolk. Heather was in splendid isolation, resting her huge arms and bosom on the bar and reading the local paper. She drew Peter a pint of bitter.

'Lunch?' What would you like? Soup is minestrone. We've got the usual sandwiches, regular or toasted.'

Peter wrinkled up his nose. 'I rather fancied something hot. Not soup though.'

'I was just about to say... there are some baked potatoes and Bryan's made some of those steak and kidney pies. Won't take a minute....'

'Brilliant! Can the soup. Pie and a baked potato absolutely dripping with butter would be excellent. And it would be the icing on the cake, so to speak, if you could rustle up a few baked beans with it.'

'Yes, of course.' Heather finished pouring Peter's bitter and then bustled off to the kitchen. She was laughing when she returned.

'What?' Peter looked up from the EDP.

'Can the soup. Icing on the cake. What are you like?'

Peter smiled. 'We do our best. We like to spread a little happiness.' He liked Heather.

A few more customers appeared and Peter took the paper and his beer off to a table by the window. He was watching two magpies and a pair of crows squabbling over the bloody remains of a hedgehog on the road when he caught a brief glimpse of a Mini passing. Bright red and travelling very fast, it could have been Margaret's.

He still had half an eye on the ornithological altercation and half on the newspaper when the birds scattered as the Mini drove into the car park from the opposite direction. It was Margaret. He watched her get out. She looked across at the Granada as though checking that it was Peter's.

He went to the door to meet her.

'Margaret. How are you? I thought I spotted the car... wondered whether it was you.'

'Yes. I saw yours as I passed. I'm just on my way back from Mundesley.'

Peter gave her a chaste kiss on the cheek, at which Margaret smiled.

'Would you like a drink?'

'Please. Hello, Heather.' Margaret perused the bar for inspiration. 'I've got a meeting later. I'd better not have anything alcoholic. I… I'd like an apple juice please.'

'Have you eaten?'

'No. But I've got a bread roll and a widely travelled banana in the car. The banana resembles the finger of worn leather glove. Frankly I can't work up much enthusiasm….'

'I've just ordered. Baked potato, steak and kidney pie and beans.'

'Oh,' Margaret paused, 'that sounds more like it.'

Peter nodded. 'And I'm not in any hurry.' He grinned. 'Especially not now.'

Margaret turned to Heather. 'Any more baked potatoes?'

'Yes, what would you…?'

'I'll have the same except peas instead of beans…. It'll save me cooking later.'

'Coming up.'

Margaret took off her black leather coat and placed it on the alcove seat beside her. She was looking much more like her old self, Peter thought.

'I'm glad I've seen you. I wanted to invite you to dinner one evening. I haven't done any entertaining for ages and even though I say so myself, I'm quite a decent cook.'

'That sounds nice. Is it to celebrate anything… or for any particular reason?'

'Not really. Perhaps something in the way of an apology?' Margaret peered up at Peter and reached over to take his hand.

'Ah. No need for any apology.'

They agreed that a Saturday evening would suit them both best and dinner was arranged for two weeks hence.

*

Peter's day improved further. That evening he spotted Kingsley, Archie and his Uncle George setting out across the field behind the cottages towards Bluebell Woods. His cousin had a bow saw tucked under his arm. Uncle George was carrying a two-man crosscut saw. Both saws were partly concealed by sacking. They were off on one of their periodic jaunts under cover of darkness to fetch timber for their woodpile. If they went sufficiently late in the day it would be dark by the time they returned. There was little chance of anyone seeing just exactly what they brought back. They weren't above cutting off a living branch or two if they happened to be handy.

Peter wondered briefly what use Archie would be on such an expedition. More of a hindrance than a help, he thought, but his mind was quickly onto other matters. His cousin never bothered to lock his car when he visited his parents. With some impatience Peter waited until it was almost dark and then sauntered quietly the short distance along Back Lane to the Rover. The driver's door was unlocked.

He returned to his garage and collected the plastic bag he had secreted there earlier. Back at the Rover he had a bit of a moment when he opened the door fully and the courtesy light came on. However he switched it off quickly and then very carefully squeezed the contents of the plastic bag onto Kingsley's accelerator and clutch pedals. With any luck his cousin would spread Marmalade's poo liberally all over his shoes, socks and trouser legs and the Rover's carpets. And the beauty of it was, Peter thought, Kingsley would think that he had trodden in something nasty himself.

*

10981 W. Kiowa,

Ventura, California, 93004 USA.

Dear Sheila, Ray & family,

What a surprise! Fantastic news. I can hardly believe that my dad's turned up after all this time-ALIVE!!!. I had to sit down when I read your letter.

You did right, giving him our address. Thanks. I do wish he'd get in touch. We haven't heard from him yet and I can hardly wait. I want to jump on a plane and head back over there and seek him out. Still, I expect he will be in touch when he is good and ready. I've waited 26 years plus! I guess I can wait a little longer.

Good old Jerry has been a big help. He got in touch with his Head Office in Houston and one of the girls there found him the address of the gas terminal in Lincolnshire.

I phoned them and they confirmed that Nick used to work there but that he is now retired and no longer employed by them. The girl I spoke to was very sympathetic but said she wasn't allowed to give out his address or phone number. She said she still sees Nick from time to time and that she would mention my call and tell him how eager I am to hear from him. It's so frustrating, but what can you do?

Anyway, I have more breathtaking news. You might recall I sent a letter to an E. Fincham in Norfolk early last year (found the name in dad's old pocketbook up in the loft) to see whether he or she could throw any light on dad's whereabouts. It was a bit of a long shot, a last ditch attempt I suppose. It turns out that it was a woman, an Ellen Fincham, and that she did know dad during the war. And get this-she last saw him at the same time that we did at the end of January 1953. What was he doing there?

She has since died but I got a very nice letter from her son Peter who said that, wait for it, he is also Nick's son-by Ellen. So I guess you could say that dad and Ellen Fincham certainly did know each other! The only sadness I have about any of this is for poor mum, and I know Ray's not too happy.

Anyway not only have I got my father back, (well, almost!!!) but I've also learned that I have a half brother. Peter works in the film industry and is over here in LA quite often. He said he would like to look us up next time he's over. Wonder what he's like. I also wonder whether he knows that Nick is alive. I think maybe I'll drop him a line.

Our other news is by comparison quite boring. We're looking forward to seeing you. Meantime if anything develops re dad or Peter Fincham, I'll let you know.

Love,

Louise & Jerry.

PS. Jerry says he'll pick up a couple of caps for the boys next time he goes down to see the Lakers.

*

They were returning through Mundesley late in the afternoon after visiting a gallery in Suffolk when Peter yawned extravagantly several times.

'Oh, for goodness sake.' He beat his hand on the steering wheel.

'Am I boring you?'

'No.' Peter grinned ruefully. 'Not at all. But I think I need some fresh air and exercise.' He rubbed a hand over his face and glanced at Gabby. 'Do you fancy a walk? Shall we go down to the beach? It's not cold.'

'Oh, good idea,' Gabby stifled a yawn. 'You've got me at it now. I could do with stretching the old pins myself.'

'It's a while since I've been down. We might as well. If I go home now I won't do anything, anyway. I'll just fiddle about and accomplish nothing.'

'Oh, I've no shortage of things to do. I've got washing and a pile of ironing, but I really can't be arsed. It won't hurt those girls to do their own stuff. Spencer spoils them rotten and they're both bone idle.'

Once they were out of Mundesley Peter turned off the coast road onto the track leading to the cliff tops beside the old army depot. He parked among the gorse, weeds and abandoned plant and equipment that had been dumped behind the Nissen huts.

'Looks deserted.'

'I thought the sea defence people were still here.'

'They must have finished, I suppose.'

The tide was out and they took off their shoes and walked arm in arm along the water's edge. After about forty minutes it occurred to Peter that they must be roughly at the back of the Lord Nelson. It was time to turn round. As they retraced their steps he regaled Gabby with how his mother was able to catch crabs with her bare hands.

'You're joking. She was pulling your leg.'

'No. It's true. It was Margaret's father, Harry Littleboy, that showed her how to do it. I saw her do it several times.'

'Have you ever tried? More to the point, have you ever had any success with it?'

Peter laughed.

'Oh, I've tried. And no, I've never caught a crab in my life. I know the theory, more or less, but I've never even had a sniff of one. I suspect that they just aren't there any more.'

They were both weary by the time they'd rubbed the worst of the sand from their feet and clambered back up the cliff. Gabby stopped twice on the way up on the pretext of gazing out to sea.

Back on top she made to get into the front of the Granada but then changed her mind.

'We'd be better in the back.'

'In the back?' Peter looked puzzled. 'What on earth for?'

Gabby smiled. She moved directly in front of Peter, looked up at him and put a finger to his lips.

'Wait and see.'

'Oh, what?' Peter frowned and shook his head. 'If I didn't know any better I'd think you'd dragged me here simply to have your evil way with me.' He climbed into the back seat of the Granada with just the merest feeling of unease. The promise of a little carnal capering held obvious attractions but he'd never really got the hang of sex in a car.

'OK,' he said, as Gabby sat down beside him and slammed the door, 'what now?'

'Well, see what you can do with these for the time being.' She thrust out her breasts and began to remove her top. 'And we'll wait and see what arises.' Gabby unhooked her bra and began to unzip Peter's jeans.

'Don't you think this is a little on the public side?' Despite his growing excitement Peter was uneasy. Gabby stopped and looked at him. She shook her head.

'You are a worry-guts, aren't you? Don't fret. How many people have you seen so far?'

Peter had to agree that it seemed pretty deserted. He lay back, closed his eyes and abandoned himself to Gabby's expert attentions. After a few minutes when she was happy with her handiwork the ever inventive Gabby detached herself.

'Let's do doggies.'

There followed an entanglement of limbs and some confusion as she negotiated her way in front of Peter. She knelt on the seat, pushed down her pants, felt for his penis and guided him into her. Peter's jeans were twisted into a knot around his ankles and he was kneeling on a seat-belt buckle but he was prepared to put up with a little discomfort.

He spotted the creature almost immediately. At first he couldn't make out what it was. A black and tan rump appeared. It was low to the ground and protruded beyond the weeds beside the black Nissen hut. All became clear as the animal turned round and more of it became visible. It proved to be Archie at full stretch, his stumpy legs pointing backwards almost horizontally as he strained at the furthest extent of a long, taut lead. Peter groaned. Somewhere still out of sight at the far end of the lead would be at least one of the members of his extended family.

He groaned again. Gabby mistook the articulation for an expression of pleasure and wiggled her bottom with renewed enthusiasm.

Distracted by Archie's appearance, Peter continued to watch. He shook his head. He had once known an elderly couple who had a Basset. Otherwise normal enough and not unintelligent they had willingly handed over a not insignificant amount of money for it. The creature had struck Peter as being of overwhelming ugliness and stupidity. At home it had no interest in anything other than food, defecation and sleep. Its owners filled it up; it emptied itself almost anywhere and left them to clear up the mess. When it was out it frequently pulled its owners over and it spent the greater part of what passed for a walk with its head stuck in other canine excreta. The creature simply lurched from one piece of foulness to the next and if its owners weren't particularly vigilant its greatest joy was to roll in something disgusting.

Peter had heard the contention that the Dalmatian held the distinction of being the stupidest of all canines. He had no experience of the breed and tended to side with the Basset baiters. A vet with whom he had a nodding acquaintance once pointed out that like all hounds they had little interest in anything other than following their noses.

Archie lurched forward another couple of feet until he was pulled up smartly. Only inches short of whatever nastiness he sought he strained every sinew trying to get to it.

The dog walker hadn't yet come into view but it was obvious to Peter that it was only a matter of seconds before someone appeared. It was equally obvious that they would have to pass close by the Granada on their way back up to the coast road.

'Someone coming,' he whispered.

'Huh?'

'There's someone coming, with a dog.'

They were both kneeling on the back seat of the Granada. Gabby looked out of the rear window.

'Oh, look at him. Isn't he sweet?'

They watched as the Basset strained a few steps further forward.

'Come on then, you'd better be quick before they get here.' Gabby tipped her backside up a little higher and squirmed encouragingly. A moment later she stopped and they both watched fascinated out of the rear window to see who would appear.

Unlike Gabby who seemed to delight in risky fornication Peter couldn't get quite the same kick out of it. At the likelihood of imminent discovery he quickly suffered a catastrophic detumescence. Still no one appeared from behind the Nissen hut.

'What on earth can they be doing?' he muttered.

Gabby looked round. 'What's happened?' she asked. 'Where's my big, strong soldier?'

'Ah, sorry,' said Peter. He sighed. 'Better get covered up a bit.'

He detached himself and with some difficulty in the confines of the rear of the Granada hitched his jeans up and buckled his belt. Gabby quickly pulled up her pants. She turned round until she was sitting and picked up her bra and top from the floor.

They were both fully dressed and sitting demurely side by side when the dog walker finally appeared. It was Kingsley's wife, May, clad in a red polka-dot dress, a turquoise anorak and Wellingtons.

'Hiya,' she called as she passed. 'Are y'all right?'

They nodded and smiled back at her and then both turned to watch her progress.

'What does she think she looks like?' Gabby snorted as she tried to keep from laughing out loud.

May and Archie were some way past the Granada when Archie suddenly checked, raised his head, sniffed the air and then, after a momentary pause rushed back the way they had come. May was obviously wise to the trick. She took a firm grip on the lead, set her heels and waited patiently.

Despite the fact that Archie was considerably overweight, by the time he reached the fullest extent of the lead he was travelling at a lively clip. It was precisely at that point that May jerked the lead hard backwards. The Basset's neck and head stopped dead, snapped back as though they had hit a wall. Archie's long, heavy body continued its forward motion and executed a glorious manoeuvre somewhere between a barrel roll and a back somersault. Even though May was obviously performing a well-practised trick the creature nearly had her over.

'Oh,' Gabby flinched, 'I bet that made his eyes water.'

'Yes. You do have to admire her skill, though. That was very deft.'

Dazed, Archie picked himself up and shook his elephantine ears.

'Come here, you little pig,' May shouted. Eventually she reeled the Basset in again.

'I did tell you, didn't I?' She shook her head sorrowfully. 'It's not as if you haven't been told. Now I shall have to tell daddy. And he's not going to be pleased, is he?'

Peter got the impression that May knew that they were watching and that a certain amount of what had passed was for their benefit. Eventually she and Archie disappeared from view heading along the track down which Gabby and Peter had come.

'Why on earth would anyone want a Basset?' Peter asked.

'Oh,' said Gabby. 'I think they're lovely. Wouldn't you like one?'

'I might, spit-roasted or in a casserole. Basset haunch might be acceptable with a few capers and onions. I suppose one might acquire a taste for them.' He paused and shook his head. 'They never used to look like that you know. During the last century they looked much more like a normal dog.'

'Well, we all looked different way back then. Children didn't look the way they do now.'

'I dare say, but kids don't walk about today looking like they're wearing their uncle's fur coat and trousers and with their ears and bollocks dragging on the ground.'

Gabby laughed.

'No, that's true. Have you ever eaten dog?'

'Hmm. I suspect I may have eaten it in the Far East.'

'Ugh!'

'You never know. People might travel miles for a decent Basset shank or rolled Basset ear stuffed with spinach and feta.'

'I wouldn't want Basset ears. Just think where they've been.' Gabby shuddered and pulled a face.

'Well, when the cod and haddock finally run out Spencer could do worse than Basset and chips.'

But Gabby had lost interest.

'Where's that little Wurlitzer?' She felt for Peter's fly and unzipped his jeans. 'Oh, poor little thing, he's gone to sleep. Let's see if we can cheer him up.' Gabby eased Peter's penis into the open and began a two handed manipulation.

'Goodness,' she said, 'there we are. Who's a big strong soldier again? Have you got a hanky with you?'

With some difficulty Peter eased a part-used handkerchief out of his jeans pocket. For just the briefest moment he wished that he had been able to produce a clean one. Then he felt as though the top of his head was coming off. Gabby deftly caught every drop of semen in the handkerchief and carefully folded it and placed it on the floor between the front seats. She cuddled up to him with her head on his shoulder.

'Was that good?' she asked after a while when Peter had more or less regained control of his breathing. He still lay back with his eyes closed.

'Mm,' he nodded and smiled. 'I think that I should quite like to die like that.'

Gabby smiled. 'I'm sure it could be arranged.' After a while she tucked Peter away, zipped his jeans and patted his crotch. She announced that she was going to see to her makeup and then it would be time for a cup of tea.

A few minutes later they passed May and Archie. May was struggling gamely enough but the straining hound was chomping energetically on some piece of plastic rubbish he'd found and dragging her steadily into the brambles that bordered the track. Peter heard her shouting as they crept past.

'Whoa! Archie, you little sod, stop it! Come here.'

'I should think you'll get another one of those in a hurry,' Peter muttered as he passed. 'That dog's got the IQ of a fence post.'

'There's no more than one brain cell attached to that lead at either end.'

Gabby laughed and wound down her window. As soon as they were out of sight of May and Archie she disposed of the soiled handkerchief, being careful to drop it where the Basset couldn't help but find it.

As she wound up the window she turned to Peter. 'Did I tell you we're off on holiday at the weekend?'

'No, where are you going?'

'Cyprus.'

'Oh, it'll be a good bit warmer there.'

'That's my earnest hope. I just want to lie by the pool with my book and a tall glass of something cool and alcoholic. And then I'll want another one, and another, and another, and….'

'Is it just you and Spencer?'

'No. We're taking the brats. Spencer wanted them to go too. Well, I've told him he can just see to them, keep them entertained. I shall be very much on holiday.'

12. Letsby Avenue

Nick drove with some care over the rutted surface of the car park at Huttoft Bank. It wasn't busy but it was extremely wet and muddy. Spotting a space free of puddles he brought the Cortina Estate to a halt beside a Thames van and an Austin 1100. Both vehicles were crumbling enthusiastically with rust and boasted ragged patches of red oxide paint at their extremities.

Despite his bulky anorak and scarf he was chilly. He shivered and left the motor and the heater running as he sat for a few minutes looking out of the window. In front of him the sky and sea were grey. There was no horizon. A thin drizzle smeared the windscreen suddenly and then stopped as quickly as it had begun. He flicked on the wipers and wondered whether a walk on the beach was such a good idea after all. The windscreen was filthy and there was insufficient moisture to lubricate the wiper blades. They squeaked and juddered. Nick sighed with annoyance and turned them off.

The greyness matched his mood despite the fact that he'd just had an excellent Sunday lunch with the Riggalls. Roast lamb with mint sauce, parsnips, carrots, peas, cauliflower in white sauce and roast potatoes, all smothered in near-black gravy. There was lemon meringue pie to follow but he hadn't really been able to do it justice. It was the first decent meal he'd eaten since going down with the flu. Food hadn't interested him for some time and he knew from the need to take in his belt an extra hole that he'd lost weight.

He was feeling a little better but he still had a horrible hacking cough. What irritated him most though was his complete lack of energy. Even reading a book was an effort. Just driving the few miles to the beach had left him weary. He felt like a limp rag and had no stamina at all.

It had been tempting to join the Riggalls in the usual comfortable sloth of their weekly post-prandial doze but he'd decided that a brisk walk on the beach in the fresh air might be a better plan. Stan was hoping that he'd be fit to help build a new shower block on the caravan site in a day or two and he was keen not to let the man down. He felt low, though. The doctor said that it was no more than a touch of depression, post-viral; and that it would pass.

'Eat,' he said, 'and have a Guinness or a bottle of Mackeson every day. Go for a brisk walk. Won't do any harm if it doesn't do any good.'

Nick tried, but he liked neither Guinness nor stout. A pint of bitter was more to his taste. It would do as well, he supposed, more or less.

He stared moodily out of the car window. The tide was going out and an east wind was whipping along the beach. There were one or two people in the distance away to the right. Most of them seemed to be accompanied by a dog or two.

Nick sighed, switched off the engine and got out of the car. He zipped up his anorak, stuffed his hands in his pockets and set off along the beach towards Anderby Creek, into the breeze. Coming back would be that much easier with the wind behind him.

He'd walked a mile or so when he stumbled on a Devil's toenail in the sand. He picked it up and examined it briefly before tossing it down. A few steps on and he came across another. He wasn't particularly superstitious but two such finds in quick succession did nothing to lift his mood.

As ever when he found himself on a beach, Ellen drifted into his mind. He had so enjoyed the times that they'd spent together on the beach in north Norfolk. What he would give now, to go back to that time. He wondered how she was getting on and whether she was still living in the cottage where he'd seen her 1953. God; it seemed an age ago now. Once again he wondered how differently things might have turned out if he'd gone back to her, either after he was demobbed or even following his mishap on the cliffs. Despite the fact that Ellen had a son there'd been no sign of any man about the place. She wore no wedding ring and she'd said she hadn't seen the boy's father for ages.

He stopped and stared out to sea, overcome by a great sadness. Suddenly he was frightened. Something was bearing down on him. He was almost certain he could hear whispering voices. There was an awful sinking feeling deep within his body and giant shutters had closed in on him too, one each side of him. They were like blinkers.

Ellen. He'd treated her so badly, never letting on that he was married and that he had a wife and child in Leeds while he was seeing her. Carrying on with her, that's what his mother would have said. He could conjure up her displeasure, her thin-lipped and disapproving looks.

When he called at Ellen's cottage in 1953 she had been so pleased to see him. She'd said she would look forward to him popping in the following day on his way home. To be truthful, he had been looking forward to it too. What a disappointment. And what a disappointment he'd been to so many people.

Both his parents died during the war while he was away. He was unable to attend either funeral. First to go was his father. They'd never been particularly close, especially when Nick was growing up. There were endless rows and arguments-and thrashings too. The old man wasn't above lashing out when Nick was young. Especially after poor, sickly little Marjorie died. His sister had never been well and she'd succumbed to heart failure at the age of four, when Nick was six. His parents had been heart-broken but he hadn't really felt anything much at all. They hadn't allowed him to go to the funeral.

He and his father grew closer once he married and left home. They went fishing together and Nick tried to take an interest in his dad's pigeons. But he had been shocked at how poorly his father looked on the last occasion he saw his

Shooting Marmalade

parents, while he was home for a few hours on leave from laying mines on the cliffs in Norfolk. In the pub the old man had looked frail and lost as he tried to get the attention of the barman. Nick had felt like weeping then. It was only a couple of months later that the old boy collapsed getting into bed. He died on the way to the hospital, of an aortic aneurism. Nick had had to look it up.

After the funeral Nick's mother left Leeds and went to York to stay with her sister. It was the end of April 1942, and sadly, the evening she arrived coincided with a Luftwaffe bombing raid on the city. The bombs had actually begun falling before any early-warning sirens were sounded. They'd been late getting out of the house. The terrace where his aunt lived took several direct hits. Both women and one of Nick's cousins had died. They were just short of the entrance to the shelter when the incendiaries struck.

He wished he'd written to his parents while he was away. His mother had begged him repeatedly to keep in touch. Just to let them know he was safe. But he never seemed to get around to it.

Suddenly Nick was gibbering. The blackness had enveloped him entirely. All his life he'd let people down, especially those closest to him. He'd really messed up a lot of lives. And at this late hour, in most cases there was little or nothing that he could do to try to make amends.

Monica was dead. He'd abandoned her, leaving her to bring up their two children on her own. Goodness knows how she had managed. Anxious, angry, disappointed and, yes, seeking a small measure of revenge for her affair with Little Jack he'd left no message when he went. It hadn't been his intention then, not to return. That occurred later. But he'd never even let her know he was still alive. He'd made no contribution to the family after 1953. As a consequence he'd completely missed seeing his children grow up. Raymond now wanted nothing to do with him, and who could blame him for that? And he'd be denied any involvement with his grandsons.

Louise? Ah. Louise. He could still hope that she might yet be pleased to see him again. It occurred to him suddenly that he could hardly remember what she looked like. But he could still recall all too easily the reproachful look in her eyes as he went out night after night to sit alone in The Murderers. There would have to be an explanation but he had no idea what he could possibly say to her that might help.

Barbara. Poor, dear Barbara was gone. He'd never treated her badly, except for the prevarication about marrying. Of course he couldn't marry her, or explain. It was easier to let things drift. What she didn't know couldn't hurt her. Although she pretended otherwise she had been hurt. He could see it in her eyes. But they'd been happy enough until her illness.

Nick sobbed and shuddered. His nose ran. He was still haunted by Barbara's yellow, gaunt and pain-racked face just before she died. She had been a comely woman, a little on the plump side, but attractive-gentle and kind. The weight had dropped off her so quickly. When she died she weighed only a little over four stones. He recalled rubbing talcum powder on her pitifully skeletal frame. It seemed as though one minute she was fine, the next he was attending her funeral. He still missed her and cursed the filthy cancer that had destroyed her.

Nick stared at the horizon, visible now but blurred with his tears. Swamped with misery, he howled out loud, grabbed by the unbearable weight tearing at his chest and the horrible mishmash of sadness, self loathing and self pity that now enveloped him like a cloak. So distraught was he that after a moment or two he sank to his knees in the wet sand and abandoned himself to his wretchedness.

He cried huge racking sobs, he wept real tears, his nose ran uncontrollably and strings of dribble coursed down his chin and onto his clothes. But still, an infinitesimal part of him seemed to remain detached, floating somewhere up above his head and behind him, surprised that he was powerless to stop this headlong rush into complete and utter desolation. Eventually, after what seemed an age, he calmed. He wiped his face and regained a measure of composure.

Nick had an appalling headache as he staggered to his feet. He blew his nose, flapped ineffectually at his trouser legs and turned to go back to the car park. After a few steps he changed direction and paused to splash his face with water in a low. As he tried to dab himself dry with the sleeves of his anorak and his handkerchief he set off again slowly to return to the car. It was fortunate, he thought, that no one was about to see him in this state.

By the time he reached the Cortina he was exhausted. He sat for some time staring out at the darkening beach. Eventually he made his way out of the car park and along the track to the road that would take him back to the edge of the Wolds. By the time he reached the caravan he had regained a measure of composure. The blackness had lifted a little. It hadn't gone but it was bearable. He assured himself that it was no more than a blip, brought about, as the doctor had suggested, by a touch of post-viral depression.

*

After a pint and a sandwich in the Lord Nelson; Peter devoted the afternoon to framing. He had enjoyed a particularly productive week, due in no small part to the fact that Gabby was away. Unsurprisingly, fewer interruptions led to greater productivity. Normally he found framing tedious but the afternoon had gone extremely well. Now he was showered and shaved, dressed in his best jeans, a clean shirt and a new leather jacket. The dab or two of *Eau Sauvage* that had stood unopened in the cupboard for a year or two he considered an inspired afterthought and he was now looking forward to dinner with Margaret.

He stopped in Cromer at the off-licence for a bottle of wine and some cigarettes. He was also fortunate enough to catch the florist as she was about to close. She packed him off with a vulgarly large bunch of assorted flowers and charged him next to nothing.

The lights were on at Margaret's as he parked the Granada on the L-shaped concrete drive. Through the half-drawn curtains the bungalow had a cheery and welcoming look. The gardens looked neat and well cared-for in the dusk.

A small tortoiseshell cat stood up, arched elaborately and then leapt down from the sitting room windowsill. It approached Peter as he got out of the car.

'Hello, puss.' He stooped to caress the top of the cat's head as the creature leaned against his calf muscles.

Margaret had obviously seen him arriving. She opened the front door before he could ring the bell.

'Peter. How lovely.'

'Hi, Margaret. How are you? You are expecting….'

'Yes. Come on in. I'm fine, thank you. And you?'

She checked as the little cat darted through the door.

'Now where do you think you're going to, Miss Mycroft?' She turned to watch as the cat disappeared. 'I thought we'd agreed that you'd be out for the evening.'

Margaret turned back to Peter.

'She's greatly exercised by our dinner.'

'As am I,' said Peter. 'It smells very promising. What did you call her? Mycroft?'

'Miss. Miss Mycroft.'

'Ah.' Peter thought for a moment and then nodded his head. He grinned. 'Sherlock's smarter older sister? She's a pretty little thing.'

'Oh, well done you. You're the first, without a prompt. Yes. She's a very intelligent little cat. A bit on the precocious side though.'

Margaret was wearing a black leather skirt that Peter hadn't seen before, with a low-cut V-necked top and very high heeled shoes. Her hair was up and immaculate and she was fully made-up and elegantly bejewelled. She had certainly made an effort with her appearance.

'How are you? You're looking well.'

'Yeah, not so shabby, thanks. I've had a good....' Peter was enveloped in the miasma of perfume that Margaret left in her wake. 'Mmm. That's very fragrant too.'

'*Diorisimo.* Thanks. Lily of the Valley, I think.'

'Mmm. Yes. It's lovely.'

'Thank you for these. Shall I put them in water? Did you get them at Kay's? They're beautiful. You said you'd had a good… what?'

'A good week. Yes. I've had an excellent week and now I'm ready for a bit of R & R. I think I've earned it.' Peter took the packet of Lucky Strike from his jacket pocket and held it a couple of inches in front of Margaret's nose.

'Oh, Luckies. You shouldn't have. Thank you.'

Margaret took the packet, ripped off the cellophane, opened it up and held the cigarettes to her nose.

'Mmm. Heavenly. Not like English. Takes me back to Apopka High.'

Like Peter, Margaret was not an habitual smoker but she did enjoy an American cigarette occasionally.

'And flowers too. I don't know.'

'And a modest bottle of plonk.'

'Oh, lovely. Come on through.'

The dining room was full of G Plan furniture and everything had been newly cleaned, straightened, dusted and polished. The table was set very attractively for two.

'I meant to ask. You haven't turned vegetarian recently, have you? It seems to be very fashionable at the moment.'

'Good heavens, no. That smells delicious. What is for dinner, if you don't mind my asking?'

'Well, let's just say I hope you like duck.'

Peter stared.

'Duck?' He expostulated. 'Oh, what? You're not serious. You can't expect me to eat duck.'

'The best Aylesbury Duckling, with roast potatoes....'

'Duckling? Oh, my God. It gets worse.'

'What?' Margaret was perplexed. 'Why's that?'

'Well,' Peter looked appalled. He paused, frowning for several seconds. 'It's like eating one of your friends.'

'How's that?'

'You can't go eating a creature that's got a name.'

'Well the duck didn't have a name.'

'How can you say that? Of course he would have had a name.'

'Well,' Margaret was becoming increasingly exasperated. 'How do you know that? What was it?'

Peter gave a short laugh and shook his head. 'We're hardly likely to find out now, are we?'

'Well....' Margaret bridled. 'I didn't know....'

'Lionel? Aubrey? Hugh? You've just cooked the poor beggar. Cooked his goose, good and proper.' Peter tried not to laugh.

Margaret stared. After a moment she grinned. 'Oh, you....' She tried to look severe, but gave up. 'What a rotten trick.'

'Should have seen your face. What a hoot.' Peter went to Margaret and put his arm round her waist. He kissed her on the cheek. 'If it tastes as good as it smells, what with the wine, cigarettes and flowers we've got everything we need for a perfect evening.'

'Not quite everything.' Margaret looked up at him.

'What?'

Margaret smiled and shook her head.

*

Dinner was, for the most part, every bit as good as Peter's olfactory organ promised. Despite downing two strong Gordons and tonic as a pre-prandial Margaret managed to orchestrate the meal so that everything was ready at the appropriate time. Nothing burned, turned lumpy or collapsed.

They started with half a grapefruit each, smothered in brown sugar and decorated with half a cherry in the centre. The clever bit was that the grapefruit were served piping hot, after being placed under the grill. Peter remarked that it was a dish he had never before encountered, but that it was both interesting and imaginative.

The main course was indeed roast duckling.

'Would you like to carve, Peter, while I get the vegetables?'

Peter looked at the duck, which was modest in size but certainly adequate for two people, and then tried the edge of the large carving knife that Margaret had put out. The blade was every bit as blunt as it looked.

'Have you got some kitchen scissors? I'll just halve it. Trying to carve duck is largely an exercise in futility. Unless, of course you wanted it to do more than just one meal?'

'No. Of course not.'

The duck was excellent, served with a sauce apparently concocted of rhubarb and port wine. It was accompanied by roast potatoes, carrots, cabbage and the whole smothered in a luxurious gravy that was utterly delicious.

'Look at this,' said Margaret, as she put down her knife and fork. 'I've eaten every bit that's edible but you'd never know it. The plate looks as though it has more on it now I've finished than it did before I started. Now why is that?'

'It's no mystery. It's called Montgomery's Revenge… after a greatly revered duck named Montgomery. But it's no more than you deserve.'

'What? Margaret laughed.

'Well….'

They drank wine throughout the meal and paused after the main course to smoke a cigarette each.

Margaret tut-tutted and grimaced. 'I normally hate it when people do this, smoke in the middle of eating. But since you brought Luckies and we're at home, it is a decadence in which I will… that I will happily indulge… in.' Margaret was becoming a little garrulous and flushed in the face.

Pudding also found favour with Peter.

'Cherry Cobbler,' he exclaimed. 'Brilliant. I haven't had this since I was in New Mexico, at a Country Club in Hobbs, a little oil town out in the desert. It was gorgeous.'

'You don't get cobblers much in the UK, do you? What were you doing in Hobbs?'

Peter laughed.

'I see more than enough old cobblers in the UK, but I know what you mean. We were in West Texas looking for a location for a movie. We wanted beam pumps, nodding donkeys; you know the kind of thing. Real roughy-toughy oilmen, roughnecks, roustabouts, drilling rigs; typical oilfield really. We found a brilliant location in New Mexico, just outside Hobbs. It was perfect, just what we needed.'

'We went to New Mexico on vacation once. To Albuquerque, Taos, Los Alamos, Santa Fe, it was great.'

'Oh, yes. I went up there. I got up to Taos.' Peter blew out smoke and chuckled. 'The first night we were in Hobbs we had a Mexican meal, Tex-Mex, just over the road from the motel. Like most food in restaurants in the States the portions were enormous. We had a mammoth starter, then a huge main course. Eventually the waitress turned up to see if we wanted dessert.

'Y'all ready for sopapias?" Peter shook his head. 'I didn't have a clue what she was saying. With her southern twang it sounded like "Y'all ready for a piss?" '

Margaret burst out laughing.

'I felt like asking, in my best English accent, of course. "Are you entirely persuaded, Madam, that the state of my bladder is any of your business?" '

Margaret giggled again. 'I always found Mexican food a bit indigestible.'

'Oh, gracious. Real Mexican food is excellent. It's a world away from Cal-Mex or Tex-Mex. Yes. We never slept a wink that night, fajitas, tacos, beans, chillies, sopapias. All very tasty but we ate far too much, far too late. Then of course we had coffee and more drinks. I spent the night totally bloated and farting like a carthorse.'

Margaret brought Stilton and grapes and then they dallied over coffee. Peter offered to clear the table and help wash up but Margaret said everything would go in the dishwasher in the morning. She couldn't be fagged to do anything with it until then.

Eventually Peter confessed that his backside was getting numb on the dining chairs so they moved through into the sitting room, which was another orgy of G Plan furniture.

Margaret brought more coffee and later, with a good deal of ceremony, she served shot glasses of sambuca, complete with flaming coffee beans. She judged this to be such a success that she was compelled to repeat it. On the second occasion she was so busy lighting a cigarette and talking that she let the flaming go on too long and burned her mouth on the searing rim of the shot glass. Her upper lip came up in a nasty looking blister that necessitated a quick visit to the bathroom.

Once the blister was attended to Margaret continued drinking sambuca, but without the benefit of the pyrotechnics. Peter moved on to a rather fine bottle of Fonseca vintage port that Margaret produced from the back of the sideboard.

'I opened it to make the sauce. You might as well take it with you when you go. I don't like port. I'll never drink it.' She had received it a year or two earlier from a grateful patient at the convalescent home.

They drank, they chatted; they told jokes and as the hour grew later, fell about increasingly with laughter. At some point, quite late in the evening they blew smoke into each other's hair and then rolled about, helpless at the sight of their apparently smouldering heads.

They were so taken with the trick that they went upstairs, taking their drinks and bottles with them, to get the full effect in the long mirror in Margaret's bedroom. After they tired of this activity Peter lay on the bed and waxed eloquent about painting and his hopes for the future. Margaret excused herself and went to the bathroom. She returned a few minutes later with her makeup renewed, her hair tidied, and having had a generous re-spray of *Diorissimo*. She was also clad only in her underwear.

Without any preamble she knelt on top of Peter, kissing him hard. She then began to undress him.

Peter laughed. 'Mrs Graver. What on earth do you think you're doing?'

Margaret sat up straight and then thrust her breasts in Peter's face.

'Do you like the lingerie? It's new. I bought it specially. I seem to recall you had a thing about stockings, suspenders and high heels.'

'Mm.' Peter groaned and squirmed beneath Margaret. 'I do. I do. I do like black stockings. And I love the suspenders, bra and panties.... What are they? Ivory? And the shoes.' He ran his hands over Margaret's buttocks.

Margaret rolled off him and removed his jeans and pants. 'Oh, for goodness sake, you're not still wearing those same old Y-fronts?'

'What?'

But Margaret had dumped the offending garment on the carpet and was astride Peter once again. She ran her fingertips lightly up and down the shaft of his penis.

'Are you sure this is... you know?'

'What?'

'I mean after losing... the... the baby, you know? Are you....'

'Oh, yes. It's fine. I'm fine.'

Intent on her work Margaret smiled. When she was satisfied with her handiwork she lowered herself onto him. They both gasped. After a few minutes Margaret got off Peter. She took the pillows from the head of the bed and lay with them piled beneath her buttocks.

'Come on, then, lover. Let's be 'avin' you.'

Peter obliged, with a will. After a while he asked, 'Do you know who lives in Letsby Avenue?'

'I do! I don't!' Margaret called, pressing Peter's buttocks into her, grinding her hips and intent on impending orgasm. 'But I feel sure you're going to... enlighten me.'

Peter too was beginning to gasp.

'Clever Dick!' he shouted, his breath ragged. 'Clever-bloody-Dick! That's who. Clever-bloody.... Ah! Ah! Ah! Aaaaaaah! Oh! Oh! Oh! Dick.'

After a short while when Peter made to get off her, Margaret clasped him to her, locking her legs tightly around his waist and buttocks. It hurt but she wouldn't let him go.

*

Peter was forced up early by his distended bladder and a pounding headache. After some paracetamol from the bathroom cabinet and a couple of glasses of water he returned to bed and went back to sleep. It was very late when Margaret appeared beside him in a white towelling dressing gown and bearing mugs of tea.

'Ah, lovely.'

'I gave up waiting for you.'

'Oh, sorry.'

Peter hauled himself up and was glad to find that the headache had gone.

As they drank their tea he got the impression that Margaret seemed a little crusty but it wasn't until after they had made love again that she became tiresome.

'Where's your friend Gabby, then? Have you seen her lately?'

'She's away, on holiday.'

'Oh, right. Well, bully for her.'

Peter looked questioningly.

'What's...?'

'I don't know what you see in her.'

'She's been very helpful.'

'Oh, I bet she has. Helping you into bed, I expect. Or at least helping you into her knickers.'

'Margaret! She's been very helpful professionally. Why do you say that?'

'Oh, please. Don't pretend you don't know what I'm talking about.'

They continued with sporadic bickering until after a piece of toast and Marmite and another mug of tea Peter announced that he really would have to be off.

'Thanks for a splendid meal. I really enjoyed last night. You'll have to come over and I'll cook you dinner.'

Margaret stood in front of him and straightened his jacket lapels.

'She can't have children, you know.'

'Who?'

'You know who. Gabby.'

Peter frowned and sighed with exasperation.

'Why would I be interested in whether someone else's wife…?' Exasperated, he shook his head. 'I don't know why you think….'

'She's older than me too. And she hasn't got anything I haven't. I really don't know why you're wasting your time and energy,' Margaret paused, 'and sperm, on her.'

*

Peter stopped at Annie's shop on the way home to pick up milk and a loaf of bread. He was standing outside the shop reading the headlines on the papers in the newspaper rack when a car pulled up behind him. As he turned to see who it was Kingsley wound down his window.

'Oh. Hello, King. How are you?'

Kingsley studied Peter for a moment. Eventually he spoke. 'You can cut the bullshit, Pedro. I know it was you.'

Peter looked perplexed. 'Know what was …what?'

'Put the shit in my car. I know it was you.'

Peter frowned. 'What? I don't know what you're talking about.'

He moved towards his car.

'Oh, yes you do,' Kingsley called after him. 'And you'll bloody-well pay for it, too.'

Kingsley turned off his engine. He got out of the Rover and called after Peter, who was about to open the door of the Granada.

'And do you know how I know?'

'No.' Peter sighed. 'But I'm sure you're going to bore me with it. Please go on.'

For a moment he saw a flicker of doubt in Kingsley's pale blue eyes. It didn't last.

'Clever bugger. You think you're so smart. You turned the courtesy light off, didn't you?'

Peter hesitated a moment. He remembered turning the light off, but he had no memory of turning the wretched thing on again.

'And you think that proves what exactly?'

'Never you mind. I'll get you back.'

Peter shook his head and opened his car door. He paused.

'Do you know, Kingsley? You've said that to me ever since we've known each other. "I'll get you back." Don't you ever get weary of it? Could you not, just for once, behave like a normal human being?'

Kingsley stared for a moment and then sniggered.

'I will. You wait and see.' With that he turned and stumped into the shop.

*

10981 W. Kiowa,
Ventura, California, 93004 USA.

Dear Peter,

Thank you for your letter. I was sorry to hear of your loss. Sounds like Ellen was quite a lady.

I needn't tell you-what a surprise to learn that you and I are related. It would be nice to meet you next time you are over, if possible. We are easy to find, off Darling Road, between Telephone and Santa Paula Freeway.

Now I have a surprise for you. I have it on very good authority that <u>Nick (our father) is still alive and well and living in Lincolnshire.</u> Or he was until recently. Apparently his name is now Nick Codling. Don't ask, I don't know. I had a letter from my sister-in-law in Princes Risborough after he appeared out of the blue one day looking for my brother Raymond.

Nick has been living in Lincolnshire and working at the Gas Terminal on the coast near Mablethorpe. We don't have an address for him since he recently retired and the terminal people won't give out his address or telephone number. In any event he seems to have moved from the last address they had for him. (The woman he was living with died.)

I don't know whether you would be interested in trying to locate him. In case you are I enclose the address of the terminal. Norfolk and Lincolnshire are quite close. You could probably do it in a day. Needless to say if you are able to find out anything I would be very interested!

Apparently Nick told Sheila (sister-in-law) that he wanted to come out here to catch up with me. That should be interesting!

I look forward to hearing from you and hopefully meeting you one day in the not too far distant future.

Roger Kirk

Yours truly, Louise.

PS. If Nick does get in touch I will tell him about you and give him your address, if you have no objection.

*

'So are you going to try to get in touch with Nick?' Kathy looked up from the crossword in the local paper.

'Yes. I'd love to meet him.' Peter was tossing darts at the dartboard in a mechanical and distracted fashion. One pinged off a wire and clattered to the floor.

'Quite apart from him being my father, I'd be really interested to hear his story, where he's been, why he disappeared off the face of the earth, how he did it, why change his name. Did he ever know about me, and if he did….'

'Yes.' Kathy said, 'it would be daft not to, now you've got a lead. Will you drive up there?'

'I nearly jumped in the car straight away. No. I'm going to try phoning first, see if I can get an address or number, or some kind of information, before I head off up there. I don't want to go on a wild goose chase. Interested as I am, I'm busy and I really can't afford to waste time just at present.'

Another dart ricocheted off the wire and stuck in a nearby table leg.

'I think you'd better stop before you hurt yourself,' Kathy said kindly.

'It's these darts. They're hopeless. They've no flights left on them. I defy anyone….' Peter gathered the darts up and placed them on the shelf below the dartboard.

'They're not much good, but I'm not leaving any decent ones out, they'll look like those within a week if they don't get knicked first.'

Peter sat down at the bar and sipped his pint.

'How's Phil getting on? I haven't seen him for a bit.'

Kathy gave a short laugh. 'Well, no use asking me. I've seen neither hide nor hair of him.'

'I was wondering whether he'd made any further progress on Dave. Last I heard he was thinking about going down to Rye.'

'Well, if he has, he certainly hasn't seen fit to let me know. But then, I'm only his mother.'

*

When he moved into Cowper's Cottage Peter decided to sleep in his old bedroom. Following Ellen's programme of extension and gentrification it was now a good deal bigger and rather better appointed than it had been when he was a child. Located at the back of the property it was quiet, with a pleasing view over the garden and the fields beyond to the old railway line.

He had never had any difficulty sleeping or with getting up in the morning on those days when he had to be somewhere. Occasionally however, particularly on a Sunday morning, he liked to lie in. As Ellen would have put it, 'he liked the streets well-aired,' before he got up, so he was more than a little irritated one Sunday morning to be woken before five o'clock. Glowering at the clock on his bedside chest he couldn't, at first, understand what had woken him.

'*Click-tick.*'

He started and stared at the curtained window.

'*Tick.*' There it was again.

Someone was in the garden, throwing pebbles at his bedroom window.

It was not a sound with which he was wholly unfamiliar. As a student he'd been woken early one morning in the same way. When he looked out of the window on that occasion he'd been horrified to see two female students on the pavement below. He and his friend Doug had left them only a couple of hours earlier. They'd all been to the Folk Club and afterwards had spent an age in Doug's car parked outside the girls' bed-sit. They'd been drinking beer out of bottles and laughing at Doug's endless jokes until very late. After much slamming of car doors, giggling and calling out, the girls had clattered down the tiled path to let themselves in the front door. Doug had beeped his horn several times in a friendly farewell as he and Peter sped away.

On that occasion Peter had dressed hurriedly, gone downstairs and let the girls in. They had walked the three miles to his place after their landlady had thrown them out. She had been waiting for them, grim-faced, at the top of the stairs. With limited facilities Peter had made them all coffee. Then they had trudged round to Doug's bed-sit and spent the rest of the day together, dividing their time between looking for flats or bed-sits and numerous public bars.

'*Click*.'

Peter rose and went to the window. He could make out a figure down below, casting about for another stone.

He opened the window.

'Hello?'

'Oh, you're awake. Thank goodness for that.'

'Margaret? Are you OK?'

'Yes. Apart from being frozen. Are you going to let me in?'

'Hang on. I'll be down in a moment.' Peter quickly disposed of the old Y fronts he was wearing and put on his dressing gown.

He was surprised to see that Margaret was smartly dressed. She looked as though she was ready for a good day out.

'Hello.' She greeted him with a big smile and threw her arms around his neck. 'It's lovely to see you.'

Peter was a little taken aback but he responded with a kiss.

'Oh, come on in. It's bitter out here.'

'Yes, there was frost on my car.'

'I'm not surprised. What are you doing here? Do want a hot drink, or anything?' Peter rubbed his face and ran his hand through his hair. He felt distinctly rumpled and disadvantaged.

Margaret took his arm and snuggled up against him as they went through to the kitchen.

'I just wanted to see you. I couldn't sleep. In the end I thought I might as well get up. Then I thought, well why not come over here and cuddle up with you. If you don't mind, that is?' She gave him an impish look.

'No; not at all. Shall I make some tea?'

'Yes, let's take our mugs up with us. I suddenly feel ready to sleep.'

Peter put the kettle on as Margaret took off her coat.

'Oh gracious! What is that smell?' Margaret cast around and then looked at her shoes. 'Oh, I've trodden in something foul. And in my good shoes.'

'What?'

Margaret took off her shoes and cautiously held one to her nose. 'Oh, it's poo. It's cat. Urrgh!'

'Oh, give them here. It'll be that stinking tom, my aunt and uncle's cat. Lives a few doors down, horrible creature. I swear I'll do for him one of these days.'

'Oh, poor pussy. Don't you like cats?'

'I don't mind your average, normal cat. I like your Miss Mycroft. She's beautiful. I just don't like this particular cat. He's evil, rotten to the core.'

Peter took the shoes from Margaret and placed them on some newspaper in the porch. 'I'll sort them out in the morning.'

'Is there any on the carpet.'

'Can't see anything. Oh, hang on a minute.' Peter got down on his hands and knees and sniffed the floor. 'Oh. Yes. There's something here. I'll see to it later.'

Margaret was sitting up in Peter's bed wearing one of his tee shirts when he appeared with mugs of tea.

'Oh, you've found something.'

'Yes. Hope you don't mind. I'm warmer now.'

After tea and sex Margaret stayed for what little remained of the night. Since she had to work until lunchtime she was up before Peter and brought him toast and coffee.

Peter hopped out of bed to go to the bathroom.

'Where's your car? You didn't walk again, did you?'

'No. I left it down at the bottom of Back Lane, round the back of the old Methodist Chapel.'

'Why on earth…?'

'I didn't want to make a lot of noise. It was very late. Didn't want to wake anyone.'

'Hmm. Very considerate of you.'

13. The Deadly Bread Roll

It was just before six o'clock on an overcast and chilly Thursday morning when Peter headed for his studio dressed in thick cord trousers and several layers of clothing. He carried with him a mug of coffee and a banana and had a half-eaten doughnut clenched between his teeth. He'd been working on a series of large abstracts for days and was sufficiently excited by them that when the local crows and magpies began their usual dawn altercation he had little inclination to roll over and try to go back to sleep. So intent was he on his painting that it came as something of a surprise hours later when he looked out of the studio window and discovered that the sun was shining. He realized at the same time that he was frozen and his back and shoulder muscles ached. Rubbing his arms energetically in an effort to stimulate warmth he went outside, stood in the sun, stretched and tried a few gentle exercises.

It had turned into a brilliant morning. One or two light, woolly clouds dotted the horizon in the west but otherwise the sky was clear, blue and sparkling. A light breeze was blowing off the land and it seemed a splendid drying day. It had occurred to Peter the previous evening that he couldn't remember when he last changed his bed. The linen basket in the bathroom was overflowing and he had meant to put the washing machine on.

He was upstairs and about to strip his bed when he glanced out of the window. The woodpecker was on the lawn. It had been about the garden often when he first arrived but its visits had tailed off through the winter. Now he was seeing it again, in and around the apple trees and beneath the holly. Leaning on the windowsill, he watched the bird for a few minutes. He found its air of soberness endearing.

Since moving into Cowper's Cottage he'd developed something of an interest in bird watching, albeit in a fairly low-key fashion. Had anybody asked him to name his hobbies and pastimes, ornithology would probably never have occurred to him. But he did take an interest in the birds in the garden, watching from the conservatory, his bedroom or the kitchen window.

It was while he was at the airing cupboard looking for pillowcases that he heard a disturbance outside. Having something of a premonition of what was happening he rushed to the window. He was right. Marmalade was on the lawn. He looked as though he was resting. Peter was relieved that there was no sign of the woodpecker.

'Ha, good for you, Woody,' he crowed. 'Well done, that woodpecker.' He turned away but rushed back to the window moments later, drawn by feeble cries of anguish from the garden. It was clear that the woodpecker hadn't escaped Marmalade at all. The cat was pressing the unhappy bird into the lawn as it struggled, flapping and squirming beneath him.

'Hey!' Horrified, Peter banged on the glass. Marmalade gave him an indolent stare but didn't move other than to look down briefly at his prey and shift his weight slightly. Peter hammered again on his bedroom window until rather belatedly it occurred to him that he could open it.

'Hey! Get off! Go on!'

Still Marmalade didn't budge. Peter waved his arms at the cat and looked around wildly. The Diana was downstairs somewhere. He couldn't remember what they'd done with it after Gabby's lucky shot. He took a wooden coat hanger out of his wardrobe and tried to hurl it at the cat but it caught the curtain.

'Damn!' Peter jarred his wrist and the coat hanger clattered onto the conservatory and the patio below.

Marmalade started at the noise, then quickly took the woodpecker in his mouth and darted into the hedge.

Massaging his sore wrist Peter charged down the stairs and out into the garden but by the time he arrived, panting on the lawn; there was no sign of Marmalade or the woodpecker.

'I'll get you, you swine,' Peter muttered. He felt like shouting so that even if the cat didn't understand the words it might at least get the message that he was angry, but he didn't want his aunt or uncle to hear. He *was* angry. The cat had taken *his* woodpecker on *his* property. It was the last straw. He picked up the coat hanger from the patio and returned to his bedroom to finish what he had been doing.

It was late in the afternoon when he discovered the decapitated body of the bird on the path near the bottom of the garden.

'Ah, you poor thing.'

He stared at it for moment and then went to fetch an old newspaper. 'What a totally pointless thing to do,' he muttered as he picked up the remains of the bird. It looked all the more pathetic since its normally brightly coloured plumage was now sodden and dull, terminating in a ragged red wound where once had been its handsome head.

Peter wrapped the remains of the woodpecker carefully in the paper and placed it in the bin.

'Of course,' he muttered, 'meting out torture and pointless death and destruction is not solely within the feline gift. Anyone can do it. In fact, Marmalade, I feel an irresistible urge to visit some pointless pain and misery on you. Except it won't be as entirely pointless as your terminating the life of a perfectly harmless bird, it'll be the purposeful settling of scores. I shall merely be seeking vengeance on behalf of my erstwhile good friend, the pecker-wood. And as all top avengers are well aware, revenge is a dish best served cold.'

Peter grimaced and nodded his head.

'Perfecto.' He had remembered the shotgun beneath the bed in the guest bedroom. 'I shall be biding my time.' Smiling grimly he went indoors to find the weapon. 'I'm going off my head, talking to myself.'

He knew nothing about shotguns. Other than the Diana air pistol the only gun he'd ever handled in his life was one of the ancient Lee Enfield .303 rifles that they had drawn with much ceremony from the school armoury from time to time on a Cadet Corps afternoon.

He dragged the fibre gun case from beneath the bed and blew away the fluff that had already accumulated. When he took the gun out it was a good deal heavier than he remembered. He found the box of cartridges Gabby had brought but promptly dumped them on the bed, defeated by the yards of sticky tape with which she had bound the broken box.

The gun certainly looked a handsome piece. He popped the Greener open, peered into the barrels, then snapped it shut and took it to the window. After aiming at one or two things out in the garden he pulled both triggers and was rewarded with two satisfying clicks.

'Right; you little sod.' He put the shotgun back in its case and placed it beneath the bed. 'Next time we'll see how you like one of these up your backside.'

*

Peter picked up the phone.

'Hiya, it's me.'

'Oh, Gab. How are you? Good holiday?'

'Not bad, apart from getting stung almost to death by a jellyfish.'

Peter heard a guffaw in the background, followed by a shout of laughter.

'It was a bread roll, Peter. It was no more a bloody jellyfish than I am.'

'Oh, go to hell.' Gabby didn't sound in the best of humours.

'Is that Spencer?'

'The idiot thinks I mistook a bread roll floating in the sea for a jellyfish. What I'd like to know is, if it was a bread roll why have I got these bloody great stings on my back? At least I did actually go in the sea. I went out. I did things. All he did for the entire holiday was lie in a heap and drink and do those stupid word search things that are designed by morons for idiots. Then he sat in the bar all night drinking and talking with a bunch of other numbskulls, who were to a man boorish, racist, sexist and unutterably stupid. They all spent the entire holiday pissed as farts.'

'Oh, well, as long as you enjoyed yourselves.'

'I did, but a bit of company wouldn't have gone amiss. I had to.... Oh, never mind, enough about bloody Spencer. What I was phoning about is this. There's an exhibition at Kings Lynn and the day after tomorrow's the last day for submissions. It's an important show and you need to be in it. Did you know?'

'No.'

'That's what I thought. Well, I can't help tomorrow, I've got stuff to do, but I'll see you the next day. You can submit up to four paintings. Presumably you've got something suitable, something framed.'

'Oh, I should think so. But I've just about finished a series of abstracts. They're acrylic and they can be ready tomorrow.'

'OK, well, I'll have a look. Anyway we need to take something up there. Are you free the day after tomorrow, for a couple of hours?'

'Yes, I can go anytime, really.'

'OK. Well, I'm going to bed. I'm suffering from a surfeit of Spencer and I'm a bit jetlagged. I'll see you then. Shall we go straight after coffee?'

'Yes. OK. Bye; see you.' As he put the phone down Peter wondered idly how jetlagged one would be, flying from Cyprus.

*

Next morning he phoned the gas terminal in Lincolnshire.

'NorSeaCo-Gas Terminal, good morning.'

'Oh, morning. I wonder whether you can help me. I'm trying to contact a Mr Nick Codling.'

'Putting you through.'

Peter's heart leapt. Perhaps Louise had got it wrong. He listened to several clicks at the far end of the line.

'Warehouse, Jackie speaking.'

'Oh, hello. I'd like to speak to Mr Codling, Nick Codling.'

There was silence.

'May I ask who's calling?'

'My name's Peter Fincham. Mr Codling is my father.'

It gave Peter a curious feeling to be asking for his father.

'I'm sorry but Mr Codling doesn't work here any more. He retired a little while ago.'

'Do you have an address or a phone number for him at all?'

'I'm sorry, but I can't help you with that kind of information. Do you want to talk to the Warehouse Supervisor?'

'Oh, OK. Yes. Thanks.'

The Warehouse Supervisor was Welsh and sounded thoroughly harassed. He confirmed that Nick had left *NorSeaCo* and that it was company policy not to give out confidential information on its employees, past or present. When Peter tried to explain he transferred the call to Personnel.

The Personnel Secretary was able to tell Peter that Nick was no longer living at his old address. She had sent him some paperwork and it had been returned unopened. London Personnel might have an address since they would be dealing with his pension but she felt that they would be unlikely to give Peter information of that sort. She knew no one locally who had Nick's current address, but suggested that Peter talk to the warehouse secretary.

After a short pause Peter found himself once again talking to Jackie.

'Jackie speaking, how may I help you?'

'It's Peter Fincham again. I'm sorry but I've been shuffled back to you.'

Jackie laughed.

'You're looking for Nick. Mr Codling?'

'Yes. As I said, I'm his son.'

'I was thinking a moment ago, you're the second person that's been looking for Nick recently. There was a woman… hang on, let me just…. Yes, a lady from America was trying to contact him. His daughter apparently. That would be your sister then…? Nice lady.'

'Louise Stark?'

'Yes. That's right.'

'We are apparently related; she's my half-sister. I've never actually met her.'

'Oh.'

'We only recently found out that Nick was still alive. Neither of us knew of the other's existence and neither of us has seen him since January 1953. We thought he was dead.'

'Gracious.'

Peter talked some more. Jackie seemed genuinely interested and in the end conceded that she might be able to help.

'He is naughty. I don't know where he's living at the moment and I know that Personnel haven't got an address for him either. I do occasionally bump into him in Alford or Louth. Having said that, I haven't seen him recently but I will keep an eye out for him. If I see him I'll let him know you're trying to get in touch.'

'Thank you. That would be excellent.'

'He won't have an address or phone number for you presumably. Not if you haven't seen him....'

Peter laughed. 'I'm not sure he even knows that I exist, that he has another son.'

'Ah. Well, if you're happy enough to give me your details I can pass them on to him when I see him.'

'Yes. OK, that would be very helpful, if you wouldn't mind.'

'I can't guarantee anything but I'll keep your details with me, in my purse, just in case. I'll give them to Vanessa too, the secretary in Personnel. She sees Nick about occasionally.'

'Excellent. Thank you so much. I really do appreciate you taking the trouble to help.

'Well, I liked Nick. We used to have a bit of a laugh.'

*

In the event Gabby was unable to accompany Peter to Kings Lynn to deliver his paintings. She gave him the address of the gallery and details of how to find it but in pouring rain it proved a good deal less straightforward than she had implied. It also became apparent to Peter that Gabby struggled with the concepts of left and right but he forbore from making mention of the fact later.

They were able to go together to the private viewing. Peter managed to fend off Gabby's offer to drive on the basis that there was nowhere for him to put his legs comfortably in the MGB. The evening started well enough but went downhill briefly after Gabby bumped into an old adversary from school. She didn't drink to excess but she certainly enjoyed a glass or two of champagne and for a moment became argumentative and a little loud. As the evening drew to a close Peter's paintings had received much interest but he hadn't sold anything. He had a quick look at the Visitor's Book. There were several nice comments but nothing constructive. He was more than a little irritated at the last entry.

Someone had written in huge and achingly stylish italics, *'Peter Finch-HAM! Nice FRAMES.'* The comment shrieked an unwritten 'PITY ABOUT THE PAINTINGS!!!'

Gabby was dismissive. 'Forget it. I saw who wrote it. It was one of those Goths that came in towards the end.'

'Good grief, yes. What on earth did they think they looked like?'

'They looked to me as though they were high as kites and that putting on their underpants in the morning would present them with an almost insurmountable challenge. Doom-brains, the pair of them. Your paintings will be sold by this time next week.'

On the way back Gabby dozed. She woke with a start as they crested the rise coming into Cromer.

'Oh' she said, yawning. 'Excuse me. I must still be a bit jet-lagged, I think. I wasn't snoring, I hope.'

'Barely at all. And then only the most delicate and lady-like inhalations. Nothing to frighten the horses.'

'Pig!' Gabby slapped Peter's shoulder.

'Jetlag is a funny thing. It sometimes takes a little while to get back to normal.'

Gabby looked out over the sea as they drove into Cromer. 'It's a lovely evening. Look at the moon and the ships' lights twinkling out on the horizon. And the pier's lit up.'

Peter glanced at the sea and then at Gabby. 'I was wondering…. Do you fancy some …?' He paused as he braked hard for a dog, hurrying across the road.

'Whoops.' Gabby laughed. 'Fish and chips?'

'Fish and chips.'

'You must be a mind-reader. I was just thinking the very same thing.' She looked at her watch. 'It's not ten-thirty yet so they'll still be open. They do good fish and chips here.'

Peter found a parking space on the steep gangway just round the corner from the Cromer branch of *Capaldi's*.

'I thought Spencer was going to rename some of the shops. He was talking at Christmas about this one being *Chips Ahoy* or some such.'

Gabby snorted. 'Oh, for goodness sake! Stupid man! I told him to stick to *Capaldi's*. People don't talk about going out to get some fish and chips; they talk about nipping out to *Capaldi's*. He's got really strong brand identity. Why would you want to change it? I know it's just local, but lots of companies would pay a fortune to have what he's got. I told him to keep them all *Capaldi's*. Nothing else makes any sense.'

'Yes, I have to say I couldn't really see the point…. If it ain't broke, don't fix it.'

'Exactly.'

They received a warm welcome from the staff in Spencer's chip shop and were each sent on their way with a huge piece of freshly cooked cod and what looked like a shovel-full of chips.

'It's a pleasant evening,' said Gabby. 'Let's go down on the prom. We can walk along a bit while we eat these.'

'Mmm. They're lovely and hot, and the fish. Mmm, delicious. It's so fresh.'

'Yes. One thing I will say for Spencer, everything is good. People know if they go to *Capaldi's* the fish is going to be fresh, the chips are newly chopped and that it's all properly cooked in good quality oil. You won't find any of these soggy messes that some places sell, old fish, sodden batter running with rancid fat, sitting about for ages after it was fried, crappy old potatoes, nasty greasy chips.'

'I had something purporting to be fish and chips in Birkenhead once. The thing that was supposed to be fish arrived as a perfect rectangle, dark brown in colour and I doubt whether it had ever swum, let alone within living memory, and the chips couldn't possibly have come from anything that grew in the ground. The whole sorry mess disintegrated almost immediately I got out of the shop, into something you might find at the bottom of a 45 gallon drum up the corner of a backstreet garage.'

'Mmm, nice.'

They walked along the promenade past the entrance to the pier. As they approached the western extremity of the prom Peter suggested they return to the car along the cliff path and through the town. As they made their way up the zigzag slope Gabby complained about her shoes and said she needed a rest. They stopped at a shelter midway up the cliff. After depositing the now cold remains of their huge fish suppers in a bin they sat side by side looking out at the lights. Gabby took Peter's arm and cuddled up to him. After a while she turned and offered her face for a kiss.

She thrust her hand inside Peter's shirt, tweaked a nipple and whispered in his ear.

'Fancy a quickie?'

Peter was somewhat taken aback.

'What, here?'

'Mmm. There's no one about. It's warm and dry.' Gabby's tone became faux wheedling. 'And I've missed you.' She plucked at a button on his shirt.

Peter was a little reticent until Gabby took his hand and placed it on her thigh.

'See,' she said, 'under my little black dress I'm wearing stockings and suspenders. New underwear, dusky pink-and silk stockings, I might add, bought at enormous expense and entirely for your benefit.'

'Well, since you put it like that....'

*

Peter stopped outside the gates of The Old Rectory.

'Are you sure you won't come in? Spencer won't be back yet. Can't offer you coffee or a nightcap?' She giggled. 'Or another... knee-trembler?'

'No, thank you very much Gab. It's a generous offer but I'm pooped.'

'OK. Well, I'll see you in the morning.' She leaned across, kissed Peter and then got out of the car. 'Goodnight, lover.'

Back at Cowper's Cottage Peter poured himself a whisky and water, thumbed through the local paper, had a quick shower and went to bed. He was woken by the doorbell. The clock said 5.45 a.m.

He lay still for a moment listening to the usual cacophony outside as doves and woodpigeons cooed and the crows and magpies renewed their dispute. His initial reaction was to ignore the caller but he knew that he wouldn't be able to. People didn't call at this hour without good reason. Reluctantly he got up, put on his dressing gown and went down. He could see a tall, dark figure through the patterned glass as he unlocked the front door. Despite the distortion his caller was instantly recognizable.

'Margaret.'

'Good morning.' She hunched her shoulders briefly and gave him the smile of a little girl seeking forgiveness. 'I hope you don't… I thought I'd just come and say hello.'

'Ah. As one does before six in the morning. Oh. Well, you'd better come on in.'

She was dressed smartly for work. Peter caught the faintest hint of *Diorisimo* as she passed him in the hall.

'Tea? Coffee?'

'No. Not for me, thank you. I've just had breakfast, but you go ahead.'

'Oh. Thanks.'

After he filled the kettle Peter excused himself and went to the bathroom. There was no sign of Margaret when he returned but he could hear movement above. He made a mug of tea and went upstairs.

'Bit prompt for a visit?' he called as he reached the top of the stairs. 'What brings you …?'

Margaret was in the centre of his bed, peeping at him over the covers. Her clothes were draped tidily over a chair. She giggled.

'Aren't you pleased to see me?'

'Well, yes. Of course.' Peter took a sip of his tea and put down the mug. He took off his dressing gown. 'Shall I join you?'

'I thought you'd never ask.' Margaret budged over to make room for him. As soon as he lay down she turned to kiss him.

Once again she placed pillows beneath her hips and wouldn't release Peter for some time after they had both climaxed.

'Oh, heavens. Is that really necessary?' Peter eventually disentangled himself and rolled off the bed. 'Aah!' He arched his back. 'I've got cramp.'

Margaret gave him a long look before replying.

'How's Gabby?'

'She's fine, thanks. Just come back from Cyprus. Been on holiday.'

He made her a cup of coffee while she dressed. When she came downstairs she was smart and very businesslike. The sexual creature of earlier had been banished. She had a couple of sips of her coffee, then picked up her handbag and went to the door. There she paused.

'She can't have children, you know.' She held Peter's gaze for a while. 'She's had it all out.' With that she left. Peter assumed she'd left her car behind the Methodist Chapel at the foot of Back Lane again.

It was still early but Peter thought that he might as well get up. As he stood in the shower with hot water coursing over his body he wondered what on earth Margaret was playing at. The obvious conclusion was that she wanted his body. She wanted him to impregnate her. But what was her interest in Gabby? Simple jealousy? As he towelled himself dry Peter wondered whether she had been spying on him, or on them. He was also a little concerned at Margaret's brittleness and the worryingly mad person that seemed to stare occasionally from somewhere deep, at the back of her eyes.

*

Peter was washing out his brushes prior to calling it a day when there was a peremptory knock and Philip stuck his head round the studio door.

'Hey-up, Toulouse. How's it hanging?'

Peter turned from the sink and grinned.

'Well, drill me and fill me, if it isn't our favourite dental cove. Haven't seen you for a while. Are you lost?'

'I think I must be, by gum.' Philip came in, closed the door and stood open-mouthed, gazing at the painting on the studio easel. 'Bloody Hell.' He looked from the painting to Peter and then back at the painting again. He noticed another painting leaning against the wall. 'Did you do those?'

'No. You were right first time, Phil. It was Toulouse. Not his usual style admittedly, but Toulouse without any doubt.'

'They're very impressive. I like that.' Philip wandered over to the easel for a closer look and then moved away, to the wall opposite. 'Need a big space for it. Is it for sale?'

'Well, eventually. Might be. It's not finished, and I really want it and the other one for the O & O show later in the year. Might make a limited edition print though. I need to look into that.'

'How much would you expect for the original?' Philip nodded at the painting.

Peter puffed out his cheeks and thrust out his lower lip while he pondered.

'I don't really know. I still have to take advice on pricing. Eight hundred maybe. Eight fifty.'

'Holy crap! I'm in the wrong business. And a print?'

'Don't know. I've never done it. Be much cheaper though.' Peter finished drying his brushes. He looked round the studio and then dried his hands.

'Of course, I might be able to do something for a friend. I'm done for today. Have you got time for a drink? Tea, coffee, wine, a beer?'

'Yes. Go on. Have you got a bottle of wine open?'

'I have, as it happens, a rather pleasing drop of that stuff that gathers in puddles round the foot of a silage heap.'

'Silage, eh? Good-oh.'

Once they had a glass of wine each Peter led the way into the conservatory.

'Busy day?'

'Yes. It's been non-stop. This is very welcome. Cheers.' Philip sipped his wine. 'Mmm, that is nice. Must have been a good year.'

'Yes. Up your pipe.'

Philip looked at Peter and shook his head. 'I've always thought that that is particularly crass, if you don't mind my saying.'

'It is. I don't. Cheers! Call me Alphonse.'

'What? I'm not sure that's much better.'

Peter laughed. 'Saw it in a book once, a children's book.'

It seemed obvious to Peter that his visitor had something to say. It didn't take long for Philip to raise it.

'We went down to Rye.' He paused. 'I think….' He paused again and savoured a sip of wine. 'I think that man is my father.'

'Ah, excellent. What does Kathy say? You'll be pleased. Did you go with Kathy? I didn't know she'd….'

'No. I went with Franz.' Philip almost swallowed the name. 'Anyway, I went to the address they'd given me but there was no one there. A neighbour told me that Mr Holt was in a nursing home in the town, The Hollies. It was no distance so I went along… and they were kind enough to let me see him.' Philip shook his head, sadly. 'He's a poor, poor thing. In a terrible state. Deaf and blind. He was badly burned and lost an arm and a leg, an ear and an eye, in the desert during the war. There's a woman visits occasionally, a Mrs Holt. She's Egyptian apparently, named Hoda, lives in Hastings. We… I went to the address they gave me for her at the home but there was no one in.'

'Hoda Holt, hey? That's a name to conjure with. Didn't Kathy get a letter from someone called Hoda? I seem to remember her saying....'

'Yes. Obviously it's the same woman, the one that nursed him in the desert. If it is, I don't know how they came to marry since he was... is, still married to mother.' Philip finished his wine. 'Anyway, I didn't get to talk to Mr Holt, for obvious reasons. There is a vicar helps out with communicating, but he wasn't there. I need to get mother down there to see him and we need to talk to the Egyptian Mrs Holt.'

'What does Kathy say?'

'Ah.' Philip grimaced. 'There lies the rub.... She doesn't want to know. She says if it is him and if he's as bad as that, and if he's married to someone else, she'd rather let sleeping dogs lie. If we go down there and it is our Dave and he has married someone else, even though he and Kathy are still married-she just doesn't want to cause any trouble. Says there must have been some good reason for it and anyway... it's been too long. What good could it possibly do? She'd rather remember him as he was.'

He stood up. 'And frankly I can see her point. But.... I'd still like to know whether he is my father.' Philip straightened his tie and organized his cuffs. 'I must be going. Thanks for the wine. Thought I'd just bring you up to date. In case you wanted to check those people out and try and find Nick.'

'Well.' Peter stood up and plumped up the cushion behind him. 'As it turns out, I too have some news. I got a letter back from that Louise Stark in California. You remember? She said Nick is still alive.'

'What? Never!' Philip stared, open-mouthed.

'Yes. He turned up apparently, out of the blue one day to see her brother in... Princes Risborough, I think she said. She's expecting him, Nick, to contact her. He apparently told her sister-in-law that he would.'

'Really. Where on earth has he been all this time?'

'It turns outs out he's been living up in Lincolnshire and working at a gas terminal. Recently anyway. I phoned to try to get in touch with him but he's just retired and-wouldn't you know it, buggered off without leaving his new address. One of the secretaries at the terminal says she sees him from time to time and she's going to give him my address when she does. So is Louise, if he goes to see her.'

*

Kathy chewed over Philip's recent discovery with Peter while he demolished a plate of steak and kidney, peas, carrots and mashed potatoes in the bar of the Lord Nelson. Peter had never seen Kathy so rattled. Normally she took things in her stride. The possibility of Dave Holt's resurrection seemed to have unnerved her more than a little.

'If it is him and he's remarried, he's a bigamist, isn't he? We were never divorced. Our marriage has never been annulled. Why didn't he come home or at least get in touch? Well, he probably couldn't. But he could end up in gaol, theoretically, at least.' Kathy pulled a face. 'Well, given his condition he probably wouldn't-but it would be bound to make trouble.' She shook her head. 'I don't want that. It sounds as though he's been through more than enough.'

'Yes.' Peter tried to scoop up the last of his gravy with his fork. 'Aren't you just a little bit curious?'

Kathy looked at him pityingly. 'Of course I am.' She paused. 'But in the end, what good would come of it?' She shook her head emphatically. 'It'll just make trouble… for everyone. Here.' Kathy passed him a spoon. 'I can't stand watching you fiddle about with that, and leave us the plate, we'll need it again.'

'Mmm, that was good.'

After his lunch Peter forced his way down the overgrown lane at the side of the pub to the cliff tops. It was some time since he'd been down to look at the sea. If somebody didn't tackle the banks and hedges before long the lane would be impassable.

The tide was in and nothing of the beach was visible. Despite the clearness of the day he wasn't able to spot a single ship. Out on the horizon a couple of gas platforms were just visible. On a crystal clear day it was possible to make out the air gap between the decks and the surface of the sea. On cue a helicopter clattered overhead, its trajectory implying a more northerly and distant destination than the platforms that Peter could see. This was the German Ocean; his mother had told him. He'd known it from geography or history at school but he'd been impressed that she too had known.

When he arrived back at the pub he found Gabby and Kathy and most of the clients from the public bar standing in the car park goggling at Gabby's new sports car. Those that were not lost in admiration seemed speechless at Spencer's folly in buying Gabby the car since her brio at the wheel was well known. Peter immediately cursed his luck since he had been foolish enough to walk from Cowper's Cottage down to the pub. There was no way that he was going to be able to return home by means other than in Gabby's new toy, with Gabby at the wheel.

Gradually the admirers withdrew and returned to the comfort of the bar.

'Well. What do you think?' Gabby fixed him with a look, hand on hip.

'It's certainly eye-catching. Isn't it like that one of what's-his-name's; we met him and the ice maiden at that pub, McKillop's?'

'Yes. It's the same model.'

'What is it, exactly?'

'It's a TVR M Turbo. Just over a year old. Only done a few miles. Oyster gold paint, metallic; and it's got a magnolia hide interior.' Gabby flicked a proprietorial hand at an imaginary speck on the aforementioned hide. 'They only made a handful.'

'What happened to the MG?'

Gabby flapped a hand dismissively. 'Oh, the clutch or something. It just stopped coming back from Cromer. Smelled as though it was on fire. And it had run out of oil or water or something and the tyres were worn out anyway. Made it skid and hit a bank a bit earlier.'

'Ah.' Peter nodded soberly and managed to suppress a snort of laughter.

'Spencer was very good about it. I will give him that. Said it wasn't my fault… and the car wasn't worth mending anyway. This is an early birthday present.'

'Ah.'

'Jump in and I'll give you a ride home.'

'Oh, it's no distance. It's hardly worth….'

'Get in.'

Peter folded himself into the low slung passenger seat as Gabby embarked on a quick guided tour of the cockpit and controls, pointing out the walnut dash and the chrome gear knob and lever. She commented on and gestured at numerous dials and switches as she started the engine, but none of these afforded Peter the least comfort.

The car barked into life. Gabby revved the engine unnecessarily hard several times and then let it settle into an even burble. She grinned at him. The exhaust seemed loud. But then, Peter realized, it would in a convertible. He grabbed his seat and held on as Gabby slewed out of the car park unnecessarily fast, scattering gravel in her wake.

'Kathy's going to be boot-faced when she sees what you've just done.'

But Gabby was leaning forward, gripping the wheel tightly, lips slightly parted and a look of exultation on her face. My God, thought Peter, she looks as though she might have an orgasm any moment. It was definitely a Mr Toad moment.

The car turned out to be as frighteningly fast as it looked. As they roared up Back Lane the sound of the exhaust clattered back at them from the cottages either side. Gabby was still accelerating as they passed George's house. It was obvious that she had no intention of stopping at Cowper's Cottage.

'We'll just go for a little spin,' she yelled as they fishtailed round the right hander at the top of Back Lane. She then bogged down in too high a gear as she tried to accelerate away.

'Haven't quite got the hang of it yet,' she shouted. 'The guy we bought it from said it took a little getting used to, but I haven't had that much of a problem so far.'

The TVR snarled, roared and screamed through the narrow lanes. Peter's fingers dug into the magnolia hide, his toes curled and as usual if Gabby was driving, his legs pedalled in a frenzy of ghostly movements at her driving excesses. Eventually they stopped at the beck, Gabby pulling off the road into a field gateway. She revved the motor one last time and then turned off the ignition.

'So, what do you think? It's brilliant, isn't it?'

'Mm, it's quite a machine.' Peter had his door open and was out with indecent haste. He rolled his eyes and puffed out his cheeks at the thought of getting back into the TVR to go home.

'Since we're here let's take a look at the beck. I've been meaning to come for a while. I thought it might make a good subject for a painting or two. There are some superb old oak trees and a really nice tumbledown bullock shed. I haven't been down here for ages.' Gabby clambered out and together they sauntered along the lane towards the five barred gate that opened into the meadows through which the beck meandered.

The beck had been popular with local children for generations. A clear, shallow stream; it issued through a sluice gate in a bank from a large pond deep within nearby woods. Several sluggish ditches that bordered the trees joined the main stream before it took a dogleg course through the picturesque meadows. A few well-mannered cows cropped the grass and drank at the stream in a natural dip in the land, beside a culvert that ran beneath the road.

The beck and the meadows were sheltered by huge thick hedgerows that had been established during Anglo-Saxon times. Occasionally the farmer turned a bull out into the field and it was always as well to check whether it was in evidence since there had been occasions when visitors had found it prudent to take to their heels.

The stream left the meadow by means of the culvert. It then took a direct course across arable land heading towards the sea a few miles away at Mundesley. It had always been considered a beauty spot and a safe place for children to play, comfortably within walking distance of the village. Like Peter, his mother, Kathy and their friends had spent a good deal of time there.

Peter was horrified when they reached the gate. The lush grassy meadows of his schooldays had gone. There was no sign of the old cattle shed. Even the ancient oak trees had been felled. It looked as though everything had been cleared and ploughed up a few years earlier. Now the entire area was shoulder-high in weeds, punctuated here and there by rusting farm implements and piles of rubbish. The remains of a silage heap stood stinking in one corner, a burned-out straw stack close beside it. Everything that had once been so attractive about the meadows was now spoiled, unsightly and derelict. Even the ancient hedges had been rooted out, presumably Peter thought, in the pursuit of agricultural optimization.

'I don't believe it.' He shook his head sadly. 'What a bloody mess. This was such a lovely place. How could they do it? It's completely ruined.'

For a while they leaned on the gate while Peter absorbed the full magnitude of what lay before them. He regaled Gabby with tales of golden days spent at the beck.

'It's funny, I suspect that on every occasion that we came down here some of us or all of us went home with wet feet, at the very least. I can remember one time I fell in full length and had to walk home soaked to the skin and frozen. No matter how nice a day it was the water was always a bit on the chilly side.'

On the way back to the car Peter paused where the culvert passed beneath the road and after a moment of indecision began to push his way through the brambles on the roadside away from the old meadows.

'What on earth are you doing?' Gabby stood in the middle of the road and goggled as Peter picked a bramble carefully off his chest.

'I just want to see whether the water cress is still there. We used to gather it. The only way to get to it though was through the culvert.'

'What? You had to go under the road to reach it?'

'Yes.'

Peter finally forced himself into a position where he could see the stream. He stood on tiptoe and craned his neck this way and that.

'There it is!' He turned to Gabby. 'Still there. I bet almost no one knows about it any more. Do you like water cress?'

'I do. I can't remember the last time I had some, apart from the odd sprig as a garnish.'

'I'll go and fetch some. It won't take many minutes.'

'You're going through the little tunnel?'

'Yes. There's still no other way. There are huge banks of brambles either side of the water cress bed and you can't get near it except by actually standing in the water.'

'Won't it be a bit chilly?'

'Oh, well. It'll only take a moment. You stay here and I'll nip through the culvert.'

Gabby shook her head and shivered at the thought.

Peter left his shoes and socks on the bank and rolled up the legs of his jeans. He gasped as he entered the water. It was painfully cold but just about bearable. He was fine until he was about to enter the mouth of the culvert. It suddenly looked awfully small and dark. He had been beneath the road many times as a child but as he approached the entrance now it dawned on him that it was going to be something of a challenge to do it again.

He stopped and crouched at the culvert entrance. The far end was clearly visible. It was no distance. He tried several times but each time he was gripped by rising fear. Finally he nerved himself for a make or break dash and he stumbled into the culvert. He hadn't taken more than a few steps into the darkness when the familiar symptoms of a panic attack washed over him. It was horribly claustrophobic in the culvert. There wasn't room for him to turn round. He flailed his arms at the walls as he realized that he was going to have to back out. The panic worsened. Then he trod on something sharp and almost fell over. He saved himself from going full length but drenched an arm and one leg of his jeans up to his waist.

With his eyes bulging and his heart pounding Peter finally staggered out of the culvert into the light. He flopped down among the weeds beside the stream. All feeling seemed to have gone from his feet. He was lying on his back shivering, with his eyes closed, trying to breathe slowly and deeply when Gabby spotted him from the road above.

'Peter! Are you all right? You're bleeding. Hang on, here I come.'

Peter could hear the sound of Gabby's tapping heels receding as she ran down to the five-barred gate. He rolled over onto one elbow and inspected himself. The knuckles on his right hand were bleeding. He must have grazed them on the bricks as he flailed about. It wasn't too bad, though. He wrapped his sodden handkerchief around his hand and tried to stand.

'What happened? Are you OK?' Gabby was beside him, helping him up.

'Oh,' Peter shook his head in irritation, 'I had another panic attack. Then I slipped and got soaked.' He gestured at his jeans. 'I'm so pissed off. I thought I was over all that.'

'Are you feeling all right now?'

'Yes, a bit better, thanks. I'm frozen though. That water is bitterly cold.'

'Come on, put on your shoes and then let's get you home and dry you off.'

Gabby put an arm around the limping Peter and helped him back to the car. She took an old travelling rug from the TVR's boot and spread it on the passenger seat.

'Wrap yourself in that. Just try not to drip everywhere.'

Peter was so cold and miserable that he paid little heed to the drive back to Cowper's Cottage. By the time they arrived he was shaking uncontrollably.

'I should take all your things off outside if I were you and then go and have a bath or a good hot shower. I'll put your clothes in the wash and make a hot drink.'

Peter was down to his underpants on the front doorstep when he became aware of something at the gate. He looked up to see Archie standing in the gateway watching them. Gabby had just got hold of his underpants and was yanking them down when his Uncle George appeared.

14. Not the norm

Margaret continued to call at Cowper's Cottage, albeit erratically and covertly. Since she often appeared long after Peter had gone to bed; he offered her a key to the front door. She refused it however, preferring to enter by the conservatory at the back of the cottage, using a key that Peter kept hidden beneath a flowerpot on the patio wall.

Infrequently they slept together until dawn. On most occasions Margaret left almost immediately after sex. She still parked her Mini behind the old Methodist Chapel and walked up Back Lane to Cowper's Cottage in the dark. The business with the key, arriving and leaving under cover of darkness, parking well away from the cottage, all smacked to Peter of oddness.

As time passed Margaret made less effort with her appearance. The stylish dresses, sexy underwear, the careful makeup and expensive perfume gave way to old sweaters, jeans and sandals. Once she arrived without the benefit of any underwear, but as Peter was prepared to admit she looked pretty good in almost anything, or nothing.

He recognized that the relationship between them had become quite bizarre. Sometimes they barely exchanged a word. Peter didn't know what to make of it and there was no one with whom he felt he could discuss things. He didn't want to bring it to Gabby's attention and Philip was rarely in evidence these days. Kathy occasionally asked about

Margaret but he tended to curtail such conversations. As close as he and Kathy were, he would have found the subject too embarrassing.

A few months earlier he had been excited at the possibility of a long-term relationship with Margaret, one which he thought eventually might even culminate in marriage. Now her behaviour could hardly be described as mainstream and Peter found himself, if not an entirely willing party, at least in a position of complicity.

One night after they'd finished making love Peter asked what she wanted from him. She'd given him a strange look as she struggled into an old, shapeless sweatshirt.

'You know very well what I want.'

She hadn't demurred when he'd said, 'a baby.' He'd tried to talk to her about what she had in mind if she did become pregnant. Where would that leave her, unable to work for some time at least, and him, as the child's father? What would she and her child want or need from him? Would he have any rights? Did they have a future together?

'Oh, let's just wait and see what happens,' was all she said.

What concerned Peter, although only rarely, was whether he was the sole partner in Margaret's quest. He had seen and heard nothing to indicate otherwise but he couldn't help but wonder. It seemed rude to ask though.

Margaret no longer voiced any interest in his relationship with Gabby. And Gabby, for her part, had never shown anything other than a perfunctory interest in Margaret. Despite a degree of disquiet about his relationship with both women Peter found that in practice they could be accommodated. Spencer scarcely entered his head and Tom Graver never had.

*

'I can't imagine why that didn't go.'

Peter was at the gallery in Kings Lynn removing the first of the two paintings that hadn't sold. He turned to find Lavinia O'Grady standing behind him with her head on one side, hand to chin. Her glasses were perched in her thick grey hair.

'Oh, hello. I didn't hear you.' Peter turned back to look at the painting. 'There was plenty of interest apparently, just no buyer.'

'You must have sold something?'

'Yes, a couple.'

'Well done. Bring that one up to Norwich. And the painting beside it-that is another of yours isn't it?'

Peter nodded.

Lavinia frowned and went over to the second painting. She put on her glasses to take a closer look at something.

'What?' Peter enquired.

'Oh, I see. That's very successful. Ah! Excuse me....'

Lavinia had caught sight of the gallery owner and hurried off.

Peter had his paintings stowed in the Granada and was on the point of getting into the car when Lavinia waved at him from the gallery door. He stopped and went over.

'Have you time for a cup of coffee?'

Peter smiled. 'A cup of coffee would be nice. Do you know somewhere?'

'There's a place just round the corner. They do some awfully good pastries too.'

They were seated side by side on a worn brown leather sofa, both with a black coffee and a Chelsea bun before them when Lavinia turned to Peter.

'So. Tell me how things are going.'

Over the next fifteen minutes she divided her attention between a huge diary, in which she made lengthy entries with a slim, gold propelling pencil, rooting about in her capacious handbag and Peter. Eventually she finished her coffee and wiped her mouth with a paper napkin. She was obviously getting ready to leave.

'When we saw you in Norwich you mentioned the autumn show…?

Lavinia was again rooting in her handbag.

'Yes. I know.' She paused for some time while she searched for something else in her bag. Eventually she pulled out yet another diary, a small one this time.

'I'll need to talk to Clem but I think we'd like to take you on.' She smiled. 'You'd have a permanent presence in O & O and we could think about something further afield. London perhaps. It would be good to enter one or two serious competitions too. What do you think?'

It was a full fifteen minutes later that she pressed a business card into his hand as they left the coffee shop.

'OK. We'll leave it like that then. Give me a call.'

*

He was passing the first of the council houses at the western end of the village when suddenly, from behind an overgrown hedge; a large figure careered out of a gate on a bicycle directly in his path, causing him to stamp on the brake pedal and swerve violently across the road.

He hadn't been going quickly since the council houses were well known as a potential hazard. They were also within a 30 limit, which had been established some years earlier after a child had been knocked over at the same spot. Fortunately there was nothing coming the other way as he screeched to a standstill. The woman hopped to an ungainly halt only a few inches in front of the Granada. She turned, took a newly lit cigarette from her mouth and glared at Peter.

'Loony!' she shouted. 'You bloody nearly killed me.'

'Oh, no.' Peter recognised the moon face despite the helmet of unfeasibly black hair. The woman was naturally ash blonde and Peter had known her all her life. Try to laugh it off, he thought. We're not dealing with the norm here.

He wound down his window and poked his head out.

'Hello, Jeannie,' he called. He cackled theatrically. 'I nearly got you that time.'

His cousin's slack mouth dropped open.

'Oh. It's you.' Jeannie bristled but her overt hostility lessened slightly, to be replaced by a look that Peter recognized all too well. It quickly ran the gamut from wounded, through self-righteousness and suspicion to low animal cunning. Finally settling once again on wounded, she was plainly irritated that she was not going to be able to give full vent to her rage and that there was really nothing in it for her.

Jeannie was George and Janice's daughter, younger sister to Kingsley and mother of several snotty-nosed kids that had apparently not all been fathered by her common-law husband Greg. She was about three years younger than Peter and they had never got on. Today she stood astride an elderly Raleigh *Pink Witch*, itself a visual feast in shocking pink, turquoise, white and rust. She was wearing a black leather bomber jacket, tight black skirt and high heeled boots, which must have made cycling some thing of a challenge. With her jet-black hair, earrings the size of dinner plates, sooty eyes and crimson lips, Peter thought she looked like something out of *Star Wars*.

'You want to be more careful.' Jeannie fixed Peter with a hard look as she dragged on her cigarette.

'And you really ought to make sure nothing's coming before you bowl out of your gate like that. If I hadn't jumped on the brakes I'd have hit you, and if something had been coming the other way….'

'Yeah, yeah, yeah.' Jeannie took another couple of quick drags on her cigarette and tossed it dismissively into the hedge. She got back on her bicycle. 'See you.'

Peter gave her a wide berth as he passed her in Church Street. Glancing in the rear-view mirror he waved in a genial fashion. Jeannie shouted something at the back of the car but Peter couldn't hear what she said. He waved again. From the ugly look that accompanied Jeannie's riposte he supposed that whatever she was shouting was less than complimentary.

He had numerous memories of Jeannie as a child, none of them pleasant. As a toddler she had spiky and unruly hair, ash blonde almost to the point of whiteness. Her nose ran interminably and she dribbled. She was loud, howled a lot and seemed always to be clutching a large, partly eaten and disintegrating sandwich. Janice favoured margarine with tomato ketchup, sugar or condensed milk as sandwich fillings for her offspring. Smeared down her front together with mucus and dribble the contents of her sandwich frequently gave Jeannie a spectacular appearance.

Like her brother, Jeannie was never a popular child. They both broke toys, tore books, lost integral pieces of this and that and invariably managed to break up any hitherto happy and peaceable little band of children that they came upon. They were both bullies. Several times Peter had heard Jeannie's ultimate threat to any female playmate that had displeased her.

'… and I'll tear your bloody dreth in any cathe, tho there.'

He had never forgotten the time when his Aunt Janice had been in hospital for a couple of weeks. It was when he was about six. Since George was then working shifts at Mundesley gasworks Kingsley and Jeannie had come to stay at Cowper's

Cottage for a few days. It had been unutterably miserable. Not only had he been forced to sleep with Kingsley but he'd had to share his toys and books with the unlovely pair.

They both slobbered and dribbled and picked their teeth and noses, wiping the copious products of their oral and rhinal investigations on anything at hand. The bedroom walls beside their pillows, the lavatory wall, the tablecloth, all of these were bad enough, but it was the sullying of his books that angered Peter most. Scarcely a page was left unmarked.

It was only minutes after they finally went home that Ellen sorted out toys to be washed. Grimacing with disgust and holding the books theatrically at arms length she took them outside and burned them. Peter had been wretched. He'd protested, despite not really wanting to keep them in the state they were in. Ellen said that she would replace them but she never did. Peter's literary tastes moved on beyond his old *Eagle* and *Rupert Bear* Annuals but he never understood how anyone could treat a book in such a fashion, particularly one that belonged to someone else.

Then there was the fire. Peter had been about nine. He had been doing homework in his bedroom one evening when he spotted a glow in the sky at the top of Back Lane, a glow that should not have been there. When he stood on his bed he could see a great column of smoke boiling up into the darkening sky, lit by what was obviously a huge fire raging below.

Before he could get downstairs to tell Ellen, the fire engine from Mundesley thundered up Back Lane. Along with numerous others drawn by the sound of the heavy vehicle and the clanging bell Peter and Ellen hurried after it. When they arrived in the field Peter was staggered by the scale of the inferno. The farmer drove up in his shooting brake and one or two of his hands arrived at the double on bicycles. Having taken in the enormity of the disaster in front of them they stood silently and resigned to one side. There was no saving any part of what had been an enormous straw stack. Such was the heat; the fire crew was unable to get anywhere near it. Like everyone else all they could do was stand and watch, shaking their heads occasionally.

A fire engine from Cromer and another from North Walsham eventually arrived, but like the Mundesley crew they were powerless. The enormous stack was alight from end to end. Driven on by a gusting north-easterly nothing could stop it. Eventually things began to die down somewhat and people began to leave. The firemen were just beginning the process of raking smouldering material away and damping down when the frightened, pale, smut-covered and tearful faces of Kingsley and Jeannie appeared out of the darkness, coming from the direction of the beck, the wrong direction entirely.

It was all hushed up, but it came out eventually. Kingsley had stolen some of his mother's cigarettes from home and he had been sitting at the foot of the stack smoking. Jeannie had been playing with matches, quite deliberately holding a flame to the side of the stack. She'd done it several times and successfully smothered the flames before things got out of hand. On the next occasion, however, fanned by the strengthening wind, the tiny flame had raced up the side of the stack and before they could react there was a column of fire reaching the very top. They could do nothing and had been forced to run. Howling and gibbering they had sought refuge in the pitch black of the railway cutting, tucked up beneath the bridge.

It was Kingsley that cracked. He led his sister back to the smoking remains and on seeing the crowd, the police sergeant and not one, but three fire engines promptly spilled the beans to the nearest fireman, blaming the entire thing on Jeannie. George and Janice had to fork out a considerable sum to the farmer in recompense and in order to keep the affair under wraps and out of the courts.

There had been straw stacks at the top of Back Lane as far back as Peter could remember, and they had always been something of a draw for the children of the village. The farmer always built them in the same place, in the corner of the huge field that extended from the coast road opposite the Lord Nelson, up past the gravel pit and down to the railway cutting.

When Peter was really young the stacks had been built of sheaves and the top thatched. He recalled one occasion when Kingsley had taken one of his plimsolls and hurled it up onto the thatch. Unable to reach it Peter had to fetch Ellen and the clothes prop from home in order to retrieve it.

It was with the introduction of a combine harvester and the baling of the straw that the stacks really became irresistible. With time, a little imagination and willing workers it was possible to rearrange the stacks into all kinds of castles, dens and tunnels. During the summer holidays weeks were spent on developing elaborate systems of tunnels and other constructions which almost invariably culminated eventually, after a tortuous route in a small, dark chamber. There, still sweating from their labours the juvenile builders would eventually conceal themselves in the warm, musty blackness, assuring themselves that no one would ever be able to find them.

As he drove into the yard at Cowper's Cottage Peter suddenly remembered something that he had long forgotten. He and Philip had been very young. One evening they had been sitting with Kingsley in one of the dark, sweaty little chambers that someone had constructed of bales. There in the blackness, after they'd been there some while, Kingsley had unbuttoned his trousers. He forced first Philip and then

Peter to tickle his balls. It had never occurred to Peter at the time that there was anything untoward about this. He hadn't wanted to do it, he couldn't see the point, but at the age of five or however old he had been there was often quite a lot that he didn't understand. It had been Philip that had gone home and told Kathy. She had gone off like a rocket. After an urgent visit to Cowper's Cottage to establish the veracity of what Philip had told her she and Ellen had gone round to face George, Janice and Kingsley.

From the initial shouts of disbelief it was clear that George and Janice didn't believe the visitors. However it took them only a moment to browbeat Kingsley into a confession.

Having both been left in no doubt of the enormity of Kingsley's misdeeds, Peter and Philip hugged themselves with delight at the raised voices and ultimately the howls of pain that emanated from a couple of doors down. Janice obviously got in a few quick slaps before George dragged their son out into the shed and thrashed him with his belt. It made a welcome change to hear the bullying Kingsley getting a deserved comeuppance.

Something else occurred to Peter as he let himself into the cottage. He'd been at the grammar school. One of his classmates asked him if he was related to Jeannie Fincham. When he admitted as much he was treated to a more than fulsome narrative of what a good sport Jeannie was.

'She's often down there at Gold Park, with what's her name, you know. They'll both let you play with their tits and give you feel. She'll play with your dick too. Round the back of the pavilion. Blast, she's a good sport. I bet she wouldn't mind letting you have a go, even if you are family. Ask Mick and Decker, they're always down there with her.'

It turned out that Mick and Decker and most of the teenage males in Mundesley were agreed that Jeannie was a good sport. The thought of touching any part of Jeannie had made Peter's skin crawl.

*

The body of the wren lay on the top step leading from the patio down into the garden. Like the woodpecker it had been decapitated. As he picked up the tiny body Peter wondered at how quickly the lustre left the plumage once life was extinct. He shook his head sorrowfully as he wrapped up the remains and placed it carefully in the bin.

'One of these days… soon,' he muttered.

*

'Damn!'

Spencer Manfredi was late. He'd reached the bend just past the church when he realized that he'd left his cigars at home. In his mind's eye he could see them on the corner of the kitchen table, along with a box of new business cards and a neatly folded handkerchief. He'd also left Gabby's coat draped over the back of a kitchen chair. He was supposed to be dropping it off at the dry cleaners. He was on the point of returning home when the Lord Nelson came into view. Kathy wouldn't have his brand but she'd have some *Hamlet* to tide him over until he reached Great Yarmouth. Gabby wouldn't be pleased about the coat but it would just have to wait.

He was clambering out of the Mercedes in the pub car park when someone hailed him.

'Mr Man Friday.'

Spencer looked around in irritation. There was only one person that addressed him in that manner. He spotted Kingsley a few cars over, opening the door of his Rover.

'All right?' Spencer nodded and headed for the public bar. He and Kingsley had nothing in common and despite no encouragement whatever on Spencer's part Kingsley continued to labour under the misapprehension that they did.

'How are you keeping? How's business?' Kingsley called after him.

'OK. Thanks.' Spencer half-turned, gave a brief wave and continued on his way.

'And er… Mrs Man Friday? Is she OK too?'

'She's fine.' Spencer called. 'Thanks.' He gestured again.

'Sure everything's all right?'

Spencer sighed. Not for the first time it struck him that the man was like a dog with a bone. He stopped, and turned to face Kingsley.

'Yes? What?' He shook his head impatiently. 'What did you…?'

'You sure you're OK?'

Spencer fixed his protagonist with a look. He patted his pockets, seeking cigars and then remembered. A few seconds passed before he continued.

'Why wouldn't we be?' He paused briefly. 'I somehow feel sure you're going to tell me.'

'Well, if you're not interested….' Kingsley sniggered to himself and shook his head sorrowfully. He began to get into his car.

'If you've got something to say, Kingsley, just go ahead and say it.'

Now inside the car, Kingsley wound down his window. He beckoned Spencer over. It was only when Spencer was close beside the car and bending over the window that Kingsley continued, in a whisper.

'What it is, old mate, is this. We've noticed that Mrs Man Friday is spending an awful lot of time with that arty-farty twat at the top of Back Lane. They do seem a bit close, if you get my meaning.'

Kingsley gave Spencer a knowing look and then drummed his fingers on the steering wheel. Spencer stared. Eventually he spoke.

'And this is your business... because of what, precisely?'

Kingsley shrugged, puffed out his cheeks and shook his head.

'Just trying to be helpful, old mate. A word to the wise. Don't want to make trouble but.... Don't like to see an old friend.... You know.' He shook his head again, sorrowfully and then turned the Rover's ignition key. The starter motor whinnied. The engine coughed once and promptly died. Kingsley tried again, with the same result.

Spencer continued to stare. Eventually he gave an emphatic nod, pointed an index finger at Kingsley, nodded again, winked and straightened up. He rapped his knuckles hard, twice, on the roof of the Rover.

'Thank you, Kingsley. I owe you one.' He turned towards the bar. Behind him, at the third attempt, the Rover stuttered into life.

*

It was a wet Saturday morning when Vanessa, the secretary from Personnel at *NorSeaCo* spotted Nick. She was pushing a grizzling son in a buggy, accompanied by a fractious daughter demanding money and her friend grinding on about a drink when she ran into him in Louth market. Despite the thin drizzle and the demands of the children she remembered the slip of paper in her purse. As she handed Nick the address and telephone number in Ventura she regaled him with an abbreviated account of his daughter's phone call.

'Oh. I've got these.' Nick gestured with the paper. 'But thanks. I'm off over there next week.'

'Oh, you lucky thing. I'd love to go to California. How are going? From Heathrow?

'No way. I'm getting a taxi up to Humberside, flying to Amsterdam and then non-stop to Los Angeles. I can get a bus from there.'

'You'll be staying with your daughter, then? That'll be nice.'

'Well, not right away. I'm booked into a hotel for a couple of days.' Nick wrinkled his nose and looked rueful. 'Just till I get the lie of the land. You know….'

'Oh.'

'We haven't been in touch for years.'

'You have told her that you're coming, haven't you?' Vanessa gave Nick an enquiring look. 'She is expecting you?'

Nick looked a little sheepish. 'I was going to get in touch but then… I thought I might surprise her. Not too sure of the reception.'

'Ah.' Vanessa shook her head.' I don't know, Nick. What are we going to do with you?' She turned to check on her daughter who was leaning disaffectedly against a pet shop window. The friend was nowhere to be seen. 'Where's Sophie?'

'I don't know,' the disaffected one replied.

Exasperated, Vanessa sighed and shook her head. 'I asked you both to wait. She is naughty.' She turned back to Nick. 'I'd better go. Nice to see you, Nick.'

'You too, Van. Take care.'

'Have a nice holiday. Hope it all goes well.'

It wasn't until she was back home and putting her shopping away that Vanessa realized that she hadn't mentioned the phone call from Nick's son. Nor had she remembered to get Nick's address.

*

Peter was intent on digging acrylic paint from beneath his fingernails as he walked down Back Lane on his way to the pub for his Sunday lunch. A peremptory 'beep' on a car horn behind him caused him to turn. Spencer glided up beside him in a large dark green Jaguar. He indicated that Peter should get in.

'Hi, Spencer. It's hardly worth it for just a couple of hundred yards.'

'Morning, Peter. Hop in.'

Peter settled himself into the passenger seat. The car smelled of leather, cigars and hair oil. Spencer looked over his shoulder and then powered off smoothly. 'I'm glad I spotted you. I wanted a word.'

'Oh. No Gabby this morning?'

'I haven't been back yet. I've been down at Lowestoft all morning.'

'To see a man about a fish?' Peter laughed.

'Something like that. I'm late. She'll be chafing for her gin and tonic.'

They pulled into the Lord Nelson car park and Spencer eventually stopped in a corner well away from any other cars and the pub.

'Is this a recent acquisition? I don't remember seeing it at Christmas.'

'No. I've had it for ages. Used to belong to what's-his-name… used to read the news.' Spencer turned off the ignition, fished in his jacket pocket and pulled out a packet of cigars.

'So, what…?' Peter half turned to face Spencer. 'What can I do for you?'

Spencer waited until the cigar lighter popped out and he had his cigar going to his satisfaction. He wound down his window and then turned.

'What it is, Peter….' Spencer paused, bobbed his head and peered up through the windscreen. 'That idiot cousin of yours, Kingsley, accosted me in this very car park a few days ago with the revelation that you and my wife are…. How shall we say? A bit more cosy than might be thought right and proper?' Spencer peered at Peter quizzically, a half smile playing around his lips.

Peter looked at Spencer in alarm. Spencer stared back, his expression unchanged. Peter looked away and began fiddling with the glove box. He felt trapped. He hated confrontation of any sort. There was little doubt in his mind who would come off worst if it came to anything physical. Spencer was probably not in great shape but he was a big man.

'Well… I….' Peter stopped and stared out of the window. 'I don't know where he got that… idea. Certainly Gabby's been very helpful, helping me get started. Without her knowledge and expertise….' Good Lord, he sounded like a bad advert. He tailed off.

Beside him Spencer smoked busily. They sat for a moment, the ticking of the clock in the dashboard the only sound. Spencer opened the ashtray and tapped ash. He straightened up and looked again at Peter. Eventually he gave a short laugh.

'If you could see your face…. It's OK, don't worry. I'm not about to knock seven shades of shit out of you.' He shook his head. 'I know very well what Gabby's like. She's an attractive woman, very sexy and she can be hard to refuse. I knew when I took her on what I was getting in to. She's high maintenance and she likes to go her own way.... But she's a bit of a loose cannon.'

Spencer cleared his throat and carefully tapped the ash off his cigar before continuing.

'We've got an understanding. I suppose it's what they call in the papers these days, an open marriage. Gabby does her thing; I do mine. It suits us very well. But there are rules. And one thing above all, I do insist on discretion. Now I try to keep my business to myself. Very discreet. People may think I'm playing away, but they won't know that I am, or with who, or where. It's quite separate from home and the family. I know it can be difficult with Gabby. After a drink or two she'll think nothing of lifting her skirt in the foyer of the Hotel Continental.' He shook his head again. 'But it's not my way. And I won't put up with it from Gabby.'

Peter cleared his throat, about to interject. Spencer held up his hand.

'I don't care what you and Gabby get up to, so long as you're discreet. It suits me very well if Gabby has some distraction. But you don't shit on your own doorstep. The last thing I need is some cretin like your cousin coming up to me and wondering if everything is all right because he or some other member of his stupid family has seen Gabby getting her kit off. Gabby finds it difficult so you'll have to keep it discreet for both of you.'

Spencer banged his hand on the steering wheel to emphasize the point.

'Sorry to preach, Peter, but that's the way it has to be.'

He looked at Peter and laughed. 'You look a bit shell-shocked mate. But it wasn't too bad, was it? And now, if you'll shift your skinny little arse, I'll go and fetch madam for a pre-prandial. You can get them in. Mine's a Black Label… and you can make it a double since you owe me.'

15. The Power of Hoodoo

Nick sat in one of the cane chairs in the window of his hotel room, sipping a chilled Coors and watching the traffic pound left and right along Highway 101. It went on almost round the clock, with a brief dip in activity during the early hours. The double-glazing muted the rumbling and swishing of tyres somewhat, but it was still louder than he would have liked. He supposed that one got used to it eventually, but he wasn't planning on staying long.

To his left lay Los Angeles, to the right Santa Barbara, Monterey and San Francisco. On the far side of the highway he had a clear view of the sandy beach and the Pacific Ocean. A short distance offshore a few tiny figures, rubber-suited youngsters, sat almost motionless on their surfboards. Whenever they spotted a likely wave there was a marked change in attitude as they readied themselves for the brief frenzy of activity that more often than not ended with them dumped in a whirl of upended board and flailing arms and legs in the shallows. On the beach a lone female jogged along the waterline with her dog. The horizon wasn't visible. It was shrouded in mist. There were islands out there, apparently, just a few miles offshore. He'd spotted the Channel Islands on a wall map in reception and asked about them. Linda, his waitress at breakfast, said that it was always the same at this time of the year.

'We'll wake up one morning and there they'll be, large as life and twice as nasty. Haven't been myself.'

'Don't they run boats out to the islands?'

'Oh, all the time, but I get seasick in the bath. If you haven't seen them before you'll be real surprised at how close they are. You feel you could just reach out and touch the suckers. So that was eggs over easy and you did say hash browns. Be right back. Y'all want more coffee?'

Nick had arrived the day before. He'd had a trouble free trip out to California. There'd been a minor hiccup when he arrived in Ventura and got off the bus at the wrong stop and had to walk some distance with his case to the hotel. But the Pierpont Inn was comfortable, the staff and guests were friendly and the food was good, although he'd been a little disappointed with his Alaskan king crab dinner. The flesh just didn't compare with the sweet taste of a fresh Cromer crab, which, he supposed, was what he had been expecting. He'd also been a little surprised to find the crab served with a very hot and peppery red sauce.

Despite being a little jet-lagged he'd had a successful day. In the morning he'd hired a car. He'd had some difficulty persuading the desk clerk that a small car, a compact, would be more than adequate for his purposes. In an astonishingly short time a maroon Ford Mustang was delivered to the parking lot. It had been with some trepidation that he set out driving on the right but he'd managed with only one incident, when he'd stopped to look at the map and then set off a short distance on the wrong side. Fortunately the road was clear except for a bearded biker clad in bandanna, leather waistcoat and sunglasses who had gestured at him with a grin, to move over.

It had taken Nick a while to find Louise's house. He found the general location easily enough but she and her husband lived in a condominium, in one of several seemingly almost identical developments. The property turned out to be one of a number set around a vast concrete yard. The buildings were all red tiles, ochre painted walls, brown stained timber and windows of wired and tinted glass. Almost every window appeared blank, boasting a blind of some sort, bamboo or rush seemingly *de rigueur*. The front gardens, such as they were, comprised small rectangles of thick ground cover, a modest palm tree, water sprinkler heads on stalks and cement paths and hard-standings.

Eventually he located 10981 West Kiowa. There were two things that distinguished it from its neighbours. It didn't have a basketball hoop fixed above the double garage door and there were several cars parked outside. The only other vehicle visible was the wreck of a Porsche 911, half covered with a tarpaulin, which someone was obviously renovating. Nick decided against ringing the doorbell. It looked as though Louise was entertaining.

It was mid morning, fine, dry and warm so Nick left his car in the guest parking lot and went for a walk around the neighbourhood. The residents obviously had the use of a sizeable outdoor pool but there was no one there this morning. He saw little sign of life at all apart from a girl on a bicycle and a lone dog, both of whom ignored him.

Eventually he found his way into an alley that ran along the back of the condominiums where Louise lived. Despite the high wooden fencing it wasn't difficult to locate her property. There was obviously a gathering of some sort in the garden at the rear. He could make out a number of female voices and smell coffee and cigarette smoke. Unfortunately there was no handy knothole in the fence at a comfortable height but eventually he found a crack between the boards about three feet from the ground. He was on his hands and knees, peering through the fence when a pickup truck entered the alley. Nick straightened up and after a last cast around, as though giving up on something he sought, he headed purposefully towards the oncoming pickup.

He needn't have been concerned. The vehicle belonged to the yard maintenance company and the Hispanic driver in the lime green baseball cap was too preoccupied with drinking a can of soda, fiddling with the radio and smoking a cigarette whilst driving, to give Nick a second look.

The Mustang was in the shade when he returned, so he wandered down to a *7-Eleven* he'd spotted earlier, bought coffee, a soda and a muffin. He returned to the car to eat, drink and keep an eye on No 10981.

The cars left just after noon, with the exception of an elderly VW Beetle. Some of the women were carrying bags, others books, yet others were unencumbered. It wasn't clear to Nick what their shared interest would be.

He was wondering whether to walk over and ring the bell when a woman appeared. She was of medium build and dressed in turquoise trousers and a sleeveless white top. Her fair hair was frizzy. She fired up the Beetle and after a moment set off, passing within a few feet of Nick without giving him a glance.

On the spur of the moment he started his car and he was about to set off after her when a huge green Chevrolet appeared in his rear view mirror. It rumbled past him and wallowed to a halt where the Beetle had stood. A tall, grey haired man in a short-sleeved safari suit and cowboy hat and boots appeared from within the car. He looked at his watch and then went into the house. Nick laughed. The safari suit reminded him of something his father used to say when his mother enquired what so-and-so was wearing.

'Oh, I don't know, a long-sleeved top hat and pump-handled waistcoat.' The old man never failed to give Nick a wink and crack up whenever he said it. The humour was lost on his mother.

A moment later the Beetle roared into sight. She could only have been as far as the *7-Eleven*. She parked beside the

Chevy and disappeared into the house. Once again Nick considered going over to ring the bell. Undecided he sat for a while longer. The sun had moved round a little and by now the Mustang was in its full glare. A heat haze shimmered over the concrete. The place was dead. All he could hear was the traffic in the distance on Telephone Road.

He decided to call it a day. He'd do what he should have done in the first place and phone Louise from the hotel and arrange a visit, for tomorrow hopefully.

Nick stopped downtown and sought out the White Bib restaurant. As advised, he ordered Red Snapper, followed by tapioca pudding for his lunch. It was really more than he needed, but Linda; his waitress had recommended it. The restaurant was almost empty but the food was very good. Later he stopped by the beach and wandered out on the pier. There were what appeared to be entire families of Mexicans fishing along the rails. He spent quite some time watching brown pelicans diving into the sea and coming up, their gullets misshapen with rock cod.

As he sipped the last of his beer Nick nodded to himself. It had been a very good day. Despite the frizzy hair and sunglasses and all the intervening years he had had no difficulty in recognizing the woman in the Beetle. It was undoubtedly his Louise. She had a look of Monica about her. He would phone her after dinner.

*

The last time Peter visited The Mallard pub he was seventeen. It was the afternoon of his final day at school. A number of leavers gathered there for one last hurrah before they went their separate ways. Two of his drinking friends were off to teacher training college. Three, like him were bound for university. One was due to depart the following day to the Royal Navy, and several were destined for the Norwich Union. They were all in the dark at the time about the one misguided soul who was about to set out on an ill-considered and brief career as an armed robber. All alternative choices of career were denied him shortly thereafter, for the duration of a lengthy prison sentence.

It was as Peter and Gabby were approaching North Walsham that he had an urge suddenly to see the pub again. It was somewhat off the beaten track and in view of his recent interview with Spencer he thought it might be prudent to keep something of a low profile. The chance of running across anyone they knew at The Mallard was remote.

Spencer had treated Gabby to much the same homily as he had Peter, but she didn't seem at all chastened.

'Typical bloody Spencer,' she'd said. 'Don't do as I do, do as I say. He's been shagging the arse off Mrs Hitler for years.'

'Hitler?' Peter had been astonished. 'Is that her real…?'

'No. Her name's Whittler. Yvonne Whittler, but I call her Mrs Hitler. Just to piss Spencer off. Actually, she's very nice. She's the manager at Yarmouth. But that's not the point. It was OK for him to take her with him for a few days golfing with his mates in Spain. Most of them took their wives. Not Spencer though. He took Mrs H. It's not as if the rest of them didn't know he was married. If that isn't indiscreet, I'd like to know what is.'

However, after a trip to deliver paintings to O & O and the promise of lunch out, all was tranquil. Peter had first visited the pub when he was in the Lower Sixth. The Mucky Duck, as it was known among the intelligentsia, opened all day every Wednesday, it being market day. By happy chance Peter and several others had Wednesday afternoons free, so they gathered at the pub after lunch and spent the afternoons sipping mild and bitter and playing darts and dominoes. There were often no more than one or two other patrons in those days, usually morose pig or cowmen waiting for their ride home with the farmer.

Peter squeezed the Granada into the last space but one in the car park. From the outside the pub looked reassuringly familiar. Inside, he found that the bar had changed beyond recognition. What had once been little more than a tiny, smoke-stained room with worn carpets and wobbly dark furniture had now been opened up and extended. It had been done rather tastefully and the pub was obviously a popular place.

Gabby looked around at the diners and took a menu off one of the tables.

'The food looks good. I don't want too much to eat, but I suspect they'll know how to concoct a passable G and T and a sandwich.'

Peter agreed. He fetched the gin and tonic and a pint of bitter from the bar while Gabby settled herself at a table. It was all very promising until their waitress appeared.

'Yes?'

He recognized the peremptory tone immediately, without looking up. Gabby recognized the person.

'Hello, Jeannie. How are you?'

'Oh, it's you two. What can I get you?' Jeannie put her head on one side and tapped her order pad impatiently with a cracked plastic pen.

'There i'n't no liver and bacon casserole left so there i'n't no point in asking. There's only the cheese ploughman's, no ham. The lamb's off. That shouldn't be on the menu anyway and the soup of the day is cleekie.'

'The soup is what, again.' Gabby looked puzzled.

'Cleekie.' Jeannie almost swallowed the word and looked away.

'Oh.' Gabby paused. 'Not Cock-a-leekie, by any chance?'

'Yeah.' Jeannie turned and stared at Gabby. 'What I said.'

'Of course. Thank you.'

Gabby bit her lower lip and couldn't meet Peter's eye. Eventually she settled for a toasted ham and cheese sandwich. Peter ordered a baked potato with chilli.

'I didn't know you worked here, Jeannie.'

'I don't. I'm only filling in.'

'Ah.'

Another girl brought their food. They were eating when Peter glanced up to see Jeannie at the far end of the bar deep in conversation with a man. Even from behind, Peter had no difficulty in recognising Kingsley. As he watched Jeannie nodded at them and Kingsley turned and stared. He didn't spot Peter and Gabby right away since he turned back to his sister with a frown, obviously asking 'where?'

'Don't look now but we're under observation.'

Gabby looked at Peter, who inclined his head towards the bar. Gabby sneaked a quick glance.

'Oh, joy. Isn't it just typical? Spencer will probably walk in any minute too with his bloody parents.'

With new directions Kingsley found them. On spotting Peter he leered and raised his pint glass mockingly before turning back to Jeannie who was pointedly ignoring a couple of Pakistanis, waiting to be served beside her brother.

'Excuse me.' One of the Asians waved a bank note. 'We've been waiting.' Jeannie ignored him and walked straight past to another customer along the bar.

'I say!' The Pakistani was now indignant. He kept pace with Jeannie along the bar and waved the note again. Jeannie just stared at him. Kingsley grinned and shook his head. Another woman appeared briskly from the kitchens.

Shooting Marmalade

'Can I help anyone? Yes, dear,' she said brightly to the Asian.

'Ah,' said Peter. 'Nothing changes.'

'What's that?' Gabby asked.

'Courteous, helpful, approachable-bloody racists.' Peter nodded in the direction of his cousins.

'Really?'

'Oh, yes.' Peter dabbed his mouth with his napkin. 'When I was little, about four or five, I suppose; there used to be a Sikh that came round, selling door to door. He was very tall, handsome, bearded, well-spoken, very well dressed, in a suit and turban, the lot. He had the biggest leather suitcase I've ever seen. Goodness knows how he ever carried it.'

Peter took a sip of his beer. 'I don't know where he came from, or how he arrived. No one ever saw. He just appeared periodically, lugging this enormous case. Well, as soon as he arrived in the lane, somehow everyone in almost every cottage from top to bottom, locked up, drew their curtains and sat quaking in the gloom, waiting for the dread knock on the door. Most places, no one ever answered. They just sat it out until he'd gone. I was round at Kingsley's once when the jungle drums hadn't worked and the Sikh appeared at their door. He surprised Janice as she was taking the ash pan out to throw on the garden. She squawked and threw it all over him and then chased him out of the gate with her broom.'

'Dear lord.'

'The idiot cousins waited until he was going back down the lane and then they ran after him and threw stones. Mum always bought something from him, laces or dusters, stuff like that.' Peter paused and nodded at Jeannie. 'They're still the same today. Can't stand anyone that's in any way different from them. Anyone with a black face, different clothes, that eats different food. "What do they want to be eating that old muck for?" Anyone from a different culture, they grunt and caper about, making monkey noises.'

'Oh, I know the type.' Gabby put on a silly voice. 'They all want bugger off back where they came from. We don't want their sort here.'

Peter shook his head. 'Isn't it bizarre? You'd think that the place would be heaving with black faces. But here, in this neck of the woods, you can go for months without seeing anything other than your bog-standard basic anaemic Norfolk white.'

'Let's say pale and interesting. But you're absolutely right.'

When he went to pay the bill Peter was pleased to see that Kingsley had left and Jeannie too seemed to have disappeared.

Outside the sun was shining brightly in the tiny car park. Peter was about to get into the Granada when, from the other side of the car, Gabby gasped.

'What?' Peter looked up. 'OK?'

Gabby was standing back, looking at the near side of the car.

'Someone's scratched your door.'

'What?' Peter hurried round the back of the car.

'Oh, great.'

It obviously wasn't an accident. The word 'HOODOO' had been scratched, in ill-formed capitals across the passenger door.

'Well, we don't need to rack our brains for the culprits, do we?' Gabby nodded at the Rover parked in the corner beside the wall. Kingsley and Jeannie sat side by side in the front seats, smoking and watching them intently.

Peter gave them a long stare and then walked round to get into the car.

'Aren't you going to say anything?'

'No.' Peter shook his head. 'No point.'

'Why's that?'

'Because they just deny it and say "prove it." And how do we do that?'

'Ah. Of course. You'll know them well.'

'Oh, yes.'

As they drove out of North Walsham towards the coast Peter suddenly spoke.

'Hoodoo,' he said. 'Of course.' *'I know a man…. No! No. You remind me of a man….'*

'What?'

'Listen.'

Peter began again.

'You remind me of a man,
What man?
A man of power.
What power?
The power of hoodoo.
Who do?
You do.
Do what?
… remind me of a man….'

Gabby joined in. Peter shook his head. 'He used to say it all the time, when he was a kid. It was enough to drive anyone potty.'

'You should go to the police.'

'And they'll say exactly what Kingsley will say.'

'Prove it?'

'Yep. But never mind. They'll get their comeuppance eventually. Ellen always said that sooner or later bad people get what they deserve.'

*

Peter realized suddenly that he hadn't seen Margaret for a while. When he checked he was surprised to discover that her last visit was well over three weeks earlier. The nocturnal visits had stopped. He assumed that she'd finally lost interest or gone on holiday. Or perhaps she had achieved her goal and was pregnant. It was possible, too, that she'd found someone else.

Thereafter, it crossed his mind from time to time that he ought to phone, but he kept putting it off. He was busy and he was happy. The painting was going well. He enjoyed it and his work sold. His relationship with Gabby was as much as he wanted or needed. They were a good fit, both physically and emotionally. There was no requirement for their relationship to be anything other than part time and discreet. The arrangement had Spencer's approval, at least tacitly. It suited them all.

Peter and Margaret had barely communicated in any way other than the purely physical for ages. Apart from the sexual activity that Margaret had craved there was next to nothing between them. Peter was more than adequately catered for in that department so it was easy for him not to phone. The longer the silence lasted, the less Margaret was in his thoughts.

He did, however give a good deal of thought to Kingsley. It irritated him that his cousin had, essentially, got away with criminal damage in scratching his car door. It was sheer spite and nastiness and just the latest in a sizeable backlog of injustices that had never been properly addressed. But no matter how much Peter thought about it he couldn't come up with a suitable riposte without stooping to his cousin's infantile level. As had frequently been the case in the past though, Kingsley never knew when to stop.

A few days later when Peter got into the Granada one morning he recoiled at the appalling smell. It reminded him of something that he couldn't immediately identify. Perhaps some farmer had been spreading chicken manure on the fields. He was halfway down Back Lane and winding down his window when he spotted the first of the mice in the back. Then he saw another. He was wondering how they had managed to get into the car when he felt something between his feet. He looked down as a rat scampered into the passenger footwell beside him and then beneath the seat.

'Aah! Bloody hell!' Peter stamped on the brakes and pulled over onto The Green at the bottom of Back Lane. He leaped out. Mice were bad enough, but rats; they were a different matter entirely. Peter loathed the creatures. One had jumped up onto his chest when he was cleaning out the chickens as a child. It hadn't been hard at the age of six to persuade himself that the rat had launched itself at his neck with the intention of tearing his throat out.

Peter opened all the car doors and ran along to the Lord Nelson where he borrowed a broom from a bemused Kathy. On returning to the car he found no sign of any rodents although there was plenty of evidence of their earlier presence. The seats and carpets had been chewed, the mice had begun a nest and there was no shortage of malodorous urine.

Once he was fairly sure that the rats at least had gone, Peter drove over to the Lord Nelson. After a cursory inspection of the damage herself, Kathy fetched buckets of hot water, cloths and disinfectant.

'Of course,' she said. 'Kingsley's doing some work down at the chicken farm. Those broiler houses are alive with vermin. It'd be a simple matter to catch a few and bring them up here in a sack.'

'Yes, especially if your sister's boyfriend works there. Isn't that where Greg is?'

They found one mouse, which Peter eventually coaxed out of the rear of the car.

'That should smell a little sweeter.'

'Yes. Thanks, Kathy. I don't know what I'd have done without you.'

'Well, now you can come on in and make me a cup of coffee and bring me up to date with all your news.'

'I will. And you can tell me how Phil's getting on. I haven't seen him recently.'

'Ha. I would if I could. I haven't seen or heard anything from him for weeks.'

Since it was a fine morning they took their coffees out to one of the patio tables that Kathy was trying on the tiny strip of terrace at the front of the pub. She had set up four tables beneath brightly coloured umbrellas immediately outside the lounge bar.

'Gives us a bit of a continental look, don't you think? They're in the sun almost all day.'

'Yes. They used to have tables out like this years ago, I seem to recall.'

'They did. These are the very same ones. We found them up in the top of one of the garages. I just had Bryan give them a coat of paint. Now, what are you going to do about your cousin?'

'I really don't know.' Peter shook his head dispiritedly. 'I don't understand why he feels the need to do it. He's always been like that though, a bully, provocative.'

'Well, he's just damaged your car twice. You can't let him get away with it. What did it cost to get the door re-sprayed? And now you've got holes in your seats and carpets.'

'Oh, don't.'

'Surely you can go to the police.'

'No. You and I know it was him but I can't prove it.'

'Maybe you should play him at his own game.'

'How do you mean?'

'Well, you could put sugar in his petrol tank, or loosen his wheel nuts so his wheel flies off. That would get his attention.'

'Whoa.' Peter held up his hands. 'That's illegal, not to mention dangerous. Could end up killing someone. No. I don't think I want to get involved in anything like that, thank you.'

'You could always go round and punch him on the nose.'

'Yes. I suppose.' Peter laughed.

They'd finished their coffee and were gathering up their cups when Kathy asked Peter whether he'd ever met Philip's friend Franz.

'No. I think he's only ever mentioned him once. To tell you the truth I doubt whether I could have told you the guy's name. Why, what do you think?'

'Well, that's just it,' said Kathy. 'I've never met him either. It's not really like Phil. When he was with Noel, they used to come here together often. But I've never seen hide nor hair of this Franz. And Phil's hardly ever here these days. It's not like him.'

Kathy had always struggled with her son's sexuality. She accepted it, but with reticence and she rarely mentioned it. Peter and Philip had never discussed the subject.

*

The weather had been stifling for days and everyone was praying for a thunderstorm to clear the air. Now, judging by the huge heavy indigo clouds over Cromer and the distant rumbling, one was on the way. Peter was returning from Great Yarmouth when he decided to stop off at the old army depot for a breath of air. He thought that he might even get in a short walk along the cliff tops before the storm broke.

To his considerable irritation he spotted Kingsley's car parked on the cliff top as he made his way down the winding track. He would have turned back there and then had there been anywhere to turn, but the track was narrow, deeply rutted and bordered on either side by gorse and brambles. It was too far and too difficult to back up so he was forced to go all the way down to the end of the track in order turn round.

There was no sign of life on the cliff tops. Kingsley's Rover was the only car in sight. Fishermen often parked by the depot but presumably they had spotted the impending storm, packed up and gone home. Peter stopped, got out and wandered over to the cliff edge. By now thunder was rumbling almost incessantly and he had seen forked lightning several times inland, over his left shoulder.

The beach was deserted except for the unmistakable figures of Kingsley and Archie. They were obviously heading back but seemed to be in no particular hurry despite the threatening weather. Peter watched them for a moment and then sauntered a short way along the top of the cliffs. He didn't want to go too far from the car.

It was as he was wandering back past the Rover that he saw that Kingsley had left his sunroof partially open. Peter went to the cliff edge to check on his cousin's progress and then looked at the sky. Kingsley was now out at the water's edge trying to encourage Archie into the sea. Peter shook his head. They seemed oblivious to what was fast approaching and stood no chance of getting back before the rain started. He wondered whether Kingsley had locked the car.

He hadn't. Peter reached inside the Rover and wound the sunroof closed. It was more than Kingsley deserved but if the roof remained open in what looked as though it was going to be a deluge, the car interior would be drenched. A sudden clap of thunder almost overhead made Peter start. As heavy raindrops splattered the Rover and wriggled down the windscreen he straightened up quickly, slammed the car door shut and ran. By the time he reached the Granada a squally wind had risen suddenly from nowhere and was gusting sheets of rain across the cliff tops. He made it into his car without getting too wet.

By the time he had turned the Granada and was heading for the track up to the coast road the rain was hammering down in earnest. He switched the wipers onto fast and they still couldn't clear the windscreen properly. The rear wiper did however clear the back window just enough for Peter to see, in his mirror, Kingsley's car begin to roll forward towards the cliff edge. He braked and watched, spellbound as the car gathered speed and quickly disappeared from view. Turning to peer through the rear window the last he saw of it was the upended rear wheels disappearing over the cliff.

'Bloody Hell!' he muttered.

Bemused, Peter drove on up the track towards the road. For a moment he worried that the falling car might have hit Kingsley and the dog, but he concluded that it must have fallen well beyond the point at which they would begin to climb the cliffs. He worried that Kingsley might have seen him and quickly decided to put some distance between himself and the site of the incident. He was fairly confident that no one else would have seen him near the Rover.

When he reached the main road he turned left, deciding to go and have a bar meal in a pub somewhere well away from the coast. He'd get a receipt too, so that he could wave it in Kingsley's face, should the need arise. It was as he was driving out of the storm through North Walsham that he allowed himself the first smile. Funny old world, he thought. Perhaps he should believe in hoodoo.

When he arrived home later Peter discovered that Kingsley wasn't the only one to have left things open. To his surprise and irritation when he let himself into the cottage he found Marmalade stalking through the hall. The cat paused briefly, gave him an insolent stare and then continued calmly on his way.

'Wheesht! Bugger off.' Peter waved his arms and chased the cat through the kitchen and into the conservatory, where he discovered that he'd left the conservatory window open. The cat left by the same means that he had gained entry.

It wasn't until much later that Peter discovered that Marmalade had been upstairs and had knocked over and broken Ellen's crystal vase on the landing. Actually it was an absurd and cheap piece of glassware that Peter had bought his mother for a birthday when he was about seven. She had always professed to like it and had said on many occasions that it was dearer to her than any crystal. It was with a heavy heart that Peter picked up the pieces.

16. A Plethora of Phone Calls

Nick woke with a start to catch the very end of an announcement from the flight deck. Glancing around, the inside of the 747 appeared reassuringly calm so it seemed unlikely that there had been news of impending doom. Below him something hummed for a moment and then stopped with a clunk which he felt through the soles of his feet. The air-conditioning hissed, there was a low murmur of voices to his right and a brief clatter of cutlery from the galley a few feet ahead.

He yawned, stretched and looked out of the window. Beneath the wing, spread out some 35,000 feet below them lay the most spectacular panorama that he'd ever seen. He assumed that they were somewhere just to the south of Greenland. One or two people were making their way over to the port side of the plane to stoop and peer out of the windows so it was probably the view to which the captain had been calling their attention. The early morning sunlit clouds and snow-clad peaks looked like something out of a fairy story. He shivered and yawned again, then stood up carefully and pulled on his sweater. That was one of the problems with air travel, he thought. You were never completely comfortable for many minutes.

The tiny Belgian slumped beside him stirred briefly. Somewhere over Canada the poor soul had finally succumbed to the vast amount of alcohol he had poured down his neck since leaving Los Angeles. The man had been a nervous wreck even before they left the gate. He could scarcely contain himself until the *No Smoking* signs were switched off. Thereafter he'd chain-smoked and fidgeted incessantly. He'd also popped tranquillizers and emptied the greater part of a bottle of gin with grim determination and little enjoyment. Nick was pleased to see him finally at rest, or at least comatose.

He settled back in his seat. It had been a good trip. The reunion with Louise had been nerve-racking at first but he felt that overall it had been a success and they planned to remain in touch. It hadn't all been plain sailing but he hadn't expected that. There had been tears of joy-and anger. There had been inquisitions, recriminations, moods and tantrums. But things had finally settled down and the last two weeks had been tranquil enough.

Nick had eventually screwed up sufficient courage to phone his daughter after dinner on the day that he'd been over to West Kiowa. He'd had to raid the mini-bar a couple of times before he made the call but he needn't have worried. Jerry Stark answered. The slow-talking Oklahoman's voice had the same effect on Nick as had the calm, confident and reassuring voice of the KLM pilot on the way over when they crossed the east coast and hit a bit of turbulence.

Louise had been far from calm when her husband handed her the phone and after the initial surprise and numerous exclamations she insisted on meeting Nick at his hotel for breakfast the following morning. He hadn't had the heart to disabuse her when she went into some detail about what she looked like and how he would be able to recognize her.

At his daughter's insistence he'd moved out of the hotel and gone to stay with them in the condominium. It was far more spacious than he had supposed and he had a double bedroom and bathroom to himself. Louise worked part time in the Lingerie Dept in J. C. Penney and otherwise seemed to have a busy life with Petroleum Wives and the church. She had been able to take time off though, without too much difficulty. Jerry too was owed some days. They'd manoeuvred an aluminium dinghy out of the clutter in the huge garage and gone fishing up at Lake Casitas where they'd sat together in the sun drinking beer that they'd cooled in the waters of the lake. Nick was mildly surprised to find his daughter so adept with a fishing pole.

The Starks also loved to barbecue. In the yard at the rear of the house, on the beach, in the park, beside the lake, they grilled fish and meat anywhere they could set up. There were few places that they went unaccompanied by a massive cool-box, a portable grill and a bag of charcoal.

Nick was introduced to the delights of smoking meat in the Stark's backyard. He and Jerry had spent most of one day sitting in the shade of the avocado tree, drinking beer and watching the smoker as a turkey was given the treatment. Periodically Jerry levered himself out of his lawn chair to check progress and replenish the hickory chips, the fire and the water bowl. When, after eight hours or more the turkey was placed on a platter Nick found it hard to believe that the pink meat was cooked properly. He took little convincing when it crumbled in his fingers. He'd never tasted anything quite so succulent and delicious. He couldn't recall ever seeing a smoker in the UK but he determined to see if he could buy or make himself one when he returned home.

The Starks' other great passion was speedway racing. Nick had been cajoled once or twice into accompanying Barbara and some of her friends to meetings at Boston in Lincolnshire. He'd concluded after his first visit that the outcome of most races was resolved as early as the first bend. The following laps often seemed almost irrelevant, little more than a procession. He hadn't been all that keen on going with Louise and Jerry but he found the handicap racing at the Ventura Fairground altogether more competitive and entertaining than anything he'd witnessed at Boston. It was hard to beat sitting in the warm evening sun, sucking on a cold beer and breathing in the fumes, not only of hot *Castrol R* and frying onions, but also from the numerous marijuana cigarettes being passed around quite openly among the good-natured crowd. It was all a long way removed from the cold, wet afternoons he'd spent hunched against the wickedly cold wind whipping across the Fens.

Nick stared out of the aeroplane window. The scenery below was almost impossibly beautiful. After one final look and a glance at his watch he settled back in the cramped confines of his seat as best he could and closed his eyes. Beside him the Belgian gasped, resettled himself and then began to snore.

Louise was quite the American these days. She had lost any trace of an English accent and looked and sounded a typical California gal. He'd looked for some sign of himself in her features but could see nothing but hints of her mother around the eyes and mouth.

Late one night she'd told him that she was unable to have children and they'd discovered, by curious coincidence, that Jerry couldn't father a child anyway. However, they seemed happily reconciled to their childless future. She'd twinkled at her husband and reached out to take his hand.

'We're a pair of duds, ain't we hon? But happy duds.'

Jerry had looked at her fondly and taken her proffered hand. Removing his monstrous Meerschaum pipe from his mouth, he'd cleared his throat.

'Well, you know what they say. Every cloud.... Or is it the other one? It's an ill wind… whatever. Just means more shrimp and ribs for us. I'll just have to force myself to come to terms with that, I guess.'

He'd grinned at Louise and then at Nick. It was clear that they were very close. Louise said that despite having no children of her own she was looking forward to spoiling Andrew and Stephen when they came over with Ray and Sheila.

They'd been sitting out in the backyard, again drinking beer under the avocado tree when Louise told him about Ellen and Peter. It was very late in the evening and Nick had been grateful to be able to absorb the news in the dusk, beyond the warm yellow light thrown by a couple of wall lights on the rear of the house. Even so, Louise noted his silence and his tears and Jerry had gone into the house and returned with three glasses of single malt.

Nick had been a little surprised at his emotional reaction, but in all the years that had passed since he last saw Ellen he had known that there remained, buried deep within him, a feeling that he would, possibly, one day, return and seek her out. The likelihood had always been remote. He recognized that. But it had existed. It had been there. Ellen's death, however, now ensured irrevocably that it was no longer possible. News of Ellen's death left a void. It would take some getting used to.

He had also been more than a little surprised to learn that he had another son. Extraordinarily, he could remember Peter quite clearly. The first time he clapped eyes on him was when the lad opened the door at Cowper's Cottage that day in 1953. Then he'd run across him and Kathy's boy again by the Lord Nelson. Nick thought that he had some vague recollection that Peter had reminded him of someone at the time.

He couldn't understand why Ellen hadn't told him about Peter, that very day. It was a long time ago but he was almost certain that he'd asked about Peter's father. He couldn't remember what Ellen had said. She'd certainly had the time and the opportunity to tell him as they sat talking beside the fire. Perhaps Peter would be able to shed some light on it.

Louise had shown him the letters from Ellen and Peter. She had even made him photocopies. Nick suddenly wanted to reread them-for the umpteenth time, but they were in his bag in the overhead locker and he didn't want to disturb the sleeping Belgian.

He would definitely be going down to Norfolk though, and in the not-too-distant future. It was with this thought in mind, high above the frozen landscape below, that he dozed off again.

*

Peter was waiting impatiently for a gap in the traffic so he could cross the road. He'd already made two unsuccessful forays when an urgent beeping on a car horn caught his attention. Unlike the last horn though, which had been occasioned by one of his ill-considered advances, this one was neither belligerent nor hostile. It was intended to attract attention. Like the others on the pavement outside Cromer church Peter cast around but didn't at first recognize any vehicle. As the traffic continued to grind past he spotted the red Mini through the exhaust fumes from an Eastern Counties bus.

It was Margaret. As she neared and saw that she had his attention she took both hands off the steering wheel and gave him a double thumbs-up. Her head was nodding nineteen to the dozen and she was grinning, as old Frank Clarke, the fisherman, would have said, 'from ear to lug hole.' She certainly seemed excited about something.

Once past Peter, the Mini slowed. Margaret appeared to be looking for somewhere to park. Even as he watched the little red car lurched up onto the pavement and stopped at a crazy angle. Peter stepped out into the traffic immediately, almost felling an elderly man on a moped. He made it across the road without further mishap and quickly ducked into Woolworth's. There was little doubt in his mind exactly what lay behind Margaret's triumphant gesturing.

If pressed Peter would have found it difficult to explain exactly why he fled. He concluded later that he simply didn't feel up to dealing with Margaret at that moment, in the busy high street. As she drove past she had looked as mad as a hatter-and now it was almost certain that she was pregnant with his child. It had always been on the cards but Peter had invariably pushed the matter to the back of his mind. He wondered what she wanted.

Back in the Granada in the car park, he broke out in a sweat as the familiar symptoms of a panic attack washed over him.

*

'You'll have heard what happened to that twat, King.' One of the darts players paused as he was about to throw and addressed Peter, standing at the bar waiting to be served. 'Your cousin.' he added unnecessarily.

'Usual please, Kathy, when you've got a minute.' Peter turned to the darts players.

'No. What's he been up to now?'

'Oh, yes. I meant to say….' Kathy laughed as she lifted down a glass.

'Well, you couldn't make it up.' The darts players snorted, grinned and shook their heads. 'He only went and left his car down by the depot. Parked it on the grass, on the slope. Silly bugger didn't put the handbrake on, did he? Car went over the cliff. In all that rain the other night.'

'Blast, boy, I wish I'd been there to see that. I'd have paid good money. I bet his face was a picture when he found it.' Another darts player returned from the lavatory and joined in the guffawing which by now was general in the bar.

'Really?' Peter felt that there was little to be gained by owning to any knowledge of the event. 'And this was in that thunderstorm, the other night?'

'Blast, he wasn't half pissed off. Not only was the car upside down on the cliffs but he had to walk all the way home in the wet, with that dopey dog of his. Pair of 'em looked like drowned rats when I passed them.'

'You didn't stop and give him a lift then, Bumble?'

'Bloody right, I didn't. I wasn't having them dripping all over the motor. No way. Serves him bloody right anyway. I still haven't forgotten what he did to my bike.'

'What did he do to your bike, Bumble?'

'When we were kids, the bastard smeared dog shit all over it while it was outside Annie's. I didn't notice at first. Got covered in it. Didn't half get wrong off the old dear when I got home. It was bloody nearly a brand new bike too. Well, new to me. Big old Humber. Got it for Christmas or a birthday. Forget which.'

'Shame about the car though. Complete right-off. Well, it would be, wouldn't it? Cliff's nearly two hundred feet high where it went over, although it didn't actually make it all the way down to the beach.'

'Yeah, well, tough titty. And he's got to move it, or pay to have it moved.'

'So what's he driving about in now?'

'He's only gone and bought Ballo's old Land Rover. That one that's sat out in his field for donkey's years.'

'I bet he had to pay through the nose to get it too, ratty as it is. Old Henry don't half drive a hard bargain.'

'Ah.' Peter turned away and studied his reflection for a moment, in the mirror behind the bar. He could discern no trace of triumph or even the hint of a smile. Kathy bustled up with a book of raffle tickets.

'Come on,' she said. 'Stump up. It's for a good cause. What are you looking so smug about?'

*

'I saw Philip when I was up in the city a couple of days ago. Wednesday.'

'Oh?'

'Yes. Late lunchtime. He was going into that pub on Riverside. By the bridge.'

'Oh, I know. The… can't remember-popular with gentlemen of a certain persuasion. Well, that would make sense, although I don't know why he would be going into a pub on a workday. He never drinks when he's working.'

'Well, he was very smart. Perhaps he had the day off.'

'He always looks smart.'

'I don't know about men of a certain what's-it, but he was with a woman. Tall, blonde, very attractive.' Gabby laughed. 'She looked a bit like a high-class hooker. Seriously though, they were very dressed. They looked as though they'd just been to a wedding or some sort of do. He didn't look as though he was going to be pulling any teeth out that afternoon.'

'Are you sure it was him?'

Gabby propped herself up on one elbow and stared at Peter.

'Of course. Not only did I recognize him but he recognized me, although he pretended that he hadn't seen me.' Gabby reached for her cigarettes, took one and lit it.

'They got out of a taxi. It was a bit stuck out in the road and there was a steady stream coming the other way. I couldn't get by. The moron behind leaned on his horn until I gave him a look. I was right behind the cab, waiting for it to move off. He helped madam out and spotted me while he was looking for change. Meanwhile she was hovering about on the pavement. Oh, that's right. I remember wondering why she felt the need for heels when she was with such a short-arse as Philip. They looked like the long and the short, with no sign of the tall. But, of course, if they'd been to a do….'

'Hmm.' Peter grunted, helped himself to Gabby's cigarette, took a drag and then handed it back. 'Well, at least he's still alive and kicking. I haven't seen him for ages and neither has his mother. She's thorough unimpressed. He did the unthinkable and missed her birthday. And Philip never forgets. Normally Goody Two-Shoes.'

They were lying side by side on the floor of the conservatory. On this occasion Peter had taken the precaution of drawing the blinds and locking the door. Gabby had arrived earlier in the evening, on her bicycle, apparently having thrown a plastic tub of leftover baked beans at Spencer. She'd missed him but the tub had emptied itself all down the back of a radiator.

'Bloody man,' she'd muttered. She hadn't gone into any details but it was clear that all was not well at The Old Rectory.

Gabby yawned, stretched and sighed. 'It's almost dark. I suppose I'd better go.'

'Couldn't you stay?' Peter wrapped his arms about her and squeezed gently.

'Umm. Nice as that sounds, I'd better not. I don't want to turn a minor skirmish into a full-scale war.'

'You could bring me breakfast in bed in the morning. We could sit side by side with our bacon and egg sandwiches….'

'With egg yolk, melting butter, fat and brown sauce dribbling down our chins into our laps. Yes. I know. Hard as it is to resist….'

'You're no fun at all, are you?'

'Sadly not. Speaking of hard… what's happened to this?'

'Never you mind. You needn't think that… aah!'

'Hmm. Now that's beginning to look a little bit more promising.'

'It most certainly does.' Peter gasped. 'I think we might just have time for a quick one.'

*

It was late when the phone rang. Peter was asleep, sprawled on the living room floor in a T-shirt, shorts and socks. Before dozing off he had been sipping a Bells and water and reading a paperback. Yawning and rubbing his face he went through to the hall. He suspected he knew who it was and wondered why it had taken so long.

'Hello?'

There was no response for a moment.

'Hello?'

'Hello, Peter.'

'Ah, Margaret. How are you?'

'I'm fine, thank you. And you?'

'Yes, OK thanks. You know. Buggering on, much as usual.'

'I wondered whether you'd seen me the other day, in Cromer?'

'Yes. Of course. I waved.'

'Oh. I… only when I stopped and got out, you'd gone.'

'Did you stop? I'm sorry. I had to get back.'

'I thought perhaps that you were avoiding me.'

'Avoiding you? Why on earth would I want to do that? Did you not see me wave?'

It was a lie. He'd legged it as fast as he could.

'Oh. No.'

'Ah, you were probably concentrating on driving. It was a bit busy. I thought you might have seen me in your mirror, though.'

'No. Sorry. I didn't.'

There was a prolonged silence.

'What…? What can I do for you, Margaret? Did you want something?'

Silence. Peter could imagine her sitting on the stairs, playing with her hair or fiddling with an earring.

'Margaret?'

'Oh, yes. No. Not really. I was just wondering how you were, having seen you the other day. Whether you had any news.'

'No, I'm afraid not. Pretty much the same old, same old. Keeping busy, you know.'

'And you?'

'What?'
'Any news? Anything to report?'
Silence.
'Margaret?'
'No. Like you really.'
'Oh. Sure there was nothing?'
'No.'

She wasn't going to tell him after all. Either that or it had been a false alarm.

*

It was a good deal later when the phone woke Peter again. Twice it rang and then stopped. He leaned over and angled the clock on his bedside chest so that he could see the time. It was 1.35 am. He sighed, turned over and dozed off again. It seemed no time at all until his eyes snapped open again at 2.20 am when he thought he heard the phone ring again, just once.

The next time it rang was just after three o'clock.

'Oh, what?' Peter sat up, passed his hand over his face then lay back and moaned. 'What do you want?'

The phone rang again, three times, before stopping. He had a splitting headache.

'Too much whisky, too many cigarettes,' he muttered. 'Too much enjoyment altogether.'

He was just contemplating going down for something for his head when the phone rang again.

'And not enough peace!' he shouted. 'Right! Enough! Enough.'

Peter lurched out of bed and stumbled down to the hall.

'Hello!' he shouted into the phone. 'Do you know what time it is?'

There was definitely someone at the other end of the line. Peter heard a gasp before the phone was put down and the line went dead. Of course, it would be Margaret again.

He went through to the kitchen, found a couple of aspirins and had a long drink of water. On the way back through the hall he decided to try Margaret's number. She picked up almost immediately.

'Hello?'

'Margaret.'

'Peter?'

'Yes. Margaret, I wondered whether you had been trying to get me. The phone's been ringing on and off in a loony fashion for what seems like hours. And it's a little late.'

'Ah. Yes. Sorry. I knew I shouldn't really.'

'Was there something that you wanted?'

'No. I'm sorry.' With that she hung up.

'Oh, God,' Peter muttered. 'Let's not play games, please. I just want to go to bed… to sleep….'

He rang back.

'Hello?'

'Margaret, don't hang up, please. What is it? What do you want to say? Do you want to tell me something?'

There followed a long silence.

'Margaret? Are you there?'

Another silence.

'Margaret. Speak to me. I can't help if I don't know….'

'I wondered how you would feel if I said I was going to be a mummy.'

There was no shilly-shallying this time. It was Peter's turn to be silent.

'Peter? Did you hear what I said?'

'Oh. Yes. I did.' Peter paused again. 'It… it just came as a bit of a shock. Three o'clock in the morning, half-asleep, stinking headache… it came as a bit of a bolt out of the blue, that's all.'

'Are you upset?'

Dear God, no! I just wish you would go away and leave me in peace.

'Ah, well. At this ten seconds I don't really know….'

'Whether your arse is punched, bored or countersunk!' Margaret shrieked at the other end of the line.

Peter sighed. 'Something like that.' He recollected how she'd cracked up when he'd used the same expression after his mother's funeral. He wondered whether Margaret too had been drinking.

He then asked one or two of what he supposed were the right sort of questions in the circumstances, was she all right, did she need anything, could he help in any way? Everything was going swimmingly until he supposed aloud that it was his child. There followed a long silence.

'Margaret?'

Eventually she spoke.

'Peter. What on earth made you think it was yours?'

'Well… I just assumed….' He paused. 'And if I'm not the father why are you phoning me at this godforsaken hour to tell me about it?'

'I thought….'

'If I'm not the father, who is?' Peter couldn't help his testiness.

'I'm…. I can't believe this,' Margaret shouted.

'Well, who is the wretched kid's father, then? If I'm not, why are you bothering me with it? Especially at this hour.' By now Peter was shouting. 'What on earth makes you think I'd give a rat's arse, anyway? If it isn't mine.'

'Oh, thank you very much!' Margaret shrieked. 'Tom! That's who. Although what business it is of yours…. Why would you think it would be anyone else? It's Tom's. My husband's.'

With that the line went dead.

'Oh. Fuckety-doo-dah!' muttered Peter. He shook his head as he replaced the phone and stumped back up to bed.

'Flipped! Absolutely bloody woofing.'

*

'For goodness sake!'

Peter reared up in bed. It was the phone again.

'I don't believe this.'

He looked at the clock. Nearly six. He counted twelve rings and the strident bell was still going. It wasn't going to stop. He staggered out of bed and down to the hall once more.

'Yes? What now?'

'Hello? Peter?' It was a male voice; obviously not Margaret this time.

'Yes. Hello? Peter Fincham. Who is this?'

After a good deal of coughing and throat-clearing and snatches of conversation at the other end of the line the voice continued.

'Sorry. Sorry about the early call, Peter. It's Spencer.'

'Oh. Yes. What…?'

'I'm up at the hospital, the N and N. It's Gabby. She's in A and E. I thought you'd want to know.'

'What's up? Is she all right?'

'She wrecked her car. She's a bit messed up, but she'll be OK.'

'What on earth happened?'

'Oh, we had a row. Yesterday evening. She slammed off out, got in the car and took off. You know what she's like. She was obviously going too fast. Hit the bank at Sidestrand. You know, at the S bends. Rolled over a couple of times. Fortunately someone came across her right after it happened. The phone box is just round the corner. They had an ambulance there very quickly. Brought her straight up here.'

'Is she badly hurt?'

'She's got a bit of concussion and some cuts and bruises. She's very sore, but they think there's nothing broken and no internal bleeding or anything like that. Made a bit of a mess of her face though. It's going to be a while before she wins any beauty contests.'

'Are they going to keep her in, do you know? Can she have visitors?'

'It looks as though she'll be in for a while. They're just about done with her in A and E. They're trying to find somewhere for her right now. I imagine she'll be able to have visitors later on.'

'Are you going to see her again... now?'

'Yes. I've just popped out for a smoke. I'll be seeing her shortly.'

'Well, give her my... regards. I'll try to get up to see her.'

'OK. Oh, Peter?'

'Yes?'

'I wouldn't drop everything, if I were you. They want her to rest. I'd try this afternoon or this evening at the earliest.'

'OK.'

*

Unable to concentrate Peter fiddled about until he eventually ruined a painting. He then spent the rest of the day clearing out his studio. In truth the painting wasn't going as well as he had hoped. He felt as though he'd lost his way a bit and the O & O Autumn Exhibition was beginning to loom large. He phoned the Norfolk & Norwich hospital a couple of times. In the early evening he was advised to try the next morning since Gabby wouldn't be up to receiving visitors until the following afternoon at the earliest.

Later he wandered down to the Lord Nelson. With the accident occurring so close, numerous people had seen Gabby's car. It was still the talk of the bar. Three regulars had come across it upside down in the road while the police and ambulance were still in attendance. Others had viewed the mangled remains of the TVR in the yard behind the garage at Overstrand. Indeed for a while during the evening of the accident some enterprising soul ran shuttle trips from the Lord Nelson to the garage to view the wreckage. There seemed to be general astonishment that anyone could have survived such a crash. However there was no surprise at all that Gabby's driving had finally caught up with her.

'Well,' someone opined, 'she was always an accident waiting to happen, wasn't she? You remember that MGB she had, it was almost round; the corners had been banged up so many times.'

'Yeah, and what about that old Citroen. The bean can. You remember it?'

'Oh, yeah. Hasn't her sister got it now? I'm sure I saw her in it recently.'

'You sure it wasn't a broomstick. I'd have thought from the look of her that would be Lady Danielle's preferred mode of transport.'

'You're right there. What the hell does she think she looks like?'

Peter tried Spencer a couple of times when he got home but nobody answered the phone. He assumed that the daughters would be staying with Spencer's sister and that Spencer himself would be tucked up somewhere down in Great Yarmouth with Mrs Hitler. He didn't like to bother the hospital again so he tried to take his mind off Gabby with the aid of the whisky bottle and an old *Carry On* film on TV.

*

'Oh, God!'

It was just like the last time, she thought. Three days of feeling lousy, the nausea, the stomach cramps and back pain so bad she almost screamed a couple of times. Then it was over. Margaret lay on her side on the bathroom floor staring dully at the pills she'd spilled earlier.

17. One of those days

The day was very much in its infancy when Peter was once again dragged unwillingly from unconsciousness. From the depths of his alcohol-induced stupor he eventually recognized the persistent rumble emanating from somewhere close at hand as a diesel engine, probably a heavy lorry. The unwelcome intrusion was accompanied by the occasional shouts and curses of coarse male voices and bangs, clanks and rattles that seemed metallic in origin. At some point someone brayed with laughter. Others joined in. Eventually after a good deal of revving and more shouting, the lorry drove away, taking the shouters and laughers with it. Peter assumed that it had been one of the trucks that visited the gravel pit at the top of Back Lane from time to time. Why it had stopped outside Cowper's Cottage he couldn't begin to imagine.

He had another pounding headache. It had been 2 a.m. by the time he finally climbed the stairs after polishing off the Bells and making a serious start on some Famous Grouse. He had also consumed several cream crackers laden with Red Leicester and more pickled onions and gherkins than was probably wise at that hour. There was an intermittent griping pain in his lower gut. His mother always kept a tin of Andrews Liver Salts in the kitchen for just such an occasion but he knew that there were none. He'd been meaning to buy some for weeks. He groaned, drained half of the glass of water beside him, turned over and drifted back to sleep.

Some time later Peter rubbed his face. He was arid of mouth, soaked in sweat and still had the unlooked-for bonus of a pounding head. Moreover his gut and bowels seemed in turmoil. He belched, quietly at first, then noisily, crawled out of bed and lumbered to the bathroom.

It quickly became obvious that it was going to be one of those days. After an explosive bowel movement that left him sore of anus and gasping he managed to poke his fingers through the lavatory paper as he cleaned himself. Then he knicked his earlobe whilst shaving and rubbed soap in his eyes in the shower.

Things failed to improve downstairs. There was no milk and he was out of aspirins. His toast burned and then disintegrated as he tried to scrape off the worse of the charred edges over the sink. He made more toast and promptly chewed the inside of his cheek and made it bleed. Inexplicably half the slice he was eating hurled itself onto the floor. He kicked at it in fury and tweaked his right hamstring.

His bowels were obviously seriously out of sorts since he then had to hobble rather urgently to the lavatory again.

Once more it was a humiliatingly messy affair. In need of the bidet he made his way upstairs to the bathroom. After cleaning himself he managed to push his toothbrush up his nose while he was brushing his teeth.

One small piece of joy occurred when he found some aspirin in the back of the bathroom cupboard. He took a couple and decided to go downstairs, phone the hospital and then sit quietly in the conservatory with a cup of coffee until, hopefully, things improved.

The phone rang before he could make his call. It was Spencer to say that Gabby had passed a reasonably comfortable night and that if he wanted to visit her he would find her in Haveringland Ward. She was due to have some dental treatment that afternoon but would appreciate a visit in the evening, if Peter could make it.

*

'Oh, for goodness sake!'

It was impossible to tell what the mess on the front doorstep had once been. Peter was on his way out to the studio and almost trod in it. He could make out mangled pieces of wet, matted fur and the bloodied remains of shredded flesh, entrails and discarded bones on the doormat. It was also clear that whatever it had once been, those parts of it that Marmalade had consumed had made an early reappearance, in the form of a pool of lumpy vomit on the tiles beside the mat and on the gravel beyond the doorstep.

'You disgusting creature.' Peter fetched the coal shovel and a bucket and set about clearing up the mess. By the time he'd finished swabbing down the quarry tiles and the mat was scrubbed and propped up against the wall to dry he was feeling decidedly seedy again.

His headache had never really gone away. Now it was back better than ever and he was still getting the occasional griping pain in his gut. He gave up any idea of painting or doing anything useful in the studio and made himself a drink of hot chocolate. He repaired with it and a couple more aspirins to the conservatory where he put his feet up and closed his eyes.

It was an urgent need for the lavatory that woke him. He stared unbelieving at his watch for a moment, then hauled himself to his feet and limped to the foot of the stairs. He'd been asleep for ages, his hamstring had seized up, and now he was going to be leaving for Norwich much later than he'd intended.

Once back downstairs he made a cheese sandwich and a mug of tea. His mother had always advocated eggs or cheese in the case of an upset stomach or bowels.

'They're binding,' she'd say.

It was as he turned the corner of the garage to open the door to get the Granada out that his day took a further dip.

'Oh, what?' Peter stared in amazement.

Parked directly in front of his garage door was the battered hulk that had, until recently, been Kingsley's pride and joy. In truth the Rover had been not so much parked as dumped. It had obviously been vandalized since Peter last saw it since it now lacked all four wheels, both nearside doors and most of the interior. Every piece of glass had been smashed and every panel was either dented, scratched or both.

Peter walked round the wreck. It was clearly immovable. There was no way that he would be able to get his car out of the garage. This would explain all the shouting, banging and rattling that had woken him early in the morning. What he now needed to have explained was why it was dumped on his property.

He had no idea when the next bus would pass or when he might get a train from Cromer to Norwich. A taxi might be possible but it would be ruinously expensive and it would take ages to arrive. Then there was the problem of getting home again.

He looked across the fronts of the cottages. There was obviously someone in a couple of doors down. He limped round and beat on the door. Janice eventually appeared.

'Oh, it's you.'

'Hello, Janice.' Despite his irritation Peter smiled at his aunt. 'Sorry to bother you, but do you know anything about Kingsley's car. It's been dumped right outside my garage and I can't get my car out. I need to go out now.'

'Well, that was Buller's what brought it. They came this morning. I don't know why they put it there. Nor what you expect me to do about it. I can't drive. You'll need to talk to Kingsley when he gets here.'

'But that's not going to be any help now, is it? Do you know where he is? Is he working locally? Can we get in touch with him?'

'He won't be back 'til late. I'm almost sure he's out near Swaffham today.'

'Oh, great. Isn't that just typical? Why's it been dumped at my house anyway? It's not mine, not my responsibility. It can't stay there.'

Janice shook her head.

'Like I say. You'll just have to wait and see King when he get home.'

Peter looked at his aunt. After a moment he shook his head.

'I know. I'll bike down to Ballo's, Henry Ball's. They've got a tractor and a truck. I'll get Henry or one of his boys to come and drag it out of the way. They can dump it up at the gravel pit. It'll only take them a few minutes.'

'You can't do that. They'll damage it.'

Peter looked at his aunt incredulously and laughed. 'Have you seen the silly thing? It's a heap of junk. It would be hard to damage it any further.'

Janice's eyes narrowed. She studied Peter for a moment. 'What do you mean?'

'Have you seen it?'

'No, I haven't. King said they were bringing it. Where is it? At yours?' With that she pushed past Peter and paddled down her path, her short, wide form an inelegant sight in a flowered pinafore and pink slippers.

'Where is it then?' She stopped beside the wreck of the Rover. 'That's not it.'

'I'm afraid it is. Look, it's got the right number plate, if little else.'

'But that can't be it.' Janice looked stunned. 'That was a lovely motor. That didn't look like….'

'I'm afraid it is. And I need my car, so it's got to be moved. I think you'll agree it would be hard to damage it any more than it already is.'

Janice stared at the wreck and then at Peter.

'You nasty little bugger. You did this. Didn't you?'

'What?' Peter was aghast.

'I bet you've just done this, out of spite. We'll have the law in you. Where have you hid the wheels? You've always had it in for Kingsley. You've been jealous of him ever since you were both little.'

Peter stared at his aunt. He shook his head. Eventually he spoke.

'Don't be so ridiculous.' With that he stalked off inside and slammed the door. Fuming, he made himself another mug of tea and tried to get a response from the Ball's smallholding on the phone. He rang for ages but there was no reply. Presumably they were all out making mud pies or whatever it was that they did in and around their ramshackle smallholding on the cliff tops. He sighed and replaced the phone.

*

Standing by the sink in the kitchen Peter stared unseeing, out into the garden. He rubbed his chin reflectively and wondered how best to proceed. The wreck had to be moved. There were other farmers who would willingly come and drag the Rover away but they would all be out somewhere. He knew very well that trying to get in touch with a farmer during daylight hours was a good trick, in the unlikely event that you could actually pull it off. They were never where people thought they were, or where they said they would be. And even if you could locate one, they were invariably on the far side of the field and in a rush to be off somewhere else.

He ground his teeth and groaned with irritation and frustration. The headache, albeit now dull, threatened to worsen and his guts still felt a little uncertain. He realized that he had absolutely no idea what to do next. It looked as though he wasn't going to be able to go to see Gabby at all.

He was on the point of turning away from the window when Marmalade appeared, stalking imperiously across the patio. The cat had obviously made his way down the side of the cottage from Back Lane and was presumably on his way into the garden.

'You nasty little beggar. You're every bit as unlovely as your stupid owners.'

Peter watched intently as the cat stopped and sniffed delicately at the tangle of honeysuckle that overhung the patio steps. Marmalade was obviously in no hurry. He eventually manoeuvred into a position that enabled him to spray copiously up the wall and over the honeysuckle roots.

'Ah! Thank you so much. No wonder it pongs out there.'

Peter glowered and muttered under his breath.

'And don't even think about crapping on my grass, matey, or you'll be getting a lead pellet in your backside. In the unlikely event that I can hit you, that is.'

Unhurried, Marmalade made his way down the steps and out of Peter's view. Several minutes passed and the cat failed to appear on the lawn below. Peter became increasingly agitated. He was on the point of running upstairs to peer down from his bedroom window when he saw the top of Marmalade's head. The cat was on the lawn.

'So. What are you up to now, you ugly so and so?'

More of Marmalade gradually came into view. He seemed captivated by something, an odour presumably, on the skeletal remains of some Honesty stalks in the border. Peter had overlooked them in his infrequent and sketchy attempts at gardening. Eventually after a last sniff Marmalade turned and reversed into the Honesty and let go more spray. He then wandered out into the middle of the lawn and was, for a moment, distracted as a pair of Collared Doves swooped over the garden. They had been heading for the apple trees. On spotting the cat they performed an urgent, but nevertheless elegant swerve and climb, presumably up onto the cottage roof.

Marmalade affected disinterest, sat down on the grass and cleaned his privates. Peter continued to watch for a while longer. The cat then lay down and made himself comfortable in the sun. He had the appearance of one in no hurry.

Reluctantly, Peter half-turned away. Then he turned back. He formed a gun with his right hand and pointed it at Marmalade. Closing one eye, he squinted along his index finger and after a moment's deliberation squeezed the imaginary trigger.

'Pow!' He was pleased with the plosive sound and reproduced it. 'Pow! Pow! Pow!' He blew on his fingers and grinned.

'Brilliant,' he muttered, 'right in the knackers. That'd make your eyes water a bit, cat, I suspect.'

The phone rang. Peter hurried through to the hall but when he picked up there was, once again, no reply.

'Oh, please. Let's not start this nonsense all over again.'

He slammed the phone down and hurried back to the kitchen window to find Marmalade stalking purposefully across the grass towards Toby's grave at the bottom of the garden.

'He's not! The little shit. Oh, yes he is.'

Peter ran through to the conservatory. He was just grabbing up the Diana and the box of pellets from the windowsill when the phone rang again. In his haste he dropped the air pistol and knocked the pellets over. They cascaded all over the sill and the floor.

'Oh, shit! Now look….'

The phone was still ringing.

'Bloody hell! I've had enough of this garbage. It's enough to make anyone demented.'

Leaving the pellets, he hurried back to the phone.

'What?' he shouted. 'Who is it? What do you want?'

All was silent at the other end, but there was obviously someone there. Peter was by now sorely irritated.

'Speak!' he shouted. 'Say something for pity's sake!'

He waited. 'Ah. Now you're really pissing me off! Bugger off and leave me alone.'

Again there was no response.

'Fine. Suit yourself.' Seething, Peter very deliberately replaced the phone and then rushed back to the conservatory.

He grabbed up the buckled box of pellets. There were still a few inside. Seeing no sign of Marmalade from the conservatory he ran through to the kitchen and peered out of the window. The cat had diverted to sniff at a bedraggled Hosta in the flower border. Peter realized he'd left the air pistol in the conservatory.

He was about to rush back for it when he remembered the shotgun upstairs beneath the bed. He paused in the hall, undecided.

'Of course,' he muttered. 'If you're going to do a job you might as well do it properly.'

Still undecided, he thought for a moment more and then turned and ran up the stairs. He stopped briefly at the landing window to check what Marmalade was up to. The cat was still entranced by the Hosta.

Peter dragged the gun case out from beneath the bed in the guestroom and popped the catches. Once again he was struck by its weight as he took the gun out of the case. He broke the weapon open and laid it on the floor while he attacked the box of cartridges. Making no impression on the excessive sticky tape which Gabby had used he dropped the parcel on the bed and went in search of something with which to cut the wrapping.

As he hurried through to the bathroom for nail scissors Peter stopped to glance again out of the landing window. The cat was still lurking about near the Hosta.

'Ah. Thinking about crapping right in the middle of it, aren't you? How like you that would be.' Peter had never liked the Hosta. It had always seemed a tedious plant but his mother had loved it and lavished much time and care on it. She'd carried on a never-ending battle with slugs or snails or whatever it was that ate it. He wasn't about to let Marmalade defecate on it with impunity.

The nail scissors were still in the same place that Ellen had kept them ever since Peter could remember. They lay in a wide shallow earthenware dish on the bathroom window ledge along with various implements for manicure, pedicure and other aspects of personal grooming. These items jostled for space in the bowl with an astounding amount and variety of articles that could only be described collectively as stuff. Peter had thought numerous times about sorting it all out but it was one of those jobs for which any normal person might be forgiven for having little enthusiasm.

Over many years Ellen had deposited in the dish buttons, safety pins of varying sizes, oddments of costume jewellery, pencil stubs, shells off the beach, paperclips, treasury tags, hair grips, keys and one of Toby's dew claws. There were screws, nails, tacks, a couple of pieces of chalk, a twist of fuse wire, lengths of fine silver necklace chain knotted inextricably to half a pearl necklace and several rubber bands in varying stages of disintegration.

In snatching up the nail scissors, in his haste Peter also caught up pieces of chain and part of a metal puzzle out of a Christmas cracker. As he turned away these items and a sizeable proportion of the contents of the bowl made to follow him. Inevitably, the bowl itself tipped and careered across the windowsill. It dropped with a clatter onto the edge of the lavatory where it shattered, depositing shards of earthenware and most of the remains of the erstwhile contents of the bowl into the water below, since Peter had, as usual, left the seat up.

'Aaaaaah!' Peter roared with frustration. 'Gordon Bloody Bennett! If the bastards don't get you going they get you coming back.' By now in something of a frenzy he disentangled the scissors and then glanced out of the window. Marmalade had frozen and was looking towards the cottage.

He had obviously heard something, either the crash of the bowl as it broke or Peter's howl of rage.

'Shit!' Peter muttered. He kept absolutely still, fearful that the cat would see him.

Eventually Marmalade looked away, distracted as another dove settled itself in one of the apple trees. Peter dashed through to the guestroom and attacked the parcel of cartridges with the nail scissors.

'Lord, love us and keep us! Why would anyone with half a brain do this?'

He groaned as he tried to chew through the parcel tape with the tiny and less than finely honed scissors. By some miracle he managed to break the parcel open without stabbing himself. His fingers were shaking as he loaded two red cartridges into the gun.

Snapping the Greener closed he hurried back to the landing window. Having exhausted his interest in the Hosta, Marmalade was again stalking across the lawn towards Toby's grave. Peter had a clear view of the garden but an apple tree partly obscured his view of Toby's grave. Also, it occurred to him belatedly that the window was extremely stiff to open. He'd be better at the bathroom window.

Back in the bathroom, crunching pearls, beads and shells underfoot Peter drew the curtain to one side. Holding his breath and taking great care, he slowly and gently opened the window. At the bottom of the garden Marmalade stepped up onto the mound that was Toby's grave. After a good deal of sniffing and general casting about he went into a crouch and began to settle himself.

'Don't do it, Marmalade' Peter whispered. 'Crapping on Toby at this moment in time could be a grave error.' He chortled quietly at his own wit. 'You could *not* live to regret it.'

Marmalade wasn't happy. He fidgeted several times and then rose from his crouched position.

'Ah. Thinking twice about it, eh?'

After more sniffing and circling Marmalade again went into a crouch and settled once more with his back towards Peter.

'I wouldn't if I were you,' Peter muttered. He brought the shotgun up, pushed the window open a little further and then very deliberately took aim. Again Marmalade fidgeted, but he remained in the crouch.

'Now would be a good time to change your mind, cat. If you walk away now, we'll say no more about it.' Peter shook his head. 'I'm going off my head, talking to myself-or the cat. Don't know which is worse.'

There was little doubt that Marmalade was now straining. Peter's finger squeezed the trigger gently.

'There's still time, matey. To reconsider. I'm only going to pull the trigger if you actually do....'

To say that Peter was wholly unprepared for what followed would have constituted a masterpiece of understatement.

*

Having no experience of shotguns in general and the Greener in particular, Peter was more than a little surprised when the gun went off. In the close confines of the bathroom the noise was deafening. Other than the curtains either side of the window, a small bathmat and some towels drying on a rail above the radiator there was little in the room to absorb sound. Almost every surface, from the emulsioned walls to the varnished floorboards and the glazed sanitary ware, was hard and bare, ideal for repelling sound.

Peter jumped in alarm. Shocked, deafened and disoriented, such was his surprise that he took an involuntary step backwards, smashing a pane in the bathroom window with the gun barrels in the process. He then trod on a small antique perfume bottle that had been dislodged from its customary place on the window ledge during his earlier difficulties with the earthenware bowl. Thus thrown off balance, he fell headfirst into the open window, jarred both elbows and losing his grip on the shotgun. Despite a despairing lunge at the unruly weapon it fell through the roof of the conservatory below and to Peter's great relief, landed on a sofa without discharging the second cartridge.

'Bloody hell!'

With the first symptoms of a panic attack beginning to wash over him Peter leaned on the window ledge and tried to take a few deep breaths. After a moment he peered out of the window. Unsurprisingly, of Marmalade there was no sign. Peter hadn't the slightest idea whether he had hit the cat or missed by a mile. Either way it was obviously unrealistic to expect the creature to be still sitting on top of Toby's grave and about to take a quiet crap.

'Aah!' Peter shook his head. He took in the mess around him and the damage he had caused. There was a diagonal crack from top to bottom in the bathroom window and at the top left corner the frame was actually coming apart. Peter stuck his head out of the window. The damage in the bathroom paled by comparison with the hole in the roof of the conservatory below.

He glanced again out at the garden trying to catch sight of Marmalade. There was certainly no dead cat to be seen and otherwise nothing seemed to be moving. He ran into the guest bedroom and found Ellen's old binoculars. Returning to the bathroom window he began sweeping back and forth in as methodical a manner as he could manage, given that his breathing was still a little fast and shallow.

There was nothing to be seen in the garden. He widened his search out into the field beyond and was on the point of giving up and going down into the garden when he thought he saw something away to the left beside the hedge that ran along the upper reaches of Back Lane. Something moved. He brought the binoculars to bear on the spot. Nothing. He swept back and forth along the hedge.

Ah! There was something.

Peter was sickened by a brief glimpse of Marmalade dragging himself along by his forelegs. His hind legs appeared immobile.

'Oh, God!'

He was going to have to go after the cat, either to rescue it, or put it out of its misery. Gathering up some cartridges he rushed downstairs to the conservatory. There he crunched through the broken glass and other debris. He noticed that there was an ugly scratch on the polished wooden stock as he picked up the shotgun but now was not the time to concern himself with that. As he slotted another cartridge into the Greener and set out down the garden it began to drizzle.

'Oi!'

Peter was halfway across the lawn when someone hailed him. He looked across the neighbouring gardens to see his uncle's potato head peering over his fence.

'Did you hear that?'

'What?'

'That bang.'

'No,' said Peter. 'What bang?'

'Sounded like a gun or something backfiring.'

'Oh. No.' Peter clamped the shotgun tightly against his body in the hope that he could keep it concealed from George.

'Rum do.' George actually scratched his head.

'Ah. Well.' Peter almost jiggled with impatience.

'Oh! Yes! Since you're…. I was going to…. What have you been… up to with our Kingsley's motor? Mother says….'

It was at this point that the light drizzle gave way to a fairly purposeful shower.

'Sorry. Got to go. Better get a jacket or something.' Peter gestured at the heavens and ran back into the cottage. He took his Barbour from the coat stand in the hall.

It was pouring by the time he set out again and he was relieved to see that there was no sign of his uncle. He had no wish to get into some fruitless exchange with George about the Rover. It would take far too long to try to get him to understand-and whether he understood or not would ultimately prove irrelevant since he would inevitably take Kingsley and Janice's side.

He rushed on down the garden and barged his way through a gap in the corner where the back fence just failed to meet the studio wall. Turning left he hurried across the newly ploughed field towards the spot where he had last seen the wounded Marmalade.

18. Eyeball to eyeball

Spencer was exhausted and not in the best of humours. He'd had little sleep, he hadn't eaten a decent meal for ages and he was awash with hospital tea and coffee. Moreover, he'd been rubbing shoulders with the sick, the barmy, the injured and the great unwashed for far too long. Spencer loathed illness, disability or incapacity of any sort and he hated hospitals. The very smell made him want to retch.

The doctors and hospital staff had been brilliant but the clients; they were something else. As Gabby was fond of saying, 'It's amazing what you see when you're out without your gun.'

It seemed to Spencer that a significant number of the people milling around at the hospital were only ninepence in the shilling and an awful lot of them were in need of a bath and a change of clothes. Some were downright rank.

He felt filthy and was desperate to get out of his clothes. A shower or a good long soak in the bath, a hot meal and a few hours in his own bed would put him right. The Lord Nelson would be his best bet. He'd eat, and then go home. A full English with lots of hot buttered toast or a roast with all the trimmings would meet the case. On balance the fry-up would be better. Kathy, Heather or the quiet cove in the back were happy enough to knock one up at any time.

He had just dropped off his parents after taking them to visit Gabby at the hospital. The sheer futility of the near fifty mile round trip irritated him. He knew very well that Gabby couldn't stand his parents but his mother had been most insistent that he take them. She had tottered into the ward ahead of him and his father waving a box of *Black Magic* above her head like a trophy, much in the manner of a cannibal brandishing a decapitated head.

'Here we are,' she'd cried. 'Fear not! We're here.'

The chocolates were distinctly tired by the time his mother handed them over. She'd been fiddling with them in her lap the entire journey. The cellophane was torn and the entire box bore rather too much evidence of greasy finger marks. And why didn't she know that Gabby never ate chocolate?

His father hadn't gone empty-handed either. He'd taken an old oilcloth shopping bag bulging with a selection of carefully chosen reading matter and a bottle of *Robinsons Barley Water*. Spencer wondered what possessed the old man to think that Gabby would be even remotely interested in his stained and dog-eared copies of *The Spy who came in from the Cold*, *The Ipcress File* and *Funeral in Berlin*. Gabby loathed anything with lemon in it and he had never seen her finish a book in all the time he'd known her. It was unlikely that she'd ever heard of Le Carré or Len Deighton.

His parents had droned at him all the way to Norwich and back. They were greatly exercised by Gabby's accident and couldn't leave it alone.

'Too fast,' his father said, shaking his head. 'You see it time and time again, these clever beggars in their big motor cars going as if they haven't got a minute to live. There's one now! Look at that!' The old man jerked forward in his seat and pointed in triumph at a red Capri that had just overtaken them. His eyes gleamed with excitement and his chin with spittle. 'Not that I'm saying Gabby is a …, of course…. I just pull over to the side, don't I, mother? On you go, I say. On you go. I'll see you later when you're wrapped round a lamp post or when you've clattered into some metal railings and come out the other side like potato chips. That's what happened that time out near Whittlesey, wasn't it, mother… or was it Guyhirn?'

Spencer had heard the litany many times and the relish with which his father talked about railings and potato chips sometimes worried him.

'Lovely new car like that too,' his mother said, 'a real beauty. It was just like something a Hollywood film star might have. You'd have thought she'd have taken a bit more care. What a waste of money that's turned out to be, Spencer. I hope you've learned your lesson. I don't know why she couldn't do with a nice little car like a Mini. Lovely little cars, they are. Plenty good enough for what she wants anyway, getting from A to B. That's all you want in the end, isn't it?'

It had been a relief to drop them off. Spencer had seen the wreckage of the TVR in the yard behind the garage. It would never take to the road again. One of the mechanics had shaken his head sorrowfully but said that Spencer would be able to buy his wife another one with the insurance.

'Yes. That would be really clever, wouldn't it? You didn't manage to top yourself the first time, Gab, why don't you have another go? There are two chances of that happening, mate. Fat and slim. She'll be lucky to get a bloody pedal-car after this.'

'Ah. You're probably right. Bloody women drivers. I wouldn't trust my wife with anything more complicated than a wheelbarrow.'

'Oh, they're not all like that. It's just that Gabby....' Spencer shrugged his shoulders and shook his head. 'She's not actually that bad a driver when she puts her mind to it, she just....' He sighed. 'I don't know....'

The mangled and muddied bodywork had sickened Spencer. He almost threw up when he picked up a shoe and something else lying among the dark smears and bloodied shards of glass in the foot-wells. It was one of Gabby's teeth.

Not that there was much between them these days, but he'd realized during the long hours at the hospital that he'd really miss Gabby if she wasn't part of his life. He had difficulty remembering the last time that they'd made love. But that wasn't everything. She'd never shared his particular predilections. Yvonne on the other hand, participated with enthusiasm and knew precisely what turned him on.... And she wasn't shy about experimenting. He grinned, clenching his buttocks and curling his toes with pleasure at the memory of their last session.

They'd been about to shut up *Capaldi's* in Great Yarmouth and go to her flat when the police called with news of Gabby's accident. He'd rushed to the hospital in Norwich. On the way, he'd found himself muttering over and over, 'Please

God, don't let her die. Please, God, don't let her be badly injured.' He had even muttered something about giving up Yvonne, and that had been a real surprise.

Gabby ran the house well and she always looked great. Or at least she did before the accident. He hoped it hadn't ruined her looks. She would be devastated. Perhaps she would leave.

No, she liked her credit card and his bank account too much to leave. He grimaced at the thought of Gabby setting up house with Peter. She would bankrupt them both inside a month. Good grief, what on earth was it going to cost him to get her teeth fixed again? It was a bit ironic since it was only just over a year that she'd finally finished a fling with that orthodontist. No, he felt that they were both happy enough the way things were. They could live together but go their separate ways. There wouldn't be any need for him to drop Yvonne.

In addition to exhaustion Spencer was also struggling somewhat with inebriation as he hurtled over the railway bridge and headed up the narrow lane towards the bend at the top of Back Lane. There was little room for error between the sides of the Mercedes and the grassy banks either side but he knew the road well. As he approached the bend he quickly drained the last dregs of whisky from his hip flask and tossed it down on the seat beside him. He'd been taking little nips since dropping off his parents. He changed down for the bend and then had to brake hard as someone rushed across the road ahead, looking neither to the right nor the left and rather too close for comfort.

'Twat!' he muttered.

It was difficult to be certain, given the smears on the windscreen and only the briefest glimpse but it looked to Spencer as though it might have been Peter crossing the road. He rather got the impression too, that he had a gun with him. This was something of a surprise, since he had gained the idea at Christmas that Peter wasn't much interested in guns or shooting.

Spencer negotiated the turn and pulled over onto the grass verge beside a mattress, a couple of crumbling cardboard boxes spilling clothes and a pile of builder's rubble, fly-tipped beneath the hedge.

'Bastards,' he muttered. 'Why would anyone with half a brain leave this here, just a stone's throw from the tip?'

He backed the car up until most of it was off the road. There was no sign of Peter through the rear window. Intrigued, he wondered what was going on. It wasn't every day you saw an armed man running across the public highway. He glanced through the windscreen at the lightening sky and turned the wipers off. The rain was now little more than a spit in the wind. As he clambered out of the car his nostrils were assailed immediately by the smell of rotting rubbish borne on the breeze from the tip.

Despite much opposition the council had turned a deep cutting, through which once ran the long-abandoned railway line, into a rubbish tip for the surrounding villages, but to date they had neglected to erect proper fencing. As a consequence the surrounding fields, hedges and trees bore much evidence of windblown paper, polythene and plastic.

Wrinkling his nose Spencer paused to light a small cigar, then turned up his collar and buttoned his jacket. Thrusting his hands deep into his pockets he set off in pursuit of whoever it was that he had seen. As he crested the roadside bank he could see the hurrying figure quite clearly although he was now some distance away. It did look like Peter. He was obviously in something of a hurry and heading for the sagging wire fence on the far side of the field. Beyond it lay the cutting and the rubbish tip.

'Odder and odder.'

As he entered the field Spencer took his cigar from his mouth and called out to Peter, but the wind was against him. He shouted again, louder, a couple of times, but to no avail. He groaned when he saw the state of the field. Wet stubble and weeds. He was going to have to take some care if he wasn't to ruin his good slip-on shoes.

*

Peter was astonished at the speed at which the wounded Marmalade was moving, and the distance that he had managed to cover. He was obviously tiring now, though. Peter kept his eyes fixed on the rabbit run through the tussocks of rough grass at the field edge where the cat had disappeared. He was breathless and sweating by the time he arrived at the rusting wire fence above the cutting.

'Bloody... hell,' he gasped. He leaned on a wobbly fencepost for a moment and then stooped to step through the wire. 'Must... stop... smoking, and drinking... and eating so... much.' He coughed and spat. 'Need... to... lose a bit.... of weight... too.'

He looked around for Marmalade.

The cutting immediately below him was about a third full of household waste and building rubbish. He could make out an old mangle lying on its side, a slew of Formica, hardboard and ply off cuts, corrugated asbestos sheets, threadbare carpets, an upturned pram and bits of bicycles amongst the general clutter and foulness. The stench was awful.

'What a bloody... mess,' he wheezed.

A movement away to his right caught his eye. A lone rat. Something moved below and to his left. It was Marmalade. Peter watched as the unhappy cat dragged himself along among the thistles, brambles and gorse bushes that had colonized the upper reaches of the side of the cutting. It was a clear enough shot but he couldn't bring himself to shoot. He continued to watch, almost mesmerized as the cat's progress became slower and slower. Eventually Marmalade stopped in a quivering crouch, beside an old cooker. His now bedraggled and wet coat stood out against the white enamel. He couldn't have been better framed for shooting if he'd tried.

It dawned on Peter that the cat was seeking somewhere to hide. If he delayed much longer the creature might gather enough strength to disappear altogether, along with his last chance of doing the only decent thing that remained in the appalling situation that he had engineered.

Hurriedly, he brought the gun up and aimed. He steadied himself and tried to calm his breathing.

'Come on, come on,' he muttered. 'No more cock-ups. For God's sake let's get it right this time… end it now.'

He held his breath and tried to concentrate but the barrels wavered about. He just could not keep them still and on target. The more he fidgeted the worse it got. Eventually he closed his eyes and pulled the trigger. When he looked the cat was still there. It had moved a little but it seemed frozen to the spot. There was no question that it was still in the land of the living. He brought the gun up again, aimed and shot quickly, but with the same result. Having ejected the used cartridges he was fumbling to reload when a voice from above and behind made him jump.

'What do you think you're up to, hotshot?'

He looked round to see Spencer's bulk framed against the thin clouds overhead.

'Oh! Spencer.'

'Did you get it?' Spencer squinted and peered rather theatrically in the general direction that Peter had aimed. 'Oh. No. I see you didn't. Never mind. Give it another one.

Don't know why you can't hit it from there. It doesn't look as though it's in any hurry. What is it, anyway, a hare?'

Peter clicked the gun closed, took aim once more and yet again managed to miss. The cat didn't move beyond flinching.

'Ha!' Spencer guffawed. 'Good grief, man. You couldn't hit a piss pot if you hung it on the barrel. Give it here,' he took a final drag on his cigar and tossed the stub aside. 'Let the maestro have a go. Show you how it's done.'

Spencer took a careful step down onto the steep embankment and immediately lost his balance, almost toppling over backwards, the smooth leather soles of his expensive slip-on shoes finding no purchase in the wet, rough grass.

'Whoa! Bloody hell, matey, that was a bit....'

He regained his balance and stood for a moment, breathing heavily. He stared hard at the shotgun in Peter's hands, a puzzled look on his face. 'That's a Greener, isn't it? I've got a... Greener, bit like that. Didn't know.... Let's have a look.'

Spencer took another step down the slope. Then another, and getting bolder, another and another. Those steps were the last over which he had full control. He slipped on the next, and as he began to topple over backwards, he flailed his arms wildly. For a fleeting moment he regained his balance. But then he overcorrected and began what quickly developed into a headlong rush down the steep side of the cutting. He was still upright, just, but falling, with his arms whirling, when his bulk collided at some speed, with Peter. The pair of them tumbled down the bank into the foulness of the rubbish tip some fifteen to twenty feet below. At some point during their fall the shotgun went off.

*

Peter was lying face down on something soft. He could turn his head, just a little, but he couldn't see, he couldn't hear properly and he could barely breathe. Trying hard not to panic, he began to take stock. He was sure he could taste blood. His head throbbed, his nose hurt abominably and his eyelids felt as though they had been stuck down with glue. He was wholly unable to breathe through his nose and his left ear hurt. It got worse if he tried to move.

There was some movement in his legs, at least from the knees down. His right arm was trapped beneath his body and his left arm felt as though it too was pinned down, beneath something heavy. Every time he gulped air he felt a sharp pain in his chest. After a moment more he began to struggle, doing his best to ignore the pain and trying to extricate himself from beneath whatever it was that pressed down on him. His chest and head hurt with every movement and it was only a few seconds until he was forced to stop.

He lay motionless again until he felt something move above him.

'Wha'?'

Turning his good ear towards the sound he became aware of a gasping, bubbling noise to his left. Whatever it was, it was close by. Exhausted by his efforts he tried to relax. The bubbling reminded him of the beck, a stream of cool, clear water, fast-flowing over a gravel bottom.

Time passed and with it came a measure of lucidity. Changing tack, after a struggle Peter managed to free his right arm and with a bit of tentative rubbing and squinting he managed to open first one eye, then the other. There was something weird about the left one but the right eye seemed to work well enough. He concluded that he must have lost consciousness, or slept, since the day was obviously several hours advanced. The sun was shining but it was low in the sky. Where he lay was in shadow.

Shooting Marmalade

He felt weak and nauseous but with an arm free he was able to lever himself up onto his elbow, inch by painful inch. His nose was still blocked and painful to the touch and his hand came away with a smear of fresh blood on it. Each breath caused the pain in his chest to sharpen to the point of making him whimper or cry out.

Slowly and painfully he contorted himself so that he could free his other arm. He had to stop several times as feeling returned to the limb. Eventually both arms were free and he was able to squirm sufficiently to look over his left shoulder to see what it was that was pinning him down.

He gave a shout of horror when he found himself eyeball to eyeball with the lifeless Spencer.

*

'Lord Nelson. Kathy speaking.'

'Hello? Kathy? Is that you?'

'Yes. This is Kathy Holt. What can I do for you?'

'It's Nick.'

'Nick?' There was a long silence. 'What? Nick…?' There was a further silence, shorter this time. 'Not Nick Nichols?'

'Yes. Nick ah…. Nick Nichols.'

'Nick that used to be in the Royal Engineers, stationed here in the war?'

'Yes. It's me. How are you?'

'Good Lord.' Kathy was stunned.

'You're probably wondering….'

'Well, you could hardly blame me if I did. Where did you spring from? We all thought you were dead long ago. Until recently, that is.'

'Well,' Nick gave a short laugh. 'It's a long story. I'll tell you all about it sometime. Listen! What I was phoning for is that I heard that Ellen had died.'

'Yes. We did wonder whether you might have turned up then, for the funeral.'

'I didn't know, Kathy. I'd have come if I'd known. I was devastated when I heard recently-in California of all places. But that's not the only reason I'm phoning. I understand that Ellen's son, Peter, is my child too. And that's another thing I didn't know either, until a little while ago.'

'Oh. Yes. Where did you…?'

'Again, it's a long story. I don't know why Ellen never said when I saw her that last time in 1953. But listen. What I wanted to know is whether you think he'd want to see me. I thought I might come down, if he's around.'

'Well, I'm sure he'd be very glad to see you. He does know that you're still alive. But I'm afraid he's not at his best at the moment. We've had a bit of… excitement here. Peter managed to get himself injured in an accident with a shotgun. Mind you the other bloke's dead.'

'What? What happened? Is he badly hurt?'

'Well, he doesn't look great but he says it looks worse than it actually is. Quite honestly he looks as though he's been hit by a bus. He's very sore, but it's not life-threatening or permanent.'

'What on earth happened?'

'Well, nobody really knows. He'd had been having a bit of a fling with this man Spencer's wife. There's one school of thought that Spencer went after him with a shotgun and slipped and somehow managed to shoot himself dead. He was drunk at the time apparently. They found his hip flask in his car. Then there are those that think he went after Peter but Peter got the better of him and shot him. There are others that think there was a struggle and yet more who say it must have been an accident. I'm one of them. I've known Peter all his life and he wouldn't hurt a fly. Anyway, the police have been swarming all over the village. It's been barmy,' she laughed, 'good for business though.'

'Oh. What does Peter say about what happened?'

'I don't think he knows. He said Spencer lost his balance. They were on the railway embankment. He lost his balance and had them both over. Mind you, there's no doubt about the gun. It was definitely Spencer's. Peter's never had a gun, hates shooting… except for some silly little air pistol he had when he was young. The police have taken it away.'

'But you think he'd be pleased to see me?'

'I honestly don't know, Nick, but I would think so. There was a time… but. You know how it is. He was pretty cut up for years when you didn't come back after that time in 1953. And he wasn't best pleased when you didn't turn up at the funeral. But if I had to guess, I'd say he'll be very glad to see you, as will I.'

'Oh, why's that?'

Kathy paused for some time before replying.

'So I can give you the almighty slap in the chops that you so richly deserve, you miserable bastard.'

*

Peter was sitting in the conservatory with a mug of cold coffee and the local newspaper before him when a battered red Citroen 2CV drove into the yard. Despite the blowing exhaust and crunching gravel he didn't hear it arrive.

There were two women in the car. Gabby sat awkwardly in the front passenger seat beside her sister, who was driving. After yanking on the handbrake and turning off the ignition Danielle took a last swig from a bottle of Coca Cola that had been wedged between her thighs. She then took a final drag on her cigarette, pulled a face at the overflowing ashtray and tossed the stub out into Peter's garden. Draining the last drops of coke from the bottle she almost threw it out too.

'Whoops,' she laughed. 'I suspect your man would have a fit.'

Gabby shook her head disbelievingly.

A little younger than her sister, Danielle was a pale, scruffy woman with long, tangled hair, dyed an unrealistic black, tied and pinned up in some complicated fashion with a piece of pink chiffon scarf. She wore huge hoop earrings and at least one ring on each finger. Her makeup was exotic in the extreme. Despite the warm weather she was clad in a worn 1960s Afghan coat in suede, embroidered with brown and pink thread and edged with goat hair. Beneath it she had on a tight purple tie-dyed T-shirt and a voluminous multicoloured skirt. Long magenta toenails protruded from a pair of worn brown sandals.

She tossed the coke bottle into the foot well behind her where it joined an already impressive jumble of discarded wrappers, receipts, cigarette packets and other rubbish. After brushing ash from her lap she got out and walked round to the passenger door.

Behind the black scarf covering her mouth Gabby wondered how on earth anyone could live like her sister. She rolled her eyes at the sea of rubbish at her feet and the filth that covered every surface of the car. Danielle's house was much the same.

Unlike her sister Gabby was stylishly dressed in an expensive leather jacket, light T-shirt and jeans, knee length fashion boots, a soft velvet hat and large sunglasses.

Danielle opened the passenger door and leaned in to undo her sister's seatbelt. After a couple of tries she managed to help Gabby out of the car. Gabby gasped with the effort of getting up from the seat.

'Sorry. You OK?'

'Oh. I think so.' Gabby spoke indistinctly and with obvious discomfort. 'I'm still bruised and stiff. There isn't anything that doesn't hurt. Thanks. Can you get my bag?'

She flinched as she straightened up. With a hand on the door and the other on the canvas roof of the car she steadied herself while Danielle retrieved her handbag. Once Gabby had the bag over her shoulder she took her sister's arm and together they walked slowly towards the cottage.

'Let's go round the back.'

'Do you want me to come in with you?' Danielle asked.

'No. I'll be OK. Thanks.'

'Are you sure?'

'Yes.'

'I don't mind. I'm not in any hurry.' Danielle smiled winsomely at Gabby, who stopped and stared at her sister.

'Look!' she said. 'Thank you for the lift. This isn't going to be easy but it needs to be just me and Peter. You know that. So let me put it this way. Fuck off!' Gabby had no intention of obliging her sister with a ringside seat.

'Oh, very nice. Very lady-like, I'm sure.' But Danielle didn't take it amiss.

Peter saw them coming and levered himself up out of his chair. He gave them a brief wave of acknowledgement through the window as he made his way to the door.

'I'm sorry. I'll see you later.' Gabby was finding her sister increasingly irritating. She'd been staying with Danielle and her husband Kelvin in their chaotic cottage since coming out of hospital. Spencer's sister was looking after the girls.

'Okay. If you're sure.'

Peter arrived at the conservatory door at the same time as his visitors.

'Hiya Peter, are you alright? Got a visitor for you.' Danielle beamed at him and then turned to her sister. Unseen by Peter she pulled a face and mouthed an exaggerated and silent 'Bloody Hell,' at Gabby.

In truth Peter was not looking his best with his face pale and stubbly and a single bloodshot eye peering out from beneath a lopsided helmet of bandages.

'I'm off then. I've got shopping to do and I'll look in on Spencer's parents, make sure they're okay.'

Peter took Gabby's arm and helped her in. He offered her a comfortable chair in the conservatory but she refused it.

'I'm better on a kitchen chair.'

Eventually Gabby was seated at the table. She kept her hat, scarf and the dark glasses on. Peter brought them both coffee and sat down opposite her. He gave her a shy smile.

'Hello, Gab. How are you?'

'Glad to see the back of the wicked witch for a few minutes.' She closed her eyes and grimaced as she shifted in her chair. 'I'm as sore as can be. What about you? How are you?'

Peter turned the corners of his mouth down. 'Feel like crap.'

'Yeah, me too.'

'I'm sorry, Gab. It's a bloody awful mess.' Peter shook his head. 'But it wasn't me.'

Gabby nodded. They stared at each other for a moment. Gabby took off the sunglasses to reveal two swollen and discoloured eyes. She suddenly snorted. Peter wasn't sure whether she was about to laugh or cry.

'Look at the state of us for God's sake. What a bloody pair, honestly. Oh, oh.' Gabby winced and then leaned forward holding her arms to her chest at the effort of trying not to laugh.

'Oh, shit, I mustn't laugh. It hurts too much.' Somewhat relieved Peter levered himself up and gave her a brief but gentle hug.

'How's your mouth? Can you manage coffee?'

Gabby pulled her scarf down to reveal her bruised and swollen mouth. She had lost several teeth and Peter could see stitches in both lips and in her chin.

'I can manage if I let it cool a bit.'

'Ah! Is that where your teeth…?'

Gabby nodded. Very gingerly she parted her lips with the tips of her fingers. 'Five. Four were knocked out and they had to take another one. I've got to have some stuff done, but I can cope.'

'Looks as though crisps or peanuts might be a bit of a challenge.'

Gabby gave a snort of resignation and began to fish in her bag for cigarettes. 'The worst thing is I can't smoke properly.'

'Can't be good for you, surely.'

Gabby narrowed her eyes and looked at Peter as though he was mad.

'Look, clever dick,' she said, 'I've just lost my husband, my car and a load of teeth. I ache all over and look like shit and I've got months of dental work ahead of me. My boyfriend's just as bad, if not worse, so don't go telling me what's not good for me. I need that like another sodding car accident.'

Gabby selected a cigarette, carefully put it in the corner of her mouth and lit it. After taking a cautious shallow drag she removed the cigarette, expelled smoke and looked up. She flicked imaginary ash from her lap and carefully smoothed her jeans over her thighs.

'So,' she continued, 'tell me. What on earth did happen?'

*

The truth of the matter was that Peter really had no idea. The last thing he remembered was the frightening sight of all eighteen stones of Spencer Manfredi bearing down on him at high speed and totally out of control. He'd tried to get out of the way, with a singular lack of success. He remembered trying to duck or turn away but he slipped on the wet grass and it was as he fell forwards that something struck him an almighty blow full in the face. It might have been the gun, knocked up by some part of the flailing Spencer that broke his nose and knocked him unconscious. Or it might have been Spencer's elbow, his knee or one of his outsize shoes, or something else entirely. They had obviously both careered down the embankment in some entangled fashion to come to rest among the rubbish below. And at some point in their ill-fated descent the gun had gone off, but by then Peter was unconscious. He had no idea whether he was still holding the gun when it fired. Whatever the fact of the matter, the muzzle was obviously somewhere beneath Spencer's chin since the discharge tore out much of his throat and removed his lower jaw.

'They said they thought he would have died instantly. Do you…?'

'I would think so.' Peter really had no idea about that either. He was a little troubled at a vague memory of the bubbling and snuffling noises that he'd heard at some point but it would serve no useful purpose to mention it.

He could remember getting up and leaving the rubbish tip. Rubbing at his face as he had staggered up, Peter had been horrified to see that he too was covered in blood, and it wasn't all from Spencer. Whatever it was that had stopped bleeding, had started again. As fast as he wiped blood away more ran down his face and dripped onto his clothes. He became increasingly aware of his eye; his ear and his scalp. He felt as though a train had hit him. Feeling tentatively at his ear he was horrified to discover that it seemed misshapen.

It had taken a real effort to look at Spencer. Peter couldn't imagine a time when he would no longer be able to recall that awful face. Spencer was clearly dead and had been for some time. Peter had taken a couple of steps up the bank but had sat down promptly as his legs buckled beneath him. Faint and nauseous he'd broken into a sweat that immediately soaked every part of him that was not already sodden with blood. He'd lain on his side on the damp bank in the darkening afternoon shuddering and retching for some time. Eventually the uncontrollable trembling stopped, only to be replaced by intermittent shudders.

Carefully avoiding looking down at Spencer's body, he'd rolled over onto his knees, crawled carefully to the top of the bank and after a few minutes rest stood up rather shakily. Somehow he managed to drag himself across the field to the bend at the top of Back Lane. It was at the roadside just in front of Spencer's car that he'd collapsed. And it was there that Andy Ball came across Peter as he was on his way home from Northrepps where he'd been felling trees for his uncle.

Alarmed at Peter's heavily bloodstained appearance and some incoherent rambling about a shooting in the old railway cutting, Andy had driven directly to Cromer hospital where Peter was seen immediately. The excited Mr Ball then drove hotfoot to the police station to tell them what he knew. He then accompanied them to the top of the railway cutting. They'd then asked him to leave, but not before he'd spotted the ghastly sight in the rubbish tip. It was to keep him in drinks for some time in the bar of the Lord Nelson.

It wasn't until much later that evening as he lay in his hospital bed that Peter wondered suddenly what had happened to the shotgun. He couldn't recall seeing it before he left Spencer, but that was hardly surprising given the circumstances.

On the lower reaches of the old railway cutting Marmalade had dragged himself a few more inches before stopping to rest beneath some rusting corrugated iron. Peter's attempts to shoot him had been poor at best but he had succeeded in hitting the tomcat with a few pellets on each attempt. That the creature was still able to move at all bore testimony to what a tough old beggar Marmalade really was.

Throughout all of the police and ambulance activity only yards away the cat remained hidden. He was still alive, just, watchful and unseen. It wasn't until well after dark that a fox brought a sudden and welcome, end to Marmalade's suffering.

As dawn broke the following morning the local crows, rooks, magpies and gulls arrived at the tip and between their routine squabbles finally exacted some sort of avian revenge on the cadaver. By mid morning the rats and ants had also gone, fully sated. There was nothing left of Marmalade but bones.

19. More Marmalade?

It had taken Nick over three and a half hours to drive down from Lincolnshire, a full hour more than he had anticipated, even allowing for a stop for breakfast. He was not in the best of humours as he trailed slowly into the village behind a long stream of traffic, at the head of which was the ubiquitous caravan. In fact there were two, in tandem. They were obviously travelling together, unflinchingly disrupting the morning traffic and raising people's blood pressure all the way from somewhere like Langley Mill to Mundesley or wherever it was that they were heading.

It was with a good deal of anticipation earlier that he had looked out for Daisy's café near Boston, where he and Stan stopped in 1953. Unsurprisingly, it had changed. Today it was a large, gaudy establishment, three times the size of Daisy's and luxuriating in the name, *Bob's All-American Diner*. It was painted in yellow ochre with red, white and blue signage and detail. The stars and stripes of the Union flag competed with the Confederate flag, the cross of St George and the Union Jack on numerous tall white poles along the roadside. Inside, over-loud country music just about submerged the humming and burping of an impressive number of slot and pinball machines. The décor was distinctly 'yee-haw,' comprising rough-sawn timber stalls, a lengthy dining bar with chrome and blue vinyl stools and seating. Bits of old American cars and settler's wagons adorned the walls and hung from the ceiling.

However, the *Wrangler's Breakfast* had been satisfying, although not in quite the same league as the groaning platter so memorably served up by Daisy. There actually turned out to be a Bob, complete with dark glasses and ponytail and resplendent in authentic cowboy attire, but judging by his accent he may well have had his origins in Denver near Downham Market rather than in Denver, Colorado.

The rest of the trip Nick had spent fuming behind trucks, agricultural vehicles and above all, the hated caravans. He didn't mind the tractors and other agricultural machinery. It was, after all, a major farming area and farmers had to go about their business. The trucks could be irritating, especially when one sluggish leviathan made a ponderous bid to overtake another but essentially they were doing something useful. What he really couldn't tolerate were the wretched caravans. Despite the fact that he lived in a static edition of the same thing, the road going versions he considered neither necessary nor useful. He was thoroughly sick of the sight of the rear of caravans and the flat caps, straw hats and bald or grey and white heads bobbing about in the cars that dragged them.

Nick was normally fairly equable but by the time he'd got to Cromer each one he spotted was like a red rag to a bull.

'Get that piece of junk off the road. You should all be banned except between the hours of midnight and five in the morning. Or better yet four o'clock.' He'd glared and moaned, but predictably, to no avail.

As he drove slowly past the church it occurred to him that Ellen would have been buried in the churchyard. For a moment he considered pulling over but there was something close on his tail and he couldn't see anywhere to park. He thought about going to the Lord Nelson first to feel things out a little, to talk to Kathy, to try to get the lie of the land. But as the turning for Back Lane came into view he decided he couldn't stand a second more behind the caravans and began indicating to make the right turn. It was with some irritation that he noticed that the red Mini immediately behind him was doing the same, the driver bobbing about behind the wheel. She seemed in something of a hurry and he couldn't quite believe it, as he waited for traffic coming the other way, when the Mini suddenly lurched out, overtook him in the face of a stream of oncoming vehicles and shot into Back Lane.

He watched in disbelief as the Mini hurtled only some thirty yards or so up the lane before braking hard and turning right. Nick shook his head. There was no sign of the Mini as he passed the Methodist Chapel.

Back Lane seemed much busier than he remembered. There were so many cars parked on either side of the road that he was obliged to proceed in a much less cavalier fashion than the Mini. Several times he had to pull in to the side to wait for something coming the other way. One of the vehicles was a police panda. As they jostled back and forth and Nick waited, he was able to get a good look at one of the unhappy souls in the back of the police car, a woman in dark glasses and with a scarf over her nose and mouth, presumably being taken in for questioning. He and the woman were face to face for a moment and he was taken aback when suddenly she pulled down her scarf, opened her mouth wide and then stuck her tongue out at him. He'd never seen anything quite like her mouth. It looked as though a bomb had gone off in it. He was close enough to see the stitches.

It was only after the police had passed that it occurred to Nick to wonder whether Peter had also been in the car, given what Kathy had told him about a shooting. There were certainly others inside but he hadn't been able to see them clearly. Not that he would necessarily recognize Peter if he saw him.

He eventually arrived at Cowper's Cottage and pulled onto the gravel in front of the house. It too, had changed a lot, he noticed. There was no reply when he rang the bell so he looked round the back. Again, there was no sign of life. He ambled down the garden and looked out across the fields. As he turned he caught a glimpse of an upstairs curtain twitching two doors down. He wondered briefly why there was a blue tarpaulin draped untidily over the conservatory roof and a piece of plywood tacked over a window above it. Peter must be having some work done. Since he needed the lavatory Nick determined to go to the Lord Nelson. He could also do with a drink and perhaps Kathy would be able to help. It would be good to see her again despite her threat to slap him.

*

The bar was almost empty. A rep sat in a corner with a pint and a cigarette, poring over numerous papers and what looked to Nick like swatches of material. The large woman perched on a stool at the end of the bar looked up from her paper as he entered.

'Morning,' she called. She looked up at the clock over the fireplace. 'Oh, no it isn't. It's afternoon already. What can I get you?' She smiled and levered her bulk off the stool and went behind the bar.

'Hello,' Nick called. 'Pint of bitter, please. I must just nip to the….' He inclined his head towards the lavatories.

'Straight glass?'

'Thanks.'

His pint was ready and waiting for him on the bar when he returned.

'Better?' the barmaid smiled again.

'Better.' Nick replied. 'Cheers. Have one yourself.' He placed a banknote on the bar.

'Thank you. I'll have a small one with you.' She poured ginger beer into a half pint glass and topped it up with bitter.

'Good health!'

'Yes. Cheers.' Nick took a long pull at his beer. 'Mm, that's good. This place always did a good pint.'

The barmaid wrinkled her brow.

'I haven't seen you here before, have I? I don't remember your face. You're not local, are you?'

'No. I was once though. I've just driven down from Lincolnshire.'

'Oh, whereabouts? It's lovely up there, especially the Wolds. My sister lives near Louth. People always say it's flat and boring but they've obviously never been there.'

'That's true, and I'm lucky enough to live there, near Alford.'

'Oh, yes. Nice little market square.'

A young couple in long black coats entered the bar, bought a half of bitter and a shandy and went away to sit in an alcove. The barmaid returned to Nick.

'I'm Heather, by the way.'

'Nick, Nick Codling.'

'Nice to meet you.'

'Is Kathy not about?'

'No. I'm afraid not. She's gone out for the day, well for a couple of days probably.'

'Oh, that's a shame. I was hoping to see her.'

'You know her then?'

Nick explained.

'Oh, so you've known each other a long while, since the war.'

'Yes.' Nick felt that there was little need to complicate things by expanding on his extended absences.

'Well, they've gone off down to Rye. In Sussex, isn't it?'

'Oh.' Nick paused a moment and sipped his beer. 'You'll know Peter, won't you, Peter Fincham? You don't happen to know where he is at the moment.'

'No. He usually pops in for a pint at lunchtime but he hasn't been too clever lately. Hasn't been in much recently. He'll be at home, I imagine.'

'No. I've tried up at the cottage. Maybe he's just slipped out for a minute. I'll go back shortly.'

Heather wiped the pumps and fiddled with cloths and beer mats and then returned to the subject of Kathy.

'Philip, Kathy's son turned up here all in a flap last night. He's found this man down there, in Rye or somewhere down that way, who he says is his father, Dave Holt.'

'Oh. Really? I knew Dave. I thought he'd been killed. I remember it seemed a particularly cruel end with the war just over.'

'Well, so did everyone else. Then Philip got this bee in his bonnet, apparently. He got in touch with all sorts down there in London and all over really. And he found this poor beggar who he says is Dave. Badly injured, can't talk, can't see, and can't hear. Between you and me he sounds like a vegetable, poor lamb. Course, he never knew his dad. Philip, I mean. Dave had gone off to war before he was born.'

'Hmm.' Nick shook his head wonderingly.

'Anyway,' Heather continued, 'like I say, Philip turned up last night saying he'd had a phone call from the home, where the old boy is, saying he was very ill and they said if he, Phil, wanted to see him before he died he'd better get his skates on. Phil came last night and pleaded with Kathy to go with him, 'cause she always said she wouldn't go, didn't want to know. She'd rather not get into that. If it was him and he didn't come back to her, when he came back, why not? But he, Phil, that is, said she'd regret it if she didn't go. But she didn't want to, at all.'

The door opened and two elderly couples entered.

'Anyway,' Heather made towards them. 'To cut a long story short, they went off together this morning. I have to say that Kathy was looking very tight-lipped. Mind you, I don't know whether that was because of the thing about Dave Holt or because she had to sit in the back because Phil had his friend with him, Franz, I think he calls him.'

'Ah.' Nick drained his glass and gave a brief wave as he left the bar. 'Well, I'd better get on. I'll maybe see you later.'

'Yes. Well. Nice to meet you. I'll tell Kathy you were in. She'll be sorry she missed you, I expect. Nick, wasn't it?'

Nick waved in acquiescence. 'Yes. Thanks. See you.'

As he walked up Back Lane he muttered to himself that Heather was very nice, but a little of her went an awful long way.

Shooting Marmalade

'Person could end up with brain damage, talking to her for many minutes.'

*

As he turned into Cowper's Cottage he came face to face with the woman who had overtaken him in the red Mini. He had little difficulty recognizing her. She was now carrying a cardboard box which she held in front of her with some care.

'Hello,' he said. He nodded towards the cottage. 'Anyone at home?'

'No. There's no one here. I've looked round the back.'

Margaret Graver approached until she was directly in front of Nick. She peeped up at him through her lank hair, gave him a knowing smile and began untying the string that loosely bound the box. Nick noticed that the box had several ragged holes cut in the top and sides.

'Take a look at this,' she whispered. 'Look what I've brought Peter.' She peered up at him again and put her index finger to her lips.

'Shhh.'

She carefully lifted one of the flaps of the box.

'Do you think he'll like it?'

Together they peered inside.

'Isn't that just the most precious thing you've ever seen?'

'Gracious.' Nick was tempted to admit that it was.

Curled up on an old sweater in the centre of the box and fast asleep, was a tiny kitten.

'Miss Mycroft had kittens. I thought he might like this one, to cheer him up. I've been trying to think of names. Perhaps he could call him Tom.'

'Or Marmalade,' offered Nick. 'That's a pretty good name for a ginger cat.'

*

Margaret left shortly afterwards, taking the kitten with her. For the last couple of days fog had rolled in from offshore during the late afternoons. She thought it likely again and didn't want to run the risk of the kitten getting chilled.

Nick continued to wait on the patio alone until, as Margaret had predicted; the mist descended. The sun at first turned milky and then surprisingly quickly was extinguished altogether. Suddenly everything was enveloped in swirling dankness and the temperature dropped like a stone. Nick wondered idly whether they called it mist, fog or haar locally.

He sat on a while longer. It was when he began to shiver that he decided that there was little purpose in staying. The Lord Nelson was a more attractive option and he could come back later.

Heading towards the pub, he had just walked past George and Janice's gate when at the far end of Back Lane a car turned off the coast road. It approached slowly through the mist which was thickening by the minute, its fog lights making little impression in the murk. Eventually it crept past him. He paused and turned to see it halt outside Cowper's Cottage. A car door opened; there was a brief exchange of some sort, which he couldn't make out, and then someone clambered out.

There was a further short exchange followed by the slamming of the door. Nick took a few tentative steps back towards Cowper's Cottage as the car drove off slowly up Back Lane. It quickly disappeared.

He halted and called out to the indistinct figure at the roadside. 'Hello? Peter?'

The figure turned.

'Yes?' Peter, hunched, peering, questioning, tried to penetrate the mist with his one good eye. 'Who's that?'

'It's Nick. Nick Cod… Nick Nichols.' He paused. 'I don't know whether….' He took a step forward and then stopped again, uncertain.

'Nick Nichols?'

Peter hadn't moved. He watched intently as Nick slowly approached.

'My dad?'

Peter seemed thunderstruck, immobile, and lost for words. The two men looked at each other. After a long pause Peter suddenly relaxed.

Nick was by now close enough to see that portion of Peter's face that wasn't bandaged. It split suddenly into a lopsided, but nevertheless, wide grin and Peter's one good eye positively twinkled, despite the mist.

Nick held out his hand, a little uncertainly.

'Hello, son.'

Peter moved forward clumsily, eyes suddenly flicking downwards, embarrassed for some reason and unable to meet Nick's gaze.

'I… I never….' He wasn't completely lost for words though as he took the proffered hand.

'Hello, Nick. Dad.'

END

Printed in Great Britain
by Amazon

47929926R00213